FORGOTTEN ROAD

Randall Arthur

FORGOTTEN ROAD

By Randall Arthur

www.RandallArthur.com

The characters and events in this book are fictional.

Published by
Life Image Publishers
P.O. Box 1160
Stockbridge, GA 30281
LifeImagePublishers@gmail.com

ISBN 978-0-9850257-1-7

Printed in the United States of America

Cover design by Heidi Mixon

Other books by Randall Arthur
www.RandallArthur.com

<u>Novels</u>
WISDOM HUNTER
JORDAN'S CROSSING
BROTHERHOOD OF BETRAYAL

<u>Children's Book</u>
ABC's On The Move

Prologue

Friday, May 17, 1996

*N*early breathless after performing for an hour and a half, he tucked the fiddle beneath his chin and raised the bow for one final song. He closed his eyes and waited until the crowd quieted.

Slowly, he drove the bow into the first notes of *Soul Dreamer*, an original ballad that had climbed the pop chart to number eleven and the country chart to number eight.

There was an immediate outburst of cheers and hollers.

"We love you, Cole Michaels!" someone near the stage shouted.

He smiled.

Mindful of his every move, he worked the bow with total passion, then sang his heart out. The audience loved him. He could see it in their posture. Their attentiveness. Their faces—especially their faces.

The faces of his beautiful raven-haired wife and his three-year-old son were glowing as well. They sat just a few yards away on the front row.

He smiled again.

He could hardly believe the moment. His pastor had assured him just under a year ago that if he would choose God, that God would in return give him everything he wanted. "It's *never* God's will," were the pastor's precise words, "that any of His children be financially poor, physically ill, mentally distraught, or socially uncomfortable. Give Him your life and trust Him. And He'll prosper you beyond measure."

And now here he was—Cole Michaels, a follower of God—standing at the brink of stardom, poised to make millions.

As he looked out over the packed three-thousand-seat Nashville auditorium, he shook his long blonde hair and interjected a giant "Thank you!" to all his new fans.

The people roared their pleasure.

Absolutely overjoyed, he turned his 6'2" frame and nodded his approval to his accompanying musicians. His lifelong dream of becoming famous and wealthy was finally, after so many discouraging years, coming true. And to think—less than twelve months ago, he had tried to accept the likelihood that his dream would over time become nothing more than the over-indulged fantasy of an old man.

He was sure the critics would rave about this particular concert. He could feel it in his bones.

*   *   *

After the minutes-long explosion of final applause, Cole—bursting with euphoria—bowed and exited the stage. Amidst the high fives, slaps on the back, and shouts of congratulation from the offstage crew, he grabbed a rag to wipe the sweat from his face just as his wife Jana—with their son Shay in tow—rushed toward him. She threw herself into his embrace. "Oh my gosh, I'm so proud of you!" she laughed, pushing herself onto her toes. "I've got goose bumps all over!" She extended her forearms for him to see.

He laughed with her. "It's unreal!" He scooped up Shay, squeezing him in a giant hug and kissing his forehead.

But, as a celebrity in demand, he was quickly pulled away.

The next forty minutes presented a nonstop barrage of accolades—from the production team, the hired musicians, the lucky fans who had won backstage passes, and the journalists from a half-dozen newspapers and magazines.

This was show business. And Cole loved it!

He signed autographs, gave high-fives, granted a couple dozen photographs, and answered questions from the journalists. As a twenty-nine year old living out his childhood dream, he shamelessly enjoyed every second of it.

* * *

A few hours later, alone with Jana and Shay in the peace of their newly purchased home in Nashville's posh suburb of Brentwood, Cole was still pumped with adrenaline. Dancing and singing, he helped put his son to bed with another round of hugs and kisses. Before leaving the bedroom, he pulled the sheet up to the three-year-old's chin. "I love you, buddy. You're my favorite boy in the whole world." He watched the little eyes close and the little lips curl into a half smile. He kissed the tip of his own finger and placed the finger on the bridge of the boy's nose. "Sleep tight. We'll see you in the morning."

He waited for Jana in the outdoor hot tub. She slid into the water beside him, wearing a red bikini and clutching a magazine. "Before we do or say anything else, I've got to read this to you."

He put his arm around her, drew her close, and inhaled the fading aroma of her expensive perfume.

With barely controlled giddiness, she folded a page backward and read. "As recently as eleven months ago, very few people in the American music industry—producers and consumers alike—had ever heard the name Cole Michaels. Today, however, thanks to the hit single *Soul Dreamer* from the *Sweet Manipulations* album that has sold over a half-million units and has received more radio air time than most fast-food commercials, there are only a few people left who have not heard of the man and his music."

She turned, looked intently into his eyes, and gave him a quick kiss. Then she continued reading. "Blonde, rugged, and good looking, the man captures the eye as strongly as his music captures the ear and the soul. Cole Michaels quite simply is the new man in town. Single-handedly, this 29-year-old Tennessee native has created a new mixture of music that is a genre unto itself. With his trademark golden fiddle and his rich baritone vocals, he has given birth to a style of soul-stirring music that is one part country, one part light rock, one part Celtic, and one part new age. It is mood music so emotional that it makes the heart beat fast. And in a strange way, his minimal lyrics—typical for his songs—fill the mind with the reminder of all that is good in life."

She rubbed her thigh against his and gave him a sexy wink.

"With his shoulder-length hair, his facial stubble, his leather trench coat, and his powerful charisma, this handsome musician has undeniably won our hearts and our pocketbooks. Ten months ago, when a prominent Nashville radio station gave *Soul Dreamer* its first airtime, the crossover single rocketed onto the charts and has continued to climb ever since. Hopefully, for the pleasure and inspiration of thousands of music lovers, Cole and his music are here for the long haul."

Cole thrust his hands into the air. "Yes!" He took the two glasses of wine sitting on the edge of the hot tub and gave one to his wife. "To you, me, and Shay! To a life of never-ending bliss and happiness!"

"And God's favor!" she said. "Let's not leave him out of the picture."

"And God's favor," he smiled. He hoisted his glass. They toasted. Then sipped.

Under a full moon, the night could not have been more momentous. When they had drained their glasses, Cole reached for his wife and drew his fingers through the softness of her hair. He pulled her onto his lap and into a smoldering kiss.

They were still lost in passion when a single word intruded: "Mommy!"

Simultaneously, they turned and saw Shay standing a few feet away in his pajamas, seemingly frozen to the floor of the deck, a look of painful confusion etched on his face. Cole and his wife looked at each other with alarm. Something was not right.

PART 1

PART 1

1

Eight Months Later
January 6, 1997

*E*arly Monday morning, just before heading back to school after Christmas break, Jesse Rainwater—wearing only his underwear—stared at his reflection in the bathroom mirror.

He ran his finger over the bruise made by his father's fist three days ago. The bruise, almost black now, covered most of his cheek from his nose to his left eye.

What lie would he tell his seventh-grade buddies at his Atlanta school today when they asked what had happened? Would he tell them he had been torpedoed by a football thrown by a college-aged relative? Would he tell them he had fallen off his bike at high speed while jumping a ramp, and planted his face on a concrete curb?

Jesse had already been feeling unloved because of the emotional and verbal abuse often heaped on him. But now that his father had bashed him with his fists three or four times, Jesse was finding it nearly impossible to handle. What had he done to cause his father to hate him so? And how was he, a twelve-year-old, supposed to deal with the boiling hate he now felt in return?

He continued to stare in the mirror. Tall for his age, at 5'5", he was not filling out as he had hoped, nor was he yet growing any body hair. Sadly, his voice wasn't even changing. He flexed his small bicep in front of the mirror. If he could just grow some muscle and bulk up, he would stop his father from hitting him.

Jesse spat at the mirror. If he could, he would love to stop his father permanently.

The piece of vomit! If the man didn't want him, why had he ever adopted him?

2

January 17, 1997

Cole Michaels rubbed the legs of his dull-orange jumpsuit and shook his head. Most of the details of his incarceration he could bear—the restrictions, the tasteless food, the noise, the lack of meaningful conversation. Those things he accepted. But he could no longer endure the presence of the threatening cellmate in the 8' x 10' two-man enclosure. Not when his only moments of reprieve during the day were the noon and evening meals, eaten quickly in the large common room. If his circumstances did not change soon, it was only a matter of time until he would be raped.

Yet he deserved it—he knew that. Nearly every minute of every day, horrific visions of floating hair, burning flesh, and body pieces invaded his mind, reminding him of what he'd done and why he was here.

But he couldn't—and wouldn't—just give up and allow a psychotic cellmate to turn him into a pathetic slave.

He rubbed at his pants again. He had overheard inmates

at one of the evening meals talking about the legal right of prisoners to be granted a work assignment outside the cell.

That afternoon, during the lunch period, he asked one of the guards if he could speak to him. "I'd like to apply for a work assignment," he pleaded.

*   *   *

Four days later, following the afternoon inmate count, Cole was approached by a different guard. He was placed in handcuffs and delivered to a windowless, concrete-block room—the office of the captain of the Middle Tennessee Correctional Facility.

"Well, well. I understand that our world-famous inmate wants to get his hands dirty," the captain said from behind his metal desk, a soggy, unlit cigar clamped in the corner of his mouth.

Cole had noticed the captain's tendency toward sarcasm before. This was the first time, though, that he'd noticed just how lonely the man looked. "I'm nobody special, sir," Cole said quietly, running his hand over his buzzed haircut. "I'm just a regular guy who's trying to bide my time without getting into any more trouble."

"Regular?" The captain laid his hand on a stack of papers lying on the desk. "These are your hospital and police records, son. I've read them. I wouldn't say this describes a regular person. Regular thirty-year-old men don't try to commit suicide over and over and over again." The captain raised his brow. "Do they?"

For a couple of seconds, Cole was speechless. And then

in a rush of rage, he felt a sudden and powerful urge to shout, *You cold-hearted idiot! You have no idea what it's like to be in my shoes!* Instead, he closed his eyes and breathed deeply to calm himself. He cleared his throat. "I'm sure I'm not the only one here who has wanted to give up on life at some point."

The captain continued to stare at Cole as he sucked on his cigar, then chewed on it a round or two. "Well, whatever," he said finally. "It's your lucky day. It just so happens that we need a new janitor. And the warden says we should give the job to you. I personally don't agree, but I've been outranked. Anyway, as of this moment you're on two weeks' probation. If there are no problems or complaints about you during that time, and you still want the job, you'll report to my office on Monday morning, February the third, and start to work." The captain yawned and seemed to lose interest. "Here's a form to fill out and bring with you. And here's a written description of the job. Oh...and a pencil."

Within thirty seconds, Cole was being escorted through corridors and security points back to his cell.

When his cuffs had been removed and the barred cell door had clanged shut behind him, Cole saw that his cellmate was lying in bed—sleeping, feigning sleep, or ignoring him. Cole sighed in relief. He treasured every moment the man was horizontal and inactive.

Cole pulled himself quietly onto his own top bunk and settled into a cross-legged position. At first he ignored the two pieces of paper in his hand and concentrated on the pencil. Not once during his months of incarceration had he ever been allowed to possess a single item that could be conceivably used as a weapon. Now he was holding in his hand a sharpened, full-length lead pencil.

Cole gripped the pencil as if it were a knife. He squinted. Was this some kind of personal test the captain was administering, hoping he would use the pencil in another suicide attempt and be returned to guild four, where the suicidal and handicapped inmates were housed? Cole scoured his memories. Had he done something to offend the captain? Why else would the man dislike him so much?

Or was it simply that, now that he was living in guild eight, he was allowed to have such things as pencils? Whatever the answer, holding a pencil in his hand felt absolutely bizarre.

Then again, maybe it was an opportunity he shouldn't pass up. Maybe he should indeed plunge it into his heart, or his temple.

His chest tightened.

Why *shouldn't* he kill himself? The only reason he hadn't tried during the past several months, since arriving as an inmate, was because he hadn't possessed the means. Now he had the tool for the job, right here in his hand.

Cole started to weep. Perhaps he wasn't a regular human being after all.

Slowly, he placed the tip of the lead against his temple. His hand began to shake. One quick thrust, and the wooden cylinder would plunge into his brain. Within a few minutes, his miserable life would be over. Why not? He certainly couldn't imagine any possible future that would be remotely tolerable, much less one that would justify his existence. The grief that was now part of his life had completely plundered every room of his soul, and had done so beyond any imaginable restoration.

He squeezed the pencil and gritted his teeth.

Through the fog of grief and guilt, a new idea emerged, vaguely at first, and then with increasing clarity: If he slipped out now, he would be cheating his murder victims out of the long-term vindication they were due. He rightfully owed them years of misery. A quick suicide would be an outright perversion of justice.

He lowered the pencil and looked at it. A tear splattered on its yellow paint. He couldn't cheat them in that way, not after everything he'd already stolen from them. No, both women and both children deserved for him to serve his full eleven-year sentence. Whether he felt like living or not, he had to honor those four people. He had to honor their memory, and the lives they'd lost. And in order to do so, he had to persevere and suffer through every month. Every week. Every day. Every minute.

He exhaled.

If he wasn't going to kill himself, then maybe he should just go ahead and jab the pencil into the heart or the head of the depraved creature on the mattress below. Maybe that was the real reason the captain had given him the pencil—as a means to protect himself. Maybe it wasn't a test after all.

Cole was surprisingly moved by the idea. Was the captain actually sympathetic beneath his tough-man exterior? Cole almost smiled at the thought. Even if the idea wasn't likely, Cole still gave himself permission to believe it. After all, he had already learned, on three different occasions, that the 6'10" cellmate, with the muscles of a weight lifter and the cold, amber eyes of a demon, could overpower him anytime he wanted. The captain must know it as well.

After a brief search, he found a hiding place for the pencil that doubled as a weapon: inside the pillowcase, on the underside of the pillow. He shoved it all the way to the end of the fabric case, next to the wall. If at any time he needed to retrieve it for protection, he resolved to use it as wildly and efficiently as he possibly could. Not because he feared he might be killed—that would actually be welcomed—but because he refused to be sexually molested by a blatant pervert.

"Thank you, captain," he whispered.

He picked up the smudged sheet of paper that described the janitorial job. It had obviously been composed and copied inside the prison office on cheap or rundown equipment. Cole read the text.

Janitorial Assignment

The inmate selected for this job must understand that the work is both a privilege and an honor. To get the job and continue the job, the inmate must maintain a record of exceptional behavior and carry out all his or her related work with efficiency and quietness. The job includes sweeping and mopping floors, washing windows, emptying trash cans, and dusting and straightening furniture. The designated areas for these work duties are the common/dining area, officers' stations, and library. The work hours are Monday through Friday, from 8:00 to 10:30 AM, and from 12:30 to 3:00 PM. The hourly wage during the first year of work is 17 cents. The hourly wage during the second year is 25 cents. The hourly wage during the third year and every year thereafter is 34 cents. All earnings will be placed in a trust fund in the inmate's name. The funds can be credited toward commissary goods and/or other approved goods ordered from outside the prison. Otherwise, all said funds will be held in trust until the inmate's release date. Upon the release date, all accrued funds in the trust will be turned over to the inmate in the form of cash, or check. The inmate doing this job will be watched carefully. If the inmate doing this job is seen at any time slacking off or violating prison rules, he will be given a warning. He will

receive a maximum of two warnings.
In the event of a third infraction, the
inmate will permanently lose the
job.

Cole shuffled the papers and started reading the bare-bones application form.

He tensed—he heard his cellmate shifting to get out of bed. Was the man going to tell him for the dozenth time that he had a "nice" body and once again try to rub his back or stroke his hand? Cole had heard the deviate use the word *nice* so many times that he was sick of it. Still in his cross-legged position, Cole dropped the papers onto his lap and covered them with his pillow. He buried his elbows into the pillow and rested his chin in his hands with his head bowed and his eyes closed, trying to feign sleep.

Within seconds, he heard urine spraying forcefully into the toilet. Seconds later, he heard the man crawling back into the lower bunk.

Cole waited patiently for ten minutes. When he heard no further sounds coming from the bottom bunk, he quietly removed the pencil from the pillowcase.

He filled out the application form. Yes, he would gladly work as a janitor for seventeen cents an hour. He would even do it for free, as long as he was permitted to be apart from his cellmate a few hours each day.

He folded the papers and hid them away, along with the pencil, in the pillowcase.

3

The next day during lunch, Cole slipped the job application into the hands of one of the security guards. "Can you deliver this to the captain, please?" The one thing Cole didn't return was the pencil. The potential weapon was still buried in his pillow case. He had no plans of giving it back unless the captain demanded it.

* * *

Five days later, Cole was again escorted in handcuffs to the captain's office. Without any fanfare, the captain said, "If you'll give me another week of good behavior, you'll start work on Monday, February the third, exactly one week from today. On that morning, you will be brought to my office at 7:50 sharp. Another worker will be here to give you a brief orientation. And then you'll begin. Any questions?"

Cole had no questions—just a sense of tremendous relief.

As he was curtly dismissed from the captain's office, he started counting down the days and the hours.

That night, after the lights were turned off throughout the guild, sleep came slower than usual for Cole—maybe because of his own excitement, or maybe because his brutish cellmate tossed, shuffled, and grunted for at least an hour. Cole feared that at any moment the man would get out of bed and, for a lack of anything else to do, start reaching for him.

But the man stayed put. So did his hands.

Lying in the dark, his eyes open, Cole surrendered to his two other nemeses: loneliness and grief. Tears seeped from the corners of his eyes. He rolled his head and rested it against the cinder-block wall. How could he have been such a fool? The horrifying images of body parts once more lodged in his head. He thought about the sharp pencil within reach. He squeezed the bed covers and wailed inside his head until sleep finally rescued him.

* * *

At 7:30 AM on February the third, Cole was sitting on the edge of his bed, breakfast eaten, ready to report to work. Thankfully, the six previous days had unfolded with no flare-ups between him and his cellmate. Instead, a fresh tidal wave of grief had pounded his soul, leaving him void of energy or will, languishing like a sick animal.

"Cole Michaels!" a guard yelled.

Cole looked up.

"Collect all your belongings. You're being moved to

guild five, where all the staff workers are housed. I'll give you three minutes to get everything together." Like most prison instructions, the order was issued in a hostile tone.

With his mind racing, Cole dropped gently from the top bunk to the floor. Why hadn't he been told in advance about the relocation? Had the decision been made just this morning? Cole glanced at his cellmate. The huge man, stretched from end to end on the bottom mattress, stared back at him with intense consternation.

Cole looked away from the monster's amber-colored eyes and started gathering his possessions: his toiletries; his unframed photographs of his wife, Jana, and his son, Shay; his underwear and socks; his extra set of prison clothes; his extra pair of tennis shoes; and a small plastic bag of fan letters that had been mailed to him at the correctional facility. Every letter had been opened and checked for contraband. Cole, though, hadn't yet read a single letter. Maybe some day.

Cole turned his back to the guard and stacked his meager pile of possessions on his bunk, carefully positioning himself between the guard and the pillow in which he'd stashed the pencil. As inconspicuously as possible, he reached into the pillowcase and retracted the pencil. In one fluid movement, he inserted the "number 2" into the bag of letters. He gathered up his belongings and stood before the bars.

As the guard unlocked the cell door, Cole felt a massive hand squeeze his left shoulder. Before he could react, he felt his cellmate's lips nudge up against his ear and whisper, "I *will* find you, baby."

"Step back, Mack...*now!*" the guard ordered. "I said *NOW!* Are you flipping deaf?" He pulled his radio and prepared to call the control center.

Cole felt his cellmate step away.

When Mack sat down on his bunk, the guard swung open the metal portal and waved Cole out of the cell. "All right, Michaels. Walk ahead of me and follow my directions."

4

"Are you okay?" Jesse Rainwater asked his mom. The two of them were alone in the kitchen. It was a Thursday morning, a school day, and Jesse was ready to walk out of the house to catch his school bus. He and his mother seldom had substantial conversations, and never talked about anything personal. Rather, his mother—this lady who had adopted him as a newborn—had in the last few years become less and less talkative and more out of it. She spent most days shut away in her bedroom or her sewing room.

None of this seemed unusual to Jesse. His mother's quiet and withdrawn personality was simply reality. He had never felt a need to probe for a reason behind her temperament. He had just accepted that her nearly lifeless nature was due to her age.

Until last night.

Around 10:30 PM, he had been pulled out of the early stages of sleep by a heated exchange of words coming from his parents' bedroom. The commotion lasted for a solid fifteen minutes until his mother emitted what sounded like a muffled cry of pain. Had his dad just hurt his mom? Had he intentionally hit her, like he had been hitting him—the despised son—lately?

As he lay awake in bed, feeling a growing anger, he considered how, for years, his mother had a history of on-again, off-again bodily pains—sore ribcage, sore back, sore hand, sore hip, sore neck. He had always assumed that these physical problems were just part of growing old.

This morning, he stared across the kitchen at his mom and waited for an answer to his question, focusing on her dangling, limp right arm. Had his dad caused the injury? Had he been hurting her all along but managing somehow to keep the abusive behavior concealed? The thought enraged him. But if that were true, why hadn't his mother told someone? Why hadn't she notified the police? Had she been under some type of threat to keep her mouth shut?

His mom ignored his question, taking a cereal bowl from one of the kitchen cabinets, using her left hand only.

Jesse raised his voice. "Well...*are* you? Are you okay?"

"What?" she mumbled distractedly, finally looking back at him.

"I'm asking about your arm, Mom." Jesse's voice reverberated with nervousness and frustration. "You are right-handed! Why are you using your left hand this morning? Why is your right arm...just hanging?"

The expression on his mom's face quickly transformed from distraction to mild panic. "Oh. I'll be all right. Don't worry about me. You go ahead and catch your bus. You're going to be late for school if you don't hurry."

Jesse cleared his throat. "Did Dad do that to you?"

His mom's face twisted with surprise and fear. "*Jesse!*" she whispered. "We will *never* say that again! Absolutely *never!* Do you hear me?"

Jesse flinched in hurt and shock. "But...I..."

"*Never!*" his mom shouted.

Not once before had his mother ever raised her voice to him.

So was she in outright denial? And a spineless weakling to boot? He vigorously adjusted the backpack strapped over his jacket. "Have it your way, then!" He stomped out the door. In the cold winter morning, he could feel his face harden with layers of disgust.

His dad *was* guilty! He knew it.

He hated the man! Absolutely hated him!

*   *   *

Less than two hours later, in the middle-school hallway during his morning break, Jesse forcefully shoved a classmate for the first time in his life. The victim was a seventh-grade geek wearing glasses. "Jerk head!" Jesse yelled. "The next time you talk about me behind my back, I'll bash your face in!" The anger festering in his head gave Jesse an unprecedented fearlessness. It also gave him a thirst to inflict pain on somebody else.

The geek recoiled in silence and looked down, frightened and submissive.

Emboldened, Jesse stepped forward and pushed the

guy into the lockers. He held a fist in the wimp's face. "Do you freaking understand?"

Wincing, the guy offered a fearful nod.

Jesse spat on the guy's shirt. "Freaks like you make me sick!" He turned and walked away.

Still seething, he felt like bullying another person or two.

5

After all the cell lights were switched off in guild five, Cole lay alone in the two-man cell and felt the familiar ache overtake his soul. Except this evening, the pain was even more pronounced. It was Saturday, March 8. It would have been Shay's fourth birthday.

Cole sighed and squeezed his head. "Why, God? Why?...I don't understand! I was going to church. I was praying. I was being a good husband. I was being a good father. I was staying away from alcohol. Did all that mean *nothing* to you?" He crossed his arms over his chest, fists clenched. "Was I lied to by my pastor? By my church? By my friends? Was it all just a joke?" He waited, but no answer came. "I'm *talking* to you! Don't you even care?" He balled his fists tighter.

He wept until he finally gave in to emotional exhaustion and lost himself in blessed sleep.

* * *

On Monday morning, March 10, Cole began his work assignment exactly at eight o'clock, as he had done for the past twenty-three days.

Emotionally flat, nearly robotic, he reported to his work supervisor and was told to proceed to the library, where he would spend the morning removing books from their shelves, dusting and polishing each shelf, dusting each book, and then returning the books to their correct order. He would return to the library for the next morning or two until all the shelving units were polished and all the books were dusted. In the afternoons, he would make his regular rounds, mopping and collecting trash.

Cole gathered cleaning supplies and made his way to the library.

Cole welcomed the freedom to move throughout the prison's various rooms and hallways, but the library was one room he did not like. It was depressing. The hundreds of volumes that lined the four walls of the medium-sized room were a visible reminder of constructive, energetic, proactive thinking, with the intent to educate one's mind—the absolute least of his survival needs. The mental process of absorbing new information seemed to Cole the most futile of exercises. For nearly ten months, he had purposely shut off every urge and every opportunity to think academically. He had wanted to do nothing but feel—whether grief, anger, or depression—and hold on to his treasured memories.

Entering the square, windowless room, with its six evenly spaced tables, he approached one of the corner shelving units. An inmate stood nearby, gathering books to head to the checkout desk. The man acknowledged Cole's presence with a nod. Cole ignored him. He placed his cleaning supplies on an empty table and began to pull books from the highest shelf. He stacked the volumes on a table in Dewey-decimal order. When the top shelf was empty, he polished the oak panel until it shone. Then he dusted the hardbacks and returned them to the shelf, placing each book in sequential order.

He repeated that process for each shelf, working downward. When he'd reached the bottom shelf, the librarian, a short, thin-nosed man wearing glasses, interrupted him. "I need to step out of the room for about fifteen minutes. If anyone comes in, tell them I'll be back shortly."

Cole saw this man every time he came into the library to empty trash, but had never spoken more than a dozen words to him. "All right," he responded lifelessly.

When the librarian left, Cole gazed around the room. He was alone. When the hydraulic door softly latched, the room became totally quiet. Cole turned and continued his work.

He removed the books from the bottom shelf and laid them on the table. The furniture polish and a rag in hand, he knelt. His eyes scanned the length of the oak plank. A round stain, most likely from a cup, glass, or can, marred the finish near the center of the board. Cole took a water bottle and sprayed the discolored circle. Then, with a clean rag, he rubbed the area with pressure. He could feel the raised residue. He rubbed harder. The stain was not going to disappear easily, and Cole—for some inexplicable reason—

welcomed it as a challenge. The stain was not going to beat him. He squirted cleaning formula onto his rag. With focus and tenacity, he scrubbed for four or five minutes. The blotch began to fade. Cole continued his attack.

Finally convinced that the mark was no longer visible, he sprayed furniture polish over the length of the shelf.

He was polishing the board with his rag when a single word spoken from above and behind startled him and sucked the air from his lungs.

"Nice," a deep voice proclaimed.

6

Already on his knees, Cole spun and threw his arms up to protect his head, peering up to see where the attack would come from.

He froze.

The face staring back at him, though, did not belong to his former cellmate. Even so, he sprang to his feet and edged away. "What the...who are..."

Cole didn't know how to explain what he was seeing. In all his life, he had never seen a face—if that's what it could be called—so twisted and deformed. It looked more like a paper sack full of potatoes that had been beaten to a pulp with a truncheon and then immersed in acid.

Whatever it was, it spoke to him.

"Excuse me. I didn't mean to frighten you," a garbled voice said. "I guess you're one of the inmates...I haven't met yet." The man stumbled through his syllables as if he were physiologically unable to string together more than a half-dozen words before he was forced to pause. Although his face was hideously scarred and deformed, the hand he extended from beneath a long-sleeved shirt appeared normal.

Cole hesitated, unable to keep himself from staring. The large head was hairless and discolored. The browless eyes squinted out of small slits between bags of puffy flesh. The nose was a small lump tilted sideways. The lips were asymmetrical and grossly misshaped. The misaligned cheeks bulged in several directions.

"That's okay," the man said. "Your reaction is normal. I was...in a plane crash eight years ago. My face was crushed and...completely burned off. The surgeons rebuilt it the best...they could. But yes...it's still a scary sight. Anyway, my name is Duke Parker. I'm the new chaplain around here." The hand was still extended.

Cole gradually regained his breath. He could feel his heart still thumping as he cleared his throat and hesitantly shook the man's hand. "Cole. Cole Michaels."

"Well, Cole, it's good to meet you. And...as I was intending to say, you're doing a nice job there." Parker nodded down at the shelf. "You're making it look almost new."

Still recovering, Cole acknowledged the man's remark with a halfhearted, "If you say so." The truth was, he couldn't care less about how the man assessed the quality of his work. Cole wondered how long the man had been standing there watching him.

"Actually, your work there tells me...something about your character," Parker said. "Your posture says you carry a lot of inner pain, yet...your work ethic says you're most likely an honest and...dependable man. And even though

I'm not on the...maintenance staff, I just want to say, 'Well done.'"

The last thing Cole wanted was another preacher in his life. He wanted to spit and say, *Character? I don't have any character. And what if I did? Who gives a rip? And what difference would it make anyway? Do you see where I am? Do you know what brought me here?* Instead he looked into the man's freakish eyes and growled, "Life is brutal, as you obviously know. No matter *who* you are, no matter *what* your character. It's all a big cosmic joke. Now, not that it's any of your business, but if you don't mind, I'll get back to work."

Cole was just turning away when the man reached out and grabbed his arm. "Wait," the chaplain said softly. "I'm just trying...to encourage you. Please know if you ever need...anyone to talk to, I'll be around. It's a sincere offer."

Yielding only silence, Cole gently but firmly pulled away. He turned and went back to his cleaning duties.

* * *

Cole floated through the remainder of the day on anger—through his work, through his lunch and dinner, and through the evening alone in his cell. He continually replayed the episode with the chaplain. No preacher, especially this unknown chaplain, had the right—without being invited—to talk to him about character and dependability. He was sure the man was simply zeroing in on him as someone to be *won over*. One pastor had already set him up for disaster with devastating and self-serving Christian babble. Cole cringed, hearing the syrupy echo of his former pastor: *God the Father desires that every one of His followers always experience the finest health, the finest material goods, and the finest lifestyle.* Cole would never allow himself to be conned by another preacher again. Never. He was just glad that his former pastor and associate pastor had months ago taken the hint and stopped visiting him.

Lying face-up on his bunk, he stared into the semidarkness. No, he had absolutely no intent, none, of placing himself under the influence of another spiritual leader.

Nonetheless, the incident with Duke Parker had inflamed the questions that had mercilessly pillaged his soul. Was God really sovereign over every event and circumstance? Was He really knowledgeable of and involved in the lives of all six billion people on the planet? Even so, why would anyone dare teach that His all-consuming character was centered around goodness and rightness? Couldn't everyone see that He was absolutely volatile, acting callously toward those who, knowingly or unknowingly, ticked Him off? Why would anyone consider Him trustworthy? Didn't He sometimes unpredictably and unsympathetically just stand back—when He was in the mood—and let life beat the hell out of people? And why did He insist on remaining silent when people cried out to Him? If he really desired to be known and respected by humankind, why did He make himself so inexplicably difficult to understand?

Cole rolled onto his stomach and pulled himself to the edge of the mattress. The unopened Gideon Bible still lay on the floor, up against the wall, where he had tossed it weeks ago. He stared at it for a few seconds. Then he made himself comfortable and eventually dozed off.

*   *   *

In the coming weeks, Cole brooded more and more over the questions that plagued him. At the same time, he tried to block Chaplain Duke Parker from his thoughts. He probably would have succeeded, had Parker's appearance not been so petrifying and pitiable.

Plus, three weeks later, on Friday, March 28, the man approached him a second time. Cole was again working in the library, mopping the vinyl floor. This time, Cole saw the chaplain heading his way focused in on him like a hawk swooping down on its prey, his horrid face distorting his attempt at a smile.

Cole looked away, his first thought to escape any kind of dialogue. His second was to wonder what anyone with such a grotesque-looking head could honestly find to smile about.

The man cleared his throat. "Morning, morning," he said, approaching Cole. Even the man's slurred voice sounded chipper. He extended a hand and said, "I just wanted to check up on you and find out if we could possibly get off to a better start."

Cole did something he had never done before. Mop and bucket in hand, he turned his back on the man without a word and walked out of the room.

7

*T*hat spring, the chaplain made three more attempts to establish some kind of dialogue with Cole. Despite twinges of guilt, Cole snubbed the man all three times.

Yet several times during the latter part of May, the one-year anniversary of his crimes, Cole almost changed his mind and had the chaplain summoned to his cell. After a full year of being tormented alone by his inner demons, he felt an irrepressible need to share with someone the agony that insatiably ate away at his soul, to unload the nightmares that prevented him from getting on with life. And who in the prison, other than the chaplain, could he even begin to trust with such gut-wrenching anguish?

But he resisted the impulse, utterly upset with himself for nearly reneging on his promise. No, if he ever decided to confide in anyone, he would make sure to choose someone other than a Christian preacher. It would be emotionally safer for him to find a confidant who was simply a good listener and nothing more—not someone who would try to influence him with pious and destructive rhetoric.

*   *   *

One Monday morning, ordered by his work supervisor to carry through with his normal schedule of duties, Cole first worked in the officers' station and the adjoining restroom. He emptied the trash cans, dusted the furniture and blinds, swept and mopped the floors, then cleaned the restroom sinks, urinals, toilets, and mirrors. Moving to the library, he emptied the trash, dusted, swept, and mopped.

At 10:30, he returned his cleaning supplies to a secured storage area adjacent to the officers' station and took his morning break. He napped in his cell from 10:40 to 11:20, then reported to the dining area with the twenty-one other inmates from guild five. The residents of the different guilds (with the exception of guild four, which held the handicapped and suicidal prisoners) were escorted to the lunch hall in shifts. The lunch period designated for guild five was from 11:30 to 12:00. With the dining tables to themselves, Cole and his cellblock occupants began their lunch in relative quiet. The smell of cornbread, cabbage, and fried bologna hung in the windowless room. As always, Cole sat at the end of one of the tables and ate in silence, refusing to converse with anyone. To make the most of his lunch break, he had learned to pace his eating. He had developed the ritual of taking small bites and chewing slowly, concentrating on each mouthful, allowing him to fill the entire thirty minutes with the productive distraction of eating.

During the last five minutes of the meal, as he plodded through a tasteless peach pie, one of the prison guards marched out of the cafeteria restroom and over to Cole.

"Michaels!" the guard snapped. "When the line-whistle blows, I want you to get your cleaning supplies and go pronto to the toilets. There's a god-awful mess in there that needs to be cleaned up."

Cole focused on the guard's face. "Yes, sir."

Waiting for the line whistle, Cole forgot to finish his pie, focusing instead on a swift response to his new orders. Normally, he would return to his cell after lunch, doze or daydream for thirty minutes, and then report back to work at 12:30. His afternoon work hours were ordinarily spent cleaning the dining hall and the restroom anyway. Today he would just get an early start, at least in the lavatory.

At the sound of the whistle, Cole and the twenty-one other prisoners fell in line for the line count and the march back to guild five. As the other inmates filed out of the room, Cole made his way instead to the restroom, just behind the serving lane. He wanted first to assess the extent of the "god-awful mess" he would be dealing with.

When he entered the rectangular lavatory, he gagged, assaulted by a stench so far beyond normal that he gasped and held his breath. He wanted to turn and run. But under orders to clean the room, he covered his nose and mouth tightly and moved ahead.

He scanned the room, immediately spotting a couple of reasons for the smell. He focused on the nearest one. One of the center sinks held a large puddle of vomit. Chunks of the mess were splattered across the edges of the sink and the floor tiles. Some had even reached the other sinks and the backsplash.

Cole guessed that someone had probably been made

queasy by the *other* problem he'd spotted, over in the stall area, and had emptied his stomach. He wondered if the one who'd fouled the sink had been the guard who'd approached him in the dining hall. He had indeed looked a little pale.

With his mouth and nose still covered, Cole approached the row of stalls. Putrid-looking water covered the floor beneath the partitions. Obviously, one of the toilets had been stopped up and had overflowed.

With his foot, Cole shoved open the door of the last stall. He winced. The toilet bowl was filled to the brim with mushy toilet paper and pungent brown liquid.

Cole backed away, all the way out of the room. Once the lavatory door closed behind him, he inhaled and exhaled deeply.

He wound his way through the hallways to the supply closet, where he gathered a plunger, a mop, a mop-bucket on wheels, a can of disinfectant, a can of aerosol freshener, a bottle of all-purpose cleaner, a pair of rubber gloves, and a handful of rags. Dreading the job at hand, he made his way back to the lavatory.

* * *

The large, amber eyes at the corner lunch table spotted Cole immediately as Cole rambled into the restroom.

* * *

In the lavatory, Cole laid out his cleaning supplies at a couple of the sinks that had not been fouled. He pulled on the latex gloves. Holding the plunger, he maneuvered on tiptoe into the stall with the stopped-up toilet, trying not to breathe deeply. He placed his feet wide apart for stability and wiped his brow with the back of his glove, grimacing. Then, gripping the plunger with both hands, he inhaled slowly, then, out of necessity, held his breath. He slowly submersed the rubber head of the plunger into the water.

At that second, his head was pulled backward with such velocity that his whole body followed. His breath exploded from his lungs. Immediately, he was choking, his neck constricted by something with the strength of a python. His legs flailed helplessly, trying to keep his body upright. He reached for his neck, trying to free it, his eyes rolling wildly—all he could see was the ceiling. The arm wrapped around his neck squeezed even harder, its power overwhelming. Cole's wide-open mouth sucked for air in vain. Changing his strategy, he began swinging with both hands and both feet to try to connect with his assailant.

Suddenly, a cheekbone and nose pressed into the skin behind his right ear. The hot air of the assailant's rapid breathing blew across the side of his face.

And then the pain came, sudden and overpowering. Everything in his body—muscles, breath, brain—surrendered to the piercing agony that shot like lightning through his entire nervous system. He felt his toes stretch and stiffen.

The pain struck again, with mind-shattering sharpness.

And then he realized he was being stabbed.

Somewhere in his lower back.

He arched.

And he was impaled again. Then again.

He gagged. He tried to scream.

And then words reverberated off his eardrums, bitter and angry, in rhythm with the stabbing pain. "I don't like it when people cheat me, man! They need to be punished! And I did promise I would find you!"

Cole could no longer breathe. He felt the world around him grow hazy. Then dark.

Blessed darkness.

As he sank into unconsciousness, he felt as if he were falling, weightless.

Just before the blackness engulfed him, he thought he heard another voice. A faraway voice. A voice seemingly speaking with intense volume. But it was all so vague.

And then nothing.

8

*J*esse Rainwater sat alone at his bedroom desk and reread the words he had just typed.

Mrs. Esther Maddox   Jesse Rainwater
English—Expressive Essay   7th Grade
Monday—May 26, 1997   Final Paper

> I was told two years ago that I was adopted. I have thought about this almost every day since. It is hard for me to believe that my mom and dad are not my real mom and dad. It is more hard for me to believe that my real mom and dad did not want to keep me. I get really sad when I think about this. And sometimes I get mad. I mostly try to hide my feelings, but last week I just could not hold them back anymore. My

mom explained something to me that I've been questioning for a long time, something not related to the adoption. And what she told me made me more angry. I don't see how I will ever get over it.

He had wanted to add: *It's a horrible, horrible secret that I will have to carry for the rest of my life. And it's already too much for me to handle.*

But he didn't.

When my dad came home, I shouted at him and told him I hate him. I know he doesn't like me. I wonder if my real father would feel the same. I also wonder if I will ever meet him. When I'm older I think I will try to find him and ask why he gave me away. But I think I already know. I will then tell him how much he has hurt me and how he has ruined my life forever.

After reading his essay twice more, Jesse was even less sure that he should submit in writing such a detailed account of his private and personal agonies.

He locked the door to his room and stood in front of his mirror.

He stared at himself for the longest time. Tall, blonde,

and thin, he looked nothing like his adoptive parents. He wondered how much he resembled the man who had biologically fathered him. Regardless, he wasn't as masculine looking as he wanted to be. Was the repulsive secret he carried somehow to blame?

He stripped.

In the mirror, he examined his anatomy with such disgust that he began to tremble. Why him? Why, of everyone on earth, was it him who had to be damned with such a horrid curse?

No one was ever going to love him.

9

Groggily, Cole tried to decide whether he was dead or alive. He couldn't feel his body. Everything around him was dark, except for the blurry glow of a few miniscule lights. There seemed to be some kind of electronic beeping in the background. He tried to speak, but his thoughts were too foggy. What little awareness he had started to fade. And then everything went blank again.

* * *

"Well, good afternoon, Mister Michaels. It's nice to finally see you awake."

Cole slowly registered a lady standing at his side.

What was happening? Where was he? He seemed to be horizontal. He scanned the space around him. Slowly, he realized that he was in a hospital of some kind. In a hospital bed. And that the lady addressing him was...a nurse.

As he tried to shift his position, he felt an acute pain in his back. He cringed.

"Be careful. You're connected to an IV and to a catheter," the African-American nurse said, laying a hand gently on his shoulder.

So, he was still alive.

For that, he felt no gratitude. Oh, for the darkness, the lack of awareness. He closed his eyes, hoping to sink back into oblivion. But now he was conscious.

He slowly opened his eyes again. "How long have I been out?" His mouth felt heavy and dry.

The nurse gave him a sip of water. "You were brought here yesterday around one in the afternoon." She looked at her wristwatch, "So you've been here for almost twenty-four hours now."

Cole visually probed the room. "Where am I? Is this the prison infirmary?"

"No, your injury was way too serious to be handled at the infirmary. So, you were brought here to Nashville General. At the moment, you're still in the ICU." The nurse gently lifted Cole's arm and wrapped a blood-pressure cuff around his bicep. She pumped air into the device.

Cole sniffed. "What...are my injuries? And what's...the prognosis?" Cole felt fatigued just trying to formulate his words.

The nurse waited until she'd registered his blood pressure. "Well, the doctor will be here to visit in an hour or two, and he'll give you the official report. But I'll tell you this—you just barely made it. One of your kidneys was lacerated. You nearly bled to death. Fortunately, the surgeons were able to save you. And it looks like everything's going to be okay, barring any infections."

"How long will I be here?" He moved slightly, and the pain ran like fire through his nerves.

The nurse pushed a button on the EKG monitor. "Why? Are you in a rush to get back?"

Cole half-smiled, seeing the irony. He coughed. "No...I was...I was just..."

"Well, today is Tuesday," the nurse interrupted. "So, you'll most likely be up and out of here by Friday."

"Up by Friday?" The way he felt at the moment, he couldn't imagine leaving so quickly.

The nurse chuckled. "The good news is, it looks like you're going to be okay. The bad news is, the physical therapist will start working with you this evening. He'll have you up and walking before dinner tonight."

Cole looked at the nurse with a 'you-can't-be-serious' expression.

The nurse just smiled.

After she left, Cole was given a light snack. He was asked to sit up to eat.

Then the surgeon, a Doctor Joseph Hallstein, dropped by to evaluate Cole's condition and to give him the official report. Hallstein raised Cole's bed, putting Cole in a more upright position as they conversed. The doctor's report was a more detailed version of the nurse's.

"How many stitches?" Cole finally asked.

"One hundred and ninety-two. There were multiple strikes in the same area that left a pretty jagged opening. But again, if there are no post-surgery infections, you'll be just fine. As a matter of fact, if it weren't for the scars, which will stay with you for the rest of your life, you'd most likely forget that you'd ever been injured."

* * *

An hour later, Cole was transferred out of intensive care into a regular room, two floors higher in the building. It was during the reshuffling that he became aware that a guard on loan from the prison had been stationed—and would remain—outside his room. During the elevator ride up, the guard—a middle-aged, chubby white man—casually mentioned to Cole that he was fortunate to be alive, that he could thank his lucky stars for Chaplain Parker who had single-handedly fought off the attacker and saved Cole's life.

As Cole settled into his new room, puzzling over what the guard had reported about the chaplain, the physical therapist showed up. The man—a huge African-American—was kind but merciless.

Cole indeed managed to walk before the evening meal.

After dinner, he was finally allowed to settle in. He had never before been so thankful to be horizontal. And to have peace and quiet. He released a long sigh of relief.

After another round of pain meds, the lights were turned out, and Cole again contemplated the story about the chaplain. How much of it was legit? In case most of it was true, Cole tried to work up an anger toward the preacher for intervening. After all, what gave the man the right to intercede where he hadn't been invited? What gave him the right to presume that his help was even wanted? Cole groaned. How much better off he would be right now if he had never awakened, if he had just been allowed to bleed to death. He cursed the man. He also cursed God for teasing him, for inviting him to the door of his greatest wish and then sadistically turning him away at the last possible moment.

But after calming down, he reminded himself of his lasting conviction that his four victims deserved full and absolute justice for the crimes committed against them. With new tears, Cole strengthened his resolve to serve out every day of his eleven-year sentence.

Nevertheless, for more than an hour, his feelings about living or dying vacillated dramatically. In the end, he reluctantly admitted that, for outright decency, the chaplain's decision to intervene had been the right one. As a convicted criminal, Cole needed to stay alive and live out his punishment. No matter what he sometimes felt. No matter what he sometimes wanted.

As his thoughts finally started to drift hazily toward sleep, he realized he had not even asked about the identity of his attacker. But there was no need. He had recognized the voice...the choice of words...and the mind-blowing strength. He wondered what had happened to the man. One good thing—Cole was sure the powers-that-be would never expect the two of them to share a cell again.

In the final stage of drowsiness, Cole wondered again about the chaplain. Had he been injured? And why would a preacher risk his life to battle such a vicious, psychotic brute? And how in the world had he managed to overpower him? Slipping in and out of awareness, he pondered a few fitting scenarios and, feeling the hint of a weak grin, finally lapsed into a deep sleep.

10

The next morning, eyes still closed and only half awake, Cole thought he was dreaming as the twisted voice of the chaplain amplified through his mind. But when he opened his eyes, Chaplain Duke Parker stood in the room talking to a nurse, a different nurse from those who had helped him before.

The nurse looked his way and said, "Well, I think our patient is finally awake." She moved to his bedside. "How are you feeling this morning?"

Cole softly cleared his throat. "Still feel...a little groggy."

"That's only because of the pain medications. All right, I need for you to sit up for me." Just sitting up was surprisingly painful, but the nurse assisted him. Then she began her daily hospital routine—the "state of mind" questions, blood pressure, temperature, the next dose of medications.

The chaplain stood silently to the side, watching.

As soon as the nurse finished and left, Cole asked, "So, is it true?"

Parker pursed his scarred lips. "What—that I stopped the guy from killing you?"

Cole nodded.

"Yes. It's true."

"That guy's a dang monster," Cole stressed. "Can I ask exactly how you stopped him?"

Parker grinned.

Cole realized, with surprise, that the chaplain actually had a nice smile. Despite the backdrop of the deformed face, his teeth were relatively straight and white.

"Well," the chaplain said, "his back was to me when...I approached him. And his feet were spread apart. So I...simply planted a strategic kick between his legs...as hard as I could."

Cole felt himself grin in surprise and satisfaction. "And that put him out of commission?"

"Well, let's just say...I'm pretty sure he won't father any children anytime in the near future. But...just to make sure he stayed down, I bashed him over the head a couple of times with my walkie-talkie. I hit him so hard that I put a giant gash in his head and knocked him out. If it makes you feel any better, he's in the prison infirmary as we speak."

Cole started to smile. Then, abruptly, to his frustration and embarrassment, he began to weep.

"If it will give you any peace of mind," the chaplain said, "in the next day or so the maniac...will be placed in solitary confinement. And then most likely, within the next five to six weeks...the disciplinarian board will have him transferred to a maximum security facility...in some other part of the state."

"I guess I owe you," Cole said, speaking with difficulty through suppressed sniffles. "I don't guess it's often that someone steps in and saves another person's life."

"Hey, it'll give me a story to tell."

"But why? Why risk your life to save a stranger? You're not one of the guards. It's not in your job description."

Parker pursed his lips again. His eyes became serious and focused. "I was eating lunch when I saw you go into the restroom with your supplies. I saw your attacker go in behind you. Something about his attitude, his movements… raised a red flag for me. Besides…I've talked to the captain about you. I'm aware that you filed a complaint against the man. I also know some of the details…of why you're here." Parker paused. "What can I say? My heart has gone out to you. When I suspected you might be in danger…I acted."

Cole closed his eyes. "I'm not worth saving, you know. I should have died a long time ago." His head drooped. "It would have been better for everybody."

"Only God can determine that," Parker replied, with conviction. "And apparently…He has decided you should live."

Cole opened his eyes. He dismissed the chaplain's statements with a puff of air. "Whatever. Anyway, I…I thank you," he said softly.

Parker nodded acceptance.

"And you're okay?" Cole asked.

"Not a scratch."

"Believe me, you're a lucky man."

Lifting his hairless brows and nodding his understanding, the chaplain said, "Maybe." Then, with a soft smile, he added, "The beast had actually broken a cafeteria tray into two or three pieces. It was one of those jagged pieces of hard plastic that he used as his weapon."

Fifteen minutes and several exchanges later, the chaplain left. And Cole was surprised to find, over the course of the afternoon, his heart softening toward the man called Duke Parker.

* * *

To Cole's surprise, the chaplain visited him again the following morning, and then again the morning after that.

And on Friday morning, an hour before Cole was released from the hospital, the chaplain appeared again. This time, Cole asked himself, *Was now the time to unbottle the questions that had for far too long grown rancid in his soul, the questions that had totally waylaid his belief in the Christian message?*

In violation of his promise that he would never again confide in a Christian preacher, he decided to take the risk.

11

"You're obviously a religious man," Cole said, as he and Chaplain Parker sat and waited for Cole to be released from the hospital. "Do you mind if I ask you some questions about the Bible?"

"By all means. I'm not promising that I can answer your questions, but I'll certainly try."

Cole registered the man's humility and respected it. It actually helped him to continue. "Okay, well, two and a half years ago, my wife decided to give her life to God." He had known it would be a hard story to tell. He found himself fighting a strong impulse to stop, to keep quiet. "And almost immediately I saw a positive difference in her life. As a wife, as a mother—and in every other aspect. I was touched by what I saw, so much so that I was persuaded to go to church with her."

Dressed and sitting shoeless in the bed, Cole made a slight adjustment in his position to try to alleviate some of his pain, but each movement brought a sharp pang that made him cringe.

"Anyway, after attending church with her every Sunday for a couple of months, I decided to give my life to God as well, to be what they call *born again*. Up to that point I'd been a struggling musician, watching my lifelong hopes of success disappear by the day. But shortly after that decision to follow God, I found the strength to stop drinking. I became a better husband and father. As if those things weren't miraculous enough, out of the blue I was offered a recording contract with a major record label. Overnight, it seemed, I finally achieved the fame and wealth I'd dreamed about since I was a kid. One of my songs even reached the top ten on the Billboard charts. My pastor kept telling me not to be surprised by the good things that were coming my way—that God was simply fulfilling His promise to prosper those who turned to Him."

Cole closed his eyes and massaged his temples. When he continued, his words were quieter but more bitter.

"So I trusted what the pastor said. He was the professional. He was the one who read and studied the Bible. Thus, I made sure that I gave God credit for every new blessing that came my way. And I made sure to thank Him every day. And since God was so predictable, since He was supposed to keep blessing me as long as I lived for him, I was determined to live for Him for the rest of my life. I was determined to be a good man. A churchgoer. I decided, as a celebrity, that I would even talk about God in public."

Cole paused again, struggling to control his emotions. He continued in a tense whisper.

"I had really expected, and even come to believe, that the rest of my life would be blessed. And then suddenly I lost everything. My son. My wife. My house. My career." Cole locked eyes with Parker and hissed, "So, was my pastor a lying cheat who was just in the religious entertainment business? Or is there really a God? And if so...is He a heartless tyrant? Or what is He?"

Parker, sitting in the visitor's chair, uncrossed his legs and scooted forward. He cleared his throat and, for a few moments, closed his eyes as if silently praying for divine help. "Yes," he finally answered, "there is a God. But I'm afraid that our western culture wants to believe...and often does believe...that God's number-one priority for His followers is that they should all experience comfort and prosperity." He paused. "In just a moment, I'll tell you why I believe this perception of God is way off center. But first, I have a question. Did your pastor really teach you...that God is predictable?"

Cole thought. "I don't remember if he used that exact word. But yeah, I'd say he implied it. Many times."

"That if you would behave in a certain way, God would predictably respond in a certain way?"

"Yeah...that God almost *had* to. That if you obeyed Him and put faith in Him, that He would respond with blessings. That He would protect you from danger. Lift you out of poverty. Take away the tension in your life. Fulfill your dreams. Heal your sicknesses. Even put you in a new car and a new house."

Parker shook his scarred head and clenched his fist. "This is the misconception of God that I'm talking about. I will say this—God's *character*...is predictable. He's predictably holy. Predictably right. Predictably full of love.

Always. But nowhere in the Bible are we ever told that God's...*actions*...are predictable. Unless, of course, He has promised a particular outcome to a particular person to help advance a particular plan. Otherwise I challenge you— pick up the Bible in your cell. You'll find that God never asked us in general to place our faith in His *predictability*. Rather, He asked us to place our faith in His *ability*. And there is a difference. For example, God will not predictably keep us from developing cancer. He does have the *ability* to keep us from getting cancer. But He also has the ability to walk with us, teach us, console us, and use us as a positive influence while we are dying with cancer. And we need to trust His ability to choose what is best for us. So, is there a God? Yes. Is He a tyrant? No. Was your pastor misleading you? Perhaps not intentionally, but, in my opinion, yes."

Cole listened carefully and thought hard.

"And not only is this *predictability* idea not supported in the Bible," Parker continued, "it's also not supported in life. I can't fathom how any Bible teacher can objectively look at the world around them and continue to say that if a person obeys God and trusts Him...God will assuredly lift that person out of poverty, heal them of their sicknesses, and put them in a nice car or nice house. I can take you to Bolivia, for example, where I grew up as a missionary kid and introduce you to the poorest people in South America. At least seventy percent of the people there live in extreme poverty, and many of them are dear Christians with a purity and a faith that is equal to anything I've seen here in the States. Yet, those precious believers have experienced financial difficulties and physical discomforts for their ENTIRE lives. Does this mean that God loves the Bolivians less than Americans or any other Westerners? No. Not one iota. And Bolivia is just one out of dozens, maybe hundreds, of countries where poverty and hardship dominate the day-to-day lives of all citizens, including Christians."

Parker's voice took on a greater degree of anger. "Plus— let's be honest—it's a known fact that hundreds of devoted believers around the world are being physically tortured and persecuted because of their faith...right now at this very moment...all with God's knowledge and permission. So, were you taught incorrectly that God's number-one priority is to endow us with comfort and prosperity here on earth? Yes! Yes, you were! God is by no means opposed to comfort and prosperity. Often, He richly bestows these blessings on us. But to make us rich and comfortable is not His number-one priority, probably not even a priority at all. Actually, God's standard according to Matthew chapter seven, verses twenty-four and twenty-five, is this: *Anyone who listens to my teaching and obeys me is wise, like a person who builds a house on solid rock. Though the rain comes in torrents and the floodwaters rise and the winds beat against that house, it won't collapse, because it is built on rock*. Those verses imply that the rain and the winds will generally *beat* down on everyone's life...even those who hear and obey His words. So, for a prosperity theologian to look at a group of Americans, who are in the top three percent of the most privileged people on the planet, and say *It's God's priority for you to have more and to never be uncomfortable*, and for that group of people to honestly believe they deserve more and that God is somehow unfair with them and not blessing them if they are not promoted to the top *one* percent... is the epitome of ingratitude. In my opinion, it's the most extreme form of sacrilege."

Parker's words—and especially his obvious and powerful anger—hit Cole with real power. He had just opened his mouth to ask a question when a nurse entered and asked him to gather his belongings. Moments later, the nurse, along with the prison guard who had been posted outside the room, accompanied Cole to the nurses' station. After Cole had signed all the release forms, the guard escorted him down to a waiting police car.

* * *

A half-hour later, Cole reported to the prison's medical facility, where he was told that he would be held and monitored for at least twenty-four hours. One of the on-site doctors removed the surgery dressing, inspected the stitching, replaced the dressing, checked Cole's body temperature, checked his blood pressure and pulse, gave him his next round of medications, and then led him to an infirmary bed.

Cole was told that he would be allowed to resume his work duties, pending his full recovery, in approximately one week. Perhaps on Monday, June 9.

He tried to rest, but for the remainder of the day, he found his mind replaying the passionate arguments of the chaplain: *"God's character is predictable. He's always holy, always right, and always full of love. But His actions are never predictable.*" Cole frowned. He borrowed a pencil and made a written list of some additional questions he wanted to ask.

12

The weather in Atlanta was ominous and foreboding. The dark sky on Monday morning, along with the thickness of the air and the muted glaze of the colors, matched Jesse Rainwater's mood as he made his way on foot to the school bus stop.

Waiting for the bus, he stepped back off the sidewalk and stood beneath the canopy of an old oak. Feeling lost and alone, he leaned against the tree and daydreamed what it would be like if the approaching storm could magically whisk him out of his nightmare and reintroduce him to society as a normal human being with a normal family. But a gust of wind blew grit in his face and reminded him that his life was real and that he was trapped in a body that would haunt him for the rest of his life.

He needed to talk to someone.

He was shocked that his English teacher had never once questioned him about the expressive essay he had turned in. Had she thought he was joking? Or exaggerating? Why hadn't she at least shown some concern and asked for details about his situation?

When he saw the school bus approaching, he realized that his face was wet with tears. He wiped his face and straightened his shoulders.

*   *   *

That morning Jesse made an appointment to meet later in the day with the school counselor. He had carried his pain on the inside for way too long. He needed someone to know his plight. He needed someone to help him.

At noon, when Jesse ambled down the hallway toward the counselor's office for his appointment, he tried to conquer his nervousness. He tried only slightly, however, to stifle his anticipation. Finally, he might find a listening ear. Someone who would understand. Someone who would come alongside him and help navigate the psychological darkness killing any hope for his future.

"Come in!" Counselor Thomas yelled through the door when Jesse knocked.

Jesse stepped inside.

"I'm glad you made this appointment—I've been meaning to talk to you," the man announced immediately. He turned from his computer and motioned Jesse toward a chair.

Jesse sat. He had no sooner opened his mouth to explain why he had asked for the appointment, than the counselor spoke again. "I'm glad you saved me the trouble of tracking you down." The man's tone was not welcoming. "It's been brought to my attention by several of the students and teachers that you've been engaged in some pretty serious bullying. So let me just ask you outright—do you have a brain deficit, or what?" His tone was angry. "Do you not have any idea what you're doing psychologically to the smaller kids when you push them around, call them names, and threaten them? Do you honestly not know that you can scar some of these kids for life? Or make them so afraid of school they'll never be able to focus on their education? Or do you really just not give a crap?" The counselor's eyes drilled into Jesse's, authoritative and unforgiving. And he wouldn't look away.

Jesse's thoughts stumbled over each other. But before he could formulate a response, Thomas launched into a tirade about middle-school bullies and the disgrace they brought to the public school landscape. "All right," he said at last, "here's the new rule. We're only two weeks away from finishing the school year. If I hear so much as a single report that you've bullied anyone else, I'll have you transferred indefinitely to the special-needs school down the road. And it won't be pretty." The man was breathing heavily. "Do you understand?"

Jesse was speechless.

"I said, do you understand!"

Jesse nodded.

The counselor looked as his watch. "Okay, was there anything else you wanted to talk to me about?"

Jesse shook his head.

* * *

Minutes later, Jesse sat alone in a toilet stall and tried to collect himself. He crunched his body into a tight knot. He didn't know whether to curse, cry, smash the wall with his fist, or just run away.

13

Cole appreciated the long weekend of rest, but by Monday afternoon, when he was back in his cell, he wondered why he hadn't yet heard from the chaplain again. The man had promised he would reconnect with him within a couple of days.

As he mulled over his disappointment, a guard appeared at his cell, and Cole was unexpectedly escorted to the captain's office.

There were three other uniformed men in the office— the head of administrative personnel, the classification coordinator, and the disciplinary chairman. The captain explained that the three officers served as the disciplinary board at the prison, and that Cole was to answer their questions about the stabbing.

"Take your time and tell us everything you remember about the attack," the disciplinary chairman said. "Start by telling us about your relationship with Mack during the five weeks the two of you shared a cell together."

Mack, Cole thought. This was only the third or fourth time he had heard his former cellmate's name. He wondered if it was his real name, or just a nickname.

Cole looked around the office at the four men facing him. The three new faces looked to be semi-educated tough guys, much like the captain. "Well," Cole said uneasily, "as you know, during my trial I was assigned to a solitary cell in guild four. I was there for about five months. After my sentencing, I was transferred to guild eight. That's when I was placed in the cell with...Mack." The name just didn't roll easily off Cole's tongue. "I entered the cell with him for the first time...I think it was January the second." Cole went on to describe in detail his cellmate's inappropriate touching and sexually charged comments during the weeks they were locked up together. He especially emphasized the last words Mack had whispered in his ear the morning he was being transferred out of the cell. "He told me, 'I will find you, baby.'"

Then he described the day of the stabbing, including the morning hours before the attack. As best he could, he provided a blow-by-blow account of the incident, including every word Mack had spat into his ear right before he blacked out—"People who cheat me will be punished, and I did promise you that you wouldn't get away."

The three disciplinary board members seemed to listen with undivided attention. One asked a few questions, exploring other ways Cole might have "cheated" Mack other than rejecting his physical overtures.

Cole assured them that there had been nothing else between them. "The man and I had absolutely no relationship. No friendship. We never talked. He refused any conversation that I ever tried to initiate."

The three men huddled together for a private discussion. The captain turned to Cole. "All right, you can step out into the hallway. The guard will take you back to your cell. Oh—and for your peace of mind, I can tell you that Mack has been locked away in solitary confinement in guild four."

Cole was led back to his cell, where he crawled into his bunk and thought back over his interview. Convinced that he hadn't left out any important facts, he decided to sleep until dinner. Lying on his stomach, he spotted the Bible on the floor next to the wall, where it had lain for months, covered in dust. Cole remembered the chaplain's challenge: *"Read it. Other than the outcomes that God promised to key people in key circumstances, you'll find that God never asked anyone to place faith in His predictability."*

Cole reached out, clasped the Bible, and drew it toward his face. He blew the dust off the binding. He gazed at the book, wondering how well Chaplain Parker really understood its teachings. Could the chaplain be trusted as a teacher of its pages? Or would he prove to be just another preacher who used its contents to advance his own personal agenda? Seriously contemplating these questions, Cole eventually slipped into a light sleep. The Bible dropped out of his hand onto the floor.

* * *

Drool on his chin, Cole awoke when a guard clipped the bars of his cell with a handheld radio and announced that dinner was served.

Cole crawled stiffly out of bed. He picked up the tray of stew, applesauce, and cornbread and ate kneeling beside his bed. As he chewed and swallowed, chewed and swallowed, his thoughts drifted unproductively.

As he neared the end of his meal, a face appeared on the other side of the bars.

No matter how many times Cole viewed the face, it always startled him and caused a churning in his gut.

"How are you doing, man?" Chaplain Parker smiled.

Cole continued to kneel, his buttocks resting on the back of his heels. He nodded and thought about how he should answer. "Physically, I'm still a little stiff. Emotionally, I guess I'm feeling a little bored."

"Are you in the mood for some conversation?"

"Sure. I'm not going anywhere."

"If you'd like, I'll sit and visit awhile."

"Please."

Parker lowered himself to a cross-legged position on the floor, up next to the bars. "I intended to come by yesterday," he said, "but my wife got a call early yesterday morning from her sister down in Chattanooga, asking her to come down and help deal with an urgent family matter. She wanted me to go along. Otherwise, I would've already been by to check up on you."

Wife. The word echoed in Cole's head. An unconventional thought struck him: The nightmarish-looking creature sitting before him was married and apparently physically intimate with a person of the opposite sex. Cole nodded again, attempting to disguise his bewilderment. "Thanks," he said. "You've been kind to take any interest in me at all."

"That's what I do. That's why I'm here."

"Not that it's any of my business, but can I ask how long you've been married?

"Twenty-one years. I've been very blessed."

"Any children?"

"Two before the accident—a boy and a girl. And one since the accident—a little guy."

"How old is the youngest?"

"Almost five now. His name is Mateo, a version of Matthew. The name means *gift of Jehovah*."

Cole shifted so that he too was sitting cross-legged. "I'm just curious—is your family one of the reasons you always seem so positive and happy? I mean...the severe scarring that you carry causes most people, I'm sure, to distance themselves from you. It's something that would drive most people into a state of depression."

Parker smiled. "Yes, my family is one of the reasons. But the bigger and more important reason for my optimistic outlook is that I am a...servant in the household of God."

"And why would being someone else's servant give you such an upbeat outlook on life?"

"Because I don't have to worry anymore."

"I don't understand."

"Well, as God's servant...I don't have to worry about acceptance. I don't have to worry about work. About the future. About possessions. About money. About purpose.

My master takes care of all that for me, even if He just gives me the barest essentials. And He happens to be a master who will never lose His property, go bankrupt, be sued, get sick, or die."

Cole buckled his nose. "And you trust Him? Even after what happened to you."

"Unequivocally."

"But what about self-dignity, self-esteem, and self—"

"And what? Self-love, self-worth, self-fulfillment, self-awareness...and blah, blah, blah?"

Cole didn't answer.

"I know...I know...I'm being sarcastic," Parker said.

Cole locked eyes with him. "And why is that?"

Parker sighed. "As a person who grew up outside the United States, I guess I see things differently." He leaned closer and pressed his hands against the bars. "I just think our western culture has exploited and fed the selfish side of the human heart to an unprecedented extreme. We've even woven this self-focus philosophy into our Christianity and have made it all sound so...biblical. Our Christian leaders have even written a whole array of books that reinforce this self-centered way of thinking. And our churches constantly host conferences to encourage these ideas. Come on, let's face it—the 'entitlement' mentality has worked its way into our Christian doctrine. That's what I was talking about the other day in the hospital. Western Christians have become so addicted...to comfort, prosperity, and selfish living that we've now built our Christian beliefs around these addictions. We truly expect God to care more about our... selfish dreams, whims, and desires than He cares about truth, justice, and rightness. It's nothing more than an 'American Dream' theology. And I'm convinced that it is a wrong perspective."

"So, you're saying it's more biblical to be a servant and give up your life—and trust the Master, no matter what—than to be a self-consumed success?"

"A self-consumed success who leaves a trail of dead relationships behind him?" Parker pursed the elongated bags of flesh around his mouth that substituted for lips. "What do you think?"

"I guess I don't know the Bible well enough to give an answer."

"Well, according to the Bible—James chapter three, verses thirteen to sixteen, to be exact—a right kind of self-understanding leads to humility. And a skewed kind of self-understanding leads to a 'me first' attitude that turns a blind eye to anyone it hurts."

Cole reflected silently.

"The fact is," Parker continued, "in our culture, we have a skewed kind of self-understanding. Does that surprise you? Listen. As fallen creatures, we're so out of sorts with God and His holiness that God would literally consume us right now if not for His...divine mercy."

"So," Cole said, "you believe we should think and behave like a servant? Not like an individual powerhouse?"

"Yes. With the knowledge that God never, never abuses his servants."

The quietness that followed was palpable.

"Here's another verse to consider," Parker said finally. "In the book of Philippians, chapter two, verses five, six, and seven: '*Your attitude should be the same that Christ Jesus had. Though he was God, he did not demand and cling to his rights as God. He made himself nothing; he took the humble position of a slave.*' How can it be any clearer than that?"

"You seem to know a lot of Bible verses."

"I've memorized a few."

Cole was surprised to hear himself say, "Do you think you could make a list of some of those verses for me to read?"

Parker hesitated briefly, then said, "Of course. I'm assuming you want a list of verses that pertain to the subjects we've been talking about—pain, comfortableness, servanthood, and egotism."

Cole nodded.

*   *   *

That evening, the chaplain delivered a handwritten list of twenty-eight scripture references—and told Cole that he would be out of town for the next six days at a conference.

Before the cell lights were turned out for the night, Cole picked up the Bible from the floor and found a relaxed sitting position on the bed. For a few minutes, he held the Bible motionless in his lap. During the eleven months that he had attended church with Jana, he had regularly carried a Bible to the weekly meetings. He had enjoyed the feel of it in his hands. Without embarrassment, he had fumbled through its pages every Sunday, searching for the pastor's announced text. He had followed with fascination as the pastor read the texts out loud and elaborated on the meaning of the words. He had seldom, however, opened the Bible during the week to read any of its chapters and verses on his own. He had been content to allow the "professionals" to read and study the *Good Book* for him. Obviously, that passive reliance had been a mistake.

Or maybe not. Maybe the Bible was in reality nothing more than an overly hyped litany of concocted legends and fantasies, and the real mistake was to now entertain the prospect of opening its pages again.

Cole looked at the sheet of paper on which the chaplain had written the list of Bible references. The reference that topped the list was Second Corinthians twelve, verses seven to ten. Well, why not? He'd been a prisoner for nearly eleven months, and in recent weeks, the unpleasant heaviness of boredom had begun to set in. So he gave himself a convenient excuse. Just for mental stimulation. So he opened the Bible and turned its pages until he found the Second Corinthians passage.

And then he started reading. Slowly.

He read and digested the words of a man who claimed that his body had been laden with a long-term painful handicap so burdensome that the man begged God to heal him. But God refused, telling the man that the weakness would persuade him as a mortal with prideful tendencies to be humbly dependent upon a higher strength. God's strength. God did promise, though, that the man would be granted enough grace to handle the situation. And that his pain would not be in vain. Rather, his life would be a monumental demonstration to a disillusioned and misled world that God's supernatural power was real and effective, and thus that God existed.

To his surprise, Cole was touched by the words. He felt an immediate and shared pathos with the man. He wanted to know the man's identity. He read the surrounding verses but found no mention of the man's name. He backtracked through the verses and chapters until he discovered that the writer was a man named Paul. He remembered hearing of Paul before, a prominent character of some kind in the New Testament.

Cole was completely lost in his study when the lights went out.

* * *

Cole spent the bulk of the next day reading and trying to comprehend the entire book of Second Corinthians. He sensed that he was grasping little of what he read. But he did find out that Paul had been appointed by God to be an apostle of Christ. Cole did not fully understand what being an apostle meant, but he was more than impressed by the man's humble heart, tireless service, widespread influence, and passionate leadership. Cole was especially impacted by the scope of the man's extraordinary hardships listed in chapters one, four, six, and eleven—multiple beatings with rods, whips, and stones, multiple jail sentences and shipwrecks, being lost at sea, poverty, hunger, sleepless nights, perpetual weariness, and periodic loss of hope. And, as impossible as it seemed, the man actually seemed accepting of those hardships, and of the fact that God had apparently allowed the hardships in his life as character builders.

When he finally broke for dinner on Tuesday evening, Cole sensed that the words of Second Corinthians had somehow breathed energy into his tired soul and bogged-down mind. Was it the reputed power of God's Word that he had experienced? Or was it simply the fact that he had exercised his mental muscles for the first time in over a year? Whichever it had been, the exercise had actually felt good. It felt like a therapeutic step for him. And an enlightening one.

After filling his stomach, Cole continued to think about the apostle Paul and his remarkable life. What he'd read had created a hunger in his soul to read more. He promised himself that over the course of the next few days he would read and analyze all the Bible references on Parker's list.

14

The rest of Cole's week was spent sleeping and studying. The recurring nightmare of body parts and floating hair only distracted him twice.

By Sunday evening, he had accomplished his goal—he had studied all twenty-five passages on Parker's list.

And he was astounded.

He had read verses stating that Jesus, during his years of ministry, had chosen to be financially poor....that many people, eager for money, have wandered from the faith and pierced themselves with many griefs...that the rich should not be arrogant or put their hope in wealth...that the rich should be generous and willing to share...that God hates human pride...that the Lord esteems those who are humble and contrite in spirit...that Christians should show true humility toward all men...that a Christian is blessed with the opportunity not only to believe in Christ but also to suffer for him...that a Christian should endure suffering as a good soldier of Jesus Christ...that King David credited his afflictions with teaching him wisdom and insight... that John the Baptist was beheaded because of his truth-telling...that the apostle James was executed with a sword because of his association with Christ...that Stephen was stoned to death because of his irrepressible faith...that each Christian has been bought with a price and no longer possesses ownership of his own body.

One particular passage in the book of Hebrews— chapter eleven, verses thirty-five to thirty-nine—he could not get out of his mind: *"Others trusted God and were tortured, preferring to die rather than turn from God and be free. They placed their hope in the resurrection to a better life. Some were mocked, and their backs were cut open with whips. Others were chained in dungeons. Some died by stoning, and some were sawed in half; others were killed with the sword. Some went about in skins of sheep and goats, hungry and oppressed and mistreated. They were too good for this world. They wandered over deserts and mountains, hiding in caves and holes in the ground. All of these people we have mentioned received God's approval because of their faith."*

As Cole ate his Sunday evening meal, he wondered angrily if his former pastor had ever read these verses. If so, how could the man have taught his brand of "American Dream" theology, as the chaplain called it, with a clear conscience? How could anyone familiar with the verses Cole had just read teach openly that God wanted all of His people to be free of pain, poverty, and discomfort, here and now and for a lifetime?

Cole squinted. Had his indignation with God during the past year been ill-founded? Had the "American Dream" theology he had been fed caused him to have wrong expectations of God? Had he as a new Christian not really been neglected or abused by God after all? To be honest, a blanket acceptance of pain and suffering made little sense to him. But obviously, in God's overall economy, pain and suffering were not always cruel or punitive initiatives. In some mysterious fashion, the Scriptures he had read seemed to almost portray both pain and suffering as some type of training for the soul—even badges of honor.

The thoughts felt like fresh, warm bath water, soaking away a lot of emotional dirt and sweat that had been caked on his spirit for far too long.

That night, lying in bed preparing for sleep, he dared for the first time to think seriously that he had been mistaken, that maybe God was not being mean to him, and had *never* been mean to him. Drifting into sleep, he felt a hint of unexpected peace, a peace that had been absent from his life for over a year. A tear of deep wonderment slid down his cheek.

* * *

The next morning, Cole returned to his janitorial work. He was still somewhat sore from the surgery, but despite the pain was able to partially bend, stretch, and lift. And the unexpected nourishment from the thought-provoking Bible verses had improved his morale.

For the first time since his incarceration, he felt the cloud of oppression that had engulfed him for so long start to quietly lift.

As he mopped the floors in the officers' station, a guard approached with the news that the disciplinary board had reassigned Mack to a state penitentiary a hundred and sixty miles eastward, near the small Tennessee town of Petros. The relocation would take place in five weeks. The investigation surrounding the attack in the men's room would now be closed.

Cole welcomed the decisions and sighed thankfully.

In the cafeteria that day, eating lunch, he was joined by the chaplain. Cole welcomed Parker back into town and asked about the conference. After the introductory pleasantries, Cole could no longer restrain his need to share. He launched into a discussion of the first Scripture reference on the chaplain's list, and included a report about his self-motivated exploration of the entire book of Second Corinthians.

"I'm impressed," Parker told him.

Cole then fired a list of questions at the chaplain—questions solely from the book of Second Corinthians, about Christ, about Paul, about the apostles, and pastors.

With tempered passion, Parker quoted a plethora of different verses from both the Old and New Testaments to answer Cole's questions.

Amazed once more by the chaplain's extensive Bible knowledge, Cole hurriedly wrote down all the new references, wanting to look closely at each of them over the next few days, just as he had done with the previous list of verses.

In no time, the lunch break was over. As Cole stood to return to work, he asked Parker if they could discuss the rest of the verses on the original list.

The chaplain smiled. "By all means. Let's do it."

* * *

Over the next week and a half, the chaplain kept his promise. He met with Cole every weekday during lunch. The meetings were more inspiring than Cole could have possibly expected, filled with animated discussions, additional revelations, and even a little laughter. Cole's mind was more and more torqued with the pleasure of productive and helpful thinking. The discussion times with the chaplain, combined with Cole's new habit of reading a trail of Bible verses every evening on his own, became a strong incentive to get out of bed each morning.

As he and Parker worked their way toward the last verse on the chaplain's initial handwritten list, Cole couldn't help but believe that his understanding of riches, servitude, and humility had been truly elevated to a far more balanced and truthful plane than the "American Dream" allurement.

His appreciation and respect for the chaplain grew significantly.

And so did his veneration for the Bible. In only a little over two weeks, the words of the Scriptures had altered his entire perspective on life. For the first time in over a year, there was light in his world. And he wanted to bask in that light. He felt like the survivor of a plane crash in the Arctic in midwinter, who for months had endured the hostile darkness and minus-thirty-degree temperatures and had finally seen and felt the absolute glorious warmth of the sun on his body again.

Humbly confessing to Parker his unworthiness, he asked if they could continue to meet regularly to scrutinize other important subjects through the light of Scripture.

Parker cocked his head and smiled. "It's for moments

like this that I do what I do." He reached out and placed a hand on Cole's shoulder. "To be honest with you, there's no greater joy for me...than to see God's Word stop someone in their tracks, lift them above their normal way of thinking, and then reshape their lives. It would be an honor for me to keep meeting with you."

With the chaplain taking the lead, the two men created a list of four topics for their study: the sovereignty of God, the veracity of the Scriptures, the fall of man, and heaven. They agreed to meet every Monday and Thursday, during Cole's lunch break.

"By the way," the chaplain added, "in all the years I've worked in the prison system...there have only been two other occasions when I've worked with an inmate who has actually acknowledged his guilt. And I just want you to know...I believe that it's your gut-level honesty about your life that has helped bring you to this place of real hunger."

Cole didn't know what to say.

The chaplain forged ahead. "I even heard that, during your trial, you stood up and interrupted your defense attorney while he was pleading your case and shouted to the judge that you were guilty and that you wanted to cease your defense." The chaplain wore a look of admiration as he spoke.

The court scene from months ago flashed in Cole's head.

Interrupting Jack Baker, his defense attorney, Cole bolted to his feet. "Your honor!" he shouted, as the courtroom went dead silent around him, "I no longer wish to pursue any kind of defense."

He clasped his hands together at his waist. "I'm a broken man, your honor. And a guilty man. Forgive me, but I can't even stop crying right now." His throat tightened so much that it almost closed, but he forced himself to keep speaking before anyone could try to silence him. "The witness is right. I killed Mrs. Cox and her little girl. Their blood is on my hands and nobody else's. Forget the officer's pursuit. The blue lights. The siren. Forget my own grief over the loss of my family. This line of defense is useless. And it's wrong. I'm guilty. I know it. You know it. Everybody knows it. As the witness so rightly declared, I deserve to be put away to the maximum extent of the law. So just save yourself some time—save the State some money—and go ahead and sentence me according to the law. I plead guilty, your honor...I plead guilty."

The blanket of silence that had covered the courtroom lasted another second—and then chaotic murmuring erupted from one side of the room to the other.

The crack of Judge Kingsley's gavel suddenly trumped all other noises, crashing hard four or five times against the monstrous desk. The gavel was followed by the Judge's stern voice: "The court will take a thirty-minute recess! And Mister Baker, I want to see you in my chambers now!"

Cole brought his mind back to the moment. His voice dropped nearly to a whisper. "There's no way I could pretend I was innocent. After all, my intent had been to go to the bar and get wasted. And then to drive home illegally. And to be honest, I didn't give a crap what the law said. My motive was to medicate my own personal pains with a total disregard for anyone else's safety." He paused. "My blood-alcohol level was point-two-eight at the time of the accident."

Chaplain Parker nodded. "I don't want to push it, but if you ever need to talk about it, just let me know."

* * *

That night—with his Bible, pencil, and pad of paper stacked beside him on the bed—Cole hunched into a fetal position and allowed his mind to be ravaged again by the replay of the gruesome details.

Intoxicated and emotionally ravaged, he fought to keep the Jeep between the lines as he drove down I-65. But his car kept swerving out of his lane. Deciding that he should take the back roads to his house, he exited the Interstate after only four or five miles. Pulling onto the exit ramp, he heard the distinct sound of a police siren behind him. He looked in the rearview mirror and saw the patrol car's blue lights. He cursed and threw up both hands. When he lowered his eyes to the roadway again, to look for a place to pull over, all of his motor functions reacted too slowly. He found himself already at the bottom of the exit ramp, headed into an intersection beneath a brilliant red traffic light.

Frozen in drunkenness and shock, he saw the small car approaching from his right just before he slammed it broadside. He heard the initial impact of crashing metal. Then everything went black.

In the midst of an inordinate stillness, he heard two or three voices—elongated and distorted, as if played on a tape recorder at frustratingly slow speeds. He saw a dull, hazy light in the far distance. But almost immediately, the light vanished as if a massive black cloud had descended around everything. All sounds disappeared as well, eerily silencing everything around him.

"Where am I?" His lips would barely move. And then the darkness that had snuffed out all his senses began to dissipate.

The vague, distant, muted images began to return. So did the muffled sounds. But this time the voices seemed to be yelling. But…why? The voices frightened him. Was he submersed in some kind of dream?

Bit by bit, his surroundings started to come into focus. His face was up against a twisted car door. He shifted his eyes. He saw a thick fabric bag lying on his chest. An airbag? And then his brain remembered. He was in the Jeep. He had collided with another vehicle. He had caused an accident.

His heartbeat went into overdrive. He tried to move, but found that he was pinned tightly in his seat.

And then he heard distinct words being barked from outside the car. "Somebody get the little girl out of there before the whole thing goes up in flames!"

"They have to be cut out!" another voice yelled, "We need the rescue squad!"

The words "little girl", "flames", and "cut out" quickened Cole's pulse even further. His chest bones felt dangerously stretched, as if wild animals were trying to break through his ribcage. He tried to squirm again, but couldn't budge. He only managed to lift his head and twist it minimally to the left.

And that is when he saw the other car.

A small gray vehicle was lying on its side about fifteen yards away. The front of the car was pointed away from him.

The driver's side, facing skyward, was completely bashed in. The metal roof of the car was spiked outward. Flames shot out of the bottom of the wreck. Three or four people, including a policeman, were on the ground on their knees at the rear of the vehicle, working frantically, trying to free someone through the misshapen rear window. Cole noticed for the first time the vivid, panicked cries of a child. The shrieks of pain and terror were coming from the car's backseat. At that instant, the fire popped and transformed itself into a full-fledged roar, engulfing more of the car. Two of the men kneeling at the rear of the car jumped up and ran. The police officer and one other person stood their ground, trying courageously to rescue the child, whose cries had now grown to hysteria.

"You guys get away from there now!" a deep voice bellowed. "She's going to blow at any second!"

The police officer and the volunteer looked up to gauge the progress of the flames. The police officer leaned back into the burning car, but the other man grabbed the officer and tried to pull him away.

People seemed to be running away from the burning vehicle in all directions. The policeman finally aborted his efforts. He and the stranger ran away from the wreck.

The shrieks of terror from the child trapped inside could be heard rising above all other sounds, haunting the dusk. For a brief instant, there was an inexplicable and intense silence. Then the car's gas tank exploded.

Cole's eyes shut in the brilliant flash. The broken windshield of the Jeep was hit with flying shards of glass. A strong smell of gasoline and smoke blitzed the air. Cole forced himself to reopen his eyes. He thought he could feel blood trickling down *his face. Peering doggedly into the smoke, he saw that the little gray car was now a blazing inferno. Through the back window frame of the wreck, Cole saw two little hands above the tilted seat. The hands were on fire.*

Straining with all his might to break free, Cole heard himself yell a bloodcurdling "No!" that seemed to last forever. Then he lost consciousness.

The prosecutor's words rang in his head: "*There's no reasonable doubt that Mister Michaels should be punished to the fullest extent of the law for this heinous and needless tragedy. With callous disregard for the safety of others, he terminated the lives of twenty-eight-year-old Allison Cox and her nine-year-old daughter Stephanie Cox—two innocent, law-abiding citizens of Davidson County who, on the Monday evening in question, were simply on their way home after a day of work, school, and daycare. And there is equally no reasonable doubt that this DUI offense is the second DUI offense in eight years for Mister Michaels and that he thus understands the consequences of such unlawful behavior.*"

Cole jerked. The Bible, paper, and pencil were knocked off the bed.

Cole entered the darkest part of the night with the Judge's declaration ricocheting in his thoughts. "*Okay, Mister Michaels, here's my decision. I will allow the defense to rest. And I will accept your plea of guilty to the Class A felony of aggravated vehicular homicide by intoxication.*"

And the Judge's eventual sentencing: "*Mister Michaels, please know that I can rightfully sentence you to a maximum of twenty-five years for your crime. But after weighing all the enhancement factors against the mitigating factors of your case, and after learning that you refused to be bonded out, and after seeing your brokenness, I am mercifully sentencing you to eleven years and eight months imprisonment, with time served. And this will be without parole. You will, therefore, be released on January the second, two thousand and eight. I truly hope you have learned your lesson."*

15

Cole and the chaplain began studying the sovereignty of God on the following Monday. Near the end of the session, the chaplain presented Cole with an old Bible dictionary and a thick Bible concordance to use in his cell.

Cole continued to study every evening on his own. He started using the dictionary and concordance as if they were a treasure map leading to the gold, silver, and diamonds of a royal family.

Throughout the summer, he and the chaplain pored over an array of Bible texts that progressively unveiled God's behavior and personality. Cole was astonished. He learned that his prior knowledge of God had been as incomplete as a dog's knowledge of space science.

What surprised him the most, though, was when Parker stressed to him one morning that regardless of one's cumulative knowledge of God's character, his understanding of God would still be severely limited. From memory, Parker quoted from the New Testament book of Romans, chapter eleven, verse thirty-three: *"Oh, what a wonderful*

God we have…How impossible it is for us to understand His decisions and His methods!" Parker continued: "Even if someone actually comprehended the true meaning of *every* jot and tittle from Genesis to Revelation…he would still be grasping only a minute portion of truth about the person and majesty of God. God is just too big for our human brains."

Cole lay in bed that evening, reviewing everything he had learned about God. For more than an hour he stared at the ceiling, lost in wonder.

Afterward, he felt a deep sense of gratitude for the chaplain's gracious help. More and more, the man—with his kind and giving spirit—was winning Cole's friendship and deepest respect.

* * *

In mid-August, Cole started attending the Sunday morning chapel services that Parker led in the dining area. About thirty inmates took part in the weekly gatherings, far more than Cole had expected.

On a Sunday in early September, Cole and Parker sat after the service at one of the tables. Cole hemmed and hawed but finally decided to unload his heart. "I know God is willing to forgive me," he confided, "but I guess I just haven't been willing, for some reason, to accept that forgiveness."

The chaplain let him talk.

"I never should have gotten in my car that night when

I left the bar." Cole scratched his head and released a puff of air. "A couple of weeks after I killed the mother and daughter in the car crash, I tried to slice my wrists with a credit card. That extended my stay in the psychiatric ward of the Vanderbilt Hospital for an extra seven days. But after everything that had happened, I just didn't want to wake up again."

The chaplain still said nothing.

Cole dug deeper into the past. "I don't know what you've heard, or what you know, about my wife's death, but after what I did to my boy, she refused to talk to me. I ended up sleeping in the living room. Five days or so after our son's funeral, I just suddenly wanted to cry on her shoulder and tell her that she had been right all along. So late one morning, with a severe hangover, I pushed aside all the bottles of Jack Daniels and went to find her. I looked in the kitchen; she wasn't there. I looked in the den, in the recreation room, on the back porch, on the front porch. I looked in the garage. Her Jeep hadn't been moved. So I figured she was still in bed." Cole coerced himself to keep talking, past the rapid constriction of his throat. "When I got to the bedroom door, I reached for the knob. Then I realized the carpet was wet. I stepped back and looked down. The carpet was soaked. It had rained a little during the night, so I looked up to see if the ceiling was leaking. But everything above the floor was dry. I tried to enter the bedroom, but the door was locked. I knocked and called Jana's name. But she didn't respond. I thought she was purposely ignoring me. So I started yelling. I went to the garage and got a long screwdriver. I came back and jimmied the door. Inside, the entire bedroom carpet was a giant puddle of water.

"I ran to the bathroom. We'd had it built special—it was sunk about two feet below the rest of the room. It was huge, but it was...totally full of water. Bathroom items were floating around everywhere. And then I spotted her. She was on her back in the tub. Underwater." There was a long moment of silence while Cole closed his eyes and let his head droop. "She was totally limp. The tub water was still running. Her hair was gently moving about in the water." He tried to say more, but his throat had closed.

He heard the chaplain take a breath as if to speak, then nothing.

"So," Cole continued a moment later, "I splashed into the tub and jerked her out of the water. I sat on the edge of the tub and held her head in my lap. I begged her to wake up. But she was...gone. It was later determined that she had taken over thirty sleeping pills, got in the tub, turned on the water, and gone to sleep." Cole squeezed the bridge of his nose. "She couldn't get over the shock of what happened to Shay." Cole lifted his head. But his eyes wouldn't focus. "We'd been married for nine years. After that...I didn't want to live anymore. When the police answered my 911 call, they found me sitting on the edge of the bed with the end of a shotgun barrel jammed in my mouth. I was put under a seventy-two-hour suicide watch at Vanderbilt's psychiatric ward. After I was released, the only way I knew how to survive was to drown myself in alcohol. An old habit, from earlier in my life. So nearly every night for five weeks I drove to the downtown bars and got wasted. And on the night of July the first, I ran the red light and killed a mom and her daughter." Cole stopped talking, lacking the energy and the will to say more.

Against prison protocol, Parker stood up, went around the table, and embraced Cole in a fatherly hug. "You've got to let Him forgive you," Parker told him. "And then you've got to let it all go. Remember…forgiveness is God's greatest gift to a penitent heart. To refuse that gift is to brazenly turn your back on the perfect heart of God."

Cole shook his head. "There's just too much to be forgiven for."

The chaplain just held him and felt him sob.

* * *

In bed that night, reliving memories, Cole closed his eyes and whispered to an imaginary vision of his wife.

"After all we've been through over the past few years, I think it's time that I asked you to marry me." He conjured up an image of the college fountain in Knoxville where he had made the proposal. He backtracked through the four years of courtship that had led up to the moment. How they had first met as juniors in high school. How her tall, lithe body and effervescent personality had attracted him like no other girl ever had. How their unquenchable passion for one another had gotten out of control and led to an unplanned pregnancy. How Jana, because of the pregnancy, had missed so many days of school during her senior year that she had to repeat the twelfth grade. How, taking the advice of parents and counselors, Jana had carried the baby to full term—all the way up to the beginning of the Christmas season—and then had immediately given the little boy up for adoption. How they had not been allowed to learn anything about the adoptive parents. How unforgettable the ordeal had been, especially for Jana.

Cole, for the first time in a long time, wondered about the little boy. He would be what— a teenager by now? Was he okay? Where did he live? What did he look like? What kind of family did he have?

He reached upward into the darkened cell, as if trying to touch Jana's presence.

"How can I ever forgive myself, babe? I hurt you so much. In so many ways."

He remembered how Jana had leapt into his arms when he had proposed, hugging him so hard that it hurt. How they had both dropped out of college to get married and shortly thereafter moved to Nashville for him to try to launch a music career. How Jana had single-handedly sustained their household with her steady work as a mail handler at one of the nation's biggest insurance companies while he had written music and sung wherever he had a chance. How their marriage, after five or six years, had been significantly strained because of his stubbornness to keep pushing, refusing to abandon his pursuit of a lucrative music career. And how Jana had out of desperation eventually turned to God, finding an unprecedented peace in her life, and had influenced him to follow in her steps. How a music contract had shortly thereafter miraculously come his way. How they had started to rebuild their lives with a naive faith.

And how everything after that...had...

Cole squeezed the sheets in his hands. "Why?" he hissed beneath his tears. "Why did I ever have to be born?"

*   *   *

Sometime after midnight, Cole crawled out of bed and lay prostrate on the floor. He groaned and sobbed, trying to muffle his voice. Then, with the deepest humility, he prayed for the first time in seventeen months. "I know I am the lowest of the low." He gasped for breath as he watered the floor with tears. "I know I don't deserve for You to even listen to me. I come to You now only because of Your great mercy." There was a long pause. He pressed his forehead against the floor. "Will You forgive me? Will You forgive me for my crimes against my wife and my son? For my anger? For my bitterness? For my blame? For my ignorance? I want to be at peace with You. I want to be clean. I want to be able to trust You again. Help me—please—I need You!"

16

"You should have never told me to prove it—you manless little piece of crap!" With one final jerk to secure the knot holding the gag, Jesse's father turned to stomp up the steps. But at the last moment, he swiveled and launched one final verbal assault. "Just to let you know—I never wanted you anyway. That was all your mother's doing. And if you ever tell a *single soul* about this, especially the police, then I *really will* hurt you." He looked toward the other side of the room. "And your mother too." The man's chest heaved. "I'll hurt her real bad." He turned and started up the stairs. "I'll be back in twenty-four hours. That'll give you both long enough to realize I'm serious about everything I say."

Jesse, gasping for breath, watched in fury and anguish as his father marched out of the basement, turning off the lights and slamming the door behind him.

Sitting in the dark, his legs, torso, and arms roped painfully to a wooden chair, Jesse took several deep breaths.

Then he fought and strained to free himself. But the chair was strapped securely to a metal pole and wouldn't bulge. Neither would the ropes binding him. He squirmed furiously one more time, then tried to relax to conserve his energy. He wanted to scream an obscenity, but the gag running through his mouth kept his tongue from forming words. All he could do was growl and groan as he bit down on the rag and exhaled in rage.

He wanted to call out to his mother to find out if she was okay. She too was tied to a chair, at a different pole. And she too had been beaten in the face, just as he had.

Jesse squinted. The blood that had dripped from his bashed nose was now drying on his upper lip. The urge was strong to wipe at it. But he could not lift his hands.

Again, he struggled against the ropes. He flexed and strained every muscle in his body. He fought. And he pushed. Eventually, he was sucking air through his aching nose as if he had just crossed the finish line in a four-hundred-meter race. He felt his head grow woozy. He backed off.

By the time his eyes started adjusting to the darkness, he realized he needed to pee. Tightening the muscles around his bladder, he looked across the basement and tried to steady his focus. He could make out the shape of his mother, but without any detail. Jesse could see only that she was very still.

Should he have stepped in to fight for her? She'd made no attempt to defend herself as she was being yanked, slapped, and punched. He wasn't sure if he should pity her or despise her. He knew for sure, though, that she would obey orders and never call the police. Not even for his—her own son's—sake.

Oh, but Jesse would make the call. And he would relish the moment. He could feel his face smirk with sadistic pleasure beneath the gag. No—on second thought, he wouldn't make the call either. What he would do was continue to fight back. Yes, and bide his time. In a few years, when he was big enough and strong enough, he would personally deliver the payback. He would make the old man regret the day he was born. He would just plan to slowly and painfully beat him to death. And then he would track down the man who had given him away at birth and do the same to him.

For several minutes, those thoughts filled his mind—until, that is, he could no longer hold back the pressure building in his bladder.

When he felt the warmth soak into his pants and puddle in the chair, his disgust for life intensified even more.

Happy birthday, he moaned to himself.

Today, December 3, 1997, was his thirteenth birthday.

17

Cole sat at the metal table in his cell and stared at his pencil. It was ten days until Christmas.

He eventually lifted the pencil off the paper.

In the past six months, his heart and mind had been transformed from stagnant pools of meaninglessness to restorative springs of hope. The day-to-day release that he had felt in his body and soul had been nothing less than miraculous.

It had been God's Word that had resuscitated him, and which was still dramatically recasting his mind. He had now memorized over fifty verses and was determined to memorize new verses every week.

His Bible, filled with notes, looked like a scrapbook with comments, cross-references, and questions written on almost every page.

He had also learned to pray. In his prayer sessions, he held nothing back; he shared everything on his heart. Those conversations with God—the first event on his agenda each morning and the last each night—had pushed his relationship with the Almighty out of a 'lifeless theory' status into an irreplaceable intimacy, intense and unlike anything Cole had ever experienced. He felt as if God was tenderly and reassuringly holding him on his lap. He even imagined that he could feel God's breath on his skin.

Yet, he still struggled with bouts of guilt and self-hate.

He looked at the pencil in his hand.

Parker had asked him specifically to put into writing everything he remembered about the car crash, Jana's suicide, and the death of his son. The idea, Parker had explained, was for him to exhaust his memory regarding the tragedies that had led to his massive self-hatred, and to record them on something that was destructible, like paper. Once finished, he was supposed to read and reread the stories until they no longer controlled his emotions and then destroy them once and for all.

He rolled the pencil in his fingers.

He had managed over the past five days to write the accounts of the car crash that had killed Allison and Stephanie, and of Jana's suicide. But instead of helping to diminish the pain, the exercise had only seemed to amplify it.

Nevertheless, he finally lowered the pencil to the paper to write down his recollection of the most horrific day of his life.

> On Saturday, May 18, 1996, the day after my Nashville concert, I decided to take out the restored John Deere and the bush hog to

cut two acres of roadside land on my new property. My plan was to eventually landscape the area and create an eye-pleasing entry to the estate. Maybe even put in a terraced fountain. When I was getting ready to walk out to the barn, Jana was on the phone with one of her church friends. She motioned for me to take Shay outside and get him away from the TV. So I took him with me.

As I changed the oil in the tractor, I let Shay play in his sandbox. Every minute or so, I would peek out of the barn and make sure he was okay.

I then drove the tractor around to the shed to connect the bush hog. All the while, I was hoping Jana would come outside and take over the responsibility of watching Shay.

She had said twice before that she didn't want Shay riding on the tractor with me when I was doing potentially dangerous work. But when the tractor was ready to roll, Shay's eyes lit up with boyish anticipation. He asked if he could ride with me. Jana hadn't appeared yet, so I...

Cole pulled the pencil away from the paper. He stood, paced the cell a few times, then stood and stared at the ceiling. Then he returned to the table.

... put Shay on the tractor with me and hoped Jana wouldn't make a big deal out of it. Shay had ridden on the tractor with me twice before and had shown both times that he could sit still.

I placed him in a standing position between my knees, right behind the steering wheel. He wrapped his arms around my thighs. That's where I had put him before. As I started the tractor and headed slowly around the house and down the driveway, I watched him to make sure he was going to be okay. He was more than okay; he was having a great time with his dad on a gorgeous Spring day.

The entire two-acre plot was over-grown with a tall thicket of briars,

> shrubs, and vines. I aligned the tractor to begin a run around the outside perimeter of the plot, then reached down and pulled the lever to lift the bush hog another three inches off the ground. The extra clearance was needed for the bush hog to cut through the heavy brush.

> As I engaged the rear drive shaft to spin the blades, I remembered that I had promised myself that I would equip the underside of the mower with a stump jumper.

Once again Cole stopped writing. He pressed the eraser hard into the table. *Oh God, why didn't I just keep the promise!* He nearly changed his mind about completing the chaplain's request. But he desperately needed to find healing. And if the chaplain was convinced that this type of therapy would help...

He took ten minutes to breathe slowly, eyes closed, trying to keep himself from emotionally breaking, and then began writing again.

> The bush hog blades spun into motion. When they made contact with the first pieces of brush, the sound of shearing was explosive.

Shay didn't even flinch. He was in kid's heaven.

After I'd made one loop around the field, I stopped to make sure Shay was okay. I was amazed at how absorbed he was, loving every minute of it. I continued circling, cutting my way inward toward the middle of the grove, feeling that everything was under control. The tractor and bush hog were functioning flawlessly. The field was flat and easy to cut. The sun was shining. A big rabbit scurried out of the brush. The day was idyllic. And we were creating a special father-son memory that we would carry with us for a lifetime.

Cole wiped at the stream of tears beginning to flow.

Occasionally, I would pat Shay on the head and squeeze him between my knees.

At one point when I slowed the tractor to make a turn, we happened to be facing the road and saw a couple of motorcycles appear around the curve on the two-lane asphalt. For the first time, Shay wiggled. He shouted, "Look at the motorcycle men, daddy!" When we saw a third and fourth motorcycle, I stopped the tractor. Then there was a fifth and sixth. Shay was so excited, it was as if I could see the grin on his face, even through the back of his head. Another bike appeared. Then another. Altogether, eighteen motorcycles roared by the field. Shay tracked them with his eyes until they all disappeared in the distance over a slight rise in the road.

I remember laughing and saying, "Man! That was a big group of bikes, wasn't it?" I even cheered to cement the moment as something special.

To my surprise, Shay turned with a glow on his face and said, "Can we get one, daddy?"

I chuckled and said something like, "That would be a lot of fun, but I'm afraid mommy wouldn't like that idea very much...at least not until you're a little older. Maybe in a few years, when you're bigger, we can talk about getting one."

I'll never forget what he said. "Will that be a real long, long time, or just a middle time?"

I had never heard anyone use the term "middle time" before. I just smiled. Since we were idling at a standstill, I lifted him onto my lap, hugged him, and said, "I promise I'll do everything I can to make it just a middle time."

He nodded a single exuberant nod.

Cole sniffed and wiped at his face again. Could that moment really have been a year and a half ago?

I put him down between my knees again so we could finish the job. We worked for another thirty minutes or so and were almost finished when Shay said he had to pee. We were only two or three cuts away from having everything mowed, but he had already fought his urge for a good five minutes or so and had started to squirm. So I stopped the tractor one more time. This time I turned off the engine.

Instantly, everything became quiet, except for the sound of some agitated bluejays and a passing bumblebee. I'll never forget it. I don't know why. Maybe it's because they were some of the last sounds of nature that Shay ever heard.

To get the two of us off the tractor, I had to stand up. But I guess I had been tensing my legs for a long time, holding him in place, because when I tried to stand, I immediately dropped back into the seat with a leg cramp. I massaged and stretched the muscle for a good half minute before I was able to get up and help Shay off the tractor.

I stood Shay in the shadow of the giant rear tire and let him do his business. He peed for a long time for such a little guy. Some of the last words I said to him were...

Cole squeezed the pencil. He battled to keep it moving.

...."Man, you did have to go, didn't you? You were a big boy to hold it for so long and not wet your pants. You did good. I'm really proud of you, buddy."

I then refastened his pants and put him back on the tractor.

But when I climbed back up, sat down, and spread my legs to make a place for him, the leg cramp struck again. I jumped up and tried to massage it out. Since we only had two more rows to cut, I told Shay that we needed to try a different seating arrangement. For the final two runs, I decided he could just stand up on the seat next to me. So I got in position, lifted him up, and placed him beside me. The seat had a backrest with mini armrests. I was sure it would be safe. I told him to hold onto my shoulder and grip my shirt.

When he was settled, I started the tractor and engaged the bush hog blades. Once we were moving and I was able to free my right hand, I reached back and put my arm around his legs as an added precaution.

As we approached the end of the first row...

Cole froze. His eyes closed and tightened. He didn't move for a long, long time—he wasn't sure how long.

Then he put the paper away. He would try to finish it later. Maybe tomorrow.

18

The following evening, after work, Cole took out his paper and pencil again. He took a deep breath, then focused on the last words he had written the day before. He thought for a long time, then pushed the lead across the surface of the paper.

> As we approached the end of the first row, I moved my right arm from around Shay's legs and put it on the steering wheel, freeing up my left hand to adjust the throttle. I intended to slow the tractor enough that at the end of the strip I could swing the machine around for the final sweep.
>
> "Okay, Shay," I told him, "I want you to hold—"
>
> And then it happened.

Cole released the pencil, placed his right hand on the back of his neck, and squeezed. He blew puffs of air, trying to hold himself together, then picked up the pencil and wept his way through the scribbling of the next paragraph. Tears blotched his paper.

> It happened so fast, too fast for me to react. The tractor's left rear wheel rolled up and over some large object. The tractor was instantly thrown into an extreme tilt to the right. In less than a second, I jerked my right arm around to grab Shay. And I tried to deny what I knew had just happened. He had been thrown off the seat. I desperately searched for him. And then, as if time froze, I saw him. He was sliding back-first down the wheel fender. In the next instant, he was sliding past the axle, wearing an expression of sheer terror.

Cole laid the pencil down and stood. He walked to the bars and took them in his hands. He pressed his head against the metal. He had spent a year and a half trying to push these images out of his head. Now he was intentionally trying to dredge them up again. Why had he agreed to do this?

It was several minutes before he could pick up the pencil again.

I locked eyes with him in that last possible moment. I made one last attempt to catch him. And failed.

In the split second before he disappeared I tried to shout to him a million times with my eyes that I was so sorry.

And then he was gone.

The tractor's left wheel slammed back down. I reached desperately with my feet to find the brake pedals. But the violent motion of the tractor jostled me, and I fumbled.

The bush hog was pulled up and over the unseen obstacle and lifted at a high angle. High enough for...

Tears were now dropping on the paper like rain.

The next moment, the air was shattered by a sound so unearthly that no parent in a thousand lifetimes should ever have to hear it—the sound of bush hog blades grinding their way through the flesh of their own child.

I screamed "NOOOO!" so loud it hurt. My body stretched and tensed as if I had been jolted in an electric chair. When I finally found the brake pedals, I shoved with every bit of strength I had. I turned the ignition off and leapt off the machine even before it lurched to a halt.

I scanned the ground on all sides of the bush hog and tractor. I saw nothing resembling my boy. I beat my face and screamed. I dove to the ground, ignoring the brush stubs that stabbed me. Flooded with adrenaline, I pushed one side of the bush hog far enough off the ground to get some light underneath, ignoring the decelerating blades. It was several seconds before my brain could accept what my eyes were already registering—particles of flesh, bone, and blood stuck en masse around the blade housing. I started to pass out. Then I noticed that the brush clippings all around me were splattered with blood. So were the tractor and bush hog. It looked like gallons and gallons. Then I saw the blood all over my clothes where I had laid in it.

Shaking, I picked a blood-covered object from my pants. I stared at it. I realized that it was a piece of bone. Skin and hair were attached to it.

PART 2

19

Amidst the ups and downs of prolonged grief, Cole continued to fight for his healing. His spiritual hunger became the driving force in his life. Throughout the remainder of the year, and well into the next, he continued to research and devour the Scriptures, memorizing dozens of passages. And he tried wholeheartedly to let the truth of those verses govern his daily decisions, actions, and reactions.

On a stormy afternoon in April, the chaplain told him with a smile, "It's been a long time since I've seen such... spiritual passion...in either a man or a woman. You've been a real inspiration to me. Not to mention the fact that you've...forced me to dig deeper into the Word just to answer your questions. I appreciate you. More than you know."

Cole did not allow the words to inflate his ego. Instead, he asked yet another question, one that he had been waiting to ask for months. "According to your understanding of the Scriptures, little boys do go to heaven when they die, don't they?" He and the chaplain had recently begun their Bible study on heaven, and now was the opportune time to seriously discuss the matter.

Parker became resolute as he answered, as if he had been expecting the question for some time. "When we studied God's attribute of forgiveness several months ago, you remember that we looked at God's interaction with King David as one of our examples. It was during the time of David's affair with Bathsheba...and his plot to kill her husband."

Cole nodded.

"As you recall," Parker stated, "Bathsheba got pregnant from that encounter. And the baby died about a week after it was born. We didn't talk at length about that particular part of the story, but...when the infant was fighting for its life, David agonized around the clock. He was so distraught over the child's suffering that he refused to eat, to leave the palace, or sleep in his own bed. For a solid week he slept on the floor...fasted and prayed. And begged God to let the baby live. For His own reasons, though, God allowed the little boy to die. At that point in the story, David— moved by the inspiration of the Holy Spirit according to First Peter, chapter one, verse twenty—made the following statement: *'Now that he is dead...why should I fast? Can I bring him back again? I will go to him...but he will not return to me.'* When David says, 'I will go to him', he is not referring to the grave. It's clear that he's talking about a hope-filled two-way reunion. So, the inference here is that he is looking forward to...a heavenly rendezvous. Therefore, the verse implies that the baby's soul went to a place of salvation. Did the baby do something special to merit a place in heaven? Of course not. Thus, the implication here is that all children, in general, before they reach the age where they can choose to lose their innocence, are...safe in God's redemptive hand. So *yes*—little boys, like Shay, do go to heaven when they die."

Cole shut his eyes and exhaled in unbelievable relief. He felt something break free inside his soul. He felt a rare smile bloom across his face as he opened his eyes again. "Thank you," he said. He grasped the chaplain's hand. "Thank you. Thank you."

The chaplain returned the hand squeeze. "Just keep trusting Him. Despite what He allows to come your way, He is still—and always will be—a good God."

Cole affirmed the exhortation with a simple nod. Then he added, "By the way, there's something I never told you. On the night before the tractor accident, my wife and I had put Shay to bed and were enjoying a restful moment in the outdoor hot tub when we suddenly saw him standing there wide-eyed on the deck. He had been awakened by a nightmare. He dreamed that a machine had tried to eat him." Cole ran his hand over his head. "I got out of the tub and sat him on my lap. I assured him that those kinds of machines didn't exist. Then I promised him that even if they did, I would never let a machine like that eat him. I told him that I would take care of him." Cole's words faded. "He believed me; and that's one of the last promises I ever made to him."

"It's still not your..." The chaplain stopped himself in

mid-sentence. Instead, he just reached out and patted Cole on the back like an understanding grandfather.

"One more thing," Cole mumbled. "I burned both the tractor and the mower."

The chaplain looked at him questioningly.

"Yeah," Cole went on, "I drenched them both in gasoline and set them on fire." Cole sniffed. "They'll never hurt anybody again."

The chaplain nodded. And suppressed a grin.

That night, Cole slipped to his knees in the dark. At his bedside, he whispered audibly as if God were sitting on the edge of the bed. "You above all others know what it's like to lose a son. You certainly understand the grief." Cole took a deep breath. "You know that I think about my son literally every day of my life. I miss him more than I can describe!" He paused, looking for strength to say the next words. "But I give him up to You. And I know that one day I *will* see him again. In the meantime...do You think You can give him a message? Will You just tell him that his dad says hi, and that I miss him." Cole felt tears surfing down his cheeks. "And will You please tell him that I've finally made peace with You...that You've healed my soul. And that I will see him again one day. And...and...will You please give that message to Jana as well? Will You please do that for me?"

Overcome with the deepest of joys, Cole felt a sense of release that produced a high he never would have imagined.

He fell asleep that night with tears drying on his face.

* * *

In the following days, Cole found the motivation to start broadening his horizons again. He began by focusing on the bags containing his fan mail. During his year and nine months in prison, he had received and accumulated three large grocery bags of cards and letters. He had not yet read a single word of any of them.

Prison authorities, though, according to state policy, had already opened every letter and checked them for contraband.

On a gorgeous Saturday afternoon in May—with his mood matching that of the restorative spring season—Cole took an envelope from one of the heaps. He looked at the return address. The writer was a woman from California.

Cole closed his eyes and for a moment tried to remember being a music star. Had he really been a celebrity? Those memories, so vague now, seemed light-years away. Almost unreachable.

He removed the letter and began to read:

> Dear Cole,
> Thank you for your CD *Sweet Manipulations*, especially the song *Soul Dreamer*. I'm sure this song has impacted many lives, and I want you to know that mine is one of them. Let me say first that I'm not a huge fan of country music of any sort. I have listened to too many rednecks croon their way through bad music and bad

grammar. Thus, my attitude wasn't too good when I first heard your song introduced on a pop station. But, as I listened to the first twenty seconds of *Soul Dreamer*, your unconventional voice and your soothing but emotional music drew me in and spoke to my heart. You see, I'm a person who has it all. I've got a great husband (married 15 years), four terrific kids, and a perfect job as a university English professor. Still, I'm so restless. And I struggle with selfishness. I married very young and immediately had children. I never had the chance, as many people do, to be by myself and responsible only to myself, and allowed to follow my own dreams. All too often, I've viewed my life as joyless, a series of must-do's: must cook dinner, must give birthday party, must wipe child's butt, must change sheets. I felt that I'd lost myself as a person and as a woman. I felt as if my personality and my worth had vanished. I began to entertain strange thoughts: "What if I just left?" I began to think seriously about walking out on my life, in despair that I had abandoned my dreams. But after listening over and over again to your song *Soul Dreamer*, which led to hours of self-examination, I'm now clued in. This life I have IS my dream; I cannot do better than this. I don't want to do better. No one can replace me as the mother of these children.

Cole felt his throat tighten. He forced a cough. He felt as if he were reading someone else's mail. This lady, this professor, was expressing her heart to a man passionately consumed by his art, a man whose talents had risen to the top of the entertainment world. But Cole was no longer that man. And had not been for a long time. He was now a man behind bars. A killer. An irresponsible citizen. A man deemed too dangerous to be free. A man who had not touched a musical instrument, composed a line of music, or written any lyrics in two years. A man who was no longer an artist.

Cole continued to read.

This life I have is a gift, and although it's also a responsibility and yes, sometimes a burden, this gift has been given to <u>me</u>. Thank you for the life-changing inspiration you've provided for me in

your songs. You're now one of my favorite musicians. Whatever happens in your life, please know that I'm thinking about you, and please keep writing music. You're one of the best. With sincerity,
Emily Britt

Cole hung his head. *Favorite musicians...one of the best...please keep writing.* He wasn't sure how to handle the compliments. Or if he should even try.

He refolded and restuffed the letter. He lifted a card out of the bag.

Dear Cole,
I've listened to *Sweet Manipulations* a hundred times. It's literally become a permanent fixture in my CD player. And believe me, it touches my heart every time I listen to it. I sometimes even cry. It is one of the best music CD's I've ever heard. In fact, I keep buying copies to give away as gifts. I'm eagerly looking forward to your next CD. I can hardly wait. One of your biggest fans.
Vicky Leeds

Touches my heart...I even cry...looking forward to your next CD. Cole put the card back into the bag, trying to recapture the feel-good sensation he used to bask in whenever he heard words of adulation about his music. But he just couldn't manage it.

Maybe one day.

*   *   *

Cole spent a good portion of his evenings throughout the long summer months reading and answering every letter and card in the three bags.

And the words in those letters affected him far beyond his expectations.

The writers, in their multiplicity of voices, managed to convince him that he was indeed a gifted musician and that he should not allow that talent to completely fade out of his life. He, therefore, determined that he would trust God to show him when and how, if ever, to use his musical skills again. After all, God was the giver of the gift. "It's all Yours," Cole whispered. "You prompt me when, or if, the time is ever right."

In late summer, Cole decided that he had finally gained enough emotional energy to try to sell his Brentwood property. He knew that the house and the land, after sitting unattended for two years, must be in a state of disarray. He could envision the grounds looking like a jungle; the exterior of the house being seized by shrubs and vines; the rooms of the house being invaded by spiders, ants, dirtdobbers, and bumblebees; and the eaves probably leaking rainwater because of clogged gutters.

He would have to let it go at a bargain-basement price. But once the property was sold, the wrongful death lawsuit filed against him by the parents of Allison Cox could finally be settled.

With the help of the chaplain, it took him a week—through bureaucratic channels—to hire a realtor and put the house on the market.

When Cole heard the realtor's eyewitness assessment of the property—not quite as bad as he had imagined—he priced the house and acreage at below-market value. He included all the furniture, appliances, tools, barn equipment, outdoor accessories, and automobiles in the deal.

To his amazement, he was notified five weeks later, in late September, that a buyer had made an offer, which Cole accepted. The closing on the house and property would take place immediately—the buyer wanted to close on the deal before the last day of September.

Six days later, with the help of a state attorney, Cole penned his signature on all the transaction documents.

On Wednesday, September 30, Cole was sitting in his cell during his break when he was given a scribbled note by one of the guards. It was a message from the realtor, passed down through the captain: *"Everything has been sold. After fees, taxes, commissions, and loan-balance payoff, $360,000 has been deposited into your bank account. Congratulations!"*

Two weeks later, Cole signed all of that money over to the attorneys acting on behalf of the Cox family, completely satisfying the balance of the settlement that had been filed against him for 1.2 million dollars.

He was suddenly penniless, but gratified.

Stretching out on the bed, he thanked God that he had been able to pay off all his debts. He had just started to pray for the Cox family when he was interrupted by Chaplain Parker at his cell door.

"Don't get up," Parker said. "I'm racing to an appointment downtown. I just wanted to stop by real quick and ask if you'd be willing to speak in the chapel service on Sunday morning, December 6—two months away. You don't need to give me an answer right now. Just think about it."

Cole sat up. "What? Me? I...."

"Just think about it." The chaplain smiled, then hurried off.

Cole lay motionless in his bed, his brain spinning like a hamster on an exercise wheel. Why would the chaplain make such a request? The chaplain knew him better than anyone. Cole had never spoken in a church service in his life. Was the chaplain planning to be out of town on that Sunday and desperate to find someone—anyone—to fill in for him? Whatever his reasoning, wasn't he aware of how nerve-wracking it would be for someone with Cole's criminal background to publicly teach God's Word? Besides, what convict sitting in a prison chapel service would listen to another convict expound on God's holy teachings? It sounded absurd. Surely, the chaplain wasn't serious. He couldn't be.

20

Jesse bored a hole in her with his eyes and pounded the wall with his fist. "I want you to tell me NOW!" he screamed.

His fourteenth birthday was less than two months away, and Jesse had grown to 5'8" but weighed only 130 pounds. Barely stronger than his mother, he shook his fist only inches from her face. He had backed her into a corner of the dining room. "I'm tired of your freaking games! I'm not going to play them anymore! So *will* you just answer my question!" Nearly hyperventilating, he pushed his fist against her forehead, forcing her head back into the corner. "Or I'll be left with only one choice—to *beat* the answer out of you, the same way your no-good husband beats you! Now, explain why you pushed to adopt me when you knew dad was a monster and would make my life an absolute hell! *What* was the freaking point?"

Jesse knew that what he was doing was wrong, but he couldn't hold back; his emotions were too powerful, and he couldn't control them.

His mother closed her eyes. "All right," she gasped, "have it your way." Her shoulders slumped; she looked as if she were trying mentally to transport herself to another zone. When she opened her eyes again, she looked at him with a mixture of pity and spite. "Ever since I was a young girl, I always wanted a baby. That was the greatest desire of my life. Your father understood that from day one. But when he would get angry with me, he would force himself on me...sexually. And then he would pull away from me. Right before he...well...you know." She wiped her hands on her apron as if administering some ceremonial cleansing. "One day, I tried to fight back. I dug my fingernails into his back and tried to...uh...hold him in place." A sadistic smile spread across her face. "It worked." The smile was instantly replaced by an expression void of emotion. "But then he went berserk. He beat me in the belly and face so severely that I had to be taken to the hospital. He told the doctors that I had been in an automobile accident. As far as I know, his story was never challenged. But then the doctors told me that, as a result of the injuries, some of my female parts were...broken and that I would never be able to get pregnant." She sneered. "Your dad, in one of his rare moments of guilt, decided he would make it up to me. So he—"

"Adopted me?" Jesse interrupted loudly. "Adopted me as a gift? Just so he could feel good about nearly beating you to death!" Pausing to catch his breath, Jesse shook his head. "So, it wasn't you that asked for the adoption after all. It was *his* decision. And you just went along with it...

just like you do with everything else he says and does! Is that the story?"

Jesse watched as his mother silently tried to figure out what to say. But her silence answered his question. In those short seconds, Jesse felt that his entire inner being was pushed across some invisible barrier. Any love or respect that he might have felt for his mother faded into an abyss. He now felt totally repulsed by her.

Feeling nauseated, he turned and lurched away. One thing was now for sure: emotionally, mentally, and socially, his life would no longer include a mother and a father. He would be responsible only for himself and his own needs.

He stomped into his room and slammed the door behind him. He would now be the ruler of his own domain. Forget everybody else!

He knew he would never be able to trust anyone again, never respect anyone again. And he would no longer hesitate to defy, walk over, or crush anyone—*anyone*—who stepped in his way.

21

Cole tried to stifle his nervousness. How had he been talked into this? He gazed blankly at the twenty-five to thirty convicts facing him in the Sunday morning chapel service. Behind them, a few well-used Christmas decorations hung disjointedly around the room. He felt just as disjointed. Trying to steady his breathing, he looked pointedly at Chaplain Parker. *This is something you need to do,* the chaplain had told him. *You've learned too much to keep it all inside your head; you need to share it with others.* For a moment, Cole and Parker locked eyes.

The chaplain smiled with his crooked mouth and nodded his reassurance.

Cole cleared his throat for the third time, looked down at his notes, and slowly began. "As you can imagine, I'm a little nervous this morning. Chaplain Parker had to ask me about a dozen times before I agreed to do this. He's definitely a determined man."

There were a few mild chuckles from the audience. Cole took another deep breath.

"Anyway, my intention this morning is not to preach at you, or even try to teach you anything. I would simply like to share an important lesson I've learned during the past few years. Two-and-a-half of those years have been spent here. Maybe my story will be an encouragement to you."

Cole looked back down at his notes.

"I've recently been convinced that most of our living is done between our ears. Therefore, I've arrived at the conclusion that *what we believe* between our ears is of the utmost importance. What we believe about God's existence, for example, is crucial. So is our belief about a whole list of other things—man's origin, man's heart, God's heart, God's laws, God's salvation, God's morality, family responsibilities, and human dignity, to name a few. What we believe, I'm learning, is more vital than we often realize. Of course, it's of great importance that our beliefs be based on things that are true."

Cole again looked at the chaplain. Parker was still smiling at him.

"Tragically, I think that most of us believe things that are not true. In other words, we believe lies. We base our lives on those lies. We are driven by those lies. And as life bears out, when we believe lies, we are led down roads of false hopes, false dreams, and eventual ruin." Cole rubbed his lips and felt some of his nervousness subside. "So where do these lies come from? From many places. From the media—magazines, newspapers, radio, and television. They come from our school teachers. They come from our family and friends. They come from our politicians. Our philosophers. Our cultural traditions. Our religious traditions. Our entertainers. Our preachers. Our own minds. They come from every possible angle of life. And if you believe in a literal being called Satan, and if you believe in the Bible's account of Satan's history, then it will make sense to you that he is behind every one of those lies."

Cole opened his Bible to a pre-marked text. Chaplain Parker used the Bible extensively every Sunday, so Cole knew that hearing it read out loud wouldn't be awkward for the men.

"Listen to these words from John's Gospel, chapter eight, verse forty-four: *'The Devil...was a murderer from the beginning and has always hated the truth. There is no truth in him. When he lies, it is consistent with his character; for he is a liar and the father of lies.'*" Cole turned to another passage. "In addition, Revelation, chapter twelve, verse nine, reads: *'This great dragon—the ancient serpent called the Devil or Satan, the one deceiving the whole world—was thrown down to the earth with all his angels.'* Using deception as his universal weapon, Satan's goal—it seems—is to deter every one of the planet's six billion people from hearing and trusting God's truths. Why? So that people will be led astray. So that they will be placed on paths that will lead to selfishness, abuse, confusion, hatred, anger, bitterness, depression, disillusionment, hopelessness, spiritual blindness, and eventual destruction. First Peter, chapter five, verse eight explains that, *'The Devil...prowls around like a roaring lion, looking for some victim to devour.'*"

Cole closed his Bible. "For example, throughout most of my own life, I followed lie after lie after lie." His voice assumed a more humble, solemn tone. "And that is why I am locked away here. I believed four basic lies. And those lies dominated my life. The first lie, which I started to believe in my late teens, was that I did not need God—that my resolve, my talent, and my intellect were more than sufficient to help me navigate through life successfully. The second lie, which I started to believe in my early twenties, was that drunkenness was an acceptable and safe way to medicate my disappointments, sorrows, and pains. The third lie, which I started to believe in my late twenties— right after I became religious—was that God would minimize my discomfort for the remainder of my life and would always honor my faith with success, prosperity, and wellness. The fourth lie, one that I started to believe right after the death of my wife and son, and after my vehicular homicide conviction, was that God could *not* be trusted, that He couldn't care less about my well-being, or anyone else's, and that life was, therefore, hopeless. Now, I have believed hundreds of lies throughout my life, but these four were the major ones. Let me tell you how these lies nearly destroyed me."

Cole took a full breath, hoping he was connecting with the men's hearts and minds. With only a brief hesitation, he launched into his stories. He eventually concluded by sharing an account of the events that had led to his suicide attempts and subsequent incarceration: Shay's death, Jana's suicide, and the car crash that had killed Allison and Stephanie Cox.

Then he explained how the Bible had in the last year exposed the four big lies and replaced them with truths. Truths that had finally set him free.

After twenty-five minutes, he said, "So, to sum up everything I've shared, I would say that right now the greatest ongoing battle in the universe is not between crime and law enforcement, not between democracies and dictatorships, not between the rich and the poor, not between nations, and not between races. Rather, the *greatest* ongoing battle in the universe is between the *lies* of Satan and the *truths* of God. The lies of the enemy, when believed, will *trap and destroy* every victim, without exception. On the other hand, the truths of God, when believed, will set a person free. John's Gospel, chapter eight, verses thirty-one and thirty-two, say, *'You are truly my disciples if you keep obeying my teachings. And you will know the truth, and the truth will set you free.'* Set you free from what? From spiritual condemnation, from spiritual confusion, from hopelessness, from fear, from unforgiveness, from anger, from depression, from bitterness, from emptiness. And the list goes on and on."

Cole could hear his words increasing in passion and conviction. And it felt good.

"It's quite simple," he said, his eyes moist with tears, "God's truths, and only God's truths, will set us free. Not education. Not wealth. Not fame. Not power. Not even parole. Only God's truths."

He exhaled deeply, thankful that he had made it through the entire message without having a nervous breakdown.

"Thanks for letting me share today. I'm truly humbled by the opportunity."

He picked up his Bible and his notes and sat down.

For a moment, silence hung heavy in the air like mountain fog.

Then the meanest-looking convict in the meeting hall stood and began clapping.

After an awkward moment, a second inmate stood and joined in the clapping. A third man stood. Then a fourth. Finally, everyone in the room was on their feet, applauding.

"You did a good job, man!" the mean-looking inmate shouted, looking Cole straight in the eye and giving him a thumbs-up.

A renewed sense of humility swept through Cole's soul. He felt tears forming. He hadn't expected any significant affirmation, much less unanimous applause. What had he said that had sparked such a show of support? He looked at the chaplain, who was clapping along with everyone else. The chaplain gave him the biggest grin ever.

Cole wiped at his eyes. "Thank you," he offered.

After the chaplain's closing prayer, Cole was swamped by a dozen inmates who extended personal thanks and handshakes. At least five of them told him that he should teach again.

That night, he stretched out on his bed and stared into the darkness. Not since he had given his last musical concert, over two and a half years before, had he experienced such a sense of purposefulness. He whispered a heartfelt thanks to his Creator.

Before he surrendered to sleep, he retrieved his hand-written accounts of the car crash, Jana's suicide, and Shay's accident. In the past year, since the chaplain had encouraged him to write them down, he had read the pages and relived the memories at least two hundred times.

He lay back down and held the papers over his heart. Tearfully, he began to tear them into strips. Overwhelmed by God's forgiveness, he ripped the papers into the tiniest possible pieces.

"It's time," he whispered.

He got up and dumped all the scraps into the toilet.

And flushed.

Finally at peace with God, his friends, the world, and himself, he lay back down and rolled onto his stomach. As he started to fade, he felt that in some strange, but monumental, way he had just entered a new phase of his life.

22

Cole's thirst for studying the Scriptures only deepened. So did his desire to teach them. The chaplain began scheduling him to share in the Sunday morning chapel services—sporadically at first, and eventually once a month. And when the prison bureaucrats introduced the Internet to the inmates via the library's computer network, Cole learned to navigate the new technology and enrolled in an online Bible college. He tenaciously completed all the required courses and over a prolonged period earned a Graduate of Theology degree. He became Chaplain Parker's untitled associate.

As a result of his mental and spiritual progress, he regained much of the weight he had earlier lost. He eventually leveled out at a trim 195 pounds. To try to maintain his physical health, he developed a regular exercise routine, incorporating mostly push-ups, sit-ups, chin-ups, and pull-ups.

One of the most notable happenings for him, though —through the migration of changes in his heart and mind—came six years into his prison term, when he decided one weekend to buy a violin. A $16,000 violin. The instrument had been the property of a concertmaster who had performed for many years with the Chattanooga Symphony Orchestra. He had died at the age of ninety-two, and the violin had become part of an online estate sale. Cole read about it in an article in the weekend edition of a Tennessee newspaper that described the colorful musician, his lengthy career, and his famous fiddle.

Cole was absolutely stirred by the vision of the photographs of the fiddle accompanying the article. His interest in music reawakened, as if out of a coma. He felt irresistibly drawn to the instrument, and even more so as he read the details of its description and history. The violin had been made in Vienna, Austria, in 1708 by Johann Georg Thir, considered by many experts to be one of the greatest violin makers in Vienna. The Chattanooga concertmaster had owned the fiddle for fifty-three years and had referred to it as the Mysterious Lady because of its distinctively dark and mysterious sound.

The violin, with its unmistakable craftsmanship, seemed to beckon Cole with some kind of inexplicable power.

On the weekend of the online sale, Cole outbid six other people, becoming the new owner—at least in promise — of the two-hundred-and-ninety-five-year-old Mysterious Lady.

Since settling his "wrongful death" lawsuit years earlier, he had seen his outside bank account grow from zero to more than $60,000 from royalties—that came to him as both singer and songwriter—from the sporadic but continuing sales of *Sweet Manipulations*. He figured the money had to be good for something.

The Mysterious Lady would replace the famous golden fiddle he had bashed across a tree trunk on the day of Jana's funeral. That memory—storming out of the house swearing and completely destroying the prized icon—still seemed fresh. It was one of those milestone memories that now symbolized an unimaginable journey of healing.

His anticipation for the Mysterious Lady's arrival intensified by the day.

The afternoon when he finally lifted the historic violin from its packing and held it in his hands for the first time was nothing less than magical. The instrument was magnificent. From its dark, reddish-brown color to its beautifully arched soundboard, it unmistakably shouted *character* and *one-of-a-kind*. For the longest time, Cole simply caressed the violin, cherishing the great prize that it was. He was enthralled as his fingers gently surveyed its every surface, taking in the soft but well-worn varnish, the ideally placed "F" holes, the grafted neck, and the exquisite scroll. Even before hearing it, he knew instinctively that the Mysterious Lady would somehow become part of his soul, part of who he was for years to come.

The first time he played it, he wept. The experience was emotional beyond all his expectations. Maybe because of past memories and past dreams. Maybe because of the instrument's unique and powerful sound. Maybe because so many years had elapsed since he had last played. Maybe because of the intrinsic and therapeutic value of music itself. Maybe because of all the reasons combined.

And once he started playing, he found that his passion for the instrument built like a crescendo and became insatiable.

He played every day, mainly in the evenings.

And not a soul objected. The inmates up and down the cell block found their spirits lifted by the nightly ritual. They were amazed at Cole's musical giftedness and at his ability to play such beautiful and diverse pieces. They quickly nicknamed him "the Blonde Fiddler."

And the name stuck.

Outside of the fiddle playing, his life became more and more typical of a highly disciplined ascetic. He embraced the restrictions and the simplicity imposed on his day-to-day existence and chose to live out his days with contentment.

And in accordance with state law, his hourly wages rose from seventeen cents to twenty-five cents, then to the maximum—thirty-four cents.

23

At the age of eighteen, Jesse Rainwater—without his parents' knowledge—drove to an adoption agency in the Atlanta district of Decatur. He explained to the female director that he was adopted, gave his adopted name, and asked if the agency could help him find the names of his biological parents.

The lady's expression conveyed sympathy, but she responded firmly, "It's not allowed by state law. I'm sorry. I can't do it. Besides, the odds are that this office did not orchestrate your adoption anyway, since it has only been open for twelve years. And the fact is, the other adoption agencies around town aren't linked together through any kind of computer network, so we don't have access to each other's files. However..."

Jesse's emotions immediately flipped to hopeful when he heard the word *however*.

"There's an agency downtown on Peachtree Street," she said, "that you can contact for help. It's the Adoption Reunion Registry." She reached toward some shelves.

"Here's one of their brochures. The address and phone number are on the back. The Registry has official records of 95 percent of all the adoptions registered in the State of Georgia."

Jesse took the brochure and thanked her. Less than an hour later, he pulled into a multi-deck parking garage a few blocks from the Registry's Peachtree address.

He found the Registry's office on the eighth floor of a skyscraper. Once inside, he asked to speak with a director and was shown to the office of an older lady, where he was invited to sit on a couch and explain the reason for his visit.

Trying to present a winning manner, he politely detailed his request.

"How old are you?" the lady asked.

"Eighteen."

"Well, we are indeed set up to assist adopted children such as yourself. But according to the laws of Georgia, we are not allowed to give you what is called 'identifying information' about your biological parents until you're twenty-one. For now, we can only provide what is called 'non-identifying information.'"

Jesse tried to conceal his instant frustration. "And what is 'non-identifying' information?"

"Just basic information about the birth parents—their physical description, health history, and possibly their reasons for giving you up for adoption."

"But no names? Or addresses?"

"No names or addresses. We're only allowed to uncover that information for you after you turn twenty-one. And then, you have to pay a search fee of three hundred dollars.

At that time, you write a letter to be given to your birth mother, asking permission for us to release her identity to you. We try to find her. If we find her, we give her your letter. If she has an interest in any kind of reunion, she will have to write a letter of response, giving us permission to release her identity. We can then give you her name and address. The process, from the time you fill out the initial application, takes four to six months."

Jesse swore inside his head. Outwardly, he strummed his fingers on the couch and faced his options. He didn't want a piece of paper to explain to him why his birth parents had given him up for adoption—he wanted the man and the woman to tell him face to face, especially the man. And he didn't want to wait years for that to happen!

Maybe he should just come back to the Reunion Registry in a year or so when the director lady had forgotten him and get a job here. He could surely manipulate the system from the inside and get his hands on his birth parents' names. But would the lady forget him? Unlikely.

"What about my birth father? When I'm twenty-one, can we try to get him to release his name as well?"

"We always start with the mother. But yes, we can try to facilitate an exchange of information between you and your birth dad as well. It will cost an additional three hundred dollars."

Jesse felt his hands ball up into fists. Two-and-a-half years he would have to wait just to *begin* the process! What crackhead fool decided that a person had to be twenty-one before he could learn the identity of his birth parents?

Jesse stood and looked around. Most likely, the names

of his biological mom and dad were stored in files just yards away. Maybe he should come back with a gun and take the information by force.

"All right," he told the lady. "I guess I have no choice but to wait until I'm twenty-one." He wiped his brow and forced himself to say, "Thank you."

Outside, he dared anyone to cross eyes with him. He felt like a walking land mine. He wanted to hurt somebody. Anybody. Man, woman, boy, girl; he couldn't care less. The urge to dominate burned through him like venom. He had to do something. To somebody.

And if not to his birth dad…

Then…yes…maybe the time had finally come to carry out his plan for his adoptive dad. After all, there were only six days left before he—the undesirable son—moved out of the man's house. Forever.

On his way home, he stopped at three nursery-and-garden centers before he found what he was looking for—a packet of castor bean plant seeds.

The packet cost a grand total of $4.53. He paid with cash. He did not want there to be a debit or credit card trail connected to the sale.

"You know these seeds are toxic, don't you?" the gray-haired man at the cash register said.

"No, I didn't," Jesse lied.

"Well, they are. So, be careful and don't leave them lying around in the reach of children or animals."

Back in the car, Jesse noticed that his hands were sweating. He turned up the fan on the AC and replayed in his head, over and over again, the words his dad had growled at him several months ago, right after breaking his arm. *"If you ever fight back again when you're being disciplined, I will not only put you in the hospital, I'll put you down! For good! You no-good piece of waste!"*

Yeah, "being disciplined"—as if punching, kicking, shoving, smashing, and bludgeoning without restraint had anything whatsoever to do with discipline. It was just hatred. Pure hatred.

But if there was one thing he was proud of, it was the fact that, ever since the basement episode on his thirteenth birthday, he had consistently and aggressively fought back. Even so, it disturbed him that he still wasn't physically strong enough to make his dad afraid of him.

"Well, we'll see!" Jesse smiled an avenger's smile.

He held up the packet of seeds.

Could it be as easy as the Internet websites had implied? Seeds that were available at garden centers everywhere. Seeds that contained a toxin called ricin, a toxin so lethal that three seeds crushed and ingested could over a seventy-two-hour period create an irreversible avalanche of physical breakdowns—fever, respiratory difficulties, intestinal bleeding, seizures, and finally death. And all without a single available antidote.

If nothing had changed, his "dad" would be leaving tomorrow afternoon for a three-day business trip to Savannah.

So, yes, now was the time to act. Now was the time to end the man's reign of abuse and terror. For his mom. Himself. And God knew who else.

Jesse threw the seed packet onto the seat and spat out the window.

That afternoon, he wrapped three castor bean plant seeds in a rag and crushed them with a hammer, then ground them over and over until the seeds were a grainy powder. He dumped the pulverized seeds into a jar of instant coffee that his dad, and only his dad, opened three or four times a day. He mixed the seeds thoroughly with the coffee granules, just in the upper part of the jar.

He took the remaining seeds and the rag he had used, drove three miles from his house, and threw it all into a concrete drainage pipe.

Driving back to the house, this time his hands didn't even sweat.

24

As one year rolled into another, and then another, the Mysterious Lady became a distinct part of Cole's identity. The newest inmates and staff knew him only as the Blonde Fiddler; they never heard him called anything else.

Although it wasn't what he asked for, or even wanted, the violin in his hands and in his broken spirit gave him an aura of refinement and deep respectability, even among some of the hardcore criminals.

He was especially surprised to learn that reports of his revived faith and fiddle playing had spread outside the prison walls. One afternoon he received a letter from a Mister Roland Powers, the CEO of a young music production company called SpiritMark Productions. Cole read it with absolute amazement.

> SpiritMark, as a company, is committed to being one of the industry leaders in the marketing of inno-

vative, contemporary, and high-quality Christian music. Poised for dynamic growth, our company is actively looking for personnel to serve at many different levels. If you don't mind, please add my name to your list of permitted visitors and send me a visitor's application form. If I am approved, I would love to visit with you face to face and perhaps talk about some of the SpiritMark positions that might be available to you after your release.

The man had also added the name of a female colleague that he wanted to bring along.

With only a year-and-a-half left to serve and with no post-prison plans, Cole—more out of curiosity than anything else—mailed the "visitor application" forms.

* * *

Two months later, Cole placed his cleaning paraphernalia in the storage bin and was escorted back to his cell for his morning break where he nervously awaited the announcement of his visitors.

Within twenty minutes, one of the guards arrived and unlocked his cell.

Since mailing off the application forms for Powers and

his colleague, Cole had anticipated this moment with more than a mild curiosity. As he and the guard approached the only room in the prison complex where outsiders were allowed—and then only after extensive bureaucratic screening—Cole wondered again how and why anyone like this Roland Powers had remembered him and had kept track of him.

When the guard opened the door and let Cole into the long, narrow room, he said, "Your visitors are at cubicle three. You have fifteen minutes."

Excited, nervous, and a little confused, Cole maneuvered into his specified chair, looking through the transparent bulletproof partition that separated him from his visitors. He felt an immediate chemical explosion inside his body. In the past decade, he had seen only five or six women—his mother-in-law, who had visited a couple of times, and the few females on the prison staff. None of the female staff had been even remotely attractive. Now, on the other side of the partition, stood an absolutely gorgeous woman who nearly took his breath away. Early to mid-thirties. Fit. With a stunning figure and outstanding posture. Stylish gray suit. Thick, honey-blonde hair cut in a bobbed, layered, carefree fashion. Radiant blue eyes. Brilliant white teeth. And lips that begged to be kissed.

The lady's attractiveness hijacked his eyes and made it nearly impossible for him to look at anything else. With great effort, he fought to visually acknowledge the man who stood at her side, obviously Mister Roland Powers.

Cole picked up the intercom phone and quickly stood up again.

The man lifted the phone on the other side. "Cole Michaels?" The voice was radio quality and professional.

"Yeah—that's me. I'm Cole Michaels."

"Well, it's an honor to meet you. I wish I could shake your hand. But...I guess we're not going to manage that under the current circumstances."

Cole dipped his head in acknowledgment.

"All right." Powers hesitated. "Is it okay if we sit while we talk?"

"Please." Cole nodded toward the chairs.

Everyone took a seat.

"All right. I'll jump right in. I'm Roland Powers, the founder and CEO of SpiritMark Productions, as I explained in my letters. And this is Lindsey Rose, the administrative assistant at our company. If you don't mind, she'll take a few notes as we talk."

Cole nodded at the lady, finding himself afraid to hold eye contact with her. His social muscles with ladies, it seemed, had atrophied due to lack of use. Still, as if magnetized, his eyes were drawn helplessly back to her figure. He caught himself brushing down his hair. He had forgotten just how weak the human psyche was when up against true beauty.

"Yeah...that's fine. Sure," he heard himself say nervously.

"Well, I'll get right to the point. Everyone on our staff is familiar with your previous work. And according to our latest research, your debut release *Sweet Manipulations* is still selling quite well, even after ten years. Obviously, its longevity on the market speaks volumes about the broad appeal of your unique voice and musical style." Powers leaned forward slightly. "Now, in the last two or three years, we've been hearing through the industry grapevine that you have become quite involved here in the chaplaincy program and that you have also resumed your fiddle playing. I have a proposal that I would like to put on the table, but first I need to find out if these rumors are true."

Cole caught himself looking at the lady again. This time he found her smiling at him. He felt like a shy fifth-grader who had been caught staring starry-eyed at his beautiful teacher. He cleared his throat. "Yes...they're both true." He wondered how anyone on the outside would know these things. Or even care.

Powers's voice took on a new energy. "Then, I have to ask—does your involvement in the chapel here in any way indicate that you've become a serious believer?"

Cole was suddenly in comfortable territory. He looked directly into the man's eyes. "Sir, I don't yet understand all the reasons you're here, but I'll say without shame that Christ and Christ alone has sustained my soul, my sanity, and my hope. And everything else that I have. Or am. So, yes. I am a serious believer. And if a person can be *more* than serious, then I am that too."

Roland Powers smiled. "Is it also true that you'll be getting out in about a year and two months?"

"Yeah. That's about right."

"Then I'll cut to the chase," Powers stressed. "My company would like to negotiate with you about producing your next CD. A CD for the Christian market. A CD with all original music. All original lyrics. All written by you. A CD that we would market heavily throughout the United

States, Canada, the United Kingdom, South Africa, New Zealand, Australia, and Europe."

Cole's mind was instantly blitzed. He was speechless.

Powers forged ahead. "With your permission, I would like to leave this proposed contract with you." Powers waited while Lindsey Rose removed a set of stapled pages from her briefcase. Powers then held the papers up. "I'll arrange for the warden to get this to you, if that's all right. It's a standard contract. Look it over during the next few days. If you are interested in our proposal, then please understand that there are items in the contract that we can modify. What I'm saying is—we really would like to work with you. And we're willing to negotiate any of the fine points. All I ask is that you try to give us an answer sometime in the next four weeks. And *if* your answer is yes, I would hope that during the next twelve months or so, you could complete most of the writing, so that upon your release we could quickly get you back into the recording studio."

Cole's mind buzzed. He had wondered several times in the previous weeks what kind of work Powers had in mind for him. But he hadn't expected anything of this magnitude. Why, after all these years, would an industry executive like this be willing to take such a gamble on him? "Yeah. Of course I'll take a look at the contract. But this is coming at me rather quickly. I mean, I can't make any promises today. But I will think through the offer and seek God's guidance. And try to give you an answer in the next few weeks."

Powers grinned. "Fantastic, that's all I'm asking. And

I'm sure as you consider the offer, you'll come up with a lot of different questions, so I'll leave my contact information along with the contract."

All too quickly, the guard stepped into the room and announced that there was one minute left.

As everybody stood, Lindsey Rose took the visitor's phone and spoke for the first time. "I don't mean to speak out of place, but I do want to say one thing."

Cole watched her, transfixed. Had he just been in prison too long? Or was this Lindsey Rose indeed an exceptionally attractive woman by anyone's standards? Again, he felt literally overpowered by her beauty. Even the way her hair moved was eye-catching to him. And the way her lips moved! He tried to shake the feelings that started to stir inside him.

The lady offered a smile that was relaxed and effervescent. "I just want you to hear it said by someone in the music industry that there is a real void in the marketplace right now for your style of music—especially in the Christian marketplace. The street needs your novel type of creativity and talent. Especially the upcoming generation that missed out on your first run. And truthfully, Roland and I, and everyone else at SpiritMark, believe that there's a potential for you to reach millions of new listeners. We're convinced the market would welcome you everywhere with open arms. So, please think long and hard about the offer. Besides, I think you would find it a lot of fun to work with us."

That afternoon and evening, Cole found that the image of Lindsey Rose would not fade from his head. Her beauty held his brain like vice grips. And her words—*"I think you would find it a lot of fun to work with us*"—would not stop recycling through his mind.

As he lay in bed that night, he wondered over and over if the invitation from SpiritMark was an open door from God. "A potential to reach millions of listeners," they had said. The opportunity, considering its scope and timing, could not have been orchestrated by fate alone, could it? One thing was for sure: Any lyrics he wrote now would be saturated with words, thoughts, and expressions that would extol God's character and God's heart to the highest.

Writing the music itself during the next twelve months would be no problem. He had already, in the past couple of years, written a dozen or more decent pieces of music without any contractual motivation whatsoever. He would mainly just need to work on the vocals.

The more he thought about the offer, the more he felt drawn to it.

25

Gripping the cell bars in a wide overhead position, Jesse rested his forehead against one of the center bars. Staring at nothing, he thought about the TV documentary he had just seen concerning the worldwide big-dollar crime of human trafficking. Could he somehow tap into that business and score some significant bucks? When he was released from jail in eight months, he would need only enough money to keep himself fed and sheltered while he hunted down his biological dad.

He grinned. Was he ready to run with the big boys and buy and sell human flesh? He would definitely research the matter and see what he could find out.

He spat through the bars into the corridor. One thing was for sure—he could hardly wait to get out of this hell hole. He looked with disgust at the huge sign posted on the corridor wall, right across from his cell:

In-House Rules
Dodge State Prison
Chester, Georgia

(1) No lewd contact at any time with any other inmate.

(2) No physical contact at any time with any member of the prison staff.

(3) No urinating or defecating on any of the prison floors.

(4) No defacing the cell walls or furnishings with graffiti of any kind.

(5) No television or radio noise after lights out.

All violators of these rules, without exception, will be disciplined by solitary confinement for a period of time deemed relevant by the warden.

Jesse upbraided himself again for being careless enough to get caught. He swore that it would never happen again so easily. He was lucky that he had only been convicted of aggravated assault and sentenced to nineteen months. If the three men hadn't pulled him away, he would have taken the broken liquor bottle and sliced the offending customer to bits. If he had, he'd have been convicted of aggravated battery and sentenced to ten to fifteen. Yeah, he was lucky. Real lucky.

And never again would he take on the demeaning work of stocking shelves at a liquor store. Or anything like it. He'd rather get his money easily and illegally. Maybe through the human trafficking racket. He could accept the calculated gamble of outsmarting the police better than he could accept the infernal drudgery of an $8.00-an-hour slave job. He smiled through the bars. After all, he had already proven for three years now that he could get away with murder.

He secretly wondered, though, whether he had actually killed his dad. Or if the man had really, as the coroner from Savannah said, died as a result of circulatory collapse and drowning. Whatever the coroner's conclusion, Jesse would always be convinced that the ricin had induced the heart failure and caused the death.

The ricin had clearly gone undetected in the postmortem blood tests, designed only to pick up traces of drugs and alcohol. Anyway, what were the chances that his dad, if he hadn't ingested the poison, would—a couple of days into his trip—lose control of his car because of a massive seizure and swerve off into the intercoastal waterway and drown inside the car before he could be rescued?

Jesse wished he could have seen it, so that he could play it over and over again inside his head, every aspect of it, in slow motion, watching while the man fought for his life and lost.

He smiled and spat into the corridor again. Dominance was a powerful drug. He kicked the bars with pent-up tension. The next person on his list was his biological dad.

Since he had turned twenty-one in prison ten months ago, he would be able upon his release to apply immediately at the Adoption Reunion Registry for help in finding his biological parents. And that is exactly what he would do, without wasting a minute.

"You want to play a hand of cards?" his cellmate asked, interrupting his thoughts.

Jesse nodded, then turned and headed for the table.

26

*P*reparing his sermon for the weekend chapel service, Cole read Proverbs chapter three, verses five and six, a dozen times or more: *"Trust in the Lord with all your heart; do not depend on your own understanding. Seek His will in all you do, and He will direct your paths."*

Cole knew that King Solomon had authored the famous words. And he knew—according to First Kings, chapter three, verses eleven and twelve—that wisdom, or understanding, was King Solomon's greatest asset.

Yet, given Solomon's great wisdom, insight, and understanding, wouldn't it have been natural for him, as a sage, to primarily depend on his own understanding?

Cole stared at the Proverbs text as an avalanche of thoughts cascaded through his mind. Yes, of course! Solomon indeed had depended on his own understanding. The entire Old Testament book of Ecclesiastes was Solomon's autobiographical confession of a lifelong attempt, using human understanding alone, to comprehend and explain the totality of life. Solomon—according to his own confession—spent decades, every day from sunrise to sunset, trying through pure mental power to unlock, decipher, and learn the mysteries of the universe around him.

But his understanding, albeit extraordinary and unparalleled, had failed him. Near the end of his life, he had come to the pitiful conclusion that *"everything was meaningless; all was vanity."* And then he realized, too late, that throughout his arduous search for truth he had totally ignored God as a scientific, social, and philosophical study companion.

Cole flipped to Ecclesiastes. He found Solomon's public warning to all who would listen: *"Don't let the excitement of youth cause you to forget your creator (like I did). Honor Him in your youth before you grow old and no longer enjoy living."* Cole paraphrased Solomon's next words and penned them in his notebook: *Here is the conclusion of the matter: As you contend with life, seek God as a partner and respect Him with all your heart.*

Cole massaged his brow. So, in essence, Solomon in the Proverbs passage was teaching from his own personal experience. He was saying, *"Do not follow my behavior. Do not depend on those things that are your greatest assets, like I depended on my own understanding. Rather, depend on the Lord."*

But didn't God equip everyone with special strengths—like wisdom, communication skills, outgoing personalities, music and artistic abilities, engineering aptitudes, and such—to depend on? For the very purpose of aiding them in life?

Cole returned to the verses in Proverbs. He was tiring out, but he urged the gears of his mind to keep turning. He scrutinized the words *"do not depend on"*.

"Do not depend on," he whispered. What did it mean?

And then it hit him. The words, in context, meant *do not lean on, or place all your weight on.* God, indeed, equipped every individual on the planet with unique skills and abilities. And He expected and encouraged everyone to use those strengths. Yet, He wanted them to know that their God-given abilities, even when maximized, were not strong enough—by themselves—to completely hold them up under the extraordinary pressures of life. They needed *Him* as well.

Then that was it, wasn't it? In this famous Old Testament passage, Solomon was actually saying: In life, do not *totally* lean on those things that are your greatest assets, as you will be tempted to do. Especially, do not put all your trust in human wisdom. Rather, in all your ways, in all your endeavors, do not fail to depend ultimately on God, whose sturdiness and knowledge are absolutely unfailing. And in return, He, as a divine partner, will help you successfully navigate the journey of life.

No sooner had Cole completed this thought than another Old Testament verse stampeded through his brain. He had vaguely memorized the words from the book of Psalms: *"Some nations trust in chariots and some in horses, but we will trust in the name of the Lord our God."*

Cole knew from previous studies that the author of this noble proclamation was King David, another of Israel's great kings. And he knew that King David's greatest asset had not been wisdom; rather, it had been his military might—his chariots and horses. And he, like Solomon, was speaking from his own personal experience. He had earlier in life trusted totally in his chariots and horses—his greatest assets—but had fortunately come to understand the error of his misplaced faith. He was now vowing to never make the same mistake again.

Cole pumped his fist. He grabbed some paper and spent over an hour writing down his thoughts. As he wrote and pondered, he found that his heart was pierced by the power, the purity, and the brilliance of God's Word. He soon felt the urgency to join David in a mutual proclamation.

So, he put into writing a vow of his own: *People like me*, he wrote on the inside cover of his Bible, *are tempted almost beyond measure to depend solely on their musical abilities and their bank accounts. For the rest of my life, though, I will choose to depend chiefly on the Lord my God.*

With tears, he repeated the vow out loud.

And then he prayed, "Help me, God. I never, never, *never* want to be guilty of taking a single step without completely depending on you."

And then his pen seemed to take on a creative mind of its own. Within minutes, he was staring at the heartfelt lyrics to a new song about man's general tendency to forget God. As he reread the lyrics several times, he realized that one of the musical pieces he had earlier composed would, with a bit of tweaking, couple beautifully with the new words.

Feeling the exhilaration of artistic expression, he thanked God for musical creativity—and recognized that such creativity was God-given, pure and simple.

He picked up his Bible-study notes in one hand and the song lyrics in the other. Since new music had been pouring out of him recently, and since his desire to rely on the Almighty was greater than ever, why shouldn't he go ahead and agree to establish a working relationship with SpiritMark Productions?

The lesson from the lives of Solomon and David had convinced him. He would contact Roland Powers within the next two days and agree to sign a contract, if Roland was still interested. Cole would then lean on God to either close or open the door of opportunity, depending upon what He deemed best.

And as God's follower, he would simply be content with whatever decision God made.

Cole spent the rest of the evening—in the backdrop of prolonged yelling and banging somewhere down the cell block—transferring his Bible study notes into a sermon outline. He could hardly wait until Sunday morning when he would have the privilege of sharing his new discoveries with his fellow inmates.

27

At Dodge State Prison in Chester, Georgia, the warden and two guards stood outside Jesse's cell.

The warden, with a completely shaved head and one eye missing from a long-ago injury, stood shoulders-straight. He looked more like the head bouncer at a high-end nightclub than a prison warden. He stared through the bars at Jesse as if Jesse were a stupid customer who had tried to deceive the club.

"All right, Mister Rainwater. Mister Rainpiss. You stepped across the line with your eyes wide open. And in my prison, that kind of behavior will not be tolerated. No exceptions! So, if you've got a brain, you might remember that you were originally sentenced to be my prisoner for twenty-four months. It was only out of the goodness of the judge's heart that he said you could go free after nineteen months if you behaved like a decent human being. Well, you've screwed that up, jackhole. Because of that nasty little head butt you gave one of my favorite convicts, you have just extended your time to the full twenty-four months. I'll make sure the judge sees to it. And a good portion of that time will be spent in segregated lockup. I hope you enjoy your stay."

To keep himself from reacting explosively, Jesse bit down on his tongue until the warden and the guards walked away. Within a few seconds, he was tasting blood.

He kicked the cell wall.

Yes, he had struck the other convict first. But it had been in self-defense. He had already explained that to the guard who had broken up the fight. But it seemed that his side of the story had been completely disregarded.

He kicked the wall again.

Why should he ever tell the truth again? To anybody? It just wasn't worth the effort. No one had ever listened to him anyway. Or even wanted to.

He looked at his cellmate who was lying down, facing away from him and feigning a nap.

He pounded his fist into his palm. If he could just add more muscle and more weight to his frame! Maybe then he would be taken more seriously—by everybody. And maybe he would be more intimidating to more people—even to people like the freaking warden.

As soon as he got out of prison, he would look into getting some kind of hormone injections.

Regardless, though, of whether he could pack on muscle, he would never let anybody just walk over him. Never. Not unless they killed him first.

28

Several of the fine points in the SpiritMark contract had been revised during the weeks of negotiating. Cole now held the latest draft in his hand, and as far as he was concerned, everything in the document was satisfactory. He read the closing paragraph one more time.

> MODIFICATION AND SEVER-ABILITY: This Agreement con-stitutes the complete understand-ing of the parties and no other representations concerning this Agreement shall be binding. No alteration, modification, or waiver of any provision in this Agreement shall be valid unless in writing and signed by both parties. If any provision of this Agreement is found to be invalid, unenforceable or illegal, the remaining terms and

provisions shall remain valid and enforceable. Each party represents and warrants that they have read this Agreement and fully understand its terms, and recognize that they have the right, and are well-advised, to consult with knowledgeable legal counsel prior to signing below.

IN WITNESS WHEREOF, the parties hereto have duly executed this Agreement effective the day and year above written.

Following that paragraph was the printed name of Roland Powers, his signature pending. Lindsey Rose's name was printed as well, as the witness, her signature also pending.

Two blank lines dominated the bottom of the page. One was for the signature of the "Singer/Songwriter/Musician-Cole Michaels." The other was for the date. For Cole, those two blank lines towered as open doors of invitation to a new chapter in life, a chapter that would at least give him some needed post-prison direction.

He picked up a pen. He took a deep breath, closed his eyes, and prayed. *God, I'm not completely convinced that this is what I should do. All I know is that You have given me my music skills and that, thanks to You, my passion, my appreciation, and my creativity for music have all resurfaced. I know the power and the influence of good music. And from now on, I really only want to use my musical talents to glorify*

Your name and do Your will. You apparently gave Roland Powers the determination to seek me out and give me this opportunity. So I'm going to accept it. And I'm going to trust that this meets with Your approval. So I ask that this contract, and all the music that it produces, will point people to You. And if signing the contract is a mistake, I trust that You will allow it to get lost in the mail—and persuade Roland Powers to change his mind about sending a new one.

Cole took another deep breath.

Slowly he penned his signature on the contract. Along with the current date, November 29, 2006.

To celebrate the moment, he retrieved the Mysterious Lady from its case and played a zestful tune that had come to him in the last couple of weeks. He submersed himself in the music. And in the new dream of being reintroduced as a professional musician, singer, and songwriter—this time to a new generation and to a new market.

When he finally put his violin back into its protective casing, he picked up the three-page administrative letter from Lindsey Rose that had been included in the envelope with the contract.

As before, his eyes were drawn to the same six sentences:

> Roland and I have really enjoyed our two visits with you. We really like you, both as a man and as an artist. We find it very appealing that you are both a very masculine figure, and one who has been broken. Your type of brokenness is rare.

So rare, as a matter of fact, that it causes people to feel emotionally safe in your presence. And that, my friend, is a compliment.

Cole wasn't sure why he kept rereading those statements. But somehow, they affirmed him as a man with potential for future relationships. Plus, as a man all alone in the world, he couldn't help but pretend that Lindsey Rose was saying something personal between the lines. The scant scent of perfume on the typed pages didn't make it any easier for him. Had the perfume rubbed innocently off her hands while she was handling the stationery, or had a whiff been sprayed purposely onto the paper?

As ludicrous as it sounded, he secretly hoped that she was trying to be personal. But then he felt guilty for even having the hope. Was it dishonoring to Jana? Was it a betrayal to her life and memory?

Cole felt his eyes twitch. Regarding women and children, he felt absolutely lost in a sea of unworthiness. Most likely, he was worrying over an issue that didn't exist anyway. The odds were that such a beautiful woman was already in a committed relationship of some kind.

How could she not be?

For whatever it was worth, though, he had noticed during her last visit that she was not wearing a ring.

In spite of being beaten down by feelings of insignificance, he decided he would still send a personal letter of response.

29

Twelve months later

The wall clock read 2:15 PM. Surrounded by three security guards in the warden's office, Jesse gladly took the ballpoint pen and signed his release papers. For him, the moment—Tuesday, November 13, 2007—was long overdue.

After he signed the forms, the personal belongings that had been confiscated from him when he entered the system two years earlier were all returned to him in a plastic bag. The bag held a set of house keys, a set of car keys, the clothes he'd been wearing, and his wallet—containing his driver's license and two hundred and seventy-five dollars in cash.

Without fanfare, he was escorted through doors, security check-points, and gates and then led out to the parking lot, where his mother was waiting.

Jesse's emotions were spinning. A few minutes earlier, he had been confined to a cage and subjugated to harsh rules. Now he was free. Free in the magnificent sunlight. Free to go anywhere on the planet his heart desired.

The transition was instant, without any preparatory

counsel or help, and without any outside assistance. The abruptness of the change was, in one sense, confusing. In another sense, it was glorious. He was speechless, unable to immediately define his thoughts and sensations.

At some point, he realized that he was in the car and his mother was talking to him.

"I'm not sure I want to talk right now," he told her.

They rode home in silence.

*   *   *

The next morning, Jesse awakened in the room that had been his bedroom for the greatest portion of his life. His mother had hired someone two years ago, when he was first jailed, to move his clothes, computer, and television back into the house from the apartment he had been renting at the time of his arrest.

He rolled onto his side, sorting through his list of plans and priorities.

He would definitely move out of the house again as soon as possible and rent another single-bedroom apartment. Time simply had not healed the black heart he possessed for his mother. During his two years behind bars, he had not regained a single ounce of respect for her. She was still a loser. He couldn't stomach the thought of living with her. And he really didn't care how she would feel about it.

In addition to finding a new place to live, he had to acquire some big bucks.

But first, he would apply at the Georgia Adoption Reunion Registry and start the process of locating his biological parents. He had waited long enough to find out the identity and location of his birth father. Now was the time for action.

He crawled out of bed and showered. The thought of finally taking a concrete step to learn the name of his real dad energized him.

When he was dressed, he stole thirty dollars from his mother's purse, giving him a total of three hundred and five dollars. Then he took his mother's car without permission and drove downtown to the Reunion Registry's Peachtree Street address.

A different lady helped him this time. At Jesse's request, she freshly explained the procedure for hiring the organization's help. Jesse showed his driver's license to prove that he was twenty-one. Then he was led to a desk and given three forms to fill out.

The first was a basic registration form where he submitted his date of birth, his social security number, his name given by his adoptive parents, his current address, his current telephone number, his e-mail address, and the full names of his adoptive father and mother.

He then signed his name and date to the following statements: *I hereby consent to the release of the above identifying information for contact with my birth parent(s). I understand that I may revoke this consent at any time by filing a written Affidavit of Non-Disclosure with the Department.*

He then looked at the "Request to Contact Biological Family" form. He signed the date in the top left-hand corner and read the first three paragraphs.

I hereby request that the Georgia Adoption Reunion Registry contact my biological parent(s) to ascertain if they wish to have contact with me. I understand that no identifying information can be released to me without the written consent of my biological parent(s). I acknowledge that I must be twenty-one years of age to make this request.

The following information is requested to be used in the event your biological parent(s) choose not to have contact with you. This may be the only chance we have to secure answers to your most pressing questions. We will attempt to gather this information for you when our contact is made.

The questions I am most interested in having answered about my biological parent(s) are:

There were blanks for writing as many as ten different questions. With his left hand, Jesse squeezed a fist full of jeans under the table. The questions he really wanted to ask were: *Why in the sick name of insanity did you give me away? Did you think I was some kind of cheap mistake? Did you really not have any feelings of love for me? Did you have any feelings at all? Did you hate me? You brought me into the world; couldn't you at least find a way to keep and feed me? Couldn't you sacrifice at least that much? Don't you want to know how much you have destroyed my freaking life with your sick, selfish decision? What kind of heartless, pathetic beings would actually give away their helpless newborn baby and then just walk away?*

Instead, he took plenty of time and composed what he felt were legitimate questions, questions that would not set off any mental alarms among the Reunion Registry's staff.

Was I born in or out of wedlock? Do I have any sisters and brothers from my birth mother? If so, how many? What gender? How old are they? How old are my birth parents now? Can my birth parents tell me any of the circumstances surrounding my birth? Do my birth mother and father have sisters and brothers? How many aunts, uncles, and cousins do I have? What is our family heritage? What do my birth parents look like? What are their personalities like? What kind of work do they do?

Jesse looked over the questions three times and decided they would suffice.

The next and final form was labeled "Brief information about me to share with my biological parent(s)." The guidelines for this section suggested that the applicant include the following information:

(1) A physical description of yourself. (2) Your current family situa-

tion. (3) Your occupation. (4) Your
motivation for searching. (5) What
do you hope to gain from doing
a search and making contact? (6)
Provide information about your
relationship with your adoptive
parents. (7) Are they aware that
you are conducting a search? (8)
How long have you known you
were adopted?

Jesse realized that he would once again have to create
honest-sounding fabrications.

My name is Jesse Rainwater. I am
the son you gave up for adoption.
I have known that I was adopted
since I was ten years old. I am now
almost twenty-three. I will soon
be moving out to live on my own.
I have a temporary job stocking
shelves at a store. My adoptive
father was killed several years ago
in an automobile accident. My
adoptive mother is a sweet and kind
lady, but I have wanted to know
for years about you, my biological
parents. My adoptive mother sup-
ports my attempt to now make

contact with you. I am tall and have thick blonde hair. I am somewhat of a leader. With your permission, I would at least like to meet you guys and learn about my heritage and fill in the gaps about my life. If you give permission for me to have your contact information, I'll gladly meet with you on your conditions. I will look forward to your correspondence.

Sincerely,

Jesse

Jesse reread the letter and decided to delete the word "blonde." He didn't want to be too descriptive. After all, he didn't want the man or woman to suspect his identity when he approached them. And approach them he would.

After he'd completed the three forms, he took the sheets of paper to the woman at the counter, paid three hundred dollars in cash, and was told that the attempt to contact his birth mother would begin in a matter of days. He was reminded again that the search could take up to four to six months. He would be notified if and when his birth mom responded to the Registry's investigation. He was given a receipt.

Finally, he'd at least taken a definitive step toward satisfying his enduring obsession. Leaving the building, he felt lighter. Now he could shift his focus to getting his hands on some money. For starters, he would steal a check from his mother's checkbook, make the check payable to himself for five hundred dollars, forge her signature, and find someone with no scruples to cash it.

He wondered, as he had done many times before, whether his sorry excuse for an adoptive father had owned a life insurance policy, to provide for his wife in her widowhood. There must have been at least some provision. His mother, who had never worked outside the home, now worked part-time as a cashier at a nearby grocery store. That job alone, however, couldn't possibly sustain her financially. So, either she was receiving her dead husband's social security checks, or she had received a survivor's benefit from a life insurance policy.

Corralled in his thoughts, Jesse decided to make his way on foot to the entrance of Atlanta's famous Underground district, two blocks to the south. He wanted to just sit on a plaza bench for a while and enjoy the sunlight on his skin.

As he walked, he energetically recalled his interest in the subject of human trafficking. He stopped, looked around. Then changed directions. This time he headed east toward the downtown campus of Georgia State University. Surely, the school had a library. And hopefully, it would be open to the public. He needed more information about the underworld of trafficking. A lot more. Surely there had been books and articles written about it.

The university campus was spread out among several of the downtown's commercial properties. Jesse asked a skinny, book-laden female who looked like a student if she could direct him to the university library.

"About three blocks that way," she said, pointing northeastwardly. "Just around the corner from Hurt Park."

Jesse nodded and headed in that direction.

He had to ask someone else for directions before he finally found the building—a five-story edifice tucked away in the middle of a city block, hidden from the street. The entrance was via a large, multileveled courtyard designated for foot traffic only, paved with rough concrete slabs and decorated with fountains.

Jesse stared at the entrance to the library, feeling nervous. He berated himself for the lack of confidence. Was he really going to allow himself to be intimidated by a university setting? Why should he? Surely he was as clever as any student on campus.

He took a big breath and walked up the steps and through the glass doors. He was greeted by a thirtyish-looking African-American male seated at a small security gate and wearing some type of badge.

"Excuse me. Are non-students allowed to use the library here?" Jesse asked, trying to calm the unrest in his voice.

"Absolutely," the man replied, "but I'll need to see a form of ID."

Jesse handed his driver's license to the man.

"All right. I'll keep the license right here in this small file box until you get ready to leave." The man looked at the name on the license and filed the card alphabetically.

Jesse didn't like the idea of surrendering his license, even for an hour or two. It made him feel vulnerable. But he nodded and pushed onward through the metal gate. He cleared his throat and tried to act composed. Immediately in front of him, in the forefront of the spacious room, were two rows of high wooden tables. Four computers sat on each table, two of them facing one side of the table and two facing the other. Without hesitation, he stepped up to the first table. Both computers facing him were available for use. An intra-net webpage for the library was displayed on the screens.

Jesse chose one and, using the mouse, moved the cursor on the screen to the search box. He typed the words "Human Trafikking" and pushed the enter key. Instantly, a new page appeared, declaring in bold red letters, "NO MATCHES WERE FOUND IN THIS CATALOG."

Jesse was confused. If the subject was as important as the television documentary had indicated, wouldn't there be a book or two about the subject?

He typed "Human Trafikking" again and hit the enter key. Again, the "NO MATCHES" message appeared.

Maybe I spelled it wrong. He deleted one of the Ks and entered the new spelling. The message flashed a third time: "NO MATCHES WERE FOUND IN THIS CATALOG."

Jesse felt self-conscious, as if the people walking past him might notice the topic of his research and become suspicious. He looked around and noticed the information desk across the room, to his right. Should he go to the desk and ask for help? No...a lazy move like that might place him on someone's mental radar. And possibly their memory. Besides, security cameras had already recorded his presence. He should quietly carry out his business and leave. There was no need to say anything to anybody. No one should remember that he was here.

He refocused his attention on the computer. He adjusted the spelling inside the search box again. This time he added a second F. The "NO MATCHES..." page returned.

"Come on!" Jesse growled through clenched teeth. Something was wrong here. He glared at the words in the search box. He strained for an explanation. He decided to add a C. He typed "Human Trafficking" and pushed enter.

Jackpot!

The screen quickly listed ten book titles. More were listed on a second page. Satisfaction and relief washed over him. At the same time, he cursed himself for his mangled spelling.

He looked around again, took a deep breath, and forced himself to relax.

30

Jesse scanned the list of titles and memorized the call numbers of the first book on the list.

Now he needed a library map. He left the computer and ambled—he hoped nonchalantly—toward the information desk. There were several stacks of paper on the long counter. Four or five people stood in line, seeking help from the two staff members behind the desk. Jesse casually walked to the side and looked over the stacks of free information. One of the available sheets was indeed a guide that outlined the library's catalog system and explained how to find any particular book amidst the thousands upon thousands of volumes.

Jesse took a copy of the guide.

Using the step-by-step key, he searched for the book that bore the call number he had memorized. He found the book on the fifth floor near the middle of a massive old room. The book was on the top shelf of a tall, brown, metal shelving unit. Jesse had to use a step stool to reach it. Before he pulled it out, he studied the titles of the surrounding volumes. Most of them focused on the sale for profit of human beings worldwide, especially the sale of women. Most of the titles fell into one of two categories— the international slave trade or the international sex trade.

Jesse was mesmerized. Until he had seen the television documentary in his prison cell twelve or thirteen months ago, he hadn't been aware that a "human trafficking" industry existed. A worldwide market? He was amazed.

And, again, he was more than a little intimidated. This was a gargantuan industry no doubt controlled by powerful and ruthless men. He should probably just drop the idea. But there was something alluring about the idea of a few individuals exercising total dominance over unsuspecting weaklings.

Jesse's mind sizzled just thinking about it. He really wanted to learn more.

Fueled by adrenaline, he continued to examine the titles on the shelf. One book in particular attracted his attention: *East European Mayhem—A Black Market for Living Flesh.* Jesse removed the book and stepped down to the floor. He opened the front cover and started reading.

> During the years of 1989 to 1991, the Iron Curtain that had for forty-five years separated Eastern Europe from Western Europe was politically dismantled. One by one, the list of republics that had been controlled by the Soviet Union for more than four decades reclaimed

their independence. Freedom swept through Eastern Europe. Every resident who had been oppressed by the puppet governments of the Russian bear was suddenly awarded fresh and endless opportunities. It was a new day. A new era. From Estonia to Romania.

Jesse sat down on the floor cross-legged and continued to read.

And then in 1991, drastic reforms in the Russian government transformed historic Russian communism into a free market. The Russian bear tried her hand at democracy, but the wealth and greed of a few corrupt and powerful individuals slowly positioned the country for a downhill slide toward an oligarchical rule. As bribery, payoffs, and lawlessness proliferated throughout all levels of leadership, organized crime surfaced as the country's covert ruler. As organized crime became more organized and more criminal, the Mafia bosses eagerly searched for new markets, especially black markets, that would help generate continuous supplies of wealth and power for years to come. They quickly discovered a gold mine—their beautiful women. All across Russia, Poland, Hungary, Romania, the Czech Republic, and the Ukraine the women were ripe for exploitation. Not only were the economies struggling to stand on their own, leaving everyone desperate for a good job and decent pay, but the family units were falling apart at an alarming rate. Abandonment and divorce became a common way to escape financially burdensome situations. As a result, thousands of girls from eighteen to twenty-one years old lost their families and their places of security. The Mafia bosses capitalized on this desperate situation.

Jesse raised his head and looked up and down the aisles. He saw only one other person on the fifth floor, and that person was at the other end of the room staring into a book. Jesse resumed his reading.

The bosses devised ingenious but simple plans to lure the girls outside the borders of their countries. They placed newspaper and magazine ads across the region, ads that offered secure and well-paying jobs as housemaids, au pairs, secretaries, photo models, catalog models, and fashion models. The jobs were always in other countries, such as Italy, Austria, Spain, France, Germany, Bosnia, Canada, Japan, and the United States. Young girls responded in substantial numbers.

Jesse read that the bosses placed the ads in the names of pseudo modeling agencies, lawyers, doctors, and executives. Phone numbers were always included with the ads. Older females were hired and trained by the Mafia to staff the phones. These phone operators would answer the inquiries from prospective victims and would extract personal, vital information from the job candidates such as their education, upbringing, physical description, previous work experience, current address, and family name. All of this information was collected under the guise of *interviews*. The phone operators would imply that a callback would be likely. The callbacks would always come a few weeks later, notifying the candidates that they had been awarded the jobs. With newly acquired passports, the young women would receive complimentary train or plane tickets from their *new employers*. The young women would then head across borders to what they believed would be exciting and promising new lives. Upon arrival at the train stations or airports of final destination, the women would be greeted by well-groomed Mafia men and kidnapped into the underworld of human trafficking. Their passports would be confiscated, and the girls would be quickly sold to expectant buyers, primarily ruthless pimps who would force the girls at gunpoint or through brutal beatings to serve as prostitutes in the seedy brothels of Europe and Asia.

Jesse lifted his head again. He was sweating. He wiped at his forehead several times, then returned to his book.

He learned that there was an ever-growing number of men lined up around the globe to purchase these female "pleasure" slaves for $5,000 to $20,000 each. These girls, forced to work six days a week, could easily net their buyers anywhere from $75,000 to $200,000 a year, tax-free. Ninety-eight percent of the girls could be successfully coerced to perform. Those who refused to work were beaten into submission, or bound in chains and left in dark basements to starve until they agreed to cooperate. The few girls who continued to fight despite the physical punishments could normally be strong-armed by ominous threats such as, "If you don't perform on demand, we will send thugs into your hometown to make a visit to your loved ones, and let's just say that your loved ones will regret the visit for years to come," or "We have already taken pictures of you at work. If you don't obey, we'll distribute copies of those pictures for all your relatives and friends to see." To give the prisoners future hope, the buyers would usually tell them up front that they could eventually buy their freedom once they earned the 'house' a specified number of dollars.

Surely, Jesse thought, all of this couldn't be as widespread as the book was making it sound.

But as he continued to read, the statistics became staggering. As many as 175,000 girls from Eastern Europe were funneled into the human trafficking industry *every year,* or 479 every day. He discovered that human trafficking was the third-largest moneymaking enterprise in the world. He found a list of countries involved—Belgium, Holland, Israel, Greece, England, the Czech Republic, Romania, Latvia, Lithuania, Estonia, Bulgaria, Serbia, Albania, Moldova, the United Arab Emirates, and even the USA.

He read in the next chapter that if a girl did escape and managed to reach the police, she would often find that the local authorities would display little or no empathy for her situation. A significant percentage of law enforcers were sincerely convinced that most of the girls who entered the business did so not as innocent females who had been kidnapped, but rather as desperate girls willing to go to any extreme to save themselves from a situation back home that was even more dire. Plus, many policemen frequented the brothels as customers, and other policemen accepted bribes from the crime bosses. After all, the girls in question were foreigners. Only on rare occasions was a trafficker or pimp ever arrested, tried, and prosecuted. Ninety-nine percent of the citizens in the pimps' hometowns remained ignorant of what was happening behind the walls of the brothels and slave houses. So the underground industry stormed forward, virtually unimpeded.

Jesse leaned backward onto the shelves behind him. He closed his eyes and tried to assimilate all he had read. After several minutes, he returned to the text and read five more chapters.

The last chapter that he read sparked an idea—a conceivable way for him to step into this secret realm of power, wealth, and deceit and claim a portion of the bounty for himself. He reread one particular paragraph four times:

> The Russian Mafia, along with its criminal progenies, have become masters of disguise. They have now jumped into the fray of cyber dating and online matchmaking with a multitude of "official" website-driven companies. Beautiful and intelligent women numbering in the thousands—from all over Russia, the Ukraine, and Eastern Europe—pay small fees to have their pictures and personal information posted on these "Mail-Order Bride" websites in the hope that rich western gentlemen will propose marriage and become their immigration tickets to better lives. A few of the ladies, indeed, are selected as legitimate brides and realize their dreams. The greater portion, however, are duped into

> bogus proposals and end up cross-
> ing borders into the waiting arms
> of human traffickers. And families
> and friends never see them again.

After reading a few more pages, Jesse put the book back on the shelf, returned to the lobby, retrieved his driver's license, and left the library.

Back at his mother's house, Jesse sat at his computer behind a locked bedroom door and typed "Russian Brides" into an Internet search engine. He was honestly surprised at the smorgasbord of website addresses that were instantly displayed across multiple pages.

He arbitrarily clicked on one of the addresses.

The website opened. Jesse looked over the home page, then clicked the tab that offered to show photos of the ladies.

Wow!

Jesse was astounded and mesmerized by the pictures. He had never thought about Russian women. But these women were outrageously beautiful. Nearly all were striking, blue- or green-eyed blondes. He spent the next two hours looking at website after website, scrolling through hundreds of pictures. He had never before seen so many attractive women. The girls that surrounded him in Georgia were, more often than not, overweight. But these Russian women all looked like svelte models. He could hardly believe his eyes.

Were there *really* so many glamorous women in Russia and its neighboring countries? And were all these ladies *really* offering themselves as brides? To strangers? In foreign countries? Was life in Russia really so deplorable that young women by the droves were taking such extreme risks to find lives elsewhere? He was skeptical.

Still, if the "mail-order bride" phenomenon was true—and it seemed to be—then he was eager to explore it.

On one of the websites, he noticed colorful tabs beside the models' profiles that spelled out the offer for him and other browsers to *Send Email.*

On the profile page of a 5' 6", 110-pound green-eyed blonde named Katja, Jesse stared and stared at the *Send Email* option. Then he stared at Katja's photo.

Taking a deep breath, he clicked the *Send Email* tab.

31

$\mathcal{A}$ week before Christmas, Cole sat on the edge of his prison mattress holding a piece of newly delivered mail. The envelope had already been opened and checked according to protocol.

The envelope contained a big card, which had been stuffed with additional items.

There was a part of Cole's soul that still, after eleven years of incarceration, felt self-conscious about the fact that some faceless employee at the prison had already read the card, especially now that the majority of his mail was coming from Lindsey Rose. Trying, though, to dismiss the issue as of little importance, he slipped the card out of the envelope. The air was immediately filled with the subtle aroma of Lindsey's perfume. He closed his eyes and inhaled. The scent, with its inviting expression of femininity, had over the past year come to be one of the definitive joys in his life.

He was still amazed that Lindsey had, from the offset, felt a chemistry between them and that she had been willing to explore it cautiously. She had said that her attraction was due to his brokenness, his vulnerability, his dry sense of humor, and his personality. Still, he found it difficult to believe that she would give him a second thought, and even harder to believe that she had remained single for so many years after the death of her first husband in a boating accident.

But the relationship had become one of the important keys of his life. Over the past twelve months, Lindsey had been able, through her multiple visits and letters, to resurrect desires and interests in him that he had thought would stay buried for the rest of his life. The exchange of feelings, thoughts, and histories had only accelerated with each interaction. By now, it was not only her outstanding beauty that held his attention, but also her keen mind, perpetually optimistic outlook, and giving soul. She had worked her way magically into his heart and mind. He felt the inner excitement of a high-school sophomore dating seriously for the first time.

He had revealed to her during one of her visits that his feelings seemed to be moving beyond just friendship. "Just wait," she had volleyed, holding up her hand. "On January the second, when you walk out of here, I might be tempted to just hug you real, real hard. And then we're going to sit down and have some long talks—some *very* long talks."

Only one thing concerned him about the growing attachment—but that one thing nagged at him with strong tugs. Even though Lindsey openly declared a personal faith in Christ, her deepest allegiances, without question, seemed to be to the American dream of success and prosperity. Her enthusiasm and drive to "have it all" were always present—and were starting to rekindle his own passions of years gone by. And he didn't want to give those passions a place in his life anymore.

Still, Lindsey had made it clear that she wasn't expecting God to give her a plateful of wealth as some kind of entitlement, or as some kind of reward for good living or honorable faith. "If you've been placed in one of the wealthiest cultures on the planet," she stressed, "and you have been given wealth-earning abilities, why not take the initiative to earn a great living? Why struggle financially when it's unnecessary?"

Sometimes he wanted to argue with her. Quite frankly, he had learned over the last ten years that a person—even in America—could exist at minimal cost and still enjoy a rich and productive life.

But the power of Lindsey's mystique and beauty were slowly chipping away at his convictions. And at this point, he didn't want to dampen the relationship. He was certain that returning to the outside world was not going to be easy, and he wanted someone out there to love, someone to share life with. And Lindsey Rose was an unexpected and undeserved treasure. Besides, what were the odds, considering his confinement, that someone as extraordinary as Lindsey would develop an interest in him? Maybe, just maybe, he convinced himself, he could influence her and help change her focus.

He inhaled another breath of perfume and opened the card. He removed a folded page of newspaper and what looked like a folded page from a magazine. He set the inserts aside and first gave his attention to the handwritten note inside the card.

> Excuse the short note—I just came in from a Pilates class and I'm rushing off to the office for a big meeting. But I just wanted to share an early Christmas gift with you. Are you ready? After three weeks of diligent correspondence, I've landed a radio interview for you on the number-one Christian radio network in America. The interview is scheduled to take place during the same week you'll be in the recording studio. This is huge, huge, huge!! Yes, I'm excited. More than excited, actually. But no one deserves this break more than you. Merry Christmas! Oh, yeah—I thought you might enjoy the enclosed articles. To the man who is very possibly stealing my heart.
> Lovingly,
> Lindsey

"Bless her," he grinned. She was definitely the kind of person who made things happen. He then sighed. He wasn't ungrateful. He was just trying to adjust his mind to the flood of events—such as the un-asked-for interviews—about to be thrust on him.

He unfolded the newspaper page. He was instantly looking at an old photo of himself, a promotional picture from twelve years ago. The picture was accompanied by an article highlighted with a yellow marker.

The Blonde Fiddler Returns

For a long time now, the name Cole Michaels has slipped from public attention. Perhaps that is all about to change. On Wednesday, January 2, 2008, after serving more than eleven years of jail time for vehicular homicide, Cole Michaels—the Nashville music star of the best-selling *Sweet Manipulations* CD—will be a free man. The highly acclaimed fiddler, vocalist, and songwriter will, soon after his release, begin recording his long-awaited second CD. This time around, he will record for the Christian market. SpiritMark, Inc., will produce the album. Hopefully, the music will rise to the same heights as his initial release. Welcome back, Cole. You have been gone way too long.

"The Blonde Fiddler returns," Cole whispered. He had spent a year now composing and finalizing twelve new songs. And he had frequently allowed himself to fantasize about stepping back into the public eye as a professional musician. But the reality of the marketing and publicity aspects of the business hadn't really sunk in yet. As he contemplated this article, from one of Nashville's leading newspapers, a rush of excitement swept through his spirit—and so did a rush of anxiety. He knew he was ready to record, and ready for the concerts that would follow. But was he ready for the marketing hype and the propaganda that was inherent in the business?

He then read the magazine article—obviously from a Christian magazine, judging by the advertisements for a private Christian academy and a general contractor for church auditoriums.

A Change Of Tune

In November of last year, Spirit-Mark Productions—one of the fastest-growing producers of inspirational music—contracted with singer and fiddler Cole Michaels (*Sweet Manipulations*—1996) to write and perform a collection of original praise and worship songs, scheduled for recording in February 2008. Cole has lived the last decade of his life behind bars because of a DUI and vehicular homicide conviction. Having undergone a spiritual awakening during his incarceration, he has earned a theology degree through an online Bible college and has been an active assistant in the prison's chapel program. His release from the Middle Tennessee Correctional Facility is slated for the early part of the new year. A spokesperson for SpiritMark says, *"Mr. Michaels has spent the last year composing music and writing lyrics for the upcoming project. The new songs are absolutely outstanding, both in quality and in the ability to move the heart. The music is unlike anything else on the market. We anticipate that the new CD will quickly rise to the top of every Christian's 'must have' music list."* If all goes according to SpiritMark's schedule, we will review the new CD in our April or May issue.

Cole dropped the glossy paper and bowed his head. At first he was speechless—and then he wept. "Dear God! My heart is…just suddenly heavy. Everything that's coming my way, when I look at it all at one time, seems almost overwhelming. The romance. The recording. The marketing. Not to mention the whole matter of readjusting to the outside. To be honest…I'm somewhat afraid. And I don't know if I should be. I really believe You've opened up all of these doors for me, or I would have already turned away from them. So, I need Your strength. Your wisdom. Your guidance. I certainly don't want to become prideful because of my gifts. Or because of how people value and praise those gifts. I'm nothing but an undeserving piece of waste—and honestly, I don't even know why You redeemed me. But if I'm going to be out there as a testimony of Your redeeming grace, then I want *You* to truly, truly be honored. In every meaning of the word." Cole grabbed his heart with both hands. "I want this next part of my life to count the most. And I don't want anything to distract from that. Not the money in my bank account. Not the public hype. Not relationships. And definitely not proud thinking. I just want to be a lamb. A lamb sacrificed on the altar of Your all-deserving and almighty name."

32

"*I*'m going to miss you, my brother," Cole said with a heavy heart, facing Chaplain Parker at one of the dining hall tables on Sunday morning. "I know I'll see you again, but I...I just can't imagine my life without you being a regular part of it." Cole shifted in his seat. "And everything in me is refusing to believe that in a few minutes I'll be taking part in my last chapel service. I just didn't think it was going to be this hard."

Parker listened and allowed Cole to unload his heart.

"I should be happy just knowing that in three days I'll walk out of here a free man. Of course, there's a part of me that's so happy I can hardly describe it. Yet, there's another part that's unbelievably sad. I mean...my life was changed here. And has continued to change beyond anything I could have ever imagined. I have found contentment here. A rhythm, a simplicity of life." Cole swallowed hard. "Anyway, what I'm trying to say is...I owe you for saving my life. For reaching out to me. For teaching me the importance of truth. For giving me so many opportunities to serve. God knows I'm indebted to you, and always will be." Cole squeezed his hands together. "The fact is—"

Parker contorted his ugly face and raised a hand. "Whoa! Whoa! You, my friend, do not owe me a single thing. Not one thing. I mean—does Big John owe you anything for investing in his life and making a difference for him?"

"No. But—"

"What about Tat? He claims that he would have tried to kill himself a long time ago if you hadn't spent so much time encouraging him and pointing him to the Gospel. And what about Eddie and Shark? Both of those guys have been transformed because of your influence."

Cole sighed.

"Look," Parker continued. "Serving one another and exhorting one another is what the body of Christ is all about. You know that."

Cole wiped tears from his eyes. "I know. I know. But right now, I am just...stupidly grateful. And I want you to know that I appreciate you more than you can ever imagine."

Parker reached out and placed a hand under Cole's chin. He lifted his head. "If you feel you owe me something... then there *is* one favor you can do for me."

"Just name it," Cole asserted.

Parker's tone became more serious. "Whatever happens out there, *do not*—I repeat, *do not* lose your focus."

Cole wiped his tears on the sleeve of his jumpsuit and nodded. "All right. With God's help, I'll try everything to not lose my focus."

Parker smiled his grotesque smile.

* * *

Cole tried unsuccessfully to steady his breathing as he sat on the edge of the bed, waiting. The moment was almost surreal. His feelings, his thoughts, and his emotions swung with adrenaline somewhere between supernatural serenity and outrageous restlessness. It was the morning of his release—Wednesday, January 2, 2008. A full eleven years had passed since he had been found guilty of vehicular homicide and sentenced. Eleven years! More than a decade. And in a few minutes, his time behind bars would be officially completed.

He was forty-one years old today.

He scanned his cell with its simple amenities. He had heard about so many changes that had been introduced to American society during his absence. What would it all look like? Would he plunge right back in as if he had never been locked away? Or would he experience reverse culture shock, something the chaplain had forewarned him about?

As he waited for someone to escort him out of the ward for the final time, the passing minutes felt inexplicably long and slow. He finally lay back on the bed and closed his eyes. He allowed his mind to flood with memories. Memories such as the loneliness and deadness that had consumed his soul eleven years ago, when he first laid his head on a prison pillow. His unrelenting obsession during those days of wanting to die. His harassment and eventual stabbing by Mack. The much-appreciated janitorial job. The visual shock of first laying eyes on Chaplain Duke Parker. The one-on-one Bible studies that followed. The unprecedented spiritual growth of his heart, mind, and spirit. The online Bible-college education with its loads of reading and writing requirements. The theology degree. The weekly chapel services with regular opportunities to learn, to make friends, and to teach. The irreplaceable Mysterious Lady with its remarkable therapeutic effect on his soul. His new songs, birthed out of personal pain. And, of course, Lindsey Rose, the blonde beauty now waiting for him just outside the prison walls—the lady whose genuine interest in him had made him feel like a man again and had given his life an extra dose of energy and enthusiasm; the stunning babe whose physical image had dominated his thoughts and persuaded his mind—contrary to everything he would have ever imagined—to become emotionally involved with a new woman. He just hoped Jana would understand.

Footsteps coming down the corridor snatched his attention back to the present. This was it.

33

Cole stood. He collected and tallied his belongings—one violin enclosed in its case and one giant duffel bag that contained his Bible, a Bible dictionary, a notebook filled with Bible study notes, his theology certificate, a collection of letters and photos from Lindsey, sheets of handwritten music and lyrics, a copy of his SpiritMark contract, his numerous fan letters, and his toiletries.

He scanned the room one last time, trying to recall and retain every thought, feeling, and lesson he had accumulated in the tiny cubicle over the past decade. He stretched his arms skyward. Anticipation surged through his body. He guessed that he was ready.

A prison guard appeared outside the bars of the cell. "You might want to change into these before you leave." The guard was holding a new set of clothes, including a new pair of shoes and a belt. Along with a jacket.

Cole looked into the guard's eyes, surprised. He was already dressed in civilian clothes—the same set he'd been wearing when he'd entered the prison years before. They had been reissued to him yesterday evening. In truth, though—they felt strange. He was so accustomed to his all-cotton prison jumpsuit that he'd have probably felt more comfortable wearing it while leaving the grounds. Not, of course, that the prison staff would let him.

"A gift from the outside," the guard explained as he handed the garments through the bars.

Cole took the clothes.

"I'll be back in five," the guard said. "Be ready to walk out with me."

Cole unfolded the clothes and laid them across the bed. The shirt was black silk. The pants were high-end denim. *Lindsey*, Cole thought. He removed his old clothes and donned the new attire, including the winter jacket. Everything seemed to fit except for the shoes, a pair of costly black loafers. They were a bit too snug. But, he could scrunch his toes and make them work, at least for the next hour or two.

As soon as he was fully dressed, he was slammed by conflicting feelings. The fashionable civilian clothes represented freedom and privilege. He should be pleased. Instead, he felt strangely uncomfortable in the expensive outfit. Maybe his feelings were part of the reverse culture shock Parker had warned him about.

But this was no time to be psychoanalytical. He could hear the guard returning. He grabbed the duffel bag of belongings with one arm and the violin with the other.

The cell door was unlocked and thrown open.

Cole turned and looked at the cubicle one more time.

Then he slowly stepped out into the corridor. Why was this so difficult?

The guard nodded for Cole to lead the way. "To the warden's office," the man ordered.

Cole started walking.

A voice from a nearby cell called, "Take care, fiddler."

All the way down the cell block, a choir of additional voices followed.

"Be careful out there."

"We're going to miss you, man."

"Good luck!"

"Thanks for all the great music. It'll be dull around here without you."

"You've been a blessing, guy. Thanks for all the encouragement."

More than a dozen inmates shouted their goodbyes. Cole was honestly not expecting such a display of support and affirmation from the cell block of criminals. The moment's significance did not escape him, though. He was both humbled and honored.

Without saying anything, Cole meekly nodded at the men as he walked.

In the warden's office, the unexpected continued. Five men stood around the perimeter of the small room. The warden. The captain. The head of administrative personnel. A senior guard. And Chaplain Parker.

The warden motioned for Cole to step to the middle of the room. "Set your belongings on the chair for a moment," he instructed.

Cole obeyed.

"Well, this is your big day," the warden said. He stepped forward and, for the first time in eleven years, cordially shook Cole's hand. "What you see right now in this room isn't normal," he explained. "These men have gathered with me to wish you the best. And to commend you for your outstanding behavior during the time you've been with us. We wish all our prisoners would follow your pattern. As a commendation and as a token of our goodwill, we've decided to give you an official letter of recommendation. Of course, you now have a criminal record, and that record will follow you for the rest of your life. And it can easily create problems for you when you're trying to secure a job. I realize that you have a recording opportunity waiting for you at the moment. But later, if you should approach other potential employers, you may find this letter useful." The warden turned. "Chaplain, will you read the letter?"

Chaplain Duke Parker grinned at Cole and unfolded a letter printed on the prison's letterhead.

> To whom it may concern. We the officials of the Middle Tennessee Correctional Facility, authorized to our post by the great State of Tennessee, hereby declare that the holder of this document, Cole Jefferson Michaels, served out his full sentence of eleven years and eight months at our prison compound and did so with humility, remorse, and out-

standing conduct. In addition, he contributed to the overall morale of our in-house community with salaried work, volunteer chapel service, and a disposition of exceptional honesty, dependability, and friendliness. It is our wish that you consider him at this time as a valid and promising candidate for the current employment offered by your company or corporation. We wholeheartedly execute this letter as a statement of support on the date of Mister Michaels' official release, January 2, 2008.

The chaplain read the five signatures penned by the men in the room. When he'd finished reading, he refolded the single sheet of paper, inserted it into its official envelope, and handed it to the warden.

"Please accept this written recommendation as our parting gift," the warden said, passing the letter to Cole. "This is only the second time in my tenure at this facility that I've permitted something like this. Please understand that you've made a significant impression on each of us."

Cole clenched the envelope as the men stepped forward one at a time to shake his hand and say goodbye. The chaplain, when it was his turn, whispered in his ear, "I love you, man. And I encourage you again—don't lose your focus out there."

The captain handed Cole a plastic bag. "Here are the things you had in your possession when you entered the prison eleven years ago."

His eyes blurry, Cole looked at the captain with a little confusion.

"It's a billfold, three credit cards, a driver's license, fifty-eight dollars in cash, and a couple of photographs," the captain stated. "Plus, here's a check made out to you personally from the correctional facility. It's for six hundred and fifty-eight dollars and seventy-one cents. The balance of your work account."

Cole nodded in slow motion and took the bag and the check.

"Now," the captain said, motioning for Cole to follow him over to the office desk. "All you need to do is sign four release documents, and you'll be a free man."

Feeling as if the moment was shrouded in some kind of fantasy, Cole signed four different release forms and laid down the pen.

The warden handed him an official discharge document. "You're free to go." He pointed to the senior guard. "Wayne, will you lead this man out of here?"

Cole placed the plastic bag, the check, and the discharge papers into his duffel, then lifted the bag and violin.

"Oh, I almost forgot," the warden said. "Happy birthday! And don't forget to smile as you walk out the gate."

Cole turned. "Thank you," he said as he looked around the room at the five authority figures. "I feel like there's so much I should say right now, but my brain is running faster than I'm able to think. I'm at a loss for words. I apologize. I..."

The warden waved off Cole's apology. "Leave, Mister Michaels! Enjoy the moment! And for God's sake, make the most of your future!"

Cole offered a wave as a final message of gratitude. Within seconds, he was following the senior guard through a pathway of heavily fortified electronic doors and gates.

When Cole finally stepped outside the last building into an outer yard saturated with sunlight and cold air, the excitement crammed into his soul felt as if it would combust.

Was this real?

And what had the warden meant about smiling when he left the compound?

Someone shouted from outside the main gate: "There he is! That's him!" The shout was followed by a barrage of camera flashes and group chatter.

What...? And then he saw; outside the main gate was a crowd of thirty to forty winter-clad people directing their undivided attention—and their cameras—at him.

Why were...?

And then he heard a familiar voice, ringing out above the rest. It was Lindsey. She was hurrying to the front of the group. He had, of course, been expecting her. She'd been planning for weeks to be here at this moment. To welcome him back to society, to be his "reorientation hostess" for a few days.

But the rest of the crowd! Who were they? Were they reporters? Paparazzi? Part of the music industry? SpiritMark?

Surely Lindsey would have warned him in advance if she had prearranged something like this. Wouldn't she? Regardless, Cole felt ambushed. This delicate moment, which he had expected to be private, was now a public event, and he didn't welcome the encroachment. But he at least now understood why the warden had urged him to smile.

The last prison gate was finally opened, under the scrutiny of four watchful guards. Cole was free. He stood less than thirty feet from the crowd of wide-eyed inquisitors. He froze. Lindsey Rose hurried toward him. He put down the violin and duffel bag, and Lindsey lunged into his arms, gripping him in a tight hug.

Cole felt a little self-conscious, standing there with Lindsey wrapped in his arms, with so many people watching. Since his marriage to Jana, this was the first woman other than Jana he had embraced with such intimacy. A tinge of guilt teased him with discomfort. Yet, the jubilation of the moment was absolutely intoxicating. So he allowed himself to be carried along by the spirit of celebration.

"Hello, handsome!" Lindsey shouted into his ear, her face pressed hard against his. He could feel her tears against his cheek. "This is absolutely unbelievable! I can't tell you..."

Cole wanted to give her his full attention, but the profusion of raised voices and animated faces was too distracting, too overwhelming.

In an impetuous move, he lifted Lindsey off her feet and spun her. There were hoots and hollers from all directions.

When he finished the spin and set her feet on the ground again, his brain started to fully register the feel of

Lindsey's body against his. After an eleven-year absence of intimate contact with anyone of the opposite sex, the physical sensation was awesome. Tantalizing, actually.

Cameras continued to click and flash all around them.

A man's voice shouted above the rest. "Cole Michaels, what's the first thing you want to say to the world, now that you're a free man?"

Before Cole could formulate an answer to the question, another voice bellowed, "Can you tell us some of the things you've learned while you've been locked away?"

Another: "What are your immediate plans?"

More questions piled unrelentingly on top of the first ones: "What are some of the things you've missed and are now looking forward to?" "Can you tell us about the songs you've been writing?" "If you had to do it all over again, would—"

Lindsey whispered excitedly into Cole's ear. "Relax... relax...it's okay." She pulled back a couple of inches and stared into his eyes at close range. "It'll be all right. Trust me. These people are here at my invitation." She winked at him. "It's free PR! Just take a deep breath and I'll walk you through it."

Feeling shell-shocked, Cole tried to black out all the other voices and focus solely on Lindsey.

"All right, listen up, everybody!" Lindsey called out. "Please, give me your attention!" She clapped hard a few times and finally brought the group to silence. "That's better. First, I want to publicly say to Cole an enthusiastic 'Welcome out!' And an equally enthusiastic 'Happy birthday!' What an awesome day this is for him!" Lindsey led a burst of applause. "Cole is a great man with a great heart," she continued. "And as all of you know, he's also a man with great talents. And he's now free to carve out a great future. Mark my words...in two-thousand-and-eight, under the SpiritMark label, his name will rise quickly to the top of the music world." Lindsey turned and winked at Cole. "Now, before we throw it open to your questions, let me explain to Cole that all of you ladies and gentlemen are journalists representing the media of radio, newspapers, and magazines, and that you're here at SpiritMark's invitation to record this exciting moment for posterity. *And*—to let the world know that he's back." Lindsey placed a hand on Cole's shoulder. "With that said, let's begin. It's cold out here."

Questions again blasted the air.

Cole took a quick breath.

"Whoa! Whoa!" Lindsey chuckled. "Let's keep it to one question at a time, please. Grace, why don't you go first."

"Thanks, Lindsey," a middle-aged woman said. "All right, well..first of all, Mister Michaels, I want to say that I loved your first CD. It's been in my music collection for years now. So, my question is, will your new CD have a similar sound? And if not, how will it be different?"

Cole looked into Lindsey's eyes for reinforcement. The whole setup had scattered his thoughts. Slowly, he said, turning toward Grace, "Well, I guess I need to say first, that I'm elated to be a free man. Believe me, after eleven years, all of this seems like a dream. And I'm somewhat confounded...and definitely humbled...that any of you are here, or that you would even want to be here. And to answer your question, I would say that, yes, the musical style of my new songs is similar to my old ones—in the sense that the music is a fusion of Celtic, soft pop, chill, and country. At the same time, though, the feel of the music is different. My first album was born out of a long-held ambition to simply produce a best-selling CD. The new music was born out of a therapeutic need to unpack all the past turmoil of my heart and soul. To be honest, the new songs were born out of a lot of deep pain. And I'm guessing and hoping that this will give the new music a stronger connection to the listeners' hearts." Cole looked at Lindsey for a sign of approval.

Lindsey was smiling without constraint.

Cole smiled nervously in response.

The interview lasted fifteen minutes. Excerpts, he was told, would be printed in newspapers and magazines and played on Christian and secular radio stations around the country.

34

$\mathcal{A}$ little past noon, Cole was chauffeured by Lindsey to the historic district of Germantown in downtown Nashville. Cole had asked Lindsey weeks before if she would find a rental apartment for him. She had jumped at the opportunity with the enthusiasm of a home-makeover expert, but had insisted that the apartment and its location be kept a surprise.

She was now giddy with excitement—making her beauty even more stunning. As they talked, she kept touching his leg.

Cole felt as if he were in a dream.

But, as they entered the streets of Germantown in Lindsey's iridescent yellow Mini Cooper, Cole found that his overall feelings, like a bungee cord, were in one moment being stretched to an effervescent high because of his newly gained freedom and Lindsey's physical presence, and then snapped back to intense melancholy because of the painful memories resurrected by the downtown area. He tried to stifle the melancholy.

"Well, what do you think?" Lindsey nearly squealed as she braked in front of a Fifth Avenue townhouse.

Cole's eyes followed Lindsey's finger. The two-story duplex left him momentarily speechless.

"The left side is yours! It's brand new. Nineteen hundred square feet. Two bedrooms. Three bathrooms. Hardwood floors. A marble fireplace. Granite kitchen counters. Maple cabinets. Stainless-steel appliances. A fenced-in backyard that's landscaped. A spacious deck. And as you can see, a cozy front porch like something out of a Norman Rockwell scene. Oh....and a sidewalk!"

Cole teared up. "I don't know what to say. It's...it's absolutely gorgeous." He felt a huge smile stretch across his face. "Absolutely gorgeous," he said again—but this time, he was looking at Lindsey. He still couldn't believe how beautiful she was!

With teary eyes, causing her mascara to run, Lindsey threw open her car door and ushered Cole toward the front porch. She put an arm around his waist and squeezed. "You're within walking distance to great cafes and stores. The Bicentennial State Park. Heck, even the recording studio is within walking distance if you ever want to spend a little energy. The location here is prime. And..."

When they reached the base of the steps, Cole saw the excitement in Lindsey's eyes ambush her rhetoric in mid-sentence. Without forewarning, she pulled him into a full-mouth kiss, a kiss so wet, so blissful, so sensual that he wanted to lose himself there indefinitely. He kissed her back without reservation.

Until...a vision of Jana popped into his head.

He fought every instinct that propelled him into the kiss and slowly detached his lips. He was reminded how the power of touch, smell, and sight could overpower a man in a nanosecond. He faced Lindsey, only inches away, in silence. He wanted to kiss her again. More than anything. Her beauty wielded a power that scared him.

"Whew," she said in an intimate whisper. "Not only are you handsome, you're also a great kisser. I'm totally infatuated now."

Cole gently drew his fingers through her blonde hair. "If you don't mind," he whispered back, "I need for you to be a little patient with me. You're so attractive that I'm afraid if I'm not careful I could rush us into something that might not be healthy."

"All right, big guy," Lindsey said. "Then I'll need for you to *help* me be patient." She leaned in and brushed her lips against his again. "This won't be easy."

Cole inhaled her aroma. "Okay," he said jovially, trying to break the spell. "It's time to see the inside of the house. You first." He playfully nudged her up the porch steps.

Lindsey laughed. As Cole watched her excitedly unlock the front door, he wondered if he should just go ahead and propose marriage and take the chance that she would say yes. After all, how could he possibly be any more smitten than he already was? And she had already told him in previous conversations that she wanted to remarry one day.

Lindsey pushed open the door. Warm air greeted them from inside. "Welcome to your new abode, Mister Michaels!" Beaming, Lindsey took him by the hand and started giving him a detailed tour of the property.

Cole's senses were quickly pushed to overload. His brain found it difficult to assimilate what he was seeing. Compared to the prison cell, the townhouse—in every aspect—was like a palace. He wondered a couple of times if the house was just too much—in size, grandeur, and quality. Besides, would he really ever use all this space? Wasn't it a waste of resources? Despite that solitary issue, everything about the place appealed to his basic appreciation for all-things-fine.

"Of course, as you can see," Lindsey said, "the only furnishings in the house right now are the mattress and bedcovers, the food in the refrigerator, the few glasses, plates, and pans, and the cutlery. Which means...starting tomorrow...we go shopping! Over the next four or five weeks, we'll need to equip you with a complete new wardrobe, a house full of furniture, a car—oh, and a new driver's license—and computers and cell phones. I've already made out a list. We're going to bring you into the twenty-first century, and set you up like the celebrity you are."

"Lindsey, I, uh—"

Lindsey interrupted him with a peck on the lips. "You don't need to say anything. I really, really want to help you with all this. Trust me, it'll be my absolute pleasure. Besides, I've already made all the arrangements." She kissed him again, this time lingering a bit longer. A lot longer.

And Cole didn't resist. He had been a free man for only a few hours, yet he was already being overrun by a torrent of outside powers. He tried, though, to push his concerns aside and simply feast on the experiences.

Lindsey eventually continued the tour, ending on the back deck. "Well, what do you think?" she said, turning toward him and taking both of his hands.

"It's a mansion. You couldn't have selected a nicer place. It's...it's nothing less than fabulous." Cole kissed her hand. "Thank you, thank you, thank you. I really mean it."

Lindsey smiled, then looked at her watch. "Oh, my gosh, I'm late." She gave him another peck. "Roland wants me back in the office for a little bit. But I'll be back in a few hours to pick you up for tonight's party. Will you be all right? I really don't want to leave you alone right now, but—"

"Believe me, I'll be fine. I'm just going to enjoy the solitude for a few minutes...and try to soak everything in."

Cole followed her outside and retrieved his possessions from the Mini Cooper. And then he was standing alone in the front yard of the townhouse. The feeling of freedom was bizarre. Feelings of euphoria overwhelmed him. Climbing to the porch, he dropped the duffel, removed the Mysterious Lady from its case, and took a seat on the top step. The temperature was in the low forties. He looked up and down the street, then up at the beaming sun. The sunlight was glorious. Tears flowed freely. It all still felt like a dream. He lifted the violin bow and softly played one of his new songs.

* * *

That night, Lindsey—acting more and more like a

young lady in love—drove him to the SpiritMark party, talking the entire way and holding his hand.

At the party, Cole was introduced to everyone on the SpiritMark staff. Roland officially opened the event: "Tonight, we want to honor our newest artist and help him celebrate both his birthday and his newfound freedom. And we would like to do so by giving him a thirty-thousand dollar check as an advance payment for a record deal that I honestly believe will be historic."

A collective cheer swept through the small crowd.

Cole humbly waved. With the thirty thousand dollars, his savings balance would now stand at more than $93,000. What would he do with all the money?

For the rest of the evening—amidst the food, drinks, speeches, entertainment, and laughter—Cole was pulled into one music-related conversation after another. Everyone was vying for his attention. He could hardly believe that he was already being treated like a star.

After the party, Lindsey drove him back to his duplex, where they talked and laughed intimately—and engaged in some restrained but passionate kissing—till the early morning hours.

35

The transatlantic e-mail correspondence between Jesse in Atlanta, Georgia, and Sasha in Khust, Ukraine, had over the past two months intensified heavily. Sasha's driving urge to elevate her life beyond her small town had become more and more obvious. For Jesse, the frequency of communication had become burdensome. But he was gratified that he had successfully manipulated the girl. He had her firmly hooked—now could he convince her to follow through? He stared at the laptop monitor in his tiny one-bedroom apartment and read her latest reply for the dozenth time.

> My Dear Ryan,
> I am hardly believing your in-vitation to come and visit you in America. Ever since I was a young girl I am wanting to see America. Are you sure this is okay if I am staying with you? You say I can visit

at any time. If yes, is it okay if I am arriving in Atlanta on Sunday, February 17? I am so happy to see you face to face, and to see your son, Cory. I am believing we will have a wonderful time. I am hardly waiting to visit with you at the club where you are DJ. I am making sure that I am looking good for you. As I say before, I am thinking you will like Ukrainian women very much. We are trying very hard to be fashionable and much nice. We also are hard working and are good to our men. We are liking children very much also. I am very, very, very excited. I am giving you my airplane information when I am getting it.

Sasha

No wonder human traffickers had been so successful in luring these girls outside the borders of their countries into the overpowering arms of hired thugs. It seemed, from his perspective anyway, that the only bait necessary was ongoing contact, fun conversation, an aura of promise, an invite, and a little patience.

Not only was Sasha apparently at his beck and call—so were two other girls, twenty-year-old Svetlana from Russia and twenty-one-year-old Alina from Russia. He had met both of them in an internet chat room and was currently wooing them, pretending—as he was doing with Sasha—to be a twenty-eight-year-old single father who was a rich DJ at a fabulous nightclub.

His limited experience confirmed all he had read—these girls were so desperate for a better life that their farfetched hopes blinded them to the risks of entrusting their lives to the easily cloaked motivations of strange men.

But Russian men, it seemed, were equally desperate. Couldn't anybody with half a brain figure out pretty quickly that the glut of "Russian Bride" websites were the tools of organized crime rings to empty the billfolds of naive and lonely men around the world? Jesse had never spent a day in college and he had figured it out. That's why he had quickly skirted the websites and found legitimate chat rooms instead.

Yet, Jesse loved the one fact about the Ukrainian and Russian people: Their young women were stereotypically eye-grabbing, by anybody's standards. No wonder they were such hot commodities on the worldwide market.

Jesse typed his reply.

> Dear Sasha,
> I'm at the club right now, so this email will be short. I would love for you to visit me in Atlanta more than anything. I can hardly wait. I believe February 17 will be a good time. But give me two or three days just to make sure. I want to take off

from work most of the time that
you're here. So, give me a couple
of days to make this happen. And
then I'll let you know if February
17 will be the best time. After all,
I would like for your first visit to
America to be the very best.
Ryan

P.S.—I'm using your latest picture as my laptop screensaver.
Everybody that sees it asks, "Is she
a model?" They can't believe how
beautiful you are.

Jesse reread the letter and changed a few words to make
it sound more mature and sophisticated. He smiled at how
innocent it all sounded. He then moved the screen's cursor
to the *Send Now* button and clicked. Yes, he was pleased.
Very pleased.

Now that his bait had been taken, the time was ripe for
his next step. He retrieved and reviewed an unembellished
one-page website that he had created but not yet launched.
The website domain he had decided upon was www.
BuyABlonde.com. His first two choices for the domain
name—*BuyABride* and *BuyAWife*—had been claimed
already. And judging by the content of those two websites,
they were managed by Russians.

With the help of an acquaintance who was a computer

hacker, Jesse had learned how to secretly plant one's web page files on another company's web server.

He now carefully walked through each of those steps, using a laptop he had bought secondhand from a flea market, one with a registration that could not be traced to him.

After an hour at the keyboard, he paused as if waiting for the fanfare and then with the strike of a few final keys, downloaded his web page files to a preselected web server, one belonging to a landscaping business in England. He had chosen the company—after hours of searching—for two reasons: It was in a foreign country, and it was a family-run business, according to the home page. He hoped that a business of that type would have no one on staff to monitor the website with a technical eye, and, at the same time, would not be prone to invest tons of money to protect the website with sophisticated firewalls and security systems.

After completing all the steps, Jesse anxiously typed the BuyABlonde.com address into his computer's online server.

He waited.

Within seconds, his created web page flashed onto the screen, featuring a high-resolution picture of Sasha with her waist-length blonde hair and magnificent green eyes.

Yes! This was freaking awesome!

He ignored the hint of guilt that pinged his conscience.

His plan now was to wait and see if anyone in cyberspace found his web page and responded with an inquiry, and second, to remove his web page files from the host computer in England after only seven days and attach them to the web server of a different company. He would change the web server every week until he found a buyer, hoping to elude law-enforcement agencies.

36

With Lindsey prodding him, Cole spent the first five weeks of freedom engaged in an intense shopping spree. She insisted that he acquire all the things a modern music star needed to support a celebrity image.

During their multiple journeys across town, Cole found himself several times mentally and physically paralyzed by the unbelievable number of consumer options. The selections were too overwhelming. Had it always been this way? He couldn't remember. More than once, he felt the need to run for the exits and throw up. At those moments, Lindsey coaxed him to breathe and to start moving again. She would take his hand and guide him up and down the aisles. Overall, she made about seventy-five percent of the buying choices for him.

When the shopping spree was finally behind him, Cole couldn't have been more relieved.

On Thursday, February 7, in the sunlight of mid-morning, Cole sat alone at his new kitchen table and, as Lindsey had asked him to do for his insurance agent, made a list of his new purchases. Lindsey had even coached him on the details he needed to include. When he had typed out a couple of pages, he reviewed them.

A 2008 ruby red metallic 6-cylinder Porsche Boxster = $45,800

A 58" Panasonic TH-58PX75U flat-screen plasma HDTV = $2,399

A Bose Lifestyle 48 Series IV home entertainment system = $3,999

A 15" MacBook Pro laptop computer = $2,499

An Apple Extreme Base Station wireless router = $179

A Nikon D40X digital SLR camera = $699

An iPhone = $399

An iPod Classic with 160 GB = $349

An HP Officejet Pro L7580 Color All-in-one printer = $269

A Leather Furniture South 96" sofa
= $2,695

A Leather Furniture South 64" love
seat = $2,550

A Leather Furniture South 53"
chair = $1,850

A Leather Furniture South 37"
ottoman = $695

An Amish Timber Ridge queen bed
= $2,058

An Amish Timber Ridge chest =
$2,331

An Amish Timber Ridge dresser =
$2,467

Two Amish Timber Ridge night
stands = $2,100

An Amish Royal Mission queen
bed = $1,399

An Amish Royal Mission chest =
$1,197

An Amish Royal Mission dresser = $1,797

Two Amish Royal Mission night stands = $1,238

An Amish Showroom Mydetown oak dining room set with one table, six chairs, and one hutch = $3,125

A Maytag Centennial top-load washer = $499

A Maytag Centennial electric dryer = $549

A Martin Kathy Ireland Mission office desk = $1,295

A brown bomber leather executive office chair = $279

Three 6' X 9' hand-tufted International Accents rugs = $1,617

Four Thomas Kinkade framed pictures: Conquering Storms, End of A Perfect Day, Hometown Morning, Mountain Majesty = $5,995

He looked up from the list and scanned what he could see of his townhome. He still wasn't done yet—there were still other items he needed to make note of: a satellite dish, mattresses, pillows, cutlery, glassware, dishware, kitchenware, plants, microwave, clocks, bar stools, cushions, curtains, a closetful of new clothes and shoes, and a LoJack tracking device for his car. Everything he'd bought so far, minus the Porsche, had cost him about $50,000 in cash. The car had been financed. There was over $40,000 remaining in his bank account.

The decor of the house was more than beautiful—it was warm, masculine, inviting, and elegant. Without the combined influence of Lindsey and SpiritMark, he would most likely be sleeping on a mattress thrown down on the bare floor.

Yet, as wonderful as the furnishings were, a hidden fear nagged at him. Had he already, contrary to the vow he made to the chaplain, started to lose his focus? Had so many purchases so soon been a mistake? Should he have practiced more restraint? Should he have insisted that he remain more monastic? He reached for his Bible lying on the table and turned to a passage he had memorized long ago—First Timothy, chapter six, verses six, seven, eight, and ten. With a somber heart, he read aloud: *"True religion with contentment is great wealth. After all, we didn't bring anything with us when we came into the world, and we certainly cannot carry anything with us when we die. So if we have enough food and clothing, let us be content. For the love of money is at the root of all kinds of evil. And some people, craving money, have wandered from the faith and pierced themselves with many sorrows."* He groaned. He then read verses seventeen and eighteen. *"Tell those who are rich in this world not to be proud and not to trust in their money, which will soon be gone. But their trust should be in the living God, who richly gives us all we need for our enjoyment. Tell them to use their money to do good. They should be rich in good works and should give generously to those in need, always being ready to share with others whatever God has given them."* He hungered to do what was right. More than anything. "To be generous and ready to share," he repeated.

Oh, how he needed his life to be still for awhile.

He had taken too little time in the past five weeks to just ponder and pray. The nonstop running from task to task was an aspect of life on the "outside" that presented another major adjustment for him. Another was the constant onslaught of noise—car radios, restaurant music, office music, store music, cell phone conversations, public televisions, home televisions, home stereos, loud speakers, laptops, sirens, horns, automated voices, and live voices. He desperately missed the downtime and the quiet that had been such a prominent part of his prison life. He squeezed the bridge of his nose. In four days, he was scheduled to enter the SpiritMark studio and begin the demanding process of recording all the songs for his new CD. How many hours a day would that require? And for how many days? He needed to start reserving his energy for the project.

He thought for a minute, and then picked up his iPhone. He called Lindsey at her office.

"Hi, it's me," he said when she'd answered. "Yeah, I'm feeling the need to just sit and relax a bit this morning. Is it okay if we postpone the lunch appointment today?" He scratched at the table with his left hand. "No, I'm fine." He scratched some more. "Yeah, I know you're disappointed. And I apologize. It's just that I need to slow the pace a little, that's all. I'm sure they'll understand." He stopped the nervous scratching. "Okay, I'll talk to you later. I love you. Bye." He broke the connection with a simple touch of his finger to the screen, then stared at the phone. The strides in technology over eleven years were astonishing.

He looked again around his townhome. As soon as his gaze hit the sofa, he knew what he wanted to do. He lay down on the thick leather and stretched out into a comfortable position. With a new-smelling pillow under his head, he rested his feet on the side arm. He sank leisurely into the posh cushions and closed his eyes.

* * *

He awoke an hour later and rubbed his face. "Yes," he yawned. He needed more moments like this, to simply enjoy the morsels of nothingness. He quoted a psalm of thanksgiving. He repeated the psalm with slow deliberation and allowed his mind to run free in the fields of meditation. Predictably, the words were a soothing balm to his mind, and they inspired him to quote, out loud and with feeling, several other passages of Scripture that he had committed to memory during the last weeks of his jail sentence. The last verses that flowed from his mental storehouse were from Psalm chapter one-hundred-and-forty-three, verses five and six: *"I remember the days of old. I ponder all your works. I think about what you have done. I reach out for you. I thirst for you as parched land thirsts for rain."*

The words *I remember the days of old* echoed in his mind, and a tear formed at the corner of his eye.

He whispered, "Remember. Days of old. Shay. Jana. Field."

He curled up and crossed his arms over his chest. He knew what he needed to do. And now, for the first time in eleven years, he was logistically free—and mentally competent—to do it.

His mind nearly drowned in the thought.

He stood, felt his pants pocket to confirm that he was carrying his car keys, then shuffled to the kitchen cabinet, pulled out a drinking glass, and filled it with bottled water from the refrigerator.

He stared out the kitchen window for several minutes as he drank, then headed for his car.

37

$\mathcal{F}$or the past few years, Cole had supposed that the sheer passage of time had dulled his sensitivity to the deep pain caused by Shay's death.

He was wrong.

As he turned the Porsche onto the two-lane country road of his former Brentwood address, he realized he had stopped breathing. He sucked down his next breath as if someone had just removed a hand from around his nose and mouth. He immediately pulled the car off the road, into the grass. As the engine idled, he gripped the steering wheel and closed his eyes. He could hear himself gasping.

Slowly, he opened his eyes and looked down the road toward his former property. He sat motionless and stared until the tension in his muscles slightly eased.

He was certainly under no illusion that Shay, in God's presence, could hear him, but he bowed his head and said, in utter brokenness, "If you can hear me, buddy, your dad needs to let you know again how very sorry I am. If we could live that day all over again, I'd gladly put myself in your place a hundred times over. Only with God's help have I been able to forgive myself." He sat for a long time in silence, reminiscing.

He eventually lifted his head and cleaned his face. He knew now that his visit to the field would not simply be a somber, introspective touch with the past. Rather, it would most likely re-ignite a multitude of nightmarish sensations and then rush his soul with a barrage of agonizing accusations. Even so, he felt irresistibly drawn to revisit the site.

He wiped at his face again and shifted the Porsche's manual transmission. He slowly accelerated down the street.

When his former driveway came into sight, he gave up any idea of being analytical. He simply allowed his feelings to dominate the moment. By the time he parked the car at the edge of the field and lowered the car windows, his body had nearly petrified. He lost track of time as his eyes soaked up the area and his lungs tasted every molecule of air.

The events of the tragic day in the spring of '96 began to file through his mind with unforced clarity. He heard a groan—his own, even though it sounded as if it were coming from someone else. Then he was walking, then crawling through the dead grass, lured to the area of the field where the tractor had tilted and where the bush-hog had mulched Shay's body into a million pieces.

When he arrived at the general area, he sat for a long time, oblivious to the 48-degree weather. Lost in memory, he found himself saying, "Can I ride on the tractor with you, daddy? All right, hold onto my legs, buddy. Look at the motorcycles, daddy. Can we get one? Maybe we can get one when you're a little older and a little bigger. I gotta pee, daddy. Okay, hold onto my shirt, we're almost finished."

Cole staggered to his feet and reached into the air as if to grab the outstretched hand of his little boy. He stood there transfixed for several moments with his arm extended. "Forgive me," he whispered. He dropped to his knees again, and this time cried openly and freely until he had no tears left to cry.

At some point, he struggled to his feet and crossed the area, scanning every inch of ground.

When he spotted what he was looking for, he froze in mid-step.

"So that was it," he muttered, staring at a barrel-sized bulge in the ground. A piece of protruding granite, partially covered in dirt and weeds. The surface of the rock looked like a miniature whale breaching in the open sea. Cole bent and rubbed his hand slowly and softly across the contour of the stone. The tractor tire had rolled up over this rock. Cole lay on the field, his face against the stone. He sighed, then found that he had some tears left after all.

*　*　*

Throughout the afternoon and evening, the bush hog accident and its aftermath remained at the center of Cole's thoughts.

A therapeutic song began to emerge.

By the next morning, he had a complete set of lyrics

on paper. He reviewed the words at the kitchen table while sipping a cup of coffee.

> When you step out of the desert
> Onto the green island of paradise
> You can't linger there forever
> You can't linger there forever
> No one can
> No one does
> So face the rocks and the sand
> Embrace the dryness
> This is your teacher
> This is your strength
> Oasis blues, oasis blues.

He decided to call the song *Oasis Blues* and include it on his upcoming CD. In fact, he would immediately change the working title of the CD to *Oasis Blues*. And, of course, he would dedicate the project to Shay and Jana.

"Tremble, O earth, at the presence of the Lord," he quoted, from Psalm one-hundred-and-fourteen, verses seven and eight, *"He turned the rock into pools of water; yes, springs of water came from solid rock."*

38

Jesse nervously drove the rental car southbound on the 675 spur southeast of Atlanta. The 675 spur connected the 285 perimeter with I-75. When Jesse passed exit 7, he drove only another mile or so and then, before he reached exit 5, pulled out of the five o'clock rush-hour traffic into the emergency lane. Before he brought the car to a complete stop he made sure the two tires on the right side of the vehicle were clearly off the pavement and unmistakably in the grass, just as he had told the man they would be. He made sure he was adjacent to the business property he had identified on an earlier scouting trip.

If he needed to escape and couldn't jump back into the car fast enough, the commercial acreage would give him an easy route to aim for by foot. The only obstacle between the expressway and the commercial landscape was a rusty chain-link fence no more than four-and-a-half-feet tall and leaning over in places. It would be easy to jump.

He turned off the engine, then on impulse started it again and let it idle.

He looked around again, as he had on his scouting trip, to confirm that there were no traffic-monitoring cameras mounted in the area. Then he reached across the seat and pushed open the passenger-side door, another prearranged signal.

He checked his watch. If everything happened according to plan, the man—using a phone number with a Virginia area code—would arrive sometime during the next twenty minutes and pull up behind him.

Jesse had communicated with the stranger once by e-mail, when the man responded to the website offer, and three times by phone since then. Both of them had been tense during all three conversations. Jesse was, of course, suspicious of the man; he had even made his calls from a pay phone at a gas station so the man could not electronically trace the number to his apartment. And the man was suspicious of him as well, or at least seemed to be. Neither had volunteered their name to the other. He had asked the stranger point-blank in each of the calls if he was, or had ever been, associated in any way with any kind of law enforcement agency—the police, the sheriff, the FBI, the GBI, the CIA, or the ATF. The man, who sounded white and in his forties, claimed that he had never been, and demanded the same assurances from Jesse.

Jesse was leery nevertheless. He had even smeared red Georgia mud across the rental car's license plate to prevent the man, if he even showed up, from reading and memorizing the plate number.

Jesse reached over to the passenger seat and picked up a manila folder containing several pages of information the man was demanding—hard copies of the last five emails between him and Sasha, and a hard copy of Sasha's flight itinerary that included her name. Jesse shuffled through the papers to once again make sure every item was in place. He read the copy of Sasha's most recent email.

> Dear Ryan,
> As you are requesting, I am changing my flight to Atlanta from Sunday, February 17 to Saturday, March 1. I am already booking the ticket, but I am waiting to hear from you before I am paying for the ticket. I am attaching the flying itinerary. I am more excited each day. So that you are easy knowing me at the Atlanta airport I am planning to wear a red sweater with a fur collar. I am wearing a white belt with my jeans and I am wearing boots with a fur top. I am first flying to Amsterdam and am changing planes there to Atlanta. I am flying with KLM. My flight number will be number 621 from Amsterdam. If I am buying the ticket, I am arriving at 14:20 in Atlanta. I am saying "thank you" again for the wonderful invitation. I am loving the poem you wrote in

your last email. I am believing you
are a very romantic man and I am
liking this very much.

Jesse laid the folder in his lap. His forehead felt damp—
was he actually sweating? *Come on, get a grip, man.* He
wiped at the perspiration and then adjusted the baseball
cap he was wearing so that the bill barely revealed his eyes.
As he did, he saw in the mirror that a pickup truck had
pulled off the highway about fifty yards behind him. His
breathing quickened. The truck, a solid black vehicle,
approached slowly. Very slowly. Jesse froze. His eyes did not
shift from the pickup. The truck continued to draw closer.
It seemed like forever before the truck rolled to a stop just
behind the car. By that time, Jesse's mind was racing.

He took a deep breath and composed himself.

As agreed, he raised his right hand—the signal that
everything was clear.

The truck's headlights flashed on and off.

All right, this was the guy.

Forcing himself to be fearless, Jesse clutched the folder
in his hand and stepped out of the car. He walked slowly
back toward the truck, holding his arms out to show that
he wasn't carrying a weapon. The highway traffic rushed by
only a few feet away, the blasts of wind buffeting his body.
He stopped halfway between the two vehicles.

The man behind the truck's windshield pushed open
the driver's side door, sat motionless for several seconds,
then stepped down out of the truck and moved toward
Jesse.

In their telephone conversations, the man's voice had sounded bland, nondescript. Jesse had thought that the bland voice was the man's attempt to mask his character and personality. But now, looking at the man, he wasn't sure. The guy was white and had a boring, forgettable face that could blend into any Caucasian crowd. He was about 5'11", partially bald, and had a slight beer belly. He was dressed in clothes that an eighty-year-old-man would wear. His expression was furtive, insecure. He looked like the kind of person who had kept a low profile all his life, maybe a recluse. The man's weak appearance made Jesse feel more courageous.

Of course, the man might actually be a high-profile leader of some kind—maybe a teacher or a banker—who had cultivated a persona of weakness as a disguise. Or maybe he wasn't even the real buyer. Maybe he was just a go-fer, a hired footman.

The man got right to the point. "Can I have a few minutes alone with the papers?" he asked with an outstretched hand as he walked up.

"Sure," Jesse said, eager to complete their business and leave as quickly as possible. He passed the manila folder to the man.

Without a word, Jesse's customer walked back to the passenger side of his truck, opened the door, and stood reading, using the passenger seat as a table.

Jesse waited tensely for several minutes, periodically scrutinizing southbound traffic to make sure no patrol car was approaching.

"All right," the stranger finally announced, returning

to where Jesse was standing. "A thousand in cash now and nineteen thousand at the time of delivery."

"That's the deal," Jesse said.

"In our next phone call, we'll work out the logistics for the exchange at the airport."

Jesse nodded.

The man reached into his pants pocket and pulled out a small stack of bills.

Jesse reached to take the money—only to see the man suddenly retract his hand. Jesse's brain skipped a groove. *What the...?*

The man looked poised to say something harsh. Instead, he grimaced, then held out the money again. "Happy Valentine's Day," he said, sounding more forceful now. "I'll expect a call in the next forty-eight hours."

Jesse took the down payment.

Within seconds, Jesse was back in his rental car. He pulled the passenger-side door closed, then fingered his newly earned money—ten crisp one-hundred-dollar bills. He smiled. He started to connect his seatbelt, then jumped as he heard the tires of the stranger's truck spin in the dirt, grab concrete, and accelerate past him out into the flow of traffic.

Jesse's eyes zoomed in on the truck's license plate. STAM-888. From out of state. Jesse memorized the number, repeating it to himself all the way home.

That evening he typed out an email to Sasha.

Dear Sasha,
Go ahead and buy the ticket. I've

cleared my schedule for March 1 through March 12. I will be at the Atlanta airport to pick you up on Saturday, March 1, at 2:20. I can't wait to see you. Even Cory is excited. He has seen your picture so much, and has heard me talk about you so many times, that he is already calling you "daddy's special lady". Now that my work schedule has been hammered out, I think I am more excited about your visit than you are. I can't wait.

Before Jesse went to bed, he relocated his www.BuyABlonde.com website to another web server, this time a server belonging to a business somewhere in Poland. He then answered emails from both Alina and Svetlana in Russia.

39

"Hello, my name is Roland Powers. And I'm a workaholic."

A shout of laughter erupted in the small conference room where the fifteen people on the SpiritMark payroll, along with Cole Michaels, were congregated.

"Seriously, though," the CEO of SpiritMark smiled, "all of us together have gone beyond the call of duty. And I know that every one of us feels it. For nearly three weeks, we have pushed hard for ten hours a day. But the good news is that all fourteen tracks for the *Oasis Blues* CD have now been laid down."

Hoots and hollers, along with whistles and applause, filled the room.

"And let me tell you," he added as the festive racket subsided, "through all my years in the music industry, I don't think I've ever been so moved by a collection of music. So I just want to give Cole and everybody else in this room a heads-up—the first twenty copies will be mine. One for my house, one for my car, one for my wife's car, one for my daughter's car, and sixteen to give away to the heads of all the other music companies on Music Row."

"Yeah!" someone shouted, followed by another squall of hoopla and clapping.

"And to add to this wonderful day of celebration," Roland continued, "our marketing department has as of last night finalized the cover for the CD—a cover of which I am extremely proud." He pushed a button on a remote control unit and watched as a huge image—an aerial view of a richly colored palm tree canopy edged by sun-baked sand—appeared on the huge monitor on the wall. A pair of tanned feet protruded from beneath the tree outward toward an open dessert. Sun rays had been digitally manipulated to maximize colors and shadows. The overall affect attracted a viewer's eyes instantly and fully. Roland gave the crowd about three seconds to absorb the view. "So, what do you think?"

"Oh, yeah!" a man's voice rose from the seats.

"Absolutely awesome" another male voice announced. "I'd like to have it as a wall mural in my home. I'm serious, man."

"Gorgeous!" "Beautiful!" "Very impressive." "I love it!" "One of the best CD covers I've ever seen!" Other accolades filled the room.

"To the art crew!" Lindsey Rose shouted, launching a round of applause.

"Will the art team stand up, please," Roland said.

Two men and a lady stood.

"Will the recording engineers and technicians stand."

Four men moved to their feet.

"And Cole, will you stand?"

Cole complied.

"As the CEO of this company," Roland said, "I want you all to know how extremely proud I am of you. I want to personally thank each of you for your hard work, your dedication to this project, and your loyalty to this company. Your skills are extraordinary. You're the best. Let's give everyone a hand."

A united applause once again filled the room.

Roland then motioned for everyone to be seated. "As you all know, these are just the initial steps in this project. We still have a long road ahead of us. The engineering team will mix the tracks and record the master disc. The art team will finalize and launch the dedicated website for the project. The marketing team will begin the process of getting radio disc jockeys all over the country to give one or two of the songs some significant air time, of procuring heavyweight endorsements from both the entertainment world and the church community, and of generating as many newspaper and magazine articles as possible. The administrative team will continue their work of scheduling teaser concerts throughout the southeast, along with arranging public appearances, television appearances, and radio interviews. And they will, of course, continue to develop the road schedule for the Oasis Blues North America tour, slated to begin in October." Roland paused and sipped a drink of bottled water. "Again, I want to remind everyone that the release date of the CD will be April the tenth. So, we've got a ton of work to accomplish in the next six weeks. And, of course, I don't need to tell you that what we're doing here right now will most likely give SpiritMark the widespread name recognition we all desire. And deserve." Roland scratched his forehead. "Cole, will you stand one more time, please?"

Cole obliged.

Roland smiled and pointed in Cole's direction. "And this man, I strongly predict, will once again become a very, very famous individual, not to mention a very, very wealthy one."

* * *

Cole decided to eat lunch alone. He told Lindsey and the others that he needed to mentally decompress. And, in truth, he felt like his brain and his body—over the past three weeks of recording—had run several consecutive marathons. He needed solitude.

But, sitting by himself at a corner booth in a downtown diner, he couldn't relax. The adjustment back to civilian life had been more complex than he had anticipated. Thankfully, the recording process—though it had drained him—had been a welcome distraction. And he couldn't be more pleased with the final tracks. He was genuinely moved by each of the arrangements. And a significant reason for that, he knew, was the Mysterious Lady. With its resplendent, epic sound, it filled him with a sense of wonder, and that wonder was reflected in his music. As he dabbed a pencil at a napkin and waited on his order—a burger and coleslaw—he could honestly imagine that the

CD, with its worshipful lyrics and sublime tunes, could easily usher a listener into a state of spiritual thirst and introspection. And that is what he had hoped for all along. Nothing more. Nothing less. Whether there would be one listener or thousands.

He recalled Roland Power's prediction that he would once again become famous and wealthy. He was curious— did everyone at SpiritMark assume this was his goal? Cole wrote the words "famous" and "wealthy" onto the napkin.

He peered at the words for a long time.

It was time to face a question he had spent the past year trying to stifle. Yes, he had wanted to produce a new CD. But did he really, really want to become a full-fledged celebrity again?

Becoming famous and wealthy just wasn't his all-consuming priority anymore. Yet he felt the momentum of the SpiritMark staff—especially Lindsey—pushing him into the celebrity pipeline, like it or not.

And wasn't this what he had signed up for when he signed his contract?

He doodled on the napkin. He had naively hoped he could help deflate Lindsey's preoccupation with the "high life" philosophy, and maybe enlist her as an additional voice of reason to his side of the table. But, Lindsey was the one perhaps pushing him the hardest to "achieve it all".

He didn't seem able to make her understand.

He didn't seem able to make *anyone* understand.

He wadded up his napkin. Had it really been God's voice he'd been hearing in prison extolling the unornamented life? Or had it been nothing more than a mental adaptation to his circumstances that had brought him to his 'simple-should-be-sufficient' convictions?

He remembered the vow he had written into his Bible in prison: People like me are tempted almost beyond measure to depend solely on their musical abilities and their bank accounts. For the rest of my life, though, I will choose to depend chiefly on the Lord my God.

He squeezed the pencil until it snapped.

40

*T*orn between his longing to hang out with Lindsey for the rest of the day and his need for more reflective solitude, Cole decided to spend the evening alone as well. Lindsey, as he'd expected, was frustrated. Reluctantly, she conceded to what had become his personal choice for crisis therapy—to retreat into his inner monastery. She gave him a lover's kiss on his stubble-covered cheek. "I wish you could just relax and enjoy what life has given you," she said. She patted him on the butt. But her smile looked forced.

When he finished at SpiritMark, Cole stopped at a movie-rental store on his way home. He had rented only one movie since purchasing his big-screen television. On this cold winter afternoon, he felt the need to rent two or three movies and enjoy an evening of escapism.

But as he perused shelf after shelf of DVDs in numerous aisles, he felt overwhelmed. Why so many choices? Wasn't it possible that having such a huge selection could become an over-indulgent abuse of resources and energy, both for the manufacturer and the consumer? He stopped, stood, and looked around, feeling, for some reason, confused and angry. And very much alone. His bare bones lifestyle in prison had obviously affected his thinking far more than he had imagined.

He soon spotted an end cap with a tiny banner that read "Staff Recommendations." There were only eight movies on the rack. Now that was a number of choices he could handle. He chose two of them. One was about an innocent man's lengthy and dramatic escape from a maximum-security prison. The other was about a businessman who had been lost for several years, alone on an uninhabited island.

At home, he turned off his cell phone and took a two-hour nap. He then fixed, for dinner, a bowl of vegetable soup and a grilled-cheese sandwich. He savored every mouthful of the simple treat while a female jazz artist, unknown to him, crooned nostalgic tunes over the new stereo system. Oh, how he cherished an occasional evening like this! Without business! And without dialogue!

When he finished his meal, he cleaned up the kitchen and sat down to watch an hour's worth of international news. After only thirty minutes of surfing back and forth between three news channels, he gave up. The bombastic sensationalism and lack of genuine news reporting frustrated him. Why couldn't the news stations just say, "There's been a report of a missing jetliner en route from Los Angeles to Manila. We don't have any hard facts yet, but we'll report back to you when we have confirmed details," instead of devoting an hour of mild hysteria to the report by bringing in multiple aviation experts to speculate on a million and one what-ifs?

Cole just shook his head.

He eventually started the movie about the castaway and stretched out on the leather couch. For the next hundred-and-forty minutes, he became totally immersed in the drama of the main character. He related to the castaway's every emotion: terror, confusion, despair, apathy, elation, and absolute broken-heartedness. By the time the credits rolled, Cole was weeping.

He too was a castaway, wasn't he?

The castaway in the movie, trapped on an uninhabited island, had no choice but to forge a new life for himself. He learned to eat whatever he could harvest from the land and the sea. He learned to build fires. He learned to live without electricity, without plumbing, and without human contact. His four years on the island transformed his life. But when he was finally found and taken back to his former life, no one could understand what he had lived through, no one could relate to him, no one understood who he was any longer. Thus, he became a castaway all over again.

Cole, too, had become a castaway—in prison. He had been forced to discover a whole new way of living. And he had been forever changed by the experience. But now, no one on the outside understood what he had lived through. No one could relate to him. On the outside, he was still a castaway.

He massaged his face and head. He turned off the television and the lights and sat in the dark. When his tears faded, he reached into his pants pocket and brought out a $3,000 engagement ring he had intended to offer to Lindsey earlier that day. He rolled the ring back and forth in his fingers.

Lindsey. He was still spellbound by her—by the way she looked, the way she talked, the way she smelled, the way she kissed, the way she felt in his arms. He loved her. He loved her mind, her personality, her optimism, her wit. He loved the way she loved him and cared for him. He couldn't think of another woman he would rather spend the rest of his life with. The memory of their evenings together over the last eight weeks streamed through his head. The walks. The home-cooked meals. The wonderful conversations. The heartfelt laughter. The Friday and Saturday night dates.

He squeezed the ring tightly in his hand. If he proposed, she would accept, probably with an explosion of tear-laced shrills; he was certain of it. She had already told him that she was ready for marriage again. And for motherhood. So why was he stumbling? He definitely wasn't afraid of commitment. Nor of responsibility. Nor of having more children. He had a house. He had money. He had a promising career ahead of him.

There was just one hitch—and it would not go away. It was their lack of shared vision. Affluence was no longer a priority for him; for Lindsey, it was. It was what got her out of bed every morning. A much slower and simpler lifestyle was vital for Cole's psychological well-being—yet that was the last thing Lindsey wanted. A spiritual hunger for God, for God's truth and God's pleasure, still burned in his belly. No such fire burned in Lindsey's belly. How could they become serious companions in life with such strong differences? His spiritual craving, along with the loss of his appetite for riches and the rat race, were causing him to doubt whether he should even devote the next year of his life to touring. He had not shared this thought with Lindsey yet. He was fearful of her reaction.

He slipped the engagement ring onto the tip of his little finger and coiled his hand into a fist. Yes, he had signed a contract to produce a CD, but his motivation had been personal therapy, ministry outreach, and a search for post-prison direction. And he had fulfilled that contract. He had not, on the other hand, signed a contract to tour the country to make money and fertilize the seeds of fame.

Perhaps it was time for him to sit down with Roland Powers, explain his inner turmoil, and ask Roland to rethink SpiritMark's plans for him. But could Cole reason with such a visionary as Roland?

He ran his fingers through his hair—purposely left uncut since his prison release. At that moment, he noticed the silhouette of one of the table phones perched in the moonlit room. Of course! He had wanted to call Chaplain Duke Parker for weeks now. Parker was one man who could understand Cole's adjustment difficulties. Parker, after all, had forewarned him. He could call Parker, spill his heart, and ask for advice.

He looked at his wristwatch—10:45. No, he wouldn't disturb Parker, or his family, at this late hour. He would call tomorrow morning. Just the thought, though, of talking with his trusted mentor gave Cole a surge of hope.

He absent-mindedly rubbed the engagement ring one more time and put it back in his pocket.

41

At 2:15 PM on Saturday, March 1, Jesse entered the north terminal at Atlanta's Hartsfield-Jackson-International Airport. On his way to the baggage claim, he concentrated on breathing deeply and evenly, trying to steady his nerves. He checked a row of flight monitors—KLM flight 621 was due to arrive on schedule at 2:20.

Jesse checked a different monitor to find out which baggage carousel was designated as the pickup spot for Sasha's luggage. The bags on Sasha's flight would be dispensed at carousel 8. He had told Sasha he would meet her at her baggage claim belt and that he would be wearing a brown cap. He had thought about holding up a handwritten sign with her name scrawled in big letters, but had decided he could not afford to give people a reason to stare at him and maybe remember his face.

The terminal was crowded—a hive of nonstop motion. Good. The more people in the terminal, the less he would stand out. He casually made his way to carousel 8. For the moment, the carousel was empty and still. Jesse walked to a nearby wall and sat on the floor to wait.

After a few moments, he looked to his left, studiously nonchalant. About thirty yards away, Sasha's buyer—having followed at a distance, as agreed—now sat on a gray plastic bench, pretending to read a newspaper. Jesse still didn't know if the man was the actual buyer or just an errand boy. Using the license plate number of the truck, he had been able to procure a name. But was it the name of the man sitting in the terminal, or someone else? Whatever, he had recorded the name on his computer, in case he ever needed some leverage.

Jesse stared down at his hands. He stretched and shook his fingers to relieve tension. He leaned his head back against the wall. Once again, he mentally ran through every phase of the plan.

He was satisfied that everything was in place.

What would happen to Sasha? Would she become a personal sex slave? Would she be imprisoned in someone's basement—a private dungeon? Forced into prostitution? Would her organs be harvested and the rest of her body dumped into a river somewhere? Jesse squeezed his forehead. The truth was, he really didn't care. And that bothered him—shouldn't he care, at least to some degree?

Carousel 8 was still motionless.

With each passing minute, the waiting got harder. Sasha's buyer was now on his feet, pacing. Jesse rested his head against the wall again and closed his eyes. He slowed his breathing and, for a while, lost himself in a mental black hole.

Finally, a couple of people—presumably passengers from the KLM flight—approached the carousel. Jesse's nerves jolted to full alert. Within a minute or two, others started to crowd around the belt. Jesse stood, surveying the clusters of people heading toward the carousel, searching for the clothes Sasha had said she would be wearing: a red sweater with a fur collar, jeans with a white belt, and boots with a fur top. Jesse willed himself to be completely focused, tuning out the chatter of everyone around him. Carousel 8 rumbled to life. Within seconds, the first suitcase came up from the belly of the airport and slid onto the carousel.

Jesse glanced to his left. Sasha's buyer was staring at him, waiting for the cue.

People were still gathering at the baggage claim belt. For fifteen minutes or more, Jesse scanned the crowds approaching the area.

And then, bam! Jesse spotted her. It had to be her. The red sweater. The jeans and white belt. The fur-topped boots. The waist-length blonde hair. He found himself visually stunned by the reach of her beauty. He'd known she was beautiful; he had seen her photos. But in person, she carried an unexpected aura of sexuality, unlike anything Jesse was accustomed too. She was beyond gorgeous. Men turned to stare at her as she walked past. Jesse took a deep breath, shook off his momentary loss of equilibrium, and concentrated on the task at hand.

He grabbed the bill of his cap and tipped it—a signal to the buyer that the target had been sighted and that he was beginning his approach. He shut his eyes for about five seconds, rehearsed his script for what was to come, and then focused totally on Sasha. He raised his hand and headed in her direction, smiling.

As he approached, he saw her spot his brown cap and break into a dazzling smile. But the smile quickly faded, leaving her looking befuddled.

"Sasha?" he said.

"Ryan?" Her tone was filled with confusion, caused no doubt by the discrepancy between Jesse's in-person appearance and the bogus photographs he had sent, as well as the obvious age difference between himself and *Ryan*.

"No, I'm Ryan's younger brother, Josh," he said. "Ryan was planning to be here, but his son, Cory, had a bicycle accident a couple of hours ago and broke his arm. They're at the hospital right now. So Ryan sent me and our Uncle Mike to pick you up. He apologizes—he knows this isn't what you were expecting. But it couldn't be helped, and he hopes you'll forgive him."

Sasha still seemed flustered. "Yes...I am remembering Ryan talking about his brother."

"Well, that's me. Oh, and he told me to wear the brown cap—he said you'd be looking for it. He's so disappointed. He bought a big bouquet of flowers, and wanted to give them to you in person. But, as I said, Cory had an accident. The little guy is normally pretty tough, but this time he begged his dad not to leave him."

Sasha nodded an uneasy acceptance.

"So, welcome to America." Jesse extended his hand.

Sasha shook it. Her smile began to return. "Thanks. I am so glad to be here. This is a dream I am having for a long time!"

"And if you don't mind me saying so," Jesse said, feigning a bit of sheepishness, "you're every bit as beautiful as Ryan said you were."

Sasha blushed, then half grinned. "What actually...did Ryan say to you?"

Jesse leaned toward her and whispered. "Well, the truth is, he's been so infatuated by your pictures and emails that, in addition to all the talk, he's even written a song about you."

Sasha looked pleased, as if she might blush. "A song? Are you saying this serious?"

"Totally serious. As a matter of fact, a few people in the music industry have heard the song and believe it has the potential to be a hit."

Sasha beamed. "I am definitely wanting to hear this song."

"Oh, believe me, you will. I'm sure Ryan will surprise you with it the first time the two of you are alone together."

Sasha smiled again. She was relaxing more and more.

Jesse stared at her for a moment, feeling himself starting to surrender to her sex appeal. Should he trash the whole plan, keep the girl, and see if anything could develop between them? But he abandoned the idea as soon as it crossed his mind. She would never accept him—once she learned his lifelong secret. He thought of his dad's favorite insult that had come at him often, the one Jesse had always hated—*manless wuss*. Besides, Jesse had already told the girl too many lies. He would never be able to explain them all.

As they waited for Sasha's suitcase, Jesse thanked her again for understanding and promised her that Ryan would make it up to her. "He's already talking about taking you to Disney World as a surprise."

Sasha was just starting to reply when she spotted her suitcase on the belt.

Jesse lifted the soft-sided case for her and led her toward the nearest exit. But then he stopped and removed a key from his pants pocket. He had bought it a couple of days before at an indoor antique mall, paying fifty cents for a ring full of them. He had soaked the key in a cleaning solution and scoured it with a metal brush to brighten it up and make it look current. "In just a minute, I'll introduce you to my Uncle Mike. I've got to get back to work, so he'll be the one to drive you to Ryan's house. Here's Ryan's house key." Jesse handed the key to her. "It opens both locks on the front door. The top lock can be a little tricky, but Mike will help you with it if you can't figure it out. Once you get inside, make yourself at home. Drinks are in the refrigerator. There are three bedrooms in the house. They're all clean, so use any one you want. If you want to take a bath, the hot tub is in the master bedroom. Ryan hopes to be home by six or seven this evening. He'll probably call you soon after you get to the house. But, if you need any help before he gets home or before he calls, just give me a ring. My cell number is posted on the bulletin board in his kitchen."

Sasha hugged him. "Thank you,' she said, "I am not believing I am here. The USA!"

Jesse was shaken by the feel of her body against his. "Oh, you're going to love it!" He then casually rolled her suitcase outside to the drop-off/pickup lanes. He pulled out a mobile phone—a prepaid one he'd bought just for this purpose, under a fake name. He called *Uncle Mike*.

"Hey, Mike," he grunted when the man answered. "We just walked outside. Where are you?" He listened to the reply. "All right...we're up near the first door." He ended the call and stuffed the phone into his pocket. "Okay," he explained to Sasha, "He's driving around. He'll be here any minute. The house is only about thirty minutes away, so the ride won't be bad." Jesse spent the next couple of minutes keeping things light, asking Sasha about her flight and about her hometown.

And then the black truck approached.

"Okay, here he is," Jesse said. "Remember, make yourself at home."

The truck pulled to the curb. Jesse put the suitcase in the truck bed and opened the passenger door. "Mike, this is Sasha. Sasha, this is Mike." Jesse helped Sasha up into the cab. She suddenly looked uncertain and uncomfortable again.

The buyer nodded and grunted.

"Thanks again, man," Jesse said to the stooge. "I owe you one."

"You owe me more than one, you little butt," *Mike* said gruffly.

"Yeah, right."

"Here, don't forget your gym bag," *Mike* added. He tossed a black duffel over Sasha's lap, out the open door.

Jesse caught the bag. He swung it just out of Sasha's sight and zipped it open about six inches. The banded stacks of hundred-dollar bills looked untouched and undisturbed since he had counted them an hour before. Jesse zipped it up. "All right, get some rest," he said to Sasha, then closed the door.

As Jesse watched the truck slowly pull away, Sasha suddenly looked rigid and more than a little nervous. How long, he wondered, would the baldheaded wacko be able to sustain the "Uncle Mike" act? Not long, Jesse wagered—and when the man couldn't fool her any longer, how would he manage to immobilize her? Inject her with a drug? Threaten her with a pistol? Hit her over the head? Whatever, Jesse wasn't going to stand around thinking about it. He walked quickly to his car in the parking ramp without looking a single person in the eye. Only when he was merging into the I-85 traffic heading north did he feel an incredible release of tension.

He'd pulled it off! He pumped his fist and shouted. He had succeeded; he'd gotten away with another crime. And he was richer by nineteen thousand dollars. Nineteen thousand freaking dollars!

* * *

Two afternoons later, Jesse stood in the back office of a sleazy downtown gym. The gym's manager, a huge black guy who was at the moment dripping with sweat, wore a faded T-shirt, every seam strained by bulging muscles.

Jesse had found out about the gym, and the gym's services, from an inmate at Dodge State Prison.

Behind locked doors, Jesse handed over $175. The man counted the bills, then unlocked the drawer of an extremely cluttered desk. He pulled out a 200-ml bottle of testosterone enanthate and gave Jesse the bottle without offering any instructions or warnings.

And Jesse didn't ask any questions. He could research it online. He tucked the bottle down into his pants and left.

*   *   *

That night, sitting on his couch with his pants down to his ankles, Jesse inserted a syringe into the bottle of steroids and drew 10 ml. When he worked up the courage, he plunged the needle into his thigh muscle and injected the anabolic cocktail.

Just as he removed the needle, his cell phone rang.

"Hey, it's Uncle Mike," the voice announced on the other end. "I'm really, really pleased with your product. I would like another one."

42

"Cole...this is Duke Parker," the voicemail relayed. "I'm sorry I haven't been around to take your calls." The voice sounded shockingly feeble and slurred. "I've spent the last fourteen days in the hospital. The news isn't good. The doctors tell me I have stage-four cancer. It's everywhere...in my lungs...in my bones. There's nothing they can do to stop it at this point. So along with my wife and Mateo...I've come down to my sister-in-law's home in Chattanooga...where I'll be cared for by Hospice. They tell me that my suffering won't last very long." There were a few seconds of silence. "Regarding your requests for advice, I promise that I'll try to ask Jesus face-to-face...to enlighten you and...help you make the right choices. And I trust that He will. Blessings, my brother. Thanks for all the treasured memories. And I salute you with the apostle Paul's sentiment, *For to me, to live is Christ...and to die is gain.*"

Cole was standing on the city sidewalk just outside the SpiritMark offices during a lunch break. With his mobile phone in hand, he replayed the message twice more. The call had come from Parker's cell number. He quickly punched the key for his iPhone to call the number. Parker's phone rang, but no one answered. Cole called again. Still no answer, not even an answering service accepting messages. He checked the time of Parker's call. It had come through over an hour ago, while Cole had been in a business meeting, his phone turned off.

He sat down on a small landscape wall and wrapped his face in his hands. He was sucked into a maelstrom of painful denial, followed by anger, then grief. Eventually he picked up his phone again and scrolled through a list of numbers until he found Parker's home number. He called. He counted twenty unanswered rings, then terminated the call. The gears of his mind were turning. He used his phone to search online until he found the phone number for the Middle Tennessee Correctional Facility. He pressed the "call" option and was immediately connected to a menu of options. He chose one.

"Hello, Middle Tennessee Correctional Complex. How can I direct your call?"

"I'd like to speak with the captain, please."

"Hold, please."

Cole waited.

"Hello, Captain speaking," the voice rang out, irritated and hurried.

"Captain, this is former inmate Cole Michaels."

"What can I do for you today, Cole?" The captain made no effort to mask his irritation.

Cole swallowed, automatically humbling himself as if back in prison. "Yeah, I just got the news about Chaplain

Parker. And I really would like to give him a call. But, I understand he's gone to his sister-in-law's home in Chattanooga. I'm calling to find out if you or someone there in the office has the sister-in-law's name, phone number, or street address."

"Hold on."

Cole waited on hold for at least two minutes. When the Captain reconnected, he still acted bedraggled. He gave Cole a phone number, wasted no time with pleasantries, and said good-bye. Cole could easily imagine the Captain fuming over some prison issue, his cigar being angrily pushed around in his lips. Cole was just glad the Captain had taken time to give him the number.

Cole called the sister-in-law's house. After twelve or thirteen rings, he was just about to hang up when someone on the other end answered. "Hello." It was the voice of an old lady.

"Is this the sister-in-law of Chaplain Duke Parker?"

"It is."

"My name is Cole Michaels. I'm calling from Nashville. I'm a ...well, the chaplain is a longtime friend of mine. He called me about an hour ago and left a message telling me about his cancer. I just want to say that I'm really sorry. Is there any way I can speak to him for a few minutes?"

There was a heavy pause on the other end. "He's been in a lot of pain in the last twenty-four hours. At the moment he's sleeping, and I don't want to wake him. He really needs to sleep while he can. If you don't mind, try to call back in three or four days, and maybe he'll feel like talking."

"I would really..." Cole was tempted to try to persuade

her to let him talk to the chaplain later that day. Against all inclinations, though, he yielded to her request. "All right," he told her, "I'll call again on Thursday morning around ten, if that's okay."

"That should be fine."

Good, he sighed. Without being rude, he had just reduced the "three or four days" to two.

* * *

That evening, Cole spent three hours rehearsing with his sound technicians and his accompanying musicians. His first live concert in twelve years was only four and a half weeks away, coinciding with the release of his CD. A six-thousand-seat entertainment center in downtown Nashville had been booked for his return to the stage. Thousands of dollars had been spent to promote the event.

For over a year, he had dreamed about this re-mergence onstage—a live comeback. At times, that dream had lifted his spirit so high that he had floated on its energy for days. But his recent doubts about the direction of his life, combined with the dispiriting news about the chaplain, robbed him of his enthusiasm. The potent mixture of bad news and badgering doubts pushed him emotionally off balance for the evening. Twice during rehearsal, he had to apologize to his technicians—once for losing his focus and not projecting his voice, and once for verbally snapping at the lead tech who'd been trying to coach him.

After the rehearsal, he joined Lindsey at her home for a late-night dinner. She greeted him at her front door in a form-fitting red dress and pearls. She looked ravishing. Cole was convinced, though, that she would look provocative even if dressed in a dirty old potato sack.

"Are you okay?" she asked, wrapped in his hug. "You don't look very well."

He told her the news about the chaplain.

Despite Lindsey's sympathy and encouragement and the gourmet meal she served him, Cole just couldn't shake his despondency.

He left earlier than he normally would have.

* * *

Alone in his bed by midnight, Cole tried to ease his heart and his mind by opening some of his old prison journals and rereading some of his notes based on Chaplain Parker's passionate revelries.

> "Our western culture is addicted to convenience, comfort, and prosperity. Everybody in our society, it seems, wants to believe, and is encouraged to believe, that God is also addicted to convenience, comfort, and prosperity. Let's just call it our *American-Dream* theology. But anyone who really knows the Bible understands that this theology is asinine."

"Nowhere in the Bible does God ask us to place our faith in his predictability. Rather, he asks us to place our faith in his ability."

"As a servant of God's household, I never have to worry. About anything. God, as owner of the house, will never lose his property, never go bankrupt, never be conquered, never get sick, and will never die. Thus, I can truly, truly relax."

As always, the truisms punched with force. Cole rubbed his fingers across the handwritten notes. He thought about the man who had taken an interest in him and had gently and graciously taught him these biblical insights. The man who had grown up as a missionary kid in Bolivia, who bore the grotesque scars of a destructive fire, who had devoted his life to bringing criminals to Jesus. The man who had physically saved him, when he was a new and vulnerable inmate, from a near-fatal beating. The man who had taught him by example how to teach and to be a spiritual influencer. The man who had encouraged him to never, never lose his focus in life. The man who was now dying with cancer.

There was something powerful about a life well lived. The chaplain had lived such a life, and his influence was undeniable.

Cole rolled out of bed, walked to the master bathroom, and looked into the mirror. "What about you?" he whispered to his reflection. "What kind of life are you going to live?" He felt the weight of the question, as if it had been asked by the Lord Himself and backed by a thousand of His angels.

Cole stared silently at his image—a trim and chiseled face and torso, with blonde hair now growing long for the first time in eleven years.

"Celebrity or servant?" he asked. "A prestigious music star who is waited on, catered to, and pampered? Or a selfless steward who offers up his life and resources to help others?"

He suddenly wanted to talk with a pastor. But he had been so busy since his release from prison that he had hardly had time to even attend a church service, much less build a relationship with a spiritual shepherd of any kind. Hopefully, on Thursday morning, he would be able to ask the chaplain one more time to help him sort out and understand his destiny.

43

Cole slept till 10:00 on Thursday morning. His body seemed to crave extended rest, probably because of his unsettled mind and the stress it placed on him. When he finally lifted himself out of bed, he jumped into a hot shower and stayed in the refreshing spray for a long time, simply because he could. He rinsed in cold water and got out.

He dressed, but didn't bother to shave.

By 10:45, he felt he had waited long enough and decided to make his call to Chattanooga. He picked up his mobile phone from the kitchen counter and rang the chaplain's sister-in-law. As he waited through the rings, he noticed his tight grip on the phone and realized just how anxious he was to find out how the chaplain was faring— and to hopefully have a conversation, even a short one, with the one person in the world who would understand his social and spiritual dilemma. No one on the *outside*, not even Lindsey, could communicate with him like the chaplain. And with no one to fill the chaplain's shoes, Cole felt more and more like a castaway with each passing day.

"Hello," a subdued voice, that of a young man, said.

"Yes, my name is Cole Michaels. I'm a friend of Chaplain Parker's from Nashville. I called on Tuesday to speak with him. But he was asleep at the time. So I made arrangements to call back this morning to see if he's available."

"I'm sorry, sir. My dad...is no longer with us. He passed away this morning at around three o'clock."

Cole felt an abrupt constriction nearly shut off his throat, as if he had swallowed a cupful of gravel.

"Sir, are you still there?" the young man asked.

"He what? I mean...I...I'm sorry...I..." Cole's head bobbed. His eyes slammed shut. "Who am I speaking with?"

"My name is Mateo. I'm the son."

Cole tried to push away a growing dizziness. "And he passed away when?"

"Excuse me, but are you somehow connected with the correctional facility?"

"I'm sorry...yes...yes I am...I was an inmate there for eleven years. During that time, your dad became the most important person in the world to me. He saved my life in...many, many ways. He...he became my best friend... he..."

Mateo said, "At around three o'clock this morning, he grabbed my hands and my mom's at the bedside and smiled a huge smile. He closed his eyes. And then he was gone." The young man stifled a groan. "It happened so fast. We're all still in a state of shock."

Cole's heart and soul felt like a one-lane road with eight lanes of traffic trying to squeeze through it. The wide band of thoughts and emotions he was experiencing was nearly paralyzing. "I...I'm so sorry," he managed to squeak. "Your father was...uh...; God, I wasn't expecting this. I'm absolutely stunned...I...I don't know what to say." Cole, stumbling awkwardly with his words, did his best to offer his condolences and said that he would call back to get details for the funeral.

After the call, Cole dropped to his knees beside the couch and wept.

When he was able to stand again, he got into his Porsche and drove slowly to the Middle Tennessee Correctional Facility. He parked in the parking lot, facing the buildings. For a long time, he sat and stared.

Against Roland Power's urging, Cole canceled the rehearsals scheduled for that evening and the next.

* * *

On Sunday afternoon, with Lindsey at his side, Cole attended Duke Parker's funeral. The service was held in Nashville, at a suburban church just three miles north of the prison. Over two hundred people gathered to pay their final tributes to the influential husband, dad, neighbor, colleague, chaplain, and friend. Seven people, including Mateo, participated in the eulogy. Each of the speakers shared stories about the chaplain and how he had personally invigorated their lives.

Cole was moved by the spoken words, but he was more moved by all of his own personal memories of the man, tattooed all over his soul.

Throughout the service Cole gazed at the coffin at the

front of the auditorium. The loss that he felt pushed him deeper inside himself.

* * *

Over the next week, Cole found that he had no energy for music, or for his career. Rather—to Lindsey and Roland's mounting frustration—he withdrew, spending his time alone. In his car. In cafes. In church sanctuaries. On the streets. And in the countryside. He prayed, read, and pondered.

He repeatedly read the vow he had written on the inside of his Bible a year and a half earlier: "People like me are tempted almost beyond measure to depend solely on their musical abilities and their bank accounts. For the rest of my life, though, I will choose to depend chiefly on the Lord my God."

He reviewed verses such as Matthew chapter ten, verse thirty-nine—*"If you cling to your life, you will lose it; but if you give it up for me, you will find it."* And Deuteronomy chapter eight, verses eleven through fourteen—*"Beware that in your plenty you do not forget the Lord your God;… When you have become full and prosperous and have built fine houses to live in and…when your silver and gold have multiplied along with everything else, that is the time to be careful. Do not become proud at that time and forget the Lord your God…"*

One afternoon, with his soul squeezed by all the introspective thinking, Cole wandered into a church-owned coffee shop downtown. As he sipped a cup of cappuccino, he haphazardly flipped through the pages of a small booklet titled "The Forgotten Road" that he found lying on his table. He quickly came across the words:

> What if He never again lets me take the road back to my home in Colorado, the home I love so dearly?

> What if He never lets me take the road back to the church I love so much?

> What if He never lets me take the road to a steady salary, and I am left with nothing but the clothes on my back?

> What if He never lets me take the road to marriage?

> What if He never lets me take the road to parenthood?

> What if He never lets me take the road to physical security, safety, and comfort?

> What if He barricades all these roads and never asks me what I think?

I do not like this list of questions. It makes me angry, afraid, tearful, and confused.

Yet, I cannot deny that He is asking me how far I am willing to walk down the road of complete abandonment to everything but Him, the road that has been gladly forgotten in today's society.

He said to the crowd, *"If any of you want to be my follower, you must turn from your selfish ways..."*

He really wants me to walk this forgotten road, doesn't he? He wants me to travel farther down this road than I have ever dreamt I could possibly go.

Am I willing to abandon my selfish ambitions, my comforts, and my life for His name's sake?

I cannot deny that I am keenly more alive when I venture even the slightest distance down this road. It does not make sense. It is not

logical. It is not normal. It seems
utterly ridiculous.

Yet, He promises that He will walk
with me. So, what more do I need?

Cole gazed around the cafe, then read the words again.
The words energized and moved him. Was it just mere
chance that he had come across these words while in the
middle of a similar battle? Or was it divine predestination?
He lingered over his cappuccino, then rose and wandered
around the city.

Shuffling beneath the skyscrapers in sixty-degree
weather, he asked himself, as he had asked many times in
past weeks, if he would be a fool to walk away from it all.
The concerts. The tour. The music video productions. The
CD signings. The interviews. The fans. The money. The
celebrity lifestyle, with all of its trappings.

That question was still battering his soul when he
returned home early in the evening. He checked the cell
phone he had intentionally left at home—he'd received
thirteen messages. "Unbelievable", he said, shaking his
head. He started to answer them, then decided they could
wait till tomorrow.

Before preparing a light meal for himself, he checked
his mailbox. There was one letter, a form letter of some
sort. The words across the back of the envelope caught his
eye: "Miraculous Bible Handkerchief Enclosed." He sat
down at the kitchen bar and opened the envelope. There
were four pages. He read:

As a theologian and minister for more than four decades, I have read and reread in the Scriptures how God instructs ministers to send Bible handkerchiefs to people's homes so that miracles will occur to those that have faith. Therefore, I loan you, in Jesus' blessed name, this paper handkerchief.

I've been on my knees praying for this address. As I prayed, the Holy Spirit said, "If you want this home to receive a miracle, mail a Bible handkerchief." Let me read what God says about these Bible handkerchiefs: *"God gave Paul the power to do unusual miracles so that even when handkerchiefs or cloths that had touched his skin were placed on sick people, they were healed of their diseases."* Acts 19:11,12.

Here is what I ask you to do, in Jesus' name. (1) Print your name in the center of the enclosed handkerchief. (2) Open your Bible to Acts 19: 11,12 and lay the handkerchief on top of the verses. (3) Leave it there under your side of the bed for TONIGHT ONLY! (4) In the morning, take the handkerchief off the Bible and place it in the enclosed self-addressed envelope, along with a seed offering, and mail it back to me.

Do not keep this handkerchief—I repeat, do not keep this handkerchief. Do not break this flow of God's Spirit from my home to your home. Rush this handkerchief back and a miracle of healing and prosperity will come into your home.

I know that the Holy Spirit is in this letter and is speaking to your spirit as you read these words. Please obey God's Spirit and allow Him to bestow a miraculous blessing on your life.

My father had an addiction to alcohol. I sent one of these handkerchiefs to my mother. She wrote my dad's name on it, left it under the bed overnight inside her Bible, and returned the handkerchief to me the next day with her seed

offering. My dad stopped drinking.
It works!

Listen to these words from a lady
in Florida. "I put the handkerchief
in the Bible...and sent it back to
you with a seed offering of $75.
Within three days I received a
miracle check for $6,000."

God tells ministers to send out
handkerchiefs to people's homes,
so that blessings and miracles will
descend upon their lives. Use this
Bible handkerchief soaked with
prayer, tonight, and return it in the
morning with your seed gift. And
the windows of heaven will open
for you. Mail it back immediately.
We are waiting.

There was an additional sheet filled with written
testimonials of how the Bible handkerchief had reportedly
wrought miracles in multiple lives. Cole looked at the paper
handkerchief, a mere piece of typing paper with colorful
patterns printed around the edges. He looked at the letter
again. Then he buried his forehead in his palms. Was this
so-called minister a real Christian, but just uneducated and
inexperienced, echoing the teachings of subtle scam artists?

Or was he a heartless liar, intentionally using his position as a spiritual leader to rob naive people?

Cole felt nauseated. The words of Chaplain Parker resounded in his head: *"I think our western culture has exploited and fed the selfish side of the human heart to an extreme. We've even woven this radical self-focus into our Christian doctrine. Western Christians, and their leaders, have become so addicted to comfort, prosperity, and selfish living that we've now built our Christian beliefs around these addictions."*

Cole ripped the paper handkerchief and ran to the restroom. He knelt over the toilet and threw up. "How do I forget about myself and look to You?" he screamed out in prayer. "How do I demonstrate to You that I don't want to be a prisoner to a screwed-up philosophy? How do I let You know that I want to be addicted to *You*, and *You* alone, and nothing else!" He raised his head and looked around at the house that Lindsey had found for him. "This is all a gift, and I'm grateful. You know I'm grateful. I'm grateful for the house, the furniture, the car. I'm grateful for everything I've been given. But I *will not* live for the acquisition of things, or money, any longer! I want to be free from that! I want to lose my life, so that I can find it! I want to find *You*!" He fell prostrate on the floor. "I'm desperate for help; don't You understand?" And then he went silent. He listened to himself breathe and tried to lose himself in the sound. He lay there for an hour or more, tears and saliva drying to his face, relaxing in the presence of God and in the decision he now knew he had to make.

44

"*I*'m sorry—you're going to do *what*?" Roland Powers asked.

Cole stood in the CEO's office at the SpiritMark studio. "I'll give the first concert, as I agreed. And then I'm...stepping away."

"Stepping away? As in stepping away for a one-month break, a six-month retreat...what actually are we talking about here, Cole?"

Cole lowered his head. "Stepping away...as in indefinitely. I'm temporarily resigning as a music star. I've made the CD according to my contract. But I've decided that I'm just not ready at the moment to go any farther down this track. So I'm going to sell everything I own and leave Nashville."

Roland grimaced. "You're going to sell everything you own and leave Nashville."

"I know...it's not an easy decision to understand. It hasn't been an easy decision to make. But everything inside me is saying this is what I've got to do right now."

"My God...you're absolutely serious about this, aren't you?"

Cole offered a self-conscious nod.

Roland tensed. "Do you realize how much time and energy, and *money*, this company has invested in you?"

Cole inhaled deeply, then put his hand in his pocket and extracted two checks. He handed them over to Roland. "One is the thirty-thousand-dollar advance you gave me. The other is a five-thousand-dollar gift. I figure that this, plus all the proceeds from the upcoming concert and the revenue from the CD, will reimburse you for all your outlay, and earn you a profit to boot."

"So, we just cancel the future concerts, the tour, the CD signings, the video productions, the interviews, the whole kit and caboodle—is that what you're saying?"

Cole squinted. "Yeah...that's...what I'm asking. I'm sorry. I—"

Roland shook his head. "I don't believe this! This is crazy! Do you know how many people would give their right arm to be in your position right now?"

Cole didn't answer.

Roland looked into Cole's eyes, apparently weighing what he saw there. "Is there any negotiating room here? I mean, can you wait a few more days and really think this through?

Cole shook his head. "Believe me, this decision hasn't been made quickly." He rubbed his hands together. "The adjustment to the outside is just too difficult for me." *I just want to be more than a slave to busyness, fame, and money,* he thought to himself for the hundredth time. "I lived the first half my life as a taker. Always thinking only about myself. I want the last half of my life to be different. I want to try giving something back."

"And you don't think that providing encouragement, inspiration, and hope through an international platform is thinking about others and giving something back?"

Cole opened his eyes and this time looked humbly into Roland's gaze. "Not when all the focus is on me, my success, and my career."

Roland grunted. "What about this invitation?" He pointed to a letter lying on his desk. "You've been invited to appear on the number-one Christian television program in broadcasting. You would be seen and heard by millions of people all over the world."

"I'm honored. I really am. But I just don't have the heart for it. I guess the simplicity of prison life affected me more than I realized."

"I don't want this to sound derogatory. But would you consider talking to a counselor—at our expense, of course?"

Cole chuckled. "I guess it all does sound a little loony.

"More than a little," Roland said softly.

There was a moment of contemplative silence.

"Have you told Lindsey?" Roland asked.

"I'm taking her out for lunch. I'm planning to break the news to her then."

45

"No, no—this doesn't make any sense!" Lindsey said, her face contorted in confusion and disbelief.

Seeing Lindsey's pain, Cole wondered once again if he was indeed an idiot. But he'd worked too hard coming to this decision; he wasn't going to backtrack now.

Lindsey's eyes begged him across the table to tell her it was all a joke, a trick. But when he said nothing—in truth, he couldn't think of anything else to say—she stood and fled from the restaurant in tears.

Cole quickly paid for the half-eaten lunch and followed.

For thirty minutes, sitting in the Porsche parked at the curb, Cole listened and tried, uselessly, to respond as Lindsey pushed her arguments, pleas, and persuasions. Her voice became hoarse. The inside of the Porsche's windows fogged over. Backed all the way up against the passenger door, she eventually screeched, "Just take me back to the office! I can't deal with this anymore!"

Cole felt lower than bedrock. He wanted to grab her and say, *Other than Jana, you're the only woman on the face of the planet who has ever kidnapped my heart. There's a big part of me that wants to walk you down the aisle and marry you right now. I want to hold you naked in my arms. I want to raise a family with you. I know I'm a fool for running the risk of losing you—you're the most vibrant, the most physically stunning, the most interesting, the most loving, the most fun woman I've ever known. I'm probably out of my mind.*

Instead, he fought back tears and whispered, "You can go with me."

Lindsey swiped her fingers through her thick blonde hair. "I can go with you? Is that an ultimatum? Either I give up my career and everything I've worked for over the last ten years, or I lose you?"

Nearly paralyzed by his own conflicting emotions, Cole looked into her eyes and tried to maintain his focus. Waiting for her answer, he reached into his coat pocket and squeezed the engagement ring.

Lindsey, breathing erratically, just stared at him with an unforgettable expression of hurt.

When waiting became too discomforting, Cole said, "Lindsey, there's no other woman I would rather spend the rest of my life with. But I just can't argue anymore. Not with you. Not with myself. Not with life." He hung his head. "I wish you could understand."

"I *can't* understand—you're totally irrational," she spouted.

Cole sighed. "If you don't mind then," he said, a catch in his voice, "I'd like to give you any of my household furniture or belongings that you might want."

"You—you want to *what?*" Lindsey threw open the

car door and stumbled outside. Without looking back, she slammed the door and ran down the sidewalk.

Cole extended his hand, as if to bring her back. His mind raced through a dozen possible options. But in the end, he threw his head back against the headrest and let her go. He grabbed a handful of his hair and squeezed.

46

It had been twenty-seven days since Jesse had given himself the first round of weekly steroid injections, and he still couldn't see any difference in the size and definition of his muscles. Though disappointed, he trusted the online research that told him he should start seeing some enhancements within the next few weeks.

With his hopes still high, he stabbed the needle into his leg and emptied the syringe. As he pulled up his pants and headed for the kitchen, he wondered if he should increase the dosage.

At the kitchen table, he opened his laptop and checked his email account. Another note from Svetlana. Yes!

> Ryan,
> I am rushing out of my apartment to go to work. I am almost late. But I have wanted to ask you if you would like to come to Murmansk and visit me. Please think about it.
> Svetlana

Jesse's fingers rested on the computer keyboard. This was a promising development, but he had to play it just right. Finally, he typed his reply.

> Svetlana,
> Are you serious? I am sitting here laughing with excitement. For weeks, I have been tempted to ask if I could come over and meet you in person. But I thought if I invited myself, you might think I was too forward. I can't tell you how pleased I am that you've invited me. I am really, really excited. So yes, let's definitely look at some possible dates for sometime this summer. I also want you to think about visiting me here in Atlanta. I could even help buy your airline ticket if that would help. I would really like to introduce you to my family and friends.

He typed five or six additional paragraphs, designed to lure and to snag. When he'd pressed *Send*, he sat back and grinned. It definitely looked as if he was going to pocket another twenty G's.

Still grinning, he stood and pulled a microwave dinner out of the freezer, then on impulse stepped outside to check his mailbox. He unlocked the metal box and pulled out a heap of junk mail and two business envelopes. He threw the junk mail on the ground and examined the two envelopes. One was a phone bill. The other was a certified letter from the Reunion Registry.

"Yes!" he shouted, oblivious to whoever might be listening. *It's about freaking time*, he thought. He ripped open the envelope and rushed back into his apartment. He sat at the small kitchen table and anxiously extracted the documents. As he unfolded the papers, his hands shook. He first read the cover letter.

> Dear Mr. Rainwater,
>
> Per our efforts to find and contact your biological mother, we discovered that she deceased in 1996. As proof of our discovery, we have enclosed a copy of the death certificate for your records.
>
> If you have further questions, please do not hesitate to call or visit our Atlanta office during regular business hours.
> Sincerely,
> Peggy Harrison, Administrator

Jesse flipped to the death certificate. "So you're dead," he grunted, mentally jarred and frustrated. He looked at the name on the document—Jana Michaels. "Hello, Mom."

He read the rest of the neatly typed details:

Certificate of Death
State of Tennessee
Sex—Female
Maiden name, if female—Jana Cooper
Race—White
Citizenship—American
Date of Birth—April 23, 1967
Date of Death—May 21, 1996
Age at Death—29
County of death—Williamson
Location of death—Brentwood
Hospital—Williamson Medical Center
Dead on arrival
State and county of birth—Virginia;
Washington County
Marital Status—Married
Spouse—Cole Michaels

Whoa. Jesse stared at the spouse's name. He stood to his feet, still clasping the paper. Was this the name he'd been wanting to know since he was ten? His mind went into overdrive. Was this the name of the piece of waste who had fathered him and then had given him away? He looked at the name again. *Wait*, he cautioned himself. Maybe this Cole Michaels was only a second or third husband and not his biological father at all. Jesse sat back down.

The certificate included Jana Michaels's social security number, her occupation (homemaker), the name of her parents, her residential address in Brentwood, Tennessee, at the time of her death, the name and address of the funeral home that had handled her body, and the name of the cemetery where she was buried.

But it was a small handwritten addition that caused Jesse the greatest wonder. The cause of death was scribbled as "suicide by medicine overdose and drowning". The document was signed by a coroner, a county custodian, and a state custodian.

"Suicide—at twenty-nine!" Jesse tried to ignore the sudden hint of sadistic satisfaction that swept through his body. He looked at the date of her death and calculated that he had been eleven at the time she had decided to check out.

What had pushed her over the edge? Had she carried a load of guilt because she'd given away her baby boy to a freaking stranger? Had she given up after being repeatedly battered by this Cole Michaels? He found that he truly wanted to know. But that, along with all the other unanswered questions—such as did he have any siblings— would just have to wait. His priority now would be to find out if Cole Michaels was indeed his biological father.

He thought about his options. He could hire the Reunion Registry again for another three hundred dollars and go through the whole process of filling out applications, composing and submitting letters, and then waiting months and months for an answer. Or he could use the information in his hand and launch his own search.

He softly hammered his fist on the table. He would do his own detective work, he decided. Besides, eliminating the Reunion Registry from any further involvement would hopefully keep his name and description from nesting in their memory.

He grabbed a pen and a piece of paper and meticulously examined the certificate one more time. He wrote down every detail he could lift from the document. When he focused again on his mother's age at the time of her suicide, he counted backward and realized that she had been only seventeen at the time of his conception. He dropped the pen.

Had she really been married at such an early age? There was no marriage date listed on the certificate. Jesse seriously doubted that she had been married when she gave birth to him. So had she been overcome by a moment of passion in someone's bedroom or the backseat of a car? Had she been too drunk or high to resist? Or—had she been raped?

"So I was a mistake," he hissed. An accident. Maybe even the despised outcome of a violent crime. "Welcome to the world," he mocked. "I'm a bastard." He suddenly felt more alone in the world than ever. He sensed a new hatred spreading inside him like a virus.

Even though Cole Michaels was probably not his biological father, he still wanted to make sure. He started to look for information about the man on the Internet, then stopped. He really wanted to be in the man's presence, and to look in his eyes, when he learned the truth. So he would simply drive to Tennessee over the upcoming weekend. Once there, he would first scope out the Brentwood address.

47

The days following his announcement weren't easy for Cole. He knew he was the cause of a lot of dashed dreams. His conscience bothered him. Still, he was sure he was making the right decision. He tried to make it easier by convincing himself that SpiritMark wouldn't really benefit from a long-term contract with him anyway—not if he projected only misery all the time. And new stars would always come along, glad to fill the company's ranks.

The hardest part of his decision, though, was to walk away from Lindsey. What was he thinking? But their subsequent and lengthy conversations about the issue had only demonstrated to him that they could never thrive as a couple with such differing visions for life. That realization didn't lessen his grief.

Still, on Friday afternoon, April 4, he readied himself to open the front door of his house for a weekend walk-through sale. He had notified the public about the sale through a newspaper ad and a homemade sign that he had stuck in his front yard. He had informed the SpiritMark employees by word of mouth and had encouraged them to invite family and friends. All the furnishings in his house, he'd told them, including his car, would be for sale. Everything was only two months old and still under warranty, and everything, except the car, would be sold for half price.

Lindsey had chosen not to accept any of his belongings. She was still too hurt. One of the SpiritMark sound engineers, however, had already declared his intention to buy the Porsche, with only 3,210 miles showing on its odometer. Cole had agreed to sell it for $10,000 less than he'd paid for it. He would use a good chunk of the proceeds from the sale of the furniture to pay off the balance of the bank loan.

Cole looked out the window again. There were over fifty people already standing outside, waiting for him to unlock the door.

He looked over his shoulder one last time to make sure everything was ready. He had gathered the sales receipts for all his items and taped them neatly across the top of the kitchen counter. The buyers could easily view the dates of sale and the original prices.

He sent up a quick prayer that God would somehow show favor on what he was doing. Then he opened the door.

*　*　*

Around 8:00 on Friday evening, Jesse crossed the city

limits of Franklin, Tennessee, about ten miles south of Brentwood.

He had stopped only a couple of times en route from Atlanta, once to buy fuel, and once to use the toilet. He was now ready to settle in for the night. He felt that ten miles was a safe distance to keep between himself and his destination. Nobody in Franklin would suspect that he had business to take care of ten miles up the road in Brentwood.

To reduce the likelihood that he would be remembered by the hotel staff, he chose a large hotel that was part of a national chain, a hotel that no doubt catered to hundreds of people every day and would, therefore, easily forget faces. Jesse was pleased to see that the front desk was staffed by a preoccupied young man. Jesse checked in with no fanfare. He went immediately to his room and locked himself away for the night.

His plans were to check out around 9:00 tomorrow morning and start his ground search. He would first visit the cemetery where his birth mother was buried, then check out the residential address in Brentwood.

48

Cole had just helped an older couple load the last three wall pictures from his house into an SUV. He was enjoying the warmth of the Saturday morning sunlight on his skin when he saw Lindsey get out of her Mini Cooper and head in his direction. He waited.

"Well, do you have anything left?" she asked.

She didn't reach out to hug him. She kept her distance, as if she had now surrendered to the inevitable. Cole stared at her beautiful face, now saddened. He fought to keep his hands from running through her hair. "The only things left," he told her, "are the stereo system, the office furniture, and some of the kitchenware. I still have my laptop, but I've decided to keep it until the last minute. I'm sure everything else will be gone by this afternoon."

"So—where will you go? What will you do?"

"I'll tell you," Cole answered as he directed her back toward the house. "But you're going to think I'm growing absolutely crazier by the moment."

"Oh, I doubt it. I think you've already given craziness a new meaning."

Cole didn't know if he should laugh or not. He didn't. "Well...on that day in 1986, an hour or so before Shay was killed, he and I saw a group of motorcycles ride down the road right past our property. Shay got so excited. I'm not sure I had ever seen him so spellbound. He just couldn't stop grinning. Anyway, no sooner had the bikes passed than Shay looked me right in the eye and said, 'Daddy, can we get one?'" Cole smiled. "The little guy was absolutely serious. Well, I laughed and told him that mommy probably wouldn't go along with the idea. I promised him, though, that maybe we could get one when he was older. He looked at me as if he knew beyond a doubt that I was telling him the truth." Cole paused slightly. "I've actually thought about that promise more than a few times during the past twelve years. So..."

"So?"

"So...I've decided to buy a motorcycle. To do it for Shay. In his honor. And for his memory."

Lindsey tilted her head and elevated her eyebrows as if she thought Cole's craziness had indeed reached a new level. "And?"

"And...I'm going to pack a tent, a sleeping bag, a few clothes, a few basic tools—along with the Mysterious Lady, of course—and I'm going to hit the road. Ride into the unknown. Try to find my real place in life."

Lindsey raked her fingers through her hair. "Why is it that you actually sound giddy as you tell me all this?"

"I've already started searching the Internet for a bike, so maybe I am a little giddy. For my son's sake." Cole looked into her eyes. "I apologize again that I've caused so much disappointment. That was never my plan. God knows I'm telling you the truth."

"You've still never gotten over them, have you?"

Cole didn't respond.

Lindsey shifted. "You could have it all, you know. Extravagant homes. Exotic cars. Big yachts. Glamorous vacations. Hundreds of thousands of fans that worship you. Not to mention a beautiful wife."

Cole pulled her into his arms. "I know," he whispered. "Instead, I'll have no home, no car, no phone, no computer, no accountant, no rousing fans...and I'll end up losing the most gorgeous and desirable partner a man could ever imagine. It's ludicrous, I know. But—"

Lindsey reached up and pressed a finger against his lips. "Just hold me," she said.

He did.

* * *

Jesse stood motionless at the cemetery on a beautiful Saturday morning, gawking at the giant tombstone engraved on the left side with the name Jana LeAnne Michaels and the dates April 23, 1967 and May 21, 1996. The tombstone was one of the larger and more elaborate ones in the area. The plot had recently been manicured. The name Cole Jefferson Michaels was inscribed on the right side of the stone.

The discovery that sparked a brushfire of thought, though, was the name engraved in the middle of the marker, between the names of Jana and Cole. Jesse read the name again: Shay Everett Michaels. He read the date of birth: January 8, 1993. And the date of death: May 17, 1996.

So he'd had a brother who had died at the age of three. He spat in the grass. Was the boy a full-fledged blood brother, or a half-brother? Regardless, he and the kid, it seemed, shared the same biological mother. So, why had the bimbo chosen to keep the younger son, but discard Jesse like a rabid animal? Why had she considered him so unlovable? A vase of roses stood at the base of the gravestone. He kicked it hard and watched the roses scatter.

As he stewed, he gradually realized that the death of his mother had come just five days after the death of her three-year-old son. He had wondered why she had committed suicide. Now he thought he knew. Whatever had killed the three-year-old—an accident, a sickness, or a premeditated act—had left her in despair, with no will to live. The bond between the two had obviously been intense. Jesse's jealousy inflated. "Good. I'm glad you're dead," he hissed as he spat at the tombstone. "I'm glad you're both dead. And I hope you both rot in hell." Jesse inhaled deeply, filling his lungs, swelling his chest. "Well, Mister Michaels," he growled, looking again at Cole's name, "it's time to find out if you're my real father or not."

* * *

By 5:00 PM the only items left in Cole's house were his clothes, his toiletries, his Bible, his laptop, his violin, a blanket, a pillow, two bath towels, one land-line phone, a plate, a fork, a pan, and a little bit of food in the refrigerator.

Everything else had been sold or given away. The two-day sale had netted him $25,000. Ten grand of that money would be combined with the thirty-three thousand put on the table by the buyer of the Porsche to pay off the car loan. Cole would keep the car for another six days, until the concert on Friday. The hand-off for the vehicle would take place sometime on that Friday, or the day after. Then Cole would be free.

Cole arranged for a cleaning lady to come on Thursday and clean the house so that it would be ready to turn back over to the landlord, then spent the rest of the evening rehearsing his song list for the concert and surfing the Internet to learn more about motorcycles. He needed to decide which type of bike would best suit his purpose for just drifting and exploring life on the outside without any material anchors.

That night, as he lay in bed, he started grinning. Never in his life had he felt so insanely hopeful, yet so pensive. In that instant he made another radical decision, one that he had actually been contemplating for some time. After he'd paid off the loan for the Porsche, he would have approximately $20,000 left in his bank account. The motorcycle and riding gear would cost, he estimated, about $10,000. He decided that he would take his checkbook on the road and would—with no strings attached—share the rest of it with those in need, especially when young children were involved. He would do it for the glory of God, and in memory of Shay and Stephanie. He might even call it his "Shay and Stephanie Fund."

"Yes!" He pumped his fist and smiled hugely. He

knew immediately who would be the first recipient of his financial help. Tomorrow he would write a check for $1,000 to Lindsey's younger sister, a single mom who worked horrendous hours at two different jobs and barely brought home enough money for herself and her four-year-old twin sons.

Cole felt more joyous by the second. He suddenly remembered the line he had read in the little booklet *The Forgotten Road*—"*I cannot deny that I am keenly more alive when I venture even the slightest distance down this road.*"

Still smiling, he whispered to himself and to God, "I want to do my best to not let my life be held hostage by fear—the fear of poverty, the fear of pain, the fear of discomfort, the fear of joblessness, the fear of rejection, the fear of sickness, the fear of loss, or the fear of walking down the forgotten road. And I want to strive to not let my life be dulled by the massive security measures that are based on fear—dead bolts, security alarms, prescribed drugs, massive insurance policies, cell phones, brokerage investments, and multiple credit cards."

He wondered again, as he often had before, whether the twenty-first-century way of fearful thinking might have been orchestrated by a sinister spirit...perhaps even by the father of lies.

Cole was so arrested by the thought that he turned on the light and grabbed his Bible. He turned to the concordance at the back and looked up the word *afraid*. Within a few minutes, he learned that the word was used in the Scriptures over two hundred times, and that in nearly half of those accounts people were being urged, in many cases by God, to *stop* being afraid. Obviously fear was a universal problem that all too often was allowed to stifle and paralyze human lives.

Cole felt an anger rise up in his soul.

The verses that dropped him to the floor and onto his knees, though, were verses twenty-three through twenty-six of Matthew chapter eight. He read the passage several times: *"Then Jesus got into the boat and started across the lake with his disciples. Suddenly, a terrible storm came up, with waves breaking into the boat. But Jesus was sleeping. The disciples went to him and woke him up, shouting, 'Lord, save us! We're going to drown!' And Jesus answered, 'Why are you afraid? You have so little faith!'"*

The passage made it very clear that fear was the exact opposite of faith. And the one thing that God wanted most from His followers was *faith*. Yet, in spite of a grand pantheon of Christian words and ideas, most westerners, it seemed, lived by fear, not by faith.

Rolling over onto his back on the rug, Cole lifted his hands in an act of penitence and worship. He felt that his recent decisions were at least baby steps in the right direction. More than anything in the whole world, he wanted his spirit to coalesce with God's Spirit. He wanted his heart to bring pleasure to God's heart. "Please!" he moaned, "I beg You—teach me how to walk this forgotten road. I don't want to be afraid. Of sacrifice. Of loss. Or of a surrendered life. I want to reach a point where I'll gladly choose to be last."

49

On Sunday morning, Jesse Rainwater used a pay phone at a gas station and once again called the number.

The day before, when he had driven out to the Brentwood address listed on the death certificate, he had learned that Cole Michaels no longer lived there. The surname Chang was stenciled on the roadside mailbox.

Immediately afterward, Jesse had stopped at a convenience store parking lot, unfolded his laptop, and searched the online white pages until he found a phone number for the Chang family listed at the Brentwood address. He had called the number nearly ten times since, hoping someone would answer. But no one ever did.

But today was a new day.

As he listened to the first ring, he tried to prepare himself mentally. He listened through several rings until the answering machine clicked on, giving instructions to please leave a message or call back later. Jesse slammed the phone back onto its hook.

He was losing patience.

*   *   *

Cole spent several hours Sunday afternoon devouring information he found on motorcycle websites. He focused primarily on product reviews.

He had already decided that the bikes that appealed to him most were the cruisers, the sport-touring bikes, and the dual-purpose adventure bikes.

And he had already learned enough from earlier reading forays to know that there were many differences between bikes, even those in the same category. So, he had created a hand-drawn chart comparing the basic differences in engine layout, riding position, fuel capacity, and horsepower.

Clicking from web page to web page, he listed all the cruisers, sport-touring bikes, and adventure bikes that visually appealed to him and then, using his chart, noted the specifics of each bike. He went back and read reviews of all those bikes.

By Sunday evening, he'd narrowed his choice to five bikes—the Suzuki Boulevard S83, the Suzuki Bandit 1250, the Triumph Scrambler 900, the BMW R1200GS, and the Kawasaki Concours 14.

He grew more excited by the moment. He could barely wait to go to the regional motorcycle shops, see the bikes with his own eyes, sit on them, and drill the sales reps with questions. He could already picture himself riding down country highways—his bike loaded with gear—feeling the freedom of the open road.

*   *   *

"Hello, can I speak with Mister Cole Michaels, please?"

"I'm sorry," a middle-aged woman answered at the Brentwood home, sounding surprised. "Mister Michaels hasn't lived here for ten years or more."

"I see. My name is Drew Ward," Jesse said. "I'm a collections agent for a lending firm in Virginia. Would you perhaps know where I can find Mister Michaels these days?"

"The last I heard, he was in prison."

Jesse was caught completely off guard. "In prison? Here locally? Or..."

"I'm not sure. I think somewhere in the State of Tennessee, though."

"All right. Thank you." Jesse hung up. He looked at his watch. It was 6:30 Sunday evening.

Within an hour, he'd checked into another hotel. Once he was settled in his room, he unpacked his laptop, deciding that the time had come to let the computer help him find Cole Michaels. He typed "Cole Michaels—Prisoner" into a search engine. To his surprise, a whole cache of Cole Michaels-related websites appeared on the screen. Jesse opened the first one on the list. The headline was: Music Star Now a Prisoner In Nashville Jail.

> Music star Cole Michaels was convicted yesterday morning in Nashville of two counts of vehicular homicide and sentenced to eleven years behind bars without parole.

Jesse paused. *A music star? Are you kidding?* He looked around the room and then back at the computer screen. He slowly read the headline and first sentence again to make sure he hadn't misread anything. A brisk tingle ran the length of his spine. Was this really the same Cole Michaels who had been married to his biological mother? The same Cole Michaels who had lived at the Brentwood address and had a son named Shay Everett? The same Cole Michaels who owned an unused grave site beside the buried slut and the little piece of dung?

He read the rest of the article, and several others from more than a dozen other websites, He learned that the music star had indeed been married to his biological mother. He also learned that Cole's first CD *Sweet Manipulations* had won many awards and had soared to the top of the music charts and earned him a lot of money. And that the man had indeed been the biological father of Shay Everett, the three-year-old, and that he had accidentally caused the boy's death in a tractor accident. That he had shortly thereafter lost Jana to suicide and had resorted to drinking as a way to escape his guilt and pain. That he had been absolutely wasted the night he had run a red light and hit a car, killing a mother and daughter. That he had been sentenced to eleven years in the slammer. That he had gotten religion in jail. That he had recently finished serving his time. That he had recorded a new CD that would debut in a few days. And that on Friday night of this week he would give his first live concert in eleven years. Right here in Nashville.

Jesse's mind was so gorged with this mother lode of information that he stopped, unable to process any more.

But he was frustrated and angered, even further, by the single bit of data that was so conspicuously absent—him.

He hissed and rose to his feet.

"So, the all-elusive question remains." He stared at images of Cole on the computer screen. "Are you, or are you not, the man who fathered *me?* And were you, or were you not, part of the decision that ruined my life?"

Jesse studied Cole's photos. There were several physical similarities between himself and the music star. They were both tall. With thick blonde hair. Green eyes. And the same cheekbones. The resemblances were noticeable enough that Jesse—pumped with adrenaline—decided that a blood connection was a strong possibility.

"There's one thing for sure, Mister Cole Michaels— music man," Jesse mumbled. "I will find out."

Unfortunately, nowhere in the smattering of websites was there a mention of Cole's current street address. Jesse checked online for a phone number or address in the greater Nashville area. Cole's name was not listed.

Jesse smirked. No problem. He would return to Atlanta, then head back to Nashville in time for the Friday evening concert. He would begin stalking Cole Michaels on the night of the music star's glorious comeback.

"And if you're guilty, it'll be a short-lived comeback, you freaking low-life scum!"

50

On Monday morning, Cole came to the SpiritMark office to finalize some technical details for the Friday concert. During his visit, one of the sound engineers pulled him into a conference room and with a look of dismay asked, "Why is it that you're just walking away? I need to hear it with my own ears. We've all worked so hard on this…"

Cole decided to be completely straightforward. "Do you mind if I ask you a few questions?"

"Shoot."

"All right. Would you say that almost everyone you know has an insatiable desire to have more and more, and they never seem to be content for very long with what they have?"

The man hesitated for only a second. "Yeah, I suppose so."

"Would you say that almost everyone you know lives with some kind of fear or anxiety—fear of losing their job, never getting out of debt, being hurt, being robbed, being rejected?"

"I'm sure there are exceptions, but, yeah, I suspect most of my friends carry those kinds of fears. Of course, they don't usually talk openly about them."

Cole nodded. "Would you say that almost everyone you know lives under an unhealthy amount of stress—due to excessive work, insufficient rest, a poor diet, a load of debt, and too little exercise?"

The man said, "Yeah, a large percentage."

"Would you say that almost everyone you know shoulders an inordinate amount of guilt—because of not focusing enough on their families, on their friends, or on giving back to society?"

"On their families—yes, for sure."

"Would you say that almost everyone you know uses some kind of prescription drugs—to curb their appetite, to fight their depression, to ease their physical pains, to enhance their energy levels, to aid their digestive system, to help them sleep, to help them stay awake?"

"Almost everyone I know. Is there a point?"

"Just one more question. Would you say that almost everyone you know possesses an entitlement mentality, at least to some degree?"

The man wrinkled his brow. "Not my grandma. But almost everyone else—yes."

"So," Cole said, "you're telling me that a normal life these days is characterized by ingratitude, fear, anxiety, stress, guilt, entitlement, and drug dependency."

The man started to say something, stopped, then

started again. "Well, wait. I don't know, I've never thought about it exactly in those terms. But yeah, maybe that is a big part of normal life these days."

"Then there's your answer. That's why I'm walking away. I don't want to be normal."

Cole turned and started to leave, then turned and said, "I want just the opposite. I want to learn to be content with very little, to live without fear, to live without stress, to live without guilt, to be grateful in life, and to be a giver, not a taker. And the only way I know how to do that is to simply bail out of the rat race."

Silence followed him out of the room.

As he finished his business at the studio over the next hour, Cole could feel the tension that his presence now created among the staff. He smiled a lot and tried to be strong.

Before he left the SpiritMark building, he swung by Lindsey's office. As he'd hoped, she wasn't there. He laid a sealed envelope, marked for Lindsey's younger sister, atop her glass desk.

Filled with a childlike anticipation, Cole then headed to a downtown store stocked with a cornucopia of equipment for outdoor adventures. He'd rather have spent the afternoon looking at motorcycles, but he had already learned that all motorcycle retail shops were closed on Mondays.

By the time he walked into the store, he felt like a middle-school kid bursting with excitement. He found a knowledgeable and friendly sales clerk, then spent two hours asking a battery of questions and making his selections. He finally walked out with a Swedish-made, double-layer, two-man tent that could be pitched in three minutes, an ultra thin, self-inflating sleeping pad, and a lightweight, down-filled sleeping bag.

He then visited two music-supply warehouses before he found and purchased a violin backpack that he felt would provide sufficient protection for the Mysterious Lady. The case had a sturdy wooden frame, a poly-foam interior with padded sides and corners, and a water-resistant nylon exterior with stout shoulder straps. Included was a plush velour blanket.

Back at his empty house, he arranged his new supplies neatly across the living room floor. Afterward, he drew a map that highlighted each of the motorcycle dealerships he planned to visit.

Before he retired to bed for the night, he checked his email and found a letter from Lindsey. The letter—written on behalf of Lindsey and her sister—was an outflow of surprise and gratitude for the unexpected present.

Cole grinned deep in his soul.

* * *

The next morning, after a night of fantasizing about motorcycles and thinking about possible routes, Cole took a long hot shower, ate some fruit, and headed for his first stop—a Kawasaki/Suzuki shop on the south side of town.

By early afternoon, he'd eliminated the Concours and the Boulevard from his list of potential purchases.

The Concours, he learned, was one of the most powerful production bikes on the market and would perhaps present too much of a learning curve for a neophyte rider. The Boulevard S83 was docile enough, but after sitting on the bike a few times, he decided that the sitting position wouldn't be comfortable for long distances. The Suzuki Bandit 1250, though, seemed to be a perfect compromise. The only downside was that the Bandit was the least appealing to him visually.

Cole skipped lunch and drove to the BMW dealership on the west side of the city. He had read rave reviews of the R1200GS. Many of them claimed that the GS, a bike in the dual-purpose adventure category, was the best all-around motorcycle in the world and the number-one choice for those who traveled the world on two wheels. When Cole saw one in the showroom, though, he was surprised at how heavy and tall it was, compared to the other bikes he had seen. The GS looked great, and he loved the sitting position, but the size of the bike intimidated him. He wasn't confident that he could ever master such a monstrous machine, especially on dirt or gravel. Still, he kept it on his list, along with the Bandit.

His next stop was at the Triumph dealer downtown. The moment he was shown the Scrambler 900—also a dual-purpose adventure bike—all the voices in his head and heart said *yes*. It was one of the most beautiful motorcycles he had ever seen. It had looked great in the photos online, too, but in person the bike was absolutely gorgeous. It was a modern classic—a retro style with a sixties look. Cole even liked the two-tone colors—fusion white and tornado red. The foot pegs were in the center. The handlebars were positioned at a comfortable height. The bike was designed for the street and for the dirt, with high-mounted dual pipes that would enable the bike to traverse shallow streams. When Cole straddled the bike, he immediately felt at home. The weight and height were perfect. Everything about the bike felt right.

"Would you like to take it for a test ride?" an older salesman asked.

"I would love to. But I don't have my license yet."

"Are you a serious shopper?"

"Oh, yeah. I'm planning to get my license tomorrow morning. And I'm hoping to have a bike by the weekend."

"Well, in that case, I can let you ride it around the parking lot."

Cole nervously explained that he very much wanted to, but would need basic instructions for operating the machine, even around the parking lot.

"I'll tell you what," the salesman said. "If you buy the bike today, I'll give you two free hours of riding lessons when I clock out at the end of the day. And then you can use the bike tomorrow morning to get your motorcycle license."

Cole asked another two dozen questions about engine capabilities, build quality, maintenance intervals, and after-market accessories. More than pleased with the answers, he left the shop, went to a nearby branch of his bank, and withdrew ten thousand in cash. He returned to the dealership and paid for the bike in full. He ordered a few accessories to be added to the bike—a skid plate, a sissy bar, and a tank bag. He bought a half helmet, a pair of goggles, a jacket with protective padding, riding boots, riding gloves, a rain suit, and a handful of bungee cords.

"Can you deliver the bike to my house when you get off work?" Cole asked the salesman.

"I'll get one of the mechanics to mount the accessories, and I'll deliver the bike in my truck around six. She'll be all set up and ready to ride."

"Yes!" Cole exclaimed. He was on an adrenaline high.

By 6:00 PM, Cole was pacing the front porch of his house, waiting for the arrival of the machine that for an indefinite period of time would be his key to exploring life in a manner unlike anything he had ever experienced before.

A few minutes after the hour, Cole saw a pickup moving slowly down the street, as if the driver were searching for an address. Then Cole saw the Scrambler 900 tied down in the bed of the truck. He waved until he got the driver's attention, then stood watching as the salesman parked the truck against the curb. To his surprise, Cole teared up looking at the motorcycle. "Maybe in a few years, when you're bigger, we can get one," he whispered. He scratched the back of his neck and closed his eyes. He imagined Shay sporting a big grin. "I really, really wish you were here, buddy. This day has been a long time coming. And now that it's finally here, it's almost dreamlike." Cole sighed. "This is for you, little man," he said as he jumped off the porch and headed toward the truck.

Cole, hyped and jittery, helped the man offload the bike down a portable ramp. He couldn't take his eyes off the machine. The last time he had felt such elation over an inanimate object was when he had taken possession of the Mysterious Lady. This felt even more personal—it was the fulfillment of a long-ago promise to his son.

Once the bike was on the street, the salesman dove right into the basic instructions on the art of motorcycling. He first introduced Cole to every major component on the machine. He then walked him verbally through the use and maintenance of each component.

Finally, the man asked Cole to straddle the bike and lift the kickstand. With the ignition switch turned off, the man showed Cole how to shift properly through the gears and watched him repeat the process five or six times.

"All right—let's move to the parking lot." He nodded toward the commercial parking area diagonally across the street. "And I'll teach you to ride." The man started the bike and rode it over to the lot.

Energized by the bike's exhaust note, Cole followed on foot, his helmet in hand.

"One of the first things you need to know," the man said as he turned off the engine, "is to always make sure the bike is in gear when it's parked. Or else it can roll off the kickstand."

Cole bobbed his head, taking mental notes.

The man got off the bike. "All right, I want you to start her up, and I want you to ride her in a straight line to the other end of the lot. Shift up to second gear and no more. Just concentrate on keeping her upright."

Cole donned his helmet, straddled the bike, and lifted the kickstand. Following step-by-step instructions, he turned on the ignition, pulled in the clutch lever, and pushed the starter button. The bike roared to life. He almost cried as the air-cooled parallel twin motor rumbled beneath him. He used his left foot to make sure the bike was kicked into first gear. He slowly twisted the throttle and gradually released the clutch lever. The motorcycle started moving. As he balanced the machine and kept it in a straight line, he was left almost breathless at how easily the machine glided under his control. He shifted into second. The bike moved with him like a professional dance partner. Cole laughed inside his helmet. This was going to be a blast!

The salesman worked with him over the next hour. He made sure Cole could shift through all five gears without a problem. He taught him how to brake, using both front and rear brakes. He taught him how to turn and weave. He taught him how to counter steer. He taught him the importance of focusing visually on his final destination while in the middle of a sweeping turn, resisting the urge to look down at the front wheel. He taught him the importance of riding off center when following closely behind another vehicle. He also taught him a mental exercise called R-A-D-A-R—Registering All Devices All Radiuses.

"The greatest safety measure you can implement," the man said, "is to always, always be fully aware of everything around you: all vehicles, pedestrians, animals and objects out in front of you; all vehicles, pedestrians, animals, and objects behind you; and all vehicles, pedestrians, animals, and objects merging into your pathway from any angle. R-A-D-A-R—registering all devices in all directions; don't ever forget it. And when you approach an intersection—it doesn't matter where—always, without exception, slow down and look to make sure that every vehicle that is supposed to be stopped *is* stopped."

Cole registered all of the man's instructions. He hadn't had so much stress-free fun in months. What an absolute hoot!

When he was finished, the salesman said, "All right. It's time for a test run. I'm going to bring the truck around, and I want you to follow me a few miles through town."

For the next fifteen minutes, as the sun was setting, Cole followed the man around a dozen or so city blocks, putting into practice everything the man had taught him. He couldn't stop laughing beneath his helmet. He thanked God over and over again that he had made the decision to buy the bike and to live freely in the moment.

"Great job," the man told him when they returned to Cole's house. "You're a natural."

"Thank you, sir," Cole smiled. "I appreciate your time more than you know."

"Just be careful. And follow the maintenance manual regarding the break-in phase, the air pressure in the tires, the tension on the chain, and the oil and filter changes. And you'll be all set."

"Got it."

"And good luck tomorrow when you go to test for your license."

Cole thanked the man again and waved goodbye.

Cole parked the Scrambler overnight in his backyard,

off the street. He was so emotionally and mentally pumped that he could hardly sleep that night.

*   *   *

The next morning, he purchased the minimum amount of insurance required for operating the Scrambler. He paid upfront for two years of coverage.

Later that morning, he earned his motorcycle license without a glitch. The sun had never shone brighter. The air had never smelled cleaner. The spring day could not have been more superb.

After lunch, Cole gleefully sorted out the puzzle of mounting all his equipment on the bike. He folded his rain suit and stuffed it into the tank bag. He took the giant duffel—loaded with his tent, sleeping pad, small pillow, toiletries, and clothes—and strapped it on the seat up against the sissy bar. He fastened his sleeping bag on top of the duffel. Once everything was tied down and secured, Cole lay back in his front yard, stared at the machine, and wondered what kind of adventures lay ahead.

Later that afternoon, he turned the Porsche over to the SpiritMark engineer. "I won't be needing it any more," he told the young buyer at the studio. "Enjoy it to the max." The title transfer and monetary transaction were completed before the SpiritMark office closed for the day.

That evening, Cole ran through another concert rehearsal. To his surprise, the whole motorcycle ordeal added electricity to his energy level.

"You're popping tonight," one of the technicians told

him. "If you can repeat this performance on Friday night, you'll have the critics chasing you down the streets for interviews."

Cole just smiled beneath a shimmer of perspiration.

He then got on his motorcycle, with the Mysterious Lady secured across his shoulders in the backpack, and rode home. He offered up his giggling thanks all the way to the house. Every second on the Scrambler, even for the brief city commutes and even in the dark, was a far cooler experience than he had ever imagined. Each ride for him was already like a blessed gift of therapy. When he was on the bike, he felt completely ensconced in God's smiling favor. The sensation was priceless.

* * *

The following morning, before he left the house, he waited for the cleaning lady to arrive. When she showed up, he gave her instructions and paid her in advance for a day's work. When he found out in a simple conversation that she was a single Hispanic mother studying on the side to earn a bachelor's in education, he offered her his laptop—the MacBook Pro. "I'm leaving on Saturday morning on a long motorcycle journey, and I don't have space for it."

The young mother had to ask three times for clarification before she understood Cole's intent. And then she started crying. "It is too much," she said. "Too expensive to just give away."

"If it can help you in your pursuit of a higher education, then it's all yours."

The lady clutched the laptop to her chest. "Thank you, thank you, thank you, Mister Michaels. Nobody has ever done anything like this for me in my life."

Cole was moved by her gratitude. He put a hand on her shoulder. "Well, it's about time, then. Just make good use of it."

She thanked him at least a dozen times more before he could manage to leave the house.

Cole finally climbed aboard the Scrambler and rushed off to the SpiritMark office for a staff meeting at 9:00 AM, chuckling the entire way, aware of the smells of newly poured concrete, freshly trimmed shrubs, and swirling water from a street cleaner. What a great machine the motorcycle was for stimulating all the senses and making a person feel alive! And he couldn't have been more thrilled with his choice of bikes. If chemistry could occur between a man and a machine, then it had indeed happened between him and the Triumph. He now felt about the Scrambler as he had felt all along about the Mysterious Lady—that it would somehow embed itself in his life and become an intimate part of his identity.

51

"*T*hank you all for being here," Roland Powers began. "As you all know, this meeting has been called to celebrate today's release of *Oasis Blues*." Roland grinned. "I thought you would all like to know that over a hundred and twenty thousand copies have already been pre-sold and will be placed on store shelves around the country today."

A high-pitched whistle erupted amidst a burst of applause.

"I don't have to tell you that for a record to be stocked in these quantities on its first day of release is monumental. Plus, we've already collected two major reviews from the web this morning. The first one is from the executive editor at *Music City* magazine." Roland held up a printout of the article. "Mister Polaski writes,"

> Very seldom as an executive editor
> have I used my editorial panels to
> review a new record. I don't even
> remember the last time I offered a

personal critique of a music project. Two weeks ago, however, someone placed on my desk a comeback CD called *Oasis Blues*, a compilation of original music by the artist Cole Michaels, known also in the entertainment world as the Blonde Fiddler. After eleven years of serving time in a state correctional facility, Cole was picked up last year by the SpiritMark label. Twelve years ago, his debut CD *Sweet Manipulations* was released to rave reviews and went gold. The new CD, scheduled for release on Thursday, April 10, takes a new direction and ventures into the gospel genre. I played the CD on my car stereo one afternoon while heading for lunch. I haven't taken it out since. I have now listened to the CD in its entirety at least a half-dozen times. I can't recall the last time a record has had such a profound hold on me. The unique and deeply rich blend of pop, country, Celtic, gospel, and chill is a collection that stirs the emotions, inspires the heart, and challenges the mind. I am recommending this record to everyone

> I know. It is music of this caliber that creates a celestial world of magic for which we all long. It is music of this genius that makes me proud to be part of the music industry. I won't be surprised if this one goes platinum. I am personally cheering it on.

Roland lowered the paper. "The article goes on to expound on the virtues of great music in general, but I think you get the point."

There was a brief aftermath of silent surprise. And then one of the marketing executives said, "Awesome! Absolutely awesome! That endorsement alone will be worth gold; it will sell another hundred-thousand copies for us!"

"And will provoke another hundred critics to review the record," someone else said.

"And—"

"*And*," Roland excitedly took the lead again, "*and*... wait until you hear this next review that we found on the website of a professional musician." He held up another printout. He cleared his throat and read.

> Everyone who knows me knows that I am not just a professional music entertainer, but also a connoisseur of music, and that I listen to music almost nonstop—in my car, in my home, on my iPod,

at my computer, in my jet. I have a bigger collection of music than anybody I know, a collection that covers the gamut from pop to opera, from hip-hop to classical, from country to R&B, and everything in between. I know the power and the subtleties of music. I think my three Grammys as a songwriter demonstrate that fact. And when I find that rare and elusive song, or collection of songs, that appeals to my technical awareness and also stirs my soul, I gladly binge on that music sometimes for weeks on end. At the moment, I am bingeing on just such a record. It is a new CD called *Oasis Blues* composed by an extremely gifted songwriter, fiddler, and vocalist named Cole Michaels. If you have never heard this man's music, I implore you to run out and buy a copy of his new CD when it hits the stores. When you hear the first song, you will want to hear the next. And the next. And the next. And that, my friends, is the hallmark of a great album. Both for the musical techies and the artists.

When Roland read the name of the country-western superstar who had written the review, there were gasps throughout the room.

"Are you kidding?" one of the men from the sales team shouted in jubilation, slapping his leg.

Pronouncements of unbelief and wonder filled the room.

When Roland was finally able to commandeer everyone's attention again, he looked straight at Cole. "What about it, guy? You've given us a winner here. Are you sure you don't want to hang around and push this project to the end? You can be the next big thing. I don't think there's any question about it. When you take the stage tomorrow night, you can announce to the world that you're back for the long haul."

Cole noticed almost instantly that Lindsey's eyes were joining in and begging him to please give consideration to Roland's words.

Cole buried his face in his palms.

"Please know," he muttered through his hands, "that I am grateful for all the encouraging words—both from inside this office and outside from the critics—I truly am. I'm even humbled by them." He lifted his head. "But...I'm just not ready to be...the next big thing. I've made promises...to God...to myself...to Chaplain Parker...and to my son. And I've got to keep them. I want to keep them."

"Well," Roland emphasized softly, "please know that you'll always have a standing invitation to come back at any time if you ever decide you'd like to make another run at it."

Cole nodded.

Roland walked over and shook Cole's hand as a public display of sincerity, then returned to the head of the room where he highlighted more exciting information about the successful launch of the project. At the end, he earnestly thanked the engineering department, the marketing department, the sales department, and, of course, Cole, for the herculean achievement.

"All right," Roland said, wrapping things up. "Tomorrow night will be a big night. A huge night. Nearly all six thousand tickets have been sold. So, everyone—get a good night's sleep. We'll go through a full dress rehearsal at two in the afternoon. I want everybody in place by one-thirty. Understood?"

As the meeting was dismissed, Roland gestured to Cole to stay behind. When the two men were alone, Roland asked if Cole was planning to keep his bank account open. He didn't want there to be any mixup as to where the royalties should be deposited.

"The account will stay the same," Cole told him, then asked if it would be possible to have his personal mail forwarded to the SpiritMark address. "I've canceled all my magazine subscriptions, and there shouldn't be any bills, but if anything else comes through, is it all right if the post office forwards it to here?"

"No problem," Roland told him. "We'll just hold it alongside your fan mail."

The two men shook hands, then embraced.

Cole wanted to talk with Lindsey before he left the building, but he was told that she had already gone to a lunch appointment. He knew she was still hurting. He was already missing her terribly as well, more than anyone realized.

When he stepped out of the studio and walked to his bike, his spirit unexpectedly lightened. He felt a swell of merriment—like an ocean wave—nearly lift him off his feet. Was he really only a day away from the live concert, and only two days away from the road trip of a lifetime? He chuckled as he threw a fist into the air and slipped on his helmet.

En route to having lunch on his own, he stopped at a downtown bookstore that occupied a small storefront. He wanted to buy a couple of books for his highway journey. He browsed until he found two adventure books, light reading to appeal to his current mood. Following the purchase, he found a deli two doors down where he gorged himself, uncharacteristically feeling like a bottomless pit.

He came home to glimmering windows, shining floors, sparkling countertops and cabinets—and a thank-you note for the laptop. Surrounded by the fragrance of lemony wood polish, he spent the evening readying himself for the concert. He not only rehearsed the music list in his head several more times, he also rehearsed everything he wanted to say—introductions to the songs, stories behind the songs, and a mighty *thank you* to his fans for their enduring loyalty. Then he lay on the floor and fell asleep praying that God would use the event to draw people to His divine hope, promise, and grace.

52

On Friday morning, Cole paid his final utility bill. He notified the utility companies and phone company that he would no longer be a resident at the address after the next morning. He called the Middle Tennessee Correctional Facility and left word that any correspondence from the prison should be sent to the SpiritMark address. He emptied the cabinets and refrigerator of all remaining foods. He stacked his motorcycle gear and everything he was taking with him at the front door. By 11:30 AM, he was ready to vacate the house. He would return to the house after tonight's concert for one final night, then depart from Nashville early tomorrow morning.

The weather forecasters were predicting that the next day would be dry with sunshine, with temperatures in the mid-seventies—perfect conditions for the first leg of what he hoped would become a life-changing odyssey.

He had already highlighted his route on a road map that would guide him on the first leg of his trip. The route would lead him on more than 300 miles of back roads from Nashville, Tennessee to Cruso, North Carolina. His destination in Cruso was a campground exclusively for motorcyclists. He would stay there for a few days, then head out on the Blue Ridge Parkway, following the famous 469-mile-long highway along the spine of the Appalachian Mountain range all the way to Waynesboro, Virginia. He inhaled deeply, imagining himself already on the Blue Ridge mountainside. He could almost smell the wildflowers along the winding roadway.

He checked his pocket for his motorcycle key and made sure his violin was strapped securely to his back. He glanced around him and thanked God for the palatial accommodation that had been his home for the past three months.

And walked out the door.

* * *

"How do you ever get over a broken dream like this," Lindsey groaned into her cell phone, ignoring her girlfriend's advice over the line that she should not be driving in such a distracted state of mind. "I've tried to give him his space. But I can't sleep. I can't eat. I can hardly get through a work day. I feel like I've lost the man of my life. I mean—if it was another woman vying for his attention, I would fight tooth and nail to not lose him. But how do I fight against a noble idea? A promise? A dream?"

"Do you want to hear my honest opinion?"

Lindsey adjusted the mobile phone. "All right, Meg.

You're going to tell me whether I want to hear it or not, so..."

"Well, I've been really nice up to this point," surged the voice. "But I'm telling you, Linds. Any man—I don't care who he is—who would turn you down and turn down the business opportunities that have come his way—not to mention the money—and choose to be a vagabond, has got to be carrying some real serious baggage. I know, I know, you don't want to hear it. But I'm telling you, I honestly believe you'll be better off without him."

"Meg!" Lindsey raised her voice and braked almost too late for a red light. "You've only met the man one time. How can you—"

"Yeah, yeah. I know. He's tall. He's good looking. He's talented. And he's potentially a millionaire. But think about it, Linds. He's been locked away behind bars for more than ten years. He refuses to become physically intimate with you, one of the hottest girls around, a girl every other man fantasizes about. He has tons of interests that are different from yours. And hellooo—he's walking away from a life of enormous fame and money that was handed to him on a silver platter by the gods. And for what? To be alone. To sleep in a tent beside the highway. Does that sound normal to you? Does that even sound sane? I'm telling you, Linds, you deserve better. I know you're in love with the man, and that you're really hurting right now. But I'll be here to help you snap out of it, I promise. We'll hang out. We'll party. And I guarantee you that within a few months you'll have forgotten all about him."

Lindsey dabbed at a tear. "I don't know, Meg. There

is a brokenness about him that gives him a rare kind of tenderness and honesty. He's the only man I've ever met who I felt would be faithful to a woman. Doesn't that mean anything any more?"

"Of course it does. But how far would that get you if he's off his rocker? I'm telling you—he's got more baggage than you want to deal with."

* * *

When Cole walked out onto the stage to commence the opening song of his dress rehearsal, every behind-the-scenes engineer and crew member went quiet. The seating areas throughout the venue were dimly lit. Cole positioned himself at center stage. He looked back over his shoulder at the three giant twenty-foot-by-ten-foot plastic stained glass window mockups suspended from the ceiling across the breadth of the stage. The windows looked as if they had been lifted from the richest cathedral in America. Bright lights shot through them from the rear, creating an awe-inspiring mosaic of colors. Cole looked out over the six thousand empty seats bathed in the fractured light. A feeling of the heavenly filled the room. He closed his eyes. This would be his first time to try out the auditorium's sound system. He bowed his head, allowing himself to be bedazzled by the moment. Thousands of man-hours had gone into bringing him to this stage, to this rehearsal, to this comeback concert—something he had dreamed about hundreds of times. And he was more than grateful to God and to everyone involved—especially Lindsey.

With his head still bowed, he smiled. He wanted to taste the richness of every individual second. In a heightened state, he understood that a live performance on this scale would, for him, most likely never happen again. But he was content. More than that, he felt an infusion of divine serenity. Tonight's once-in-a-lifetime event would, for him and his fans, simply be a blessed gift.

He lifted his head and opened his eyes. He placed the Mysterious Lady on his shoulder and raised his bow. He nodded to the lead sound engineer. A spotlight engulfed him.

53

$\mathcal{A}$s Jesse sped north on I-24 toward Nashville, he evaluated his progress with Svetlana and Alina, the two Russian beauties he was luring into his trap. Svetlana, the younger of the two, was the most naive. She was already putting money aside to buy a plane ticket to the US. To build a stronger emotional connection, since Svetlana seemed like a compassionate girl, he had added a chapter to his story, telling her that his son, Cory, had recently had a grand mal seizure that debilitated him for three days, that he was undergoing extensive medical tests, and that the doctors were telling him that they shouldn't venture far from home until the doctors were convinced things were under control. At this point, the doctors could not guarantee that more seizures wouldn't follow. To Jesse's great pleasure, Svetlana believed the story and continued to express concern about Cory's condition.

Alina, on the other hand, was more cautious. She regularly asked questions that showed her suspicious nature. But rather than walk away, Jesse had decided to keep her on the hook for another month or two, just for the challenge.

The man who had bought Sasha was waiting for his second purchase. Jesse had told him that Svetlana's arrival date should be finalized any week now.

Jesse spotted an exit sign for Murfreesboro. He was forty minutes or less from downtown Nashville. He shifted his focus from Svetlana and Alina to Cole Michaels.

*   *   *

Jesse found the downtown music hall an hour and a half before the concert was scheduled to begin. He was surprised and pleased to find that it was adjacent to an open university campus. He would be just one more young face in a neighborhood of thousands.

He parked, slipped low in his car seat, and waited. He didn't want to enter the hall early or late. He watched until a horde of people seemed to descend on the place at the same time, and that's when he shuffled into the concert hall—amidst a throng of fans.

He had an aisle seat, eight rows from the stage. He wanted to get a close look at Cole Michaels, but not conspicuously. As he made his way to the front of the auditorium, he made eye contact with no one. He found his seat, sat down, closed his eyes, and lost himself in his thoughts.

Before his Internet research, he had never heard of Cole Michaels. But obviously, the man was more well known than Jesse had imagined—any musician who could fill a giant entertainment center like this had to be on the "A" list of a lot of people. Out of curiosity, Jesse had already downloaded a couple of songs from the man's first record, which had hit the market over ten years ago. The music wasn't a style Jesse would have chosen, but the man was undeniably talented. If the guy proved to be his father, then too bad his fans weren't going to be treated to a long comeback career.

"Excuse me," someone said.

Jesse twisted and let a group of seven or eight people slip by him into the row of seats. He closed his eyes again. He considered several scenarios of how Cole Michaels could die. Suddenly the background chatter in the auditorium hushed.

Jesse opened his eyes. Lights everywhere in the building had been dimmed. Before he could readjust his position, blinding spotlights blazed from behind the stage and pierced through the biggest stained-glass windows Jesse had ever seen. The windows, like gigantic prisms, fractured the light into multicolored super-rays that reached every corner of the auditorium, creating a sci-fi movie effect. Gasps of awe were heard throughout the hall.

An imposing figure, suddenly silhouetted on the stage, moved slowly to center stage, in front of the stained-glass facade. When he stopped, a beam of light bathed him in a brilliant glow.

There stood a man dressed in a brown-leather trench coat. He sported a shag of thick blonde hair and some facial stubble. He was holding a violin. Tall and trim, the man looked like a magazine model.

Before Jesse could get a more detailed look, everyone around him leapt to their feet and applauded. He stood and clapped, too, to blend in. He took a quick glance over his shoulder. It seemed that everyone in the hall was standing, clapping, whistling, screaming, waving, or taking photos with their cell phones. The expressions of adoration persisted for two to three minutes. Jesse didn't know whether to be impressed or jealous. When the clapping finally abated and the audience took their seats, Jesse stared again at the celebrity on center stage. Without any appearance of arrogance, the man positioned the violin on his shoulder and lifted his bow. Everyone went stone silent.

Within the first ten to fifteen thrusts of the bow, it was obvious to Jesse that the man was an exceptional musician. Jesse was no expert on musical composition, technique, or expression, but the music he was hearing tempted him to give in, to let it take him somewhere sublime. And for most of that first song, he found himself under the music's spell, entranced by the special effects of smoke and lighting. He almost forgot why he was there. When he realized what was happening, he fought the music's seductive powers.

Near the end of the instrumental solo, when the smoke faded, he finally got an up-close, live, uninterrupted look at Cole Michaels. He was stunned by the real-life resemblance between himself and the man on stage. Same height, same thick blond hair, and nearly the same face. He knew for sure, at that moment, that the man was his biological father. The circumstantial evidence, now combined with the physical similarities, made him certain.

When the final note of the song faded, the crowd roared again.

Cole Michaels took a humble bow. He stepped forward and, for the first time, he spoke. The room became miraculously quiet once more.

"Thank you, thank you," Cole effused.

The crowd cheered.

Cole paused and smiled until the applause tapered off. "I've looked forward to this night for a long time. A very long time. Thank you for your patience and your support. I am deeply touched."

Six or seven wild fans blasted the room with shrill whistles.

"As many of you know," Cole continued somberly, "twelve years ago, my destiny was forever changed when I lost the two most important people in my life—my wife, Jana, and my son, Shay. I was unable to handle those losses, so I escaped into drunkenness. And then I did something that no one should ever do. While under the disabling effect of alcohol, I drove. Not just once. But repeatedly, day after day. Until the inevitable happened. Until I collided with another car. I walked away from the accident. But a single mom named Allison and her daughter, Stephanie, did not. Two tombstones now mark their graves, not far from here. As punishment for my crime, I rightly spent eleven years behind bars. While I was locked away in prison, my life was slowly transformed by the influence of a single extraordinary man, a chaplain named Duke Parker. Because of Duke, I found hope. And I found purpose. Because of his intentional and persistent influence, I chose to keep living. And, as you might guess, music became an important part of my recovery. A little over a year ago, a great little company called SpiritMark gave me the opportunity to write some new songs birthed out of my years of heartache and renewal. And now those songs have been recorded in a new CD called *Oasis Blues*. I want to thank everyone at SpiritMark for helping this project come to life. And—in memory of Jana, Shay, Allison, Stephanie, and Chaplain Duke Parker who passed away just four weeks ago—I would now like to present to you some of those songs."

What about me, you scumbag? Jesse wanted to shout. He wanted to stand and point a finger at the man and ask him in front of everybody, *Why didn't you want me? Why don't you even want to acknowledge me when you publicly talk about your family? Do you have any idea what kind of hell you've put me through? Do you perceive, even for one freaking second, how much I hate you?* Part of him wanted to get up and leave. Another part wanted to storm the stage and extinguish the man's life on the spot. His whole body quaked. He strained to bring himself under control. Only when he heard Cole begin his next number, assisted by musicians playing a keyboard and penny whistle, did he relax a little.

For the first time, Jesse heard Cole sing. The man's vocals were as keen as his violin playing. But Jesse realized, as the concert unfolded, that every time he heard Cole Michaels open his mouth—either to sing or to speak—he was repulsed. He could handle, even appreciate, the instrumental music. But the man's words, especially when he sang and spoke a few times about God, only stoked the rage flaring in his soul.

By the end of the two-hour concert, Jesse was emotionally and mentally spent. It had taken all of his discipline to simply sit and watch. Now, he was ready to trail the man to his home and begin the process of human demolition.

* * *

Cole played the last note of the concert's final song. As it faded, the audience sprang to their feet and burst into thunderous applause.

Cole bowed before the thousands of animated, appreciative faces. Sweat dropped from his brow. The moment seemed out of this world, utterly extraordinary. He turned and gestured toward the other musicians on stage, soliciting a cheer for them as well. The applause swelled. After a full minute of enthusiastic ovation, Cole tried to speak. But this time, the people would not let him. They wanted an encore. Cole could hardly believe the spectacular reaction. Standing there on stage in front of six thousand people, he thought of all the work and anticipation that had been invested in this moment, and choked up. The evening had been everything he had hoped for, and more.

He raised his violin again. The song he gave as a departing gift was a rip-roaring jig, a short, feel-good explosion of high energy. When he ripped the last chord, he was barely breathing, but his smile was huge.

Hollers, whistles, and clapping broke out one final time.

Cole had planned to take this moment to tell his fans that he was walking away from his career, retiring as a professional musician on the very night of his comeback, and that he wished them the very best. But Roland had asked him to withhold the information.

54

Jesse was parked with a clear view of the theater's back door. He had expected that Cole Michaels, when he exited the building, would crawl into a chauffeur-driven limousine. So he was more than a little surprised to see the man walk out the door and make his way to a motorcycle.

Are you kidding me?

He watched as Cole said goodbye to a few people and donned his helmet.

This might just give Jesse a one-in-a-million opportunity. His target would be alone, on a dangerous machine, at night.

Yes!

Maybe he wouldn't have to spend several days staking the man out, learning his patterns, after all. Maybe he could just "accidentally" run him off the road tonight into a utility pole, a parked car, a store front, or a deep ditch.

But wait—would an accident like that ensure the traitor's death? Maybe, if they were going fast enough. Did Michaels live in the city or out in the country? A long ride out of town, at higher speeds and with tighter curves, would definitely present greater prospects for a fatal mishap.

On the other hand—Jesse had waited half his life for this moment. He really wanted to introduce himself to the man eye-to-eye first and ask a few questions before he killed him.

When Jesse saw the fiddler start the bike, he started his car. But Cole made no attempt to pull away. He just sat with the motor idling.

Jesse watched. A limo pulled up beside the motorcycle and stopped. Michaels talked to someone through an open car window. The conversation was short and energetic. Then the limousine pulled away and Michaels followed.

Jesse gave the two vehicles a good head start, then pulled out. The anticipation surging through his body created a nerve-wracking high. After three or four turns, it became obvious that Michaels was sticking with the limo. Jesse cursed and slammed his dashboard. Within minutes, both the limo and the motorcycle turned into a gravel parking lot not far from downtown. Adjacent to the lot was a two-story brick building, a bar and grill.

Jesse parked on the opposite side of the street and slumped in his seat. He watched as six people crawled out of the limo. Michaels joined them and they headed into the restaurant. They were all talking, nudging, and laughing.

It was now just a waiting game. Jesse knew he could be patient. But tonight, his adrenaline was pumping and his patience would be tested. The minutes, he knew, would tick away with the speed of a glacier.

For an hour, people continued to come and go from

the joint at a regular pace. When the foot traffic finally slowed down, Jesse thought seriously about sneaking over to the gravel parking lot and sabotaging the motorcycle. If he'd had a working knowledge of a bike's mechanical systems, he might have done it. But he wanted Michaels to die, not just break down.

* * *

Finally, around midnight, Jesse's target came out of the restaurant, still with his party. Jesse tensed and held his breath as the group lingered, talking and laughing, around the limo. Within a few minutes, everyone—except Cole and some lady—crouched into the limousine and departed.

Michaels and the woman stood a long time in the parking lot, absorbed in an intense conversation. Eventually, Michaels held the lady in his arms, and they both appeared to cry. Then he walked her slowly to a Mini Cooper. She got in and drove away. Michaels went to his motorcycle, put on his helmet, and drove out of the parking lot.

Jesse finally sighed. He couldn't have been happier. His target was emotionally distracted. And alone. Jesse started his car and pulled away from the curb. He fell in behind the bike, keeping a distance of a hundred yards or so.

Jesse felt himself smiling.

His smile turned to extreme soberness, however, after a couple of more turns, when he saw the motorcycle's brake lights come on and saw the bike turn into a yard at a downtown address.

Jesse made a right-hand turn instead of continuing past

the yard. He circled at least four blocks before returning to the house where the bike had stopped. There it was, parked in the grass at the side of the house. In a slow pass, he took a visual snapshot of the property. He made note of the street name at the next corner, as well as a couple of nearby landmarks—a commercial parking lot and a law firm.

Jesse kept driving, figuring out his next move.

Ten minutes later, he returned to the parking lot across the street from the target's house. The motorcycle was still in the yard. Jesse stared at the townhouse. Not a single light was on, inside or out. The neighboring houses were dark as well. Again, Jesse felt the ecstasy of mind-boggling anticipation. Maybe he should break into the house tonight. His target was physically fatigued and apparently emotionally preoccupied.

But was he alone?

Could there be a wife or girlfriend in the house, someone the man had shacked up with since his prison release? If so, she might even have young kids. But wouldn't a wife have attended the concert—especially a comeback concert? Jesse mulled over the possibilities. Was the man perhaps still a widower? Could the woman he had lingered with and hugged at the bar be his new love interest? Or could she be a mistress? Jesse wondered again if there might be a wife curled up in the bed with Cole right now.

Or possibly there was another man, a buddy, that was sharing the house.

Jesse banged the lining of his car roof.

There were just too many unknowns. Maybe Michaels had a watchdog. Maybe there was a security system. If he was going to achieve his goal, and do it undetected and uncaught, then he needed to return to his original plan—and do some serious reconnaissance.

He drove off to find a hotel—someplace not too close. He would be back tomorrow. He had a head full of new information. It was time to do some careful planning.

55

Cole didn't fall asleep until 2:00 AM. He awoke three-and-a-half hours later. He lay still for fifteen minutes or more, trying to will his body to go back to sleep. But it was useless. It seemed that the combination of hypnotic contentment and ecstatic expectations had somehow lifted him above physical exhaustion.

At 5:45, he crawled out of his sleeping bag, peed, and got a drink of water from the kitchen sink. He dressed, rolled up his pad and bag, and sat in the middle of the living-room floor, with a wide view of the place he had called home for the last three months. He opened his Bible to Psalm ninety-five and read aloud verses three, four, and five, which he was currently memorizing.

> *For the Lord is a great God, the great king above all gods. He owns the depths of the earth, and even the mightiest mountains are His. The sea*

*belongs to Him, for he made it. His
hands formed the dry land too.*

Cole knelt. "Father, my emotions are at their limits
right now. As I get ready to experience the mountain
peaks, the dry land, the sea, and the depths of the earth in
a way that I never have before, I beg you to guide me down
providential paths. And may my life extol you loudly and
joyously every mile of the way."

Cole moved all his gear to the front porch. In the pale
dawn, he methodically loaded the Scrambler. He set the
tank bag, stuffed with his rainsuit, astride the gas tank, held
in place by strong magnets. His highlighted map was already
tucked inside the transparent map sleeve at the top of the
tank bag. He strapped the mammoth duffel bag—holding
his clothes, shoes, toiletries, tent, checkbook, motor oil,
and chain wax—across the passenger seat, up against the
sissy bar. He lashed the sleeping bag atop the headlight at
the front of the bike. The Mysterious Lady, secured in its
protective case, he strapped tightly to his back. When all
the gear was in place, he checked the bike's oil level, the
chain, and the air pressure in the tires.

He then made one final sweep of the house. Then he
stood at the front door for a few seconds, reliving memories
of Lindsey and the SpiritMark chronicle. He closed his eyes
and sighed. With every nerve in his body firing, he locked
the door behind him, deposited the key into the mailbox,
and turned his back on a life of stardom.

He stood by the Triumph lost in thought for several
minutes. Then he slipped on his helmet and straddled the

bike. As he started the motor, he whispered a prayer of thanksgiving, then pulled away.

By the time he made the first turn at the end of the block, his emotions overcame him. Tears flowed beneath his helmet. He shook his head to clear his vision.

Before he left town, he made one final stop. He swung out of his way and rode to the cemetery where Jana and Shay were buried. As the sun broke over the horizon, he walked across the dew-covered lawn to their gravesite and sat on the ground facing the massive tombstone. "I sure missed you guys at the concert last night," he said. He called up their faces, maneuvering back through twelve years of memory. "Well, I suppose the decision I've made seems crazy to you." He chuckled. "And maybe it is, at least from an earthly perspective. But I'm more at peace than I've ever been. Anyway, I wanted to come by and say I love you guys. And"— he pushed his hand deep into the pocket of his jeans and extracted the unused engagement ring—"I didn't know what else to do with this. So I want to honor your memory as the only woman I've ever shared my life with." Cole took his motorcycle key and dug a small trench at the base of the gravestone, just beneath Jana's name. He put the ring at the bottom of the hole and covered it with dirt. "I love you," he mumbled again.

*   *   *

At 8:00 AM, Jesse pulled into the parking lot, between two other cars, facing his target's house across the street. Michaels's motorcycle was gone. Did he work on Saturday?

Or had he left early to run weekend errands? Or did he even live here? Maybe he had just overnighted at this address with a friend. Or another mistress.

The blinds were still closed.

Jesse slammed his head back against the headrest.

He decided to sit and watch the house until noon. If he didn't see any activity by then, he would return on Monday morning at 7:00. He would somehow determine if Michaels truly lived here and had a work routine.

56

The sweet smell of honeysuckle filled the Saturday morning air. The temperature couldn't have been more perfect.

Cole had never felt such exuberance. He was riding down a two-lane country highway alongside a winding river. He felt like he was floating at shoulder level directly into the surrounding scenery at sixty miles an hour, as if he were part of it. The fluidity of the movement—with all its sweeps, elevations, and descents—was completely under his control. The sensation was incredible.

"*Yes!*" he shouted.

As he rounded one of the sweeping curves, he shot past a sand-covered river embankment. He slowed and, since he had been riding for over an hour, he turned and rode back to the picturesque setting to stretch his muscles. He pulled the bike off the road into the grass and parked. The flowering plants in the area were already in bloom, and the fragrances were heavenly. He strolled down to the sand and pulled off his boots and socks. For fifteen minutes, he stood ankle deep in the whirling water and enjoyed the view. Then, at peace and without a worry, he lay on his back in the sand, barefooted, and let the soothing sunlight lull him into a brief nap.

A loud splash in the river snapped him out of his slumber. He raised up and looked around, but didn't see any cause for the noise. He stretched and enjoyed another few minutes, then slipped into his socks and boots and remounted the bike.

His destination for the day was Dayton, Tennessee, eighty miles east. He planned to overnight there and continue the next day toward Cruso, North Carolina.

As he leaned repeatedly into a sudden string of curves, he tried to practice his counter steering. He made sure to cast his focus all the way through to the final point of the turn. The bike was a joy—he was amazed at how flawlessly it ran, weaved, and swooped.

"Thank you, Jesus!" he bellowed.

On a few straight stretches, he experimented with some hard roll-on accelerations. The Scrambler's torque was remarkable.

"Yes!" he shouted again.

To be free on the road like this, with the wind whipping all around him, was therapy for his heart and mind. He couldn't keep a smile off his face. This was his first foray outside the greater Nashville area in twelve years, and he was loving every second of it.

As he climbed a low-grade slope, he swished by an old wooden farmhouse and smelled freshly cut grass. The next minute, he squinted as the pungent smell of cow manure filled his nostrils. He shook his head. "Whew!" He laughed out loud.

The hills, creeks, meadows, and forests along the route sketched a collective picture of nature that could only be labeled as *majestic*. His long-term deprivation of the outdoors, he learned, had evoked a new appreciation for the earth.

He soon entered the city limits of a small town called Sparta. He slowed the Triumph to the posted 35-mph speed limit. Beautiful old homes, most of them well maintained, flanked the street—almost like a welcoming committee. The peaceful, lazy neighborhood beckoned him to get off the bike and stay awhile. Even though it was only around 10:30 AM, he decided that he would stop in town and eat lunch. He had skipped breakfast, and his gut was telling him it was time for some food. Plus, he wanted to take in the character of the little town at his leisure.

As he glided toward the city square, he saw his reflection off to the right in a row of storefront windows. He did a double take, careful to keep the bike on a straight path. The image of a motorcycle and rider loaded down for cross-country travel conjured up a menu of words such *as explorer, drifter, loner, risk taker, wanderer* and *wayfarer*. He felt like a bona fide member of some elite community of adventurous trekkers. He liked the idea. It somehow made him feel more manly.

When he approached a green light at the town square, he looked through the intersection and made sure all perpendicular traffic was fully stopped at the red lights. He proceeded carefully into the square and made one and a half trips around the courthouse that sat augustly in the heart of the town. During his loop, he spotted a cozy-looking homestyle restaurant. He parked in front, dismounted, pulled off his helmet and backpack, and stretched.

"That's a nice bike you got there, son," a man's voice said.

Cole turned and was welcomed by the extended hand of a clean-shaven old gentlemen wearing overalls. Cole shook the man's hand. "Thank you, sir," Cole said, trying not to grimace at the power in the old man's grip.

"What year is she?" the man asked.

"Brand-new 2008 model."

The man looked doubtful. "My younger brother had an old Triumph back in the sixties that looked just like it. That bike gave him a lot of good memories. I hadn't seen one like it in thirty years. I never would've guessed they're still making 'em."

"Yeah, the company made a real comeback a few years ago," Cole said, repeating information he had discovered in his motorcycle research. "Most of their bikes these days look real modern. But they make two or three models that are replicas of their most famous bikes from the past. And this is one of them."

The man asked if he could take a closer look. They talked motorcycles and road trips for a good fifteen minutes. *Good ol' southern friendliness*, Cole thought as he finally waved goodbye to the man and headed into the restaurant.

A bell hanging at the top of the door frame clanged when Cole walked in. "Welcome to Billy's," a woman sang out from behind the serving counter, barely looking up as she rushed to gather an order. Cole nodded and looked around. Most of the tables were empty, probably due to the hour. He took off his jacket and chose a table up front in the sunlight. A few minutes later, he ordered sweet tea, fried chicken, fried okra, black-eyed peas, and sweet potatoes.

Feeling a little grimy, he went to the restroom and washed his face and hands. By the time he got back to his table, a glass of ice tea, served up in a mason jar, was waiting for him. He took a sip. "Ummm..." The tea he'd drunk in prison had been absolutely pitiful compared to home-brewed tea like this. Ahhh...life's little delights.

While he waited for his food, he enjoyed the farm-theme decor: The large photographs that hung on the walls, highlighting farmhouses, barns, tractors, and crops. The collection of farm implements that stood in the corners—a churn, a plow, a wooden gate, and a stuffed burlap seed sack. And the table centerpieces that were made of hay, dried corn husks, cow bells, and tractor hitches.

Cole felt lost in nostalgic wonder.

"Here you go," the server announced, setting Cole's food on the table.

"Thanks. And I'm just curious—what is Sparta known for? I'm just passing through and I'm interested to learn something about the town's history."

"Well," she said, "for years, Sparta has been known for its high-school basketball teams. The girls' and the boys' teams were both ranked number one at the same time about ten years ago. And, let me see....have you ever heard of Lester Flatt?"

"The bluegrass musician?"

"That's the one. A country music hall-of-famer. He's one of our own."

"You mean Sparta was his home?"

"Born right down the road. There's a big memorial to him just around the corner. Not only that, he's buried down the highway there at Oak Lawn Cemetery."

"Are you kidding?"

Encouraged, the waitress went on. "Have you ever heard of Benny Martin?"

"Of course," Cole said. "He was one of the greatest bluegrass fiddlers of all time—maybe one of the greatest fiddlers, period. Now I know *he's* not buried here, because he was buried just outside Nashville six or seven years ago."

"No, but he *was* born here. Another one of our boys."

"Come on."

"I swear on my mother's grave."

"How ironic is that!" Cole responded, looking through the window at the violin backpack hanging from the rearview mirror of his bike.

"I don't understand."

"Oh—nothing. It's just that—no, never mind."

"Anyway, you better enjoy your food before it gets cold."

Cole devoured everything on his plate, then ordered homemade peach cobbler with vanilla ice cream for dessert.

When he finally pushed himself away from the table, he fetched his violin and backpack and took an unhurried stroll to see the Lester Flatt memorial.

* * *

At noon, Jesse gave up for the day. He had been waiting uncomfortably in his car for four hours, and not a soul had gone into or out of the house.

He cursed in frustration and squeezed the car seat in his fists.

He was fortunate, though, that the parking lot where he sat was located behind, and not in front of, the adjacent commercial buildings. There were no windows on the backside of the commercial properties, thus none of the business tenants could spot him and wonder why a strange man was sitting in his car for hours on end in their parking lot.

Jesse gazed across the street at the house one more time.

He would stick to his initial plan. He would return early on Monday morning and hope that with the beginning of the work week, he might catch a break—and Cole Michaels.

57

By mid-afternoon Saturday, Cole saw—according to the road signs—that he was nearing Dayton. He debated whether to spend the night in a hotel or in the tent. The debate didn't last long—he decided to use his tent. Like a kid, he was looking forward to the experience. He hadn't camped in a tent since he was in his twenties. And one of the things he had learned recently while walking barefoot in a Nashville park was that there was something extremely cathartic for him about his skin being in physical contact with the ground. His newfound appreciation for grass, dirt, rock, and sand was no doubt a reaction to spending ninety-nine percent of his prison years surrounded by linoleum, concrete and steel.

The idea of lying on the ground, even with a thin layer of nylon beneath him, seemed inviting.

He was wondering where to pitch the tent when he sped past a little white wooden church sitting on several acres of manicured grass bordered by a rocky brook. *That wouldn't be a bad place to camp,* he thought, but pushed on toward the city.

In downtown Dayton, he looked for, and found, a hardware store. He browsed through the store, looking for something to make a lanyard to secure his motorcycle key around his neck. Some spools of leather captured his interest. One of the spools held yards and yards of leather with the dimensions of a thick boot strap. Cole had no idea what the strands of leather would normally be used for, but he bought a piece about thirty inches long. Outside the store, he threaded the leather through the eye of his motorcycle key and tied the ends together. "Voila", he said—an inexpensive and durable keychain necklace.

At a neighboring grocery store, he bought a freshly baked loaf of bread, along with two bananas, some peanuts, and a quart of orange juice. When he checked out, he asked the elderly cashier if she knew of any campgrounds in the area. She didn't.

So Cole packed the food into his duffel and rode back out to the little white church. He looked around the property but found no one, so he rode across the grass and parked at least a hundred yards from the building, next to the brook. He hung the motorcycle key around his neck. As he unloaded his gear, he realized that tomorrow would be Sunday—people would gather at the building for a church service. He decided to stay through the night anyway. He would set his alarm for an early wake-up and be well on his way before people started to arrive.

Pitching the tent was as easy as he had been told it would be. The fact that a two-man tent could be so lightweight and easy to assemble was remarkable. He staked the tent with its door facing the creek, then unrolled the self-inflating sleeping pad—another piece of camping paraphernalia that he found impressive. Whistling, he positioned the pad inside the tent and rolled out the sleeping bag on top of the pad. He brought the rest of his gear into the tent. The interior was actually roomier than he had expected. He was more than satisfied.

Cole climbed out of the tent, took off his shoes and socks, and ambled around in the grass. He found himself looking back at the Scrambler. It was indeed an exquisite piece of machinery, begging to roam the planet. He only wished that Shay was around to enjoy it with him.

The brook then beckoned him. The water was wide, shallow, and clear—the proverbial *babbling brook*. He waded out to the middle and washed his face and hair. His hair was growing longer and thicker by the week. So was his beard. As he pressed water out of his bangs, he saw out of the corner of his eye a shadow moving through the water. Startled, he jumped toward the bank—only to look back and see that the shadow was a plate-sized turtle now rapidly swimming upstream over the rocks to get away from him. He laughed at himself. He followed the turtle and watched it for fifteen minutes or more.

Afterward, he lay in the grass and read the first four chapters of one of his books—it was about a 1996 Mt. Everest expedition. The narrative was spellbinding and made him glad all over again that he had set out on his own great adventure. The buoyant feelings of breaking away from the norm and daring to live life on the edge prompted him to ask God for divine opportunities along the way to encourage, inspire, and help a multitude of people who would otherwise be overlooked.

When he put the book down, he pulled out the bananas and bread for his evening meal. In perfect seventy-degree weather, he sat barefoot on the river bank and slowly dined on the simple fare. He could not have been happier. When his belly was content, he fetched his fiddle and returned to the water's edge.

He sat cross-legged and played a few strings to warm up. Then he lay back on the ground, holding the Mysterious Lady to his chest and reflecting on last evening's concert. The rapport he had felt with the audience had seemed more palpable than at any other moment in his career as a musician. He had needed that experience, he realized, to bring proper closure to his run as a celebrity. And the glorious memory would last for a lifetime. He thanked God for SpiritMark and the projects they had afforded him. The creative work had helped him find his new bearing. He was more than grateful.

Feeling inspired and refreshed, he sat up and again played one of his new tunes. Fiddling outdoors beside a picturesque stream, with sunrays massaging his shoulders, was nothing short of enchanting. He became so entranced by the moment that one song pulled him into another. He ended up playing ballads, jigs, hymns, and popular twenty-first-century praise songs.

He was just positioning his bow to play an arietta when he was startled by a man's voice. "Excuse me, Mister. I don't mean to interrupt, but do you know you're on private property?"

Cole spun around.

Two old men stood just feet away, staring at him. Cole slowly stood. "Man...you caught me off guard!" He lowered his violin. "I didn't mean to trespass. I was just passing through and needed a patch of grass to sleep on. I thought it might be okay if I lay here for a few hours."

"Well, this isn't a campground," one of the men explained in a southern drawl. He sounded like a grandfather gently correcting his grandson.

"Yes, sir," Cole said respectfully.

"Mind if I ask you who you are, son?" The same man spoke. "I mean, judging by your equipment here and those Gospel tunes you were playing, you're obviously not just a homeless drifter."

Tunes, plural? Cole wondered how long the two had been standing there. "My name is CJ," Cole answered, using his first and middle initial to conceal his identity. He reached out his hand, which the men shook in turn. "Actually, I recently retired from a career in music, and now I'm just taking time off to explore the country."

"Well, I'm Pastor Ralph Johnson, pastor of the church here. And this is one of my deacons, Lamar Easley. We saw you over here and thought we should find out what you were up to."

Cole nodded.

"That next-to-last piece you were playing there — Holy, Holy, Holy," Pastor Ralph continued, "that's one of my all-time favorites. You did a beautiful job with it."

"Thank you."

"Let me ask you this, CJ—are you saved?"

"Yes, sir, I am. I became a Christian a little over ten years ago."

"You mind if me and my deacon sit and talk with you a little bit?"

"No, I don't mind."

The three men sat in the grass. Cole fielded a slew of additional questions. He was careful, however, to conceal his celebrity status. He wanted the men to look on him as just another guy—no one special. The three of them talked about salvation, music, life in the South, and church. They talked for close to an hour. Cole enjoyed it—*new places, new people, new adventures,* he told himself.

"What are your plans for tomorrow morning?" the pastor asked.

"Well, I'm planning to head out early for the Blueridge Parkway, over toward Cruso, North Carolina."

"What about church?"

Cole had no ready answer, at least not one he thought the pastor would appreciate. The silence was awkward.

"Christians shouldn't be missing church—every Christian should know that." The pastor's voice veered toward sternness. "We all need to be under the preaching of God's Holy Word. None of us can afford to slack off on being in God's house on God's day. I'm a real stickler on that—always have been, always will be. So, if you're not planning to be in church anywhere else, why don't you plan to be with us?"

Cole's first inclination was to turn down the offer. But his time was his own—he had no real deadline. And it had been a while since he had attended a worship service. "Sure.

All right," he said. "But I'll look a little scruffy. I only have jeans."

The pastor grinned. "I think we can make an exception in your case."

"Does that mean I can keep my tent here for the night?"

The pastor and the deacon looked at each other. "Sure," the pastor granted, "Just don't build any fires."

"Done."

"Oh, and one more thing," the pastor added, "I'm just curious—do you sing as well as play?"

"I sing a little bit."

"How about the song 'Holy, Holy, Holy' that you were playing—do you know the words?"

"I do."

"Before me and my deacon head back, do you think you could sing a verse or two for us?"

Cole smiled and closed his eyes. Completely relaxed, he eased into the song softly and humbly as if he was singing in a heavenly audition. He kept his eyes closed and let the lyrics pour through his heart. When he reached the final words of the third verse—

> *Only Thou art holy;*
> *there is none beside Thee;*
> *perfect in power, in love, and purity*

—he felt overcome once again by the realization of God's love for him. He opened his eyes to sing the final verse. The pastor and the deacon were both moved. The pastor was even dabbing at his eyes.

No sooner had Cole ended the song than Pastor Ralph exhaled slowly and said, "Never in my life have I ever felt that hymn so deeply." He paused as if to gain control of his emotions. "Would you be willing to sing that song for my people tomorrow, just like you sang it then?"

"It's one of my favorite hymns as well. I'll be glad to sing it for you and your people."

Deacon Easley leaned over and whispered something into the pastor's ear. The pastor nodded. Easley then looked at Cole and said, "Besides being one of the deacons here at the church, I'm also the song leader. We really like your singing, there. So, if you know four or five other old hymns, we'd love for you to take my place tomorrow morning and lead us in worship."

Cole thought about it, then agreed.

They talked briefly about the order of the service, and then the pastor and deacon headed back toward the parking lot.

Cole sat still for a few minutes and reflected on what had just happened. Only God could have orchestrated something like that. Would this road trip, all along the way, be sprinkled with such divine interventions?

Before sunset, he decided to stretch a little. He jogged around the acreage, did some push-ups and sit-ups, then bathed in the cold water of the brook.

When he finally crawled into his sleeping bag for the night, his heart and mind were at peace. His first day on the road could not have been more perfect.

58

Cole was introduced to the Sunday morning worshippers as "an unexpected visitor—a gifted fiddler and singer," and as "a motorcyclist who's just wandering the States."

Cole especially liked the last description.

The congregation, about thirty people, welcomed him with curious smiles. All but two or three of them appeared to be sixty or older. No one seemed to recognize him as the Blonde Fiddler. *Good.* He didn't need, or want, any fanfare.

According to plan, Cole led them in a medley of worship songs, including "Holy, Holy, Holy." With each song, the people seemed to ascend more and more into a spirit of praise. Some raised their hands. Some sang at the top of their lungs. One heavyset woman knelt and cried uncontrollably.

When all the songs were sung and the service turned back over to Pastor Ralph, the aged minister asked everybody to bow their heads. He thanked Cole for his heart-touching ministry. He then prayed robustly for a renewed sense of God's presence to anoint their church. Afterward he announced, "This wasn't planned—it wasn't even discussed. But I feel led to help this young man out in his journey. So I'm going to ask the ushers to come to the front and we're going to collect a special love offering. Every cent that's given will be placed directly into CJ's pocket. Ushers come ahead and gather at the front."

From the front pew, Cole tried to subtly motion to the pastor that an honorarium wasn't necessary. But the pastor ignored him.

When the offering plates were returned to the altar, Pastor Ralph thanked Cole again, then launched into a fiery sermon entitled, "Peter's Denial of Jesus; Are You A Coward Like He Was?" As the sermon unfolded, Pastor Ralph preached harder and harder. Eventually he was sucking air like a water pump low on water. Sweat covered his face. When he reached his second point, he yanked off his coat and threw it into the choir loft. By the third point, he had snatched off his tie as well. His face turned sunburn-red. Cole wondered if the man might have a heart attack.

As the pastor neared his conclusion, he wiped the sweat from his face and brow with a plain white handkerchief and sipped water from a big glass. He eventually gave an altar call. By that point, he was hoarse.

Eight people came forward during the invitation and knelt at the altar to "make things right with God".

Cole had never before experienced a church service so deeply Southern, so traditionally rural, yet he was charmed by what he saw, heard, and felt. He sensed that he had somehow made an important connection with his Southern heritage, like meeting a long-lost relative for the first time. He knew that he should highly value the experience. And he did.

When those at the altar returned to their seats, the pastor shouted, "It's been a great day—Amen? God's been in our midst, and He's gotten through to some hearts. Well, Glory! All right—Brother Lamar has an announcement to make. And when he's finished, you're dismissed. I'll see you back here tonight."

Deacon Easley walked to the platform. "I know everybody's hungry for lunch, so I'll make this quick. Some of you've already heard, but Jimmy and Louise Marker— the missionaries from right here in Rhea County that we help support—flew back from Nicaragua with their youngest daughter, the seven year old, on Friday afternoon. The little girl is going to have emergency brain surgery tomorrow morning in Chattanooga. The surgery will cost around forty thousand dollars. The Markers don't have any medical insurance. So, all the churches in the county have been asked to take up a collection this morning and help out with this hospital bill. So, we're going to ask the ushers to place the offering plates on the vestibule table. And if any of you feel led to drop in a few dollars, I know Jimmy and Louise would appreciate it. If you need to make out a check, make it out to United Global Missions and designate it to the Marker Surgery Fund. All right, we're finished."

Almost instantly, Cole was swarmed by people who wanted to talk with him. But his attention was fixed on the seven-year-old girl. No matter how hard he tried to focus on the pleasantries of the jovial congregants, he just couldn't shake the image of the little girl and her family out of his head. Here was another opportunity to draw from his Shay and Stephanie Fund and help a child in need. As he tried to talk to the people around him, he kept repeating in his head the name of the mission agency—United Global Missions. He didn't want to forget it.

When he was finally able to break free, he rushed out to the Triumph, loaded and parked in front of the church building, and retrieved his checkbook. He tore out a check and wrote it out to the mission agency. As a couple of older men headed his way, he scribbled *One-Thousand* in the dollar space and signed his name.

"That there's one of the prettiest motorcycles I've seen in a long time," one of the men said as he drew close.

Cole chatted with the men for a few minutes, answered three or four of their questions about the parallel twin, and listened to a few of their motorcycle stories from years gone by. Then he slipped back into the church foyer and dropped his folded check into one of the offering plates. He was in a rush now to get on the bike and ride, before the church treasurer had a chance to see the check and discover his true identity.

Before he could depart, though, a few more people—including Pastor Ralph—cornered him and told him what an extraordinary blessing he had been to their congregation. They all invited him to please come back and visit again.

He slowly worked his way through the crowd out into the churchyard. When he finally mounted the Scrambler, he was halted by the pastor one more time. "Don't forget your love offering!" brother Ralph said, holding out a white envelope. "It's a hundred and eighty dollars and some odd change. I wish it could be more. But maybe this will help."

Cole tried to turn down the gift, but the pastor insisted. Cole finally took the envelope and expressed his deepest thanks. He wondered if there was a way to sneak back into the building and add the cash to the offering for the Markers. But just then he saw one of the ushers on the church steps wave a check in the air and yell, "Pastor Ralph!" Cole hurriedly said goodbye to the kind old pastor and started the Scrambler. He slipped on his helmet, engaged the clutch, and eased out onto the highway. He never looked back.

As he wound through the town of Dayton, he prayed for Pastor Ralph, Deacon Easley, the congregation, the Marker family, and their little girl. His visit with the church had been delightful. But he was more than jubilant to be twisting the throttle again and zipping along the asphalt on his wonderful machine.

* * *

The afternoon-and-early-evening ride to Cruso, North Carolina, was invigorating. As a new rider, the infamous eleven-mile stretch of Highway 129 known as the *Dragon's Tail*, with its three hundred and eighteen extremely sharp curves, gave him all the excitement he could handle. He was tense all over—almost like having a full-body cramp— throughout the entire eleven miles. But he had never enjoyed tension so much. He then took a stroll over Fontana Dam, the highest dam in the eastern half of the United States, and enjoyed the surrounding scenery for more than two hours. He walked the streets of Cherokee, North Carolina, the reservation center for the Eastern Band of Cherokee Indians. And he immersed himself in the foothills of the Smoky Mountains as he wound his way to the motorcycle-only campground in Cruso.

On every road, the Scrambler performed so superbly that it felt like a customized prosthetic made in heaven. He had never imagined that he could enjoy the bike more than he had enjoyed it during his first week of ownership in Nashville. But the fun factor had now climbed off the chart.

When he entered the campground at Cruso, he crossed a wooden bridge spanning a beautiful river and found an exceptionally manicured resort. There was an office building, an open pavilion, a bathhouse, several rustic cabins, and a wealth of trees. Interspersed between the buildings and trees were tent sites on lush green grass. The rushing river dominated the front side of the grounds, and a good-sized pond the back. The place was more picturesque and inviting than he had expected.

He registered as a guest and within fifteen minutes was setting up his tent near the bank of the river. Since he intended to stay for a few days, he toured the campground and read a brochure that clarified the resort's rules and policies.

That evening, he mixed for the first time with other riders. He enjoyed lengthy conversations with three different groups from three different states. He was impressed by the distances people had ridden. If they were typical of the general motorcycle community, he was in for a treat; they were all colorful, outgoing, intelligent, full of life, and full of great stories. What an awesome brotherhood! He just wished that Shay, as a fifteen-year-old, could enjoy the experience with him.

Before he retired for the night, he took a long, hot shower. Inside his tent he balanced his checkbook. After spending $10,000 for the motorcycle, $1,000 for the insurance, and after giving away $1,000 to Lindsey's sister and $1,000 to the missionary family, the checkbook registry showed a remaining balance of $7,000.

Putting the checkbook away, he read four more chapters of the Mt. Everest adventure.

He fell asleep in a state of pure splendor.

59

Jesse was back in the parking lot on Monday morning at 7:00, spying on the townhouse across the street where he had last seen Cole Michaels. The motorcycle was still not present, at either the front of the house or the side. Was it parked around back? Or was this house, as he had speculated lately, not even where Michaels lived? Or maybe one of the cars parked on the street in front of the house belonged to Michaels, and maybe he did live here. So many maybes, and no answers.

Jesse squeezed his forehead. Patience and time would produce the answers he needed. And his need for revenge, he was sure, would sustain his ability to wait on those answers.

He was so focused on the townhouse that he was taken by surprise when a car pulled into the parking space to his left. He immediately leaned toward the glove compartment and opened it, as if searching for something. He remained that way until he heard the car door slam and heard the clicking of high heels moving away. He chided himself—he had to be more careful. When he sat up, he hunkered in the seat to create a smaller profile.

At around 8:00 AM, his senses were pinged by the sight of two men, one in a business suit and the other in jeans and a T-shirt, park on the street and climb the steps to the front door of the townhouse. The man in the suit had a key and unlocked the door. Jesse watched for forty-five minutes as the men appeared and disappeared—on the porch, at a ground-floor window, at a second-floor window, outside in the yard—as if they were inspecting the place.

Why would they...? Wait—could the place be empty? For sale?

* * *

Two days later, Jesse decided that he'd spent far too many hours watching in vain from the parking lot when a moving van pulled up in front of the house. Two uniformed men unloaded the truck and toted cardboard boxes and furniture inside.

Maybe, Jesse mused, Michaels was in the process of actually moving into the house. Sure—it was possible. Maybe he had stopped by the place last Friday night to take measurements, or check the color of the walls, or examine one of the appliances, or do a host of other things that a soon-to-be tenant might need to do before moving into a new house.

Jesse's hopes were dashed a few minutes later, though, when he saw two twenty-something women arrive at the address and carry in tons of female clothing.

He watched the place for three more days until he detected definite routines. The girls and only the girls lived there.

He was now totally confused. On the Friday night that he had trailed Michaels, had he somehow wrongly identified the parked motorcycle at the side of the house? He replayed the night in his head again and again. No, he was certain he hadn't misidentified Michaels, the motorcycle, or the house.

Desperate, he retreated to his hotel room and searched the Net again, as he had done the three previous days, for any new magazine, newspaper, or website articles about Michaels that might hand him a new puzzle piece. This time, the search paid off. After hours of probing, he came across a blog, buried deep in the Cole Michaels website listings, written by a man claiming to be the keyboard player at the comeback concert. A paragraph in the blog said:

> At our dress rehearsal on the afternoon of the concert, I overheard Cole tell a brokenhearted love interest that he was sorry for the hurt he was causing by walking away from their relationship, by walking away from his partnership with SpiritMark, by walking away from his tour, and by walking away from his career. Yes, his career. I heard the woman say, "I still can't

believe you're leaving. Neither can anyone else." I have not tried to verify this—and neither have I seen it officially verified anywhere else—but I believe that Cole, for some reason, is indeed calling it quits and that he's leaving Music City. I don't know what would provoke a star with such potential to just walk away from the stage and the cameras, but this truly seems to be the case. Maybe it's somehow related to his criminal past. One can only assume, though, that Cole Michaels must have a monumental reason, if this is indeed what he's decided to do.

Jesse stared at the laptop screen. *Walking away from his career. Calling it quits. Leaving Music City.* Jesse finished the article but found no additional clues. He threw the pillow across the room. He pounded the wall. Was it true? Had Cole Michaels packed his bags and left the city? Had he, Jesse Rainwater, somehow missed his target by only eight hours? The mere thought was freaking unbelievable. He threw another pillow.

Now what could he do?

On Monday morning, he called the corporate office of SpiritMark from an outdoor pay phone. "Hello," he said, trying to squelch his anger. "My name is Kit. I'm from

Birmingham, Alabama. I'm the venue coordinator for the Jamboree Festival that our city hosts every year in October. I'm just passing through your area and I wanted to get in touch with the manager for Cole Michaels and find out what it would take to get Mister Michaels to come to Birmingham and be one of our key performers this year."

"I'm sorry, but Mister Michaels isn't booking any more appearances this year," a young female voice responded. "Is there any other way I can help you today?"

A scripted brush-off. If the rumor of Cole's walkout was true, then the receptionists would be coached to give just that kind of terse response. "Is there any way I can negotiate directly with the manager and see if there could be an exception?"

"Hold please."

Jesse waited on hold for a minute or more.

"Hello, can I help you?" a male voice finally picked up.

"Yes, I was just asking if I could be put in touch with Cole Michaels' booking manager. I would like to discuss the possibility of booking Mister Michaels for a performance in Birmingham, Alabama, at our Jamboree Festival in October."

"I'm afraid Mister Michaels has just begun a self-imposed hiatus for an unspecified amount of time, so no booking is being done for him right now. But if you'll call back in six months or so, we can let you know at that time if there have been any changes."

Jesse took a risk. "Is there any way I can speak with Mister Michaels directly?"

"I'm sorry, sir. Mister Michaels isn't accepting any calls

at this time. But if you'd like to write a letter to him and mail it to our office, we'll make sure it gets into his mail stack."

"All right, thanks for your help." Jesse hung up. He went back to his car and fumed. Obviously, the rumor was true. Cole Michaels had indeed stepped away from the entertainment business. The question now was, *Was he still living in Nashville?*

Jesse, however, wanted to resolve one other bit of curiosity. He bought a cheap suit and tie, changed into it, then ate an early lunch and drove back to the parking lot across the street from the townhouse. He already knew that the newest residents were gone during the day and didn't return until about 5:00 PM. The postman, he had observed, normally delivered mail to the address between 1:00 and 2:00 PM.

He waited in his parked car until around 1:15, when the mail carrier dropped a handful of mail into the mailbox at the porch. As soon as the mailman moved on, Jesse drove his car out of the parking lot and parked around the corner, out of sight of the commercial buildings. He walked straight to the townhouse, hoping anyone watching would mistake him for the man in the suit who had gone into the house a week ago. He climbed the steps to the front porch and lifted the mailbox lid. He withdrew the bundle of mail. He sifted through it—one of the envelopes was addressed to Cole Michaels at this address. Jesse returned the stack of mail to the box and casually returned to his car. At least he now knew: Cole Michaels had indeed lived at the townhouse and had now apparently moved elsewhere.

But where? If the man was still residing in or around Nashville, Jesse might be able to uncover the new address. But if he had left Nashville, as the Internet blog had implied, then how could he be tracked down?

Jesse checked into a different hotel. He took a hot shower, occasionally pounding his fist against the tiles and growling to himself and to fate. He tried to think. Surely, someone at the SpiritMark company knew Michaels' exact whereabouts. Jesse could probably befriend one of the SpiritMark employees and tactfully extract the information from him. But that employee might remember him and his inquiries when Michaels' death became a headline. Jesse's description would surely be submitted to the police as a possible suspect. And that was too risky.

One more idea emerged, though.

In less than two hours, he was dressed again in his suit and sitting in his car fifty yards down the curb from the SpiritMark office. He watched for at least an hour. Only a few people entered and exited the building. He hoped that he might see Michaels, so that he could trail him again. But he had no such luck.

After sixty minutes, Jesse began to feel vulnerable. There were just too many people on the busy street. He knew someone could, and would, notice him if he loitered much longer. So he left.

But he returned the next two days, at different times of the day, and lingered for an hour each time. He hoped against hope that he would spot his target. But Michaels didn't appear.

Furious, Jesse returned to Atlanta.

* * *

Jesse constantly trolled the Internet for new Cole Michaels clues. Two weeks after his return to Atlanta, he found a report on the website of a pop-industry online magazine. The headline and paragraph that snagged his attention read:

Blonde Fiddler Leaves
Fans Feeling Abandoned

Cole Michaels' promised comeback has produced the *Oasis Blues* CD that is climbing the charts faster than a quick-burning fuse. His comeback concert in Nashville on Friday, April 11, truly reintroduced the world to a one-in-a-million singer, songwriter, and musician. And his fans want more. They want him; they want a live tour. Michaels, though, to the surprise of his SpiritMark label, abruptly abandoned plans for a concert tour, along with any interviews or celebrity appearances. According to inside sources, the "Blonde Fiddler" has stepped down indefinitely from his career as a professional musician and has chosen a life of

living on the road as a motorcycle
drifter. This decision has left a lot
of fans who had hoped for a real
honest-to-goodness comeback feeling cheated.

Jesse read the paragraph, along with the rest of the
article, several times, but not a word hinted at where Cole,
geographically, might be found.

Just drifting? My God—if that was true, the man could
be anywhere in North America, or even South America!

For days afterward, Jesse found himself feeling empty
and unshakably depressed. He tried to fight his demons
with alcohol and with a renewed effort to succeed in the
human trafficking trade.

*   *   *

In less than two months, Svetlana—at Jesse's urging—
flew into Atlanta. At the airport, the Cory-had-an-accident-
and-Uncle-Mike-is-here-to-take-you-to-the-house scheme
was repeated, with equal success. Jesse held another duffel
containing $20,000 as he watched Svetlana, with a look of
sudden uncertainty, whisked away in the black truck and
into the unknown.

That same night, Jesse tasted the rush of self-mutilation
for the first time. Ignoring copious amounts of blood, he
carved a skull into the soft tissue of his upper thigh. He
later gloated in front of the mirror, admiring both the knife

job *and* the twenty extra pounds the steroids had recently packed on.

When Svetlana's buyer left a message a few weeks later saying he was ready for a third girl, Jesse upped his price to $30,000 per girl. The unseen buyer reluctantly agreed.

Jesse, full of dour revulsion for everyone, picked up his pace of establishing online contact with new Russian and East European girls.

PART 3

60

Four Months Later
August 2008

On an unusually warm New England afternoon, Cole registered for two nights at a hotel in Gorham, New Hampshire, ten minutes from Mt. Washington. When he checked into his room, he stretched out across the bed and tallied the number of nights he had slept in a hotel bed since leaving Nashville. Only ten, at the most. On all the other nights, he had slept either in his tent or in a campground cabin.

He pulled back the bed covers and sniffed the fresh sheets and pillows. What a treat! For added pleasure, he filled the bathtub and soaked in hot steamy water for nearly an hour.

He relaxed and reminisced.

During the past four months, he had logged a little over 8,000 miles on the Triumph. He had traveled the entire span of the Blueridge Parkway and Virginia Skyline, with scores of three-to-four-day stops along the way. He had bisected Maryland, Pennsylvania, New York, and

Massachusetts. And he had ridden the coastal roads of Maine.

His journey had already been filled with enough unusual experiences to fill a full-length adventure documentary.

In Spruce Pine, North Carolina, he had stopped to help a ninety-year-old widower cut two acres of grass and ended up staying for four days to help reattach a falling gutter, seal a wooden deck, and paint the outside of the two-bedroom cinderblock house.

In Crossnore, North Carolina, he had visited a faith-based orphanage that he learned about from a road sign. A group of thirteen men from Tennessee were on campus volunteering their labor to renovate bathrooms and erect a greenhouse. Cole joined the men for two days, until their work was finished. In the process, he lost his heart to several of the small children. Before he said goodbye, he wrote a $25,000 check and gave it to the finance office. Two days before his visit to the orphanage, he had on impulse while feeling nostalgic, called Roland at SpiritMark to see how Lindsey was doing. After hearing that Lindsey was still moping, he heard Roland say, "Well, have you had your fill of living by the seat of your pants—are you about ready to come in and salvage your career?"

"Are you kidding? I'm having the time of my life out here," he'd replied.

"Well, I almost hate to tell you this, because it'll probably just add to your lunacy. But we've just deposited $250,000 worth of royalties into your account. Over two hundred thousand copies of your CD have already sold." When Cole hung up, he vowed that he would remain true to his original plan, and give away most of his money. The first big donation had been to the orphanage.

In Glendale Springs, North Carolina, he had given a $5,000 Saturday morning breakfast tip to a sixty-eight-year-old grandmother who was still in the work force, waiting tables at a chain restaurant for $2.75 an hour plus tips.

In Meadows-Of-Dan, Virginia, he had stopped on impulse to help two exhausted elderly women who were trying to dig up shrubbery roots along the edge of a driveway. Not satisfied with the cracked hoe the ladies were using, he went next door to borrow a sturdy mattock and a shovel. The neighbor who loaned the tools spontaneously decided to join the project. Soon another neighbor joined in, and another, and another. The whole group then helped the ladies trim all of the shrubs that surrounded the house, remove dead limbs from several huge trees, and fix a roadside mailbox that was falling over. Responding to an over-the-phone tip, a journalist for the county's small-time newspaper showed up, took photographs, and wrote a human-interest article about the kind stranger on a motorcycle who rode into town and sparked a neighborhood rally to help two old spinsters.

In Waynesboro, Virginia, he had joined a large volunteer group in the construction of a house sponsored by an international nonprofit organization. The new house was presented at a 60% discount to an underprivileged family that had lost their original home, and all their belongings, to a flood. Cole befriended the family's only two children, eleven-year-old twin boys. He even gave the two boys a few motorcycle rides. The father of the home was an uneducated mill worker who had worked hard all his life. At the end of the build, Cole gave the man a check for $45,000 to pay off the balance of the mortgage. He had never seen such a crusty old character break down and cry so much.

In the middle of a torrential downpour along a stretch of interstate in Pennsylvania, he had nearly lost control of his motorcycle at 65 mph when the back tire picked up a screw and lost air like a cheap party balloon. He barely managed to keep the bike upright as it twisted, shook, and wrestled its way to a full stop in the emergency lane. He stood trembling on the edge of the highway, in the rain and 30-mph gusts of wind, and stuck out his thumb to hitchhike. An African American construction worker in a pickup truck, pulling a trailer loaded with a miniature bulldozer, stopped and came to his rescue. The man jumped out in the rain and helped Cole roll the bike up onto the trailer behind the bulldozer and transported him and the bike to a motorcycle shop in the next town, forty miles away. Cole took the man's phone number and arranged three days later to take the man and his wife out to a steak dinner at a high-end restaurant.

In a gas station parking lot outside Boston during the evening hours of the summer solstice, he had found himself gawking at a man yelling at a woman and a little girl. When the out-of-control man began wildly slapping and shoving the pair, Cole ran over and stood between him and the woman and girl, who turned out to be the man's wife and daughter. When the man threatened him and began to swing, Cole wrestled him to the concrete and held him there until the police arrived. Because there were several eyewitnesses, the wife beater was taken into custody and Cole was allowed to go. He did, however, have to give his name and answer some questions for a police report. When the police realized he was Cole Michaels the celebrity, a buzz swept through the crowd. It took him thirty minutes to pry himself from the autograph seekers and wannabe music stars.

In Boothbay Harbor, Maine, he had sat out on a dock overlooking the mighty Atlantic one afternoon and played some old Celtic melodies on his violin. A middle-aged couple sat nearby and listened for nearly an hour. The couple introduced themselves as Ray and Fay Christler. When they discovered that he was exploring the back roads and small towns of America, and that he was a Christian, they invited him to lodge with them for the night. They cooked him a gourmet seafood dinner and conversed into the late hours of the night. Ray had years ago served jail time for being the leader of a drug cartel in the US Virgin islands, and after his release had met Fay at a nightclub where she performed as a guitarist and singer. They moved in together and, as two wrecked individuals, quickly made a mutual descent into extreme alcoholism. Afterward, Ray reached a low point in his addiction when he decided that suicide was his only means of escape. He was puking in an alley one night and planning his death when he had an encounter with God. His life was immediately transformed. His changed heart eventually influenced Fay to seek and find God on her own. Her life too was redeemed. From then on, Fay fell in love with God and shifted her focus from singing nightclub music to writing and singing songs about the unfathomable love of God. Cole asked if he could hear one of her songs. Fay obliged. Cole wept through it, and revealing his identity as an industry star, asked her to sing a half-dozen more. Cole was so moved by her lyrics, her voice, and her style of guitar playing that the next morning he called Roland Powers at SpiritMark and helped set up an appointment for Fay to travel to Nashville and audition for the company. While they were on the phone, Roland told him that his CD had gone gold and that an additional $400,000 had been deposited into his bank account.

Stretched out in the tub, Cole smiled. He considered his collection of experiences, though, to be worth far more than the money now in his bank account. The experiences were priceless, even irreplaceable. He whispered a prayer of thanks for the awesome four months.

His plans for tomorrow were to ride his motorcycle to the top of Mt. Washington—the highest mountain in the Northeastern United States—and add another adventure to his list. Two bikers at a campsite in Maine had told him, "You have to ride to the top on the auto road." Their description of the seven-and-a-half-mile climb had sounded so thrilling that he didn't want to pass up the opportunity.

Getting out of the bathtub, he felt invigoratingly fresh and unwound. He lay down on the hotel bed and switched on the television. He watched a news channel for about five minutes, but found that it just frustrated him. The news media was always the same. Watch out, here comes a terrorist group! Watch out, here comes a horde of illegal aliens! Watch out, here comes prostate cancer! A tornado! Salmonella! A killer-bee swarm! A shortage of the flu vaccine! The bankruptcy of social security! The collapse of the nation's infrastructure! Watch out! Watch out! Watch out! Be afraid! Be afraid! Be afraid!

Cole pressed the "off" button on the remote and shook his head. He thanked God that he lived free and unplugged and that he could peacefully breathe in and enjoy the moments of the day, then soundly sleep away the moments of the night. He whooped a sigh of praise and called the lobby. "Can you tell me if there's a library in town?"

Within fifteen minutes, he was at the local library browsing through a book about Mt. Washington.

* * *

After an exhilarating and unforgettable ride to the wind-blasted, 6,288-foot summit the next morning, Cole —upon completing his descent—pulled over to the side of the road just outside the Mt. Washington Park entrance.

It was still early in the day. The weather was gorgeous. He looked northward toward the hotel where he was booked for one more night, then southward toward yet-unexplored roads. He guessed from an earlier look at a state map that he could make a loop around the mountain in about three hours.

New possibilities and drifters' fantasies whispered his name.

He put the Triumph in gear and headed south.

* * *

Jesse Rainwater shoved himself away from his desk, stood, and hurled a knife at the brick wall across the room. The knife banged the wall and ricocheted across the wooden floor.

Breathing hard, he stared at the Boston newspaper article on the computer screen.

What was he supposed to do now? Drive to Massachusetts and search the highways? No point in it—Michaels was surely already long gone. Jesse snarled. The wife and child protector, the wannabe hero, would eventually have to stop drifting and land somewhere.

And when he did, the media or the blogs would eventually log another story, another record deal, another address.

Jesse took another sip of whiskey and threw the glass across the room. He picked up the desk chair and slammed it on the floor.

A few minutes later, he sat on the toilet and gave himself another steroid injection. Several weeks ago, he had begun doubling the dosage. Even though his face was now potted with acne, a side effect of steroid use Jesse had read about, he could see the reshaping of his body taking place right before his very eyes.

He had gained another fifteen pounds. And he was definitely stronger.

Online research had also warned him, though, that extended use of the anabolic aid could possibly cause mood swings and aggressive behavior.

Good. He welcomed aggression.

61

One morning in late September, Cole stepped out of a cabin in New England and saw that the gravel road leading through the campground was gently dusted with frost. The limbs of the surrounding evergreens sparkled with the icy granules.

Cole packed his bike and headed southward.

He lazily wound his way along the coast through New York City, Norfolk, the outer banks, Wilmington, Myrtle Beach, and Charleston.

In Charleston, he volunteered for two weeks at a downtown shelter for the homeless. He served in the soup kitchen, painted several interior walls, and helped do laundry. He also played his violin and shared his story in a couple of the nightly services. He left behind a check for $20,000.

When he pulled out of Charleston, he chose to head inland for a change. For most of his life, he had heard about the Natchez Trace Parkway that ran 444 miles from Nashville, Tennessee to Natchez, Mississippi. He had only explored the northern tip of the parkway, and that had been years ago. He decided that he would like to cover the parkway in its entirety. It would be an easy ride, with beautiful autumn colors lining the paved corridor.

He pointed the bike toward Nashville.

*   *   *

Cole arrived in Nashville on a Tuesday afternoon and checked into a three-star hotel. Being back in Nashville was an awkward experience for him. The familiar surroundings somehow made his several months on the road seem almost like a dream.

Before he turned in for the night, he rode past his former townhouse and the SpiritMark office, just to convince himself he hadn't been dreaming.

The next morning, he stopped at SpiritMark to pick up any mail being held for him. He tried to slip into the building unobserved, but a commotion erupted when the new receptionist announced his arrival to Roland Powers. Word spread quickly —"Cole is here." All those who knew him stopped what they were doing and gathered around him in the front office. Cole noticed, though, that Lindsey wasn't among them.

Questions and comments flowed one after the other for about fifteen minutes. "How are you doing?" "You look great." "Where all have you been?" "Congratulations on the CD; it looks like it's going platinum." "Have you come back to stay?" "If you'd let us, we could schedule twenty or thirty interviews for you by tomorrow." "Oh, by the way, you have a ton of new fan mail."

Cole patiently responded to every question and comment and explained that he was only passing through and wouldn't be giving any interviews. He did volunteer, though, to stay an extra day and type out a general response letter that could be copied and mailed to all the fans who had written personal letters. "I'll cover the cost of the mailing," he promised.

He was shocked, a little later, when he was taken to a storage room and shown bag after bag of fan mail. "There are probably twenty thousand letters here," he was told.

"Is it okay if I just sit and read a little?" he asked.

"Absolutely; go for it."

He sat on the floor and read. Most of the letters were expressions of praise for his latest music, along with enunciations of support. Some were outpourings of pain, begging him to pray and to even offer advice. A few were from musicians, with self-produced CDs enclosed, asking him to listen and to help make connections with producers in the industry.

After reading twenty or so letters, Cole stopped reading and looked at the collection of bags stuffed with cards and envelopes. He was stirred. If he had the storage space on his Scrambler, he would haul the bags around with him and read and answer every letter. He feared that a general form letter sent to the whole bunch would feel impersonal, even insensitive, but under the circumstances it would have to do. It would be better than no response at all.

He read a few more letters.

The only other mail being held for him were a few credit-card solicitations and some bank statements.

Before he left the building, he dropped by Roland's office. "I don't know if you have the time or interest," he told Roland, "but here are a few CDs that some hopeful musicians would like for you to listen to. My collection of fan mail contains quite a few of these."

"That's typical," Roland nodded. "I'll see if I can find someone to preview a few of them."

"Anyway, I'll work on the form letter and try to get it back to you later this afternoon." Cole heard the sudden awkwardness in his voice as he continued. "How is Lindsey these days?"

Roland looked up with an expression of empathy. "No one told you? She's engaged. She and her new beau are planning their wedding for sometime next year. She's in Memphis this week, meeting the guy's family."

Cole felt a landslide of loneliness unexpectedly sweep down over his heart. And he didn't know why. He was the one who'd chosen to end their romance. Had he secretly hoped that Lindsey would keep waiting for him anyway? Had he secretly thought that he might one day change his mind about marrying her? "Someone's a lucky man," he managed to say softly.

"Extremely lucky, if you ask me. And the man is lucky enough already. He's the son of a ship-building tycoon. He's thirty-eight, and if he doesn't want to, he never has to work another day in his life. The downside is, I'll probably lose my girl. I really wish you guys could have worked it out so that we could've been one big happy family right here in Music City. But—such is life."

Cole didn't know what to say. "Yeah. Such is life," he echoed.

That afternoon, in the sanctuary of his hotel room, he worked doggedly to write the text for a meaningful form letter. All the while, his thoughts were riddled with questions about Lindsey. Where had she met this new man? Was she making a rebound decision that was way too hasty? Why was she planning to marry him anyway—because of his money? Had Cole made a mistake by walking away from her? Should he have been more patient with her?

Amidst the morass of sorted thoughts and feelings, he finally managed to finish his letter. He read it one more time to make sure it covered all the necessary points.

> Dear Fans and Supporters,
> First, please forgive me for responding to your personal, heartfelt letters with a form letter. But please know that because of my personal quest to find a more substantial way to give back to humanity, I have stepped out of the entertainment business. I have chosen to live on the road and explore life like I have never known it before. Due to my constant movement, I do not have ready access to my incoming fan mail. And due to my two-

wheeled mode of transportation, I do not have the storage capacity to carry any of it around with me. But, you certainly deserve more than my silence. So I am sending out this letter to say a heartfelt "thank you" for your support of the *Oasis Blues* project and of me as a musician. I am humbled by your positive comments. And my heart goes out to everyone who has shared your personal stories of heartache and pain. It is my honest conviction, though, that each of you have the ability to make a wise and healthy choice—in any and every situation—if you will simply analyze your circumstances in the light of God's Word and allow His guidelines to determine your beliefs, reactions, and attitudes. I also wish to wholeheartedly thank the SpiritMark staff for their dedication to the *Oasis Blues* CD and for all they have done to enthusiastically promote the record. I have been blessed beyond measure by such a wonderful network of fans and associates. From my heart to yours. Sincerely, Cole Michaels

He made one final edit and submitted the letter at the SpiritMark office just minutes before closing time. He arranged for Roland to deduct the cost of the printing and postage from his next royalty check.

A sales rep who passed him in the hallway offered to take him out to dinner, but Cole turned him down. The news about Lindsey had shaken him, and he wanted to be alone.

That evening, he rode to the Middle Tennessee Correctional Facility's parking lot and to Duke Parker's gravesite. Cole was reminded once again that every decent and revolutionary thing about his current life had been birthed out of pain. Pain, like no other tool, it seemed, had the power to chisel one's heart into radical shapes.

"Thank you, Duke, for hearing my cry and not giving up on me."

He rode the few miles to Shay and Jana's burial site. He talked to Jana for a while, then shifted his attention to Shay's grave. "Well, bud, I've been on the road for quite a few months now. And every mile has been an absolute blast. I want to thank you. I probably would have never gotten a bike had we not seen all those motorcycles from the field that day, and had your eyes not lit up like they did. Anyway, I'm really learning a lot. I've learned that most Americans—even though they travel great distances in their cars—pretty much stick to the interstate system. And all they basically see en route to their destinations are the cookie-cutter exits with the same hotels, gas stations, and restaurants. It's quite a boring landscape, if you experience it that way. But on the motorcycle, I spend most of my time on back roads and secondary highways. So I've been able to experience an endless number of small towns—the wonderful mom-and-pop restaurants, the privately owned campgrounds and motels, the quaint retail shops, the colorful personalities, the steadfast churches. Plus, I've learned quite a bit about local histories. It's all given me a whole new appreciation for our country. So...I definitely owe you one."

He choked up a little. "Oh—here's a story you might like. A few weeks ago, when I was in Wilmington, I volunteered to help out at a foster home for young teens. The staff gave me permission to give all thirteen kids a ride down the street and back. For twelve of them, it was their first time on a motorcycle. I wish you could have seen their excitement. Of course, I was probably as excited as they were. I'd given rides to a few people along the way, but never to such a large group. Anyway, I noticed immediately that one of the girls was absolutely huge. The thought of putting her on the back of the bike scared the wits out of me. But I had to at least try. Well, when it was her turn, three people had to help her get on. The rear shocks completely bottomed out under her weight. Somehow, with God's help, I managed to keep the bike upright as I made the little circuit. When I returned to the campus and geared down to make the turn into the entryway, the girl screamed and started waving her hands like a wild woman. It startled me, which threw me off balance so bad that I knew if I tried to make the slow turn I'd fall over. So, I kept the bike straight and twisted the throttle. In that instant, I felt her jerk backwards. I just knew she was going over. At the last moment, though, she grabbed my shoulders and I strained with all the power I could muster to keep us from falling off. A lot of the kids, and some of the staff, saw what happened. Once I was back in the parking lot and the girl was safely off the bike, she explained that a bee had landed on her nose and that's why she had started swatting and carrying on. Someone started laughing. And before you know it, all thirteen kids were laughing so hard that some of them were rolling in the grass. It was one of the funniest moments I've ever experienced. Anyway, I thought about you after it happened. I was wishing you could have been there."

* * *

After a night of poor sleep, Cole crawled out of bed at 8:00 AM. He ate a light breakfast and rode to the Triumph dealership that had sold him the bike. It was time for some maintenance. The tires needed to be replaced, the oil and filter needed to be changed, the carburetors drained, the chain lubricated, all the fluids checked, and all the bolts and levers tightened.

"Well, now that you've ridden the bike all over tarnation," the mechanic asked as he commenced the work, "would you say that you like it more and more, less and less, or about the same?"

Cole replied without a skip. "I like everything about the bike—the weight, the engine, the handling. I can honestly say that I like it better today than I did when I first bought it. And that's saying a lot. Besides...at this point, it's part of me. We've created too many great memories together."

The mechanic just smiled and shook his head.

By 11:00 AM Cole was rolling down the Natchez Trace Parkway and saying goodbye to Nashville for a second time.

Unlike the Blue Ridge Parkway that twisted its way through the clouds and around the peaks of a sprawling mountain chain, the Natchez meandered peacefully along the forest floor and through expansive meadows. Enveloped in the Scrambler's two-cylinder rumble, Cole lost himself in the easy miles. The temperature was in the high fifties. And the brilliant autumn colors were a testament to the Almighty's artistic pizzazz. *Stunning* was the word that kept popping into Cole's head. Yet he couldn't shake the strange and lingering sense of loneliness brought on by the news about Lindsey. He tried ineffectively to dismiss her from his mind as he swept through the countryside.

62

*B*y Christmas, Cole had crossed Louisiana, Texas, New Mexico, Utah, Nevada, California, Arizona, and had entered the northern states of Mexico. His restless turmoil regarding Lindsey had kept him moving like a swarm of locusts in a feeding frenzy.

Even the news during the Christmas holidays that *Oasis Blues* had surpassed one million copies in sales and had officially gone platinum, and that an additional $650,000 had been funneled into his bank account still wasn't enough to pacify his troubled heart.

It wasn't until after the turn of the year that he finally acknowledged to himself that Lindsey was going to marry someone else. With difficulty, he gradually found an inner peace about the loss and started slowing down and sipping the road again—enjoying shorter distances and overnighting longer in the smaller towns.

And once again, he intentionally sought out child-related organizations, children's hospitals, orphanages, and families that deserved a financial boost. For three months, he carved a zigzagging path through Texas and Louisiana and gave away more than $250,000. One uneducated and impoverished mother actually fainted when he gave her a check for $50,000. And the mother's wheelchair-bound little girl almost twitched out of her chair with glee.

When he slowed down and savored the moments, he could easily visualize his two-wheeled, open-air journey as riding through a novel. Each mile presented a new page with unpredictable plot twists, colorful characters, and picturesque narratives. The evolving story was normally awe-inspiring, occasionally mundane, but always intriguing.

On a blissful Thursday afternoon in April, he entered the small town of Mountain View, Arkansas. He had already decided that the Ozark mountains in the northwestern corner of the state presented some of the best motorcycle roads he'd found to date. They were well maintained, virtually empty of traffic, and full of rollercoaster-like climbs, drops, twists, and turns. And the small towns that dotted the landscape brimmed with a special charm and hospitality that appealed to his inclination for the simple and meaningful. But the moment he approached the town square of Mountain View, he knew he'd found something exciting. Hundreds of people were in motion, many in the process of setting up craft booths, street kitchens, outdoor tables, music stages, and rows of chairs. He had descended on the preparation for an annual three-day folk festival. He decided to stay put and set up a base camp for a few days.

He pitched his tent at a nearby campground, then returned to the town square to stroll and observe. He saw instruments everywhere—guitars, fiddles, banjos, mandolins, and even a few dulcimers. Many of the instruments were in the hands of their owners. Others were propped against trees, lying on tables, or lying on blankets covering the ground. He discovered that he had just stepped into the "Folk Music Capital of the World", and that the upcoming festival would provide an endless number of public stages where amateur and professional musicians alike could freely display their skills and passion for folk music, hill music, bluegrass, and gospel. The atmosphere was already charged with anticipation—in a laid-back, *hillbilly* sort of way.

The festival officially began around dinnertime. By then, the town square and all the side streets were filled with hundreds of families. Groups of musicians—in varied combinations of young, old, male, and female—were performing in every conceivable corner of the town. They were staked out around the courthouse lawn, on street corners, in parks, on makeshift stages, on sidewalks, in private yards, on porches, and inside cafes and restaurants. Every group drew an audience. Cole had never seen, or heard, anything like it. He meandered for hours. Purchasing one snack after another from the food vendors, he grazed his way through the crowds and reveled in the celebration of music.

The next morning, he returned to the town square carrying his violin. He found an empty chair leaning against the rear wall of the courthouse. He sat down and unpacked the Mysterious Lady. He tuned the strings, then started singing and playing gospel tunes. Within ten minutes, a crowd of fifteen to twenty people were standing around him. He then sang one of his own songs from the *Oasis Blues* recording. The crowd quickly doubled in size.

"Are you Cole Michaels?" a lady asked excitedly when the song was finished.

Cole nodded.

Word of his identity spread quickly. As he continued to play, the crowd around him grew even larger.

Within half an hour, Cole was besieged by a group of four adult male fiddlers who, he discovered, were renowned musicians in their own right, in certain geographical regions. The four men, regular attenders of the annual festival, were admirers of his work. They welcomed him into their circle of friends and became his buddies for the weekend. They introduced him to other musicians. They fed him. They told him about sights worth seeing in the area. They tried, with much laughter, to hook him up with two different single ladies. They talked about the history and nuance of the festival. They played and sang together. And they became his surrogate managers as they set him up in venues around town and introduced him to the crowds for several solo performances. The three-day extravaganza slipped by in no time.

Cole logged the weekend of conversations, faces, and gigs in his treasure chest of unforgettable memories and pointed the Scrambler southward. He had now been on the road for a full year.

This has been the most fun year of my life, he told the Almighty while scooting down Highway 65. *I've finally been able to give something back. And it feels good. I would like to keep giving, helping, supporting, and encouraging, if that's okay with you. If it is, then just continue to open doors.* He extended his left hand in response to the wave of a motorcyclist speeding northward. *Even surprise me with opportunities that pull me out of my comfort zone.*

Over the next three days, he rode in torrential downpours. He finally emerged from beneath the cloud cover when he crossed into Florida. The welcomed sunlight bathed him with warmth and allowed him to relax. As he passed the first few Florida houses sitting off the road on sandy turf, he wondered what secrets of love, betrayal, and heartache the rural homes concealed. No sooner had he formed the thought than his heart skipped a beat. A gigantic cat...a bobcat...what?..burst out of the brush, clawing its way across the asphalt at an unbelievable speed right in front of him. He squeezed the bar grips with all his might. There was no time to attempt an evasive maneuver or to even brake. He screamed. And *bam!* He felt the thud. The bike shuddered from stem to stern. But he was still moving and still upright. He looked in his rearview mirror and saw the cat tumbling and spinning behind him. He slowed his speed and gasped for breath. "YES!" he blurted beneath his helmet. "I'm okay!" He rode down the road a mile or so and stopped. He dismounted and let the tension seep from his body. And then he laughed for a good minute or two. "Well, that's a story to tell," he said as he got back on the bike. "A bobcat! Unbelievable!"

Hours later, as he approached the town of Pensacola, he saw what looked like a minimum-security prison sitting on a slight rise just off the highway. A sign encased in bricks along the roadside confirmed his guess. Jolted by an idea, he turned into the parking area and stopped. He walked inside the main building and found the visitor's checkpoint. He introduced himself as a minister and asked if he could speak with the chaplain on duty.

At the chaplain's arrangement, Cole was able—every morning for the next five days—to visit with a selected inmate, an illegal alien named Emilio, who hadn't had a visitor in over three years. Cole talked through most of the first visit. For the second and third session, he led interactive conversations about hope, forgiveness, and salvation. Emilio dominated the fourth visit, sharing his story, his fears, and his loneliness. Cole prayed with him for the first time. During the final visit, Cole shared his own testimony and encouraged Emilio to forsake all other hopes and cling to Christ for redemption and wholeness. Emilio tried unsuccessfully to hold back his tears. He thanked Cole over and over for the visits and promised that he would begin reading the Scriptures for the first time in his life. When Cole left the building for the final time, he deposited $5,000 into Emilio's prison account. "Woo him, dear Jesus—change his life," Cole begged.

A few days later, following a Sunday morning visit at a large church in St. Petersburg, Cole sat with two of the church members for lunch, a Christian businessman and his partner. "The reason we wanted to treat you to lunch," the lead guy said when everyone had ordered, "is to discuss possible investment strategies with you. In the Sunday school hour, I heard you allude to the fact that when you stepped away from the entertainment business you also stepped away from the built-in support that comes with the industry—such as managers, brokers, partners, and so on." The man took a sip of water. "Did I read between the lines correctly?"

Cole smiled. "Yes, you did."

"So, you don't have any accountants or money managers in your life at this point?"

Cole smiled even broader. "None."

"Well, in that case, I'd like to encourage you to think about some new ways to invest your money. I've been in the brokerage business for twenty-seven years, and right now during this economic downturn everybody I know is looking for a way to get a healthy return on their money. If you don't mind, I'd like to—"

"Not me."

"Not you—I'm sorry?"

"I guess I'm not everybody."

"You mean you're not looking for the best investments that produce the best returns?"

"I think I'm already invested wisely."

"Can I be so forward as to ask what instruments you've invested in?"

"The poor, the needy, children's hospitals, orphanages, foster homes."

The man scratched behind his ear. "No, no—I understand the need for philanthropic interests. That's a different point. I'm talking about—"

"None of my money is invested in brokerage in-struments," Cole interrupted. "And that's really not what I'm interested in right now. To be honest, I'm currently in the process of giving my money away."

The look on the men's faces uniformly transformed to confusion and disbelief. "Giving your money away?" the lead guy echoed in a softer tone.

"Giving it away," Cole repeated.

The two men looked at Cole as if the sharpness of his mental facilities might actually be in question. "What about tax shelters, retirement funds, real-estate investments, CDs?"

Cole shook his head.

"Don't you think you would be a good steward to safeguard at least a portion of your money in some kind of strong investment program?"

Cole shook his head again. "Not really. I'm a very simple man with simple needs."

"And what happens when all your money is gone?"

"As long as I'm healthy, I'll find work that'll earn me a few bucks here and there."

"And when all your money is gone and you're not healthy?"

Cole remembered words spoken long ago by Duke Parker. He shrugged. "I'm a servant in God's household, so I don't have to worry. He takes care of his servants, even if it's with meager provisions. I'll be okay."

"And you don't think your responsibilities as a Christian steward extend farther than that?"

"True religion with contentment is great gain," Cole quoted from First Timothy chapter six. "We didn't bring anything with us when we came into the world, and we certainly cannot carry anything with us when we die. So if we have enough food and clothing, let us be content. Tell those who are rich in this world not to be proud and not to trust in their money. Tell them to use their money to do good. They should be rich in good works and should give generously to those in need. By doing this they will be storing up their treasure as a good foundation for the future."

The two Christian businessmen raised their eyebrows at each other. This rich celebrity was obviously a religious fanatic, maybe even a borderline nut case. Not a potential client, at least not today.

They rushed through the rest of the mealtime.

*   *   *

"My name is Kit," Jesse said. "I'm the program director for the Jamboree Festival in Birmingham, Alabama. I called last year at this time to try to book Cole Michaels for an October performance. I was told that he was on a self-imposed hiatus for an indefinite period of time and that I should call back at a later date. So, that's what I'm doing. Can you tell me if he's back in town and if he's accepting bookings these days?"

"I'm sorry, sir," the SpiritMark receptionist told him. "Mister Michaels is still on our inactive list. I wish he wasn't. We could definitely keep him busy. I don't know what else to tell you, except to maybe call back again sometime."

When Jesse hung up, he punched the plastic panel in the phone booth so hard that the plastic splintered. He felt something break inside his hand.

"Damn everybody to hell!" he screamed.

* * *

On an isolated plot of land near Florida's west coast, Cole spent two hours one afternoon hustling, spinning, and sliding the bike through twenty acres of loose sand. He was still dazzled by the bike's agility off pavement. The daring foray into off-road antics made him feel like an action hero in an adventure movie—like both a manly man and a fearless kid. The grin in his soul far outsized the grin on his face. The adrenaline-filled afternoon was fun to the max.

Two weeks later in Key West, he volunteered—as a result of a chance meeting with a group of chatty church folks in a downtown cafe—to teach kids in a week-long vacation Bible school, along with nine other teachers. He was asked to teach both a music class and a Bible class.

During the five-day event, he excitedly taught fourth and fifth graders. For his Bible lessons, he chose to teach on the subject of Christlike character. He emphasized the nearly forgotten characteristics of kindness, generosity, forgiveness, sacrifice, and faith. There were seventeen kids in the Bible class. At the end of the week, two unchurched boys in the class chose to become followers of Jesus. Cole bought them each a leather-bound Bible and gave them pointers on savoring and digesting its pages.

He was on a spiritual high for days afterward.

One evening, as he was searching for a particular campground in the Orlando area, he rode past a church sign that piqued his attention. The words on the roadside marquee read: *All motorcyclists welcome to join our first annual motorcycle mission adventure. Call for details.* Cole made a mental note of the church's name and location. He also made a mental note of the pastor's name—Jason Faircloth.

A motorcycle mission adventure. He would call. He was definitely interested.

63

The Sunday morning church service was well under way when Cole entered the auditorium. He had decided to collect the information about the motorcycle adventure in person.

He hadn't intended to be late, but he had witnessed a traffic accident involving a pickup and an SUV and had stopped to help out at the scene until the police arrived. Fortunately, no one in either vehicle had been seriously injured—just shaken up.

Once inside the sanctuary Cole slipped quietly into a seat on the last row and tried to be as invisible as possible.

A man was singing a solo on the platform. Cole was unfamiliar with the song. He looked around. The ambiance was a little disappointing. The sanctuary could easily accommodate six hundred people. Yet there were no more than a hundred present. And they were scattered like tossed grass seed. Everything felt a little too stodgy, a little too cold and lifeless. *And this is the group that's going to coordinate a motorcycle mission adventure?*

Should he just leave?

When the soloist finished, another man approached the microphone. "Thank you, Sid," the man said. "All right, as most of you know, it's no secret that Genesis Bible Church has been struggling for quite some time. We're just excited that we now have a seasoned pastor who's going to give us a couple of years of his life to try to help us become a healthy church again." The man led the congregation in a quick round of applause and motioned for the new pastor to take over the mic. "Jason Faircloth," he beckoned.

A man rose from one of the front pews and ascended the steps to the platform. When the man reached the microphone and faced the people, he stared out at the audience in silence, as if trying to connect one-on-one with everyone in the room. From Cole's back-row perspective, the man looked to be beyond retirement age. He had to be at least in his late seventies. Yet, there was something austere and powerful about him. The power did not reside in his elderly physique. Rather, it radiated from his inner presence. His white hair was unusually long. And he wore a white, neatly trimmed beard. To Cole, the man looked like an unorthodox philosopher with the collective approval of ages past. He looked seriously wise, even without saying a word.

"There is nothing more beautiful," the old man eventually said, "than a healthy church where one witnesses the constant reproduction of converts, disciples, teachers, preachers, pastors, missionaries, and other churches. On the other hand..." The man paused at length to arrest everyone's attention. "...there is nothing on the planet more disappointing, disheartening, and disillusioning than a diseased church where one witnesses only sterility and impotency. This is only my third Sunday with you, and I'm truly honored to be here, but it's time that we go ahead and place a fact openly on the table. The average church in America is sterile and impotent. In the last ten years alone, hundreds of thousands of Americans have permanently given up on the local, organized church as they know it. I'm talking about people who for decades tirelessly invested their time, money, and energy in their churches. Why? Why have they walked away? Shall we talk about it?" Jason actually waited until he saw a stream of consenting nods.

"Okay," he continued. "But before we do, let's reduce the level of formality and create an atmosphere that will help us relax. We learn in James chapter two; verse three, and in Acts chapter twenty, verses eight and nine, that in the New Testament culture, the church gatherings were more family oriented than what we normally allow. We see in these verses, for example, that when they met together, some of them sat in chairs, some of them stood, some sat on the floor, and some even sat on the window sills. They simply made themselves comfortable. So, if you don't mind, I would like for us to take that approach this morning. I know this is out of the ordinary, but I would like for our experience today to be different than what you've grown accustomed to. So at this time, I'd like to ask everyone to please come to the front and cluster around the platform. Feel free to sit on a pew, sit on the floor, sit on the steps, sit on the platform, or sit against the wall. Feel free to stand, lie down, or kneel."

Pastor Faircloth waited.

Six or seven people immediately stood and headed toward the platform, as if ready to try something new. Others hesitated, as if not so sure. But slowly, across the auditorium, there was a gradual progression of people toward the front.

That's a cool move—I like it, Cole thought, gazing at the man behind the mic. He gladly joined the procession toward the front. As a visitor, he didn't want to assume intimacy, so he sat on the floor at the outer periphery of the congregants.

Within three or four minutes, a hundred people covered the down-front area like vagabonds bunched up around a fireplace. They were sitting, reclining, lying, standing, and kneeling. The floor was covered, as well as the pews. The seating configuration seemed to transform the crowd from a stale, passive audience to an engaged, expectant family.

"Thank you," Jason said kindly. "Now, let's establish a few respectful guidelines. I would like for our discussion to be interactive. So, number one—let's invite only one person at a time to speak. Number two, you're welcome to whisper among yourselves as long as your conversations pertain to our topic. And number three, if there is a long silence between a question and an answer, let's just relax and let it be. Silence is okay."

Jason lifted his eyebrows and opened his palms as a solicitation for agreement.

A host of people bobbed their heads.

"All right," Jason proceeded. "So, why is the average church in America sick? Any input?"

A lady sitting on the front pew raised her hand.

"Yes," Jason said.

"The preaching has become too one-sided. Instead of teaching the whole counsel of God, a lot of preachers just harp on money all the time."

A man sitting on the platform steps punched his hand into the air.

Jason acknowledged him.

"Or they spend too much time building their sermons around the *milk* of the Word when they should be focusing on the *meat*."

Another hand. "And they use the church as a bully pulpit to push their own personal agendas down people's throats."

An additional hand. "Plus, they normally don't preach hard truths anymore. They don't want to offend the unchurched seekers. Honestly, they've become too politically correct, too easy, too soft. I mean, when is the last time you heard a sermon on hell?"

Jason retook the lead. "Okay, who else in the room believes that church leaders are at the core of many of the church's problems?"

Probably sixty percent of the men and women hoisted their hands.

Cole raised his hand as well. He actually wanted to speak up and tell about the arrogant pastor in Nashville who had led him to develop an erroneous understanding of God that became a faith-shattering crucible. But he held his tongue and just listened.

Jason hung his head as if carefully measuring his next words. "I want to give you several reasons," he finally said, "why at least a good portion of the church's disabilities can indeed be traced back to its leaders."

The group hung on his words.

Jason lifted the microphone from its holder. "First, and perhaps paramount, is the fact that pastors in general tend to be very poor listeners. They assume that because of their theology degrees and higher calling that no one else in the church can match their understanding of theology, churchology, or methodology. It seems that all too often they turn a deaf ear to constructive criticism. They resist correction as adamantly as preadolescent schoolboys resist a bath. I would honestly guess that fewer than ten out of every one-thousand pastors have ever even exercised the forethought to go to their congregations and proactively ask what they can do, or stop doing, to become more effective leaders, and to do so with the honest intent of listening and making personal changes."

Jason nodded toward a man who had raised his hand.

The guy volleyed. "Sadly, I think this is exactly what a lot of people are realizing, but—for some reason—are afraid to talk about. I know of another congregation right now, for example, that's having a serious issue with their pastor. They've tried several times to bring it to his attention, but the man—as you say—just outright refuses to listen, or even acknowledge that he might in any way be at fault."

Jason pulled a chair to the edge of the platform and sat down. "Unfortunately, this is why so many pastors around the country find themselves in contention with a good portion of their congregations. The congregations try desperately to communicate with their pastors. But instead of listening and cultivating a spirit that is subject to correction, the pastors defend their positions and justify their decisions. Then they blame everybody else if their agendas lead to failure or hurt, and then lash out at their critics and accuse them of being divisive. But, in truth, it's usually the pastors' childish pride that is the cause of the divisiveness."

"Does God address this issue anywhere in the Bible?" an older woman asked with a hint of despair.

Jason snapped his fingers softly and pointed back to the woman. "Thank you for driving us to the Scriptures. And yes, God does address the issue of our attitude toward correction. So, let's hear what He says. Turn to the Old Testament book of Proverbs. And by the way, I personally had to learn these verses the hard way. For many years, until I lost everything that was precious to me, I was one of those pastors who thought he knew it all." Jason then gave those who had brought their Bibles a moment to find Proverbs, then he continued. "God makes it clear in the verses we're about to read that if a man characteristically refuses correction, he is a fool who will produce chaos and death. But if a man will allow himself to be corrected, he is a wise individual who will produce peace and life."

A young man interrupted with an up-stretched hand.

"All right," Jason said

"If God makes it so clear, as you say, that those who refuse correction are fools, then does that imply that most of our churches are led by fools?"

A moment of uneasiness filled the hall.

Cole was mildly shocked by the questioner's candor. Surely, these people must have been mutually victimized by a formerly abusive pastor. Cole looked to see how Jason would respond.

Jason didn't flinch. He hung his head and squeezed the bridge of his nose. When he looked up, his countenance was that of a sympathetic shepherd. "Tonight I will simply let the Spirit of God speak through His Word. So here are the verses. Chapter ten, verse seventeen. Chapter twelve, verse one. Chapter thirteen, verse eighteen. And chapter fifteen, verse thirty-one." Once again, Jason gave the people a moment of stillness, this time to write down the references.

Cole grinned. He liked the old man. He liked his appearance. His words. His savvy. Cole zestfully turned to the first few verses, marking pages with his fingers.

When everyone was ready, Jason turned with the people to the first verse. He read the words with reverence, and followed suit with the remaining verses.

He then led the way as all the verses were examined and discussed over a thirty-minute stretch.

At the completion of the study, Cole was invigorated. He hoped everyone else felt the same. Personally, he had not experienced a shared Bible study so enjoyable and thought-provoking since his days with the chaplain. He felt that God's Word had once again irrigated his soul. Cole definitely wanted to meet this Jason fellow and talk with him one-on-one.

Before offering a benediction, Jason announced to the congregation that over the next three weeks they would explore additional reasons why pastors carried a significant share of the fault for the church's ill state of health.

In spite of the tough subject matter, Cole saw an undeniable meekness in the old man.

"By the way," Jason wrapped up, "because of the church's poor condition overall, I predict that within fifteen years, you will see hundreds of church properties all over this country sold and used for community centers, art galleries, fitness studios, night clubs, flea markets, entertainment venues, and a host of other purposes. And your spiritual stamina will be tested. But if you understand *why* this is happening, then hopefully you will understand how to help sustain the offshoot remnants that will rise up and fight for their lives."

Jason bowed his head and shut his eyes. "Our father, during the next two years, help me be a good listener, subject to correction. And please give me the moxie to model for these people what a healthy church leader should look like, and may this church become a place of potency where dynamic reproduction becomes an everyday occurrence."

As the people dispersed, gravitating into groups of conversation, Cole sensed that the dark, low-hanging clouds of pessimism and weariness that he felt when he first entered the place had temporarily lifted. The old leader's transparent heart and bold voice had apparently just created a spark of hope.

Cole jostled his way through the intermingling crowd and made his way to the edge of the platform. He wanted to thank Jason personally for his gritty analysis of church leadership and his spirited resolve to be a more desirable breed of pastor. He waited for nine or ten other people to exchange words with the man, then he walked up on the platform and extended his hand.

"My name is Cole," he announced with a handshake. "I'm a visitor, just passing through the city, and was drawn to the meeting by the posting on the marquee about the motorcycle missions trip. But I wanted to let you know that I was touched deeply this morning by what you said and how you said it."

The man's soothing smile and piercing eyes conveyed a genuine desire to connect. "I'm just curious," he said, "what led to your brokenness?"

Cole was mildly shocked by the bizarre question, which, oddly, didn't seem to cross any boundary of privacy. "I...uh...yes, I was broken, as you say. But that was...over thirteen years ago. How could you possibly know?"

The man looked him in the eye with an uncanny glimmer of grace. "You still carry the mark."

Cole chuckled. "I guess I'm not sure what that mark is."

"The mark," Jason mused. "It's a capable person with a distinct aura of deep humility and atypical gratitude. It comes through in the eyes, the demeanor, the tone of voice, the choice of words, the physical stance."

"Interesting. That's something similar to what a former girlfriend once told me," Cole said.

Jason smiled.

"You know," Cole said, "I think I honestly see the same thing in you."

Jason patted Cole's shoulder. "What are your plans for lunch?"

It was another unexpected question. Cole shrugged. "Uh...I'm free."

"Can I take you out to eat?"

"Sure—as long as I can pick up the check."

Within the hour, the two men were sitting at a small table in a nearby deli.

64

"Why did today's discussion impact you so deeply?" Jason asked as they bit into their sandwiches. "Is it because you were hurt by a church leader somewhere along the way?"

Cole considered carefully before answering. "*Misled* is a more accurate description." He took several minutes, at Jason's encouragement, and told the story of the Nashville pastor who had immersed him as a new believer into the "American Dream" gospel. He described the family catastrophes that soon followed and how his misunderstanding of God, as a result of those catastrophes, created a bitterness in his heart that ate away at him for more than a year. He told how Chaplain Duke Parker spiritually rescued him. "I'm not the most experienced churchgoer," he said. "But many of the churches I've attended over the last year and a half have been led by men who were less than energizing. So in light of my own experiences, and in the light of what you said this morning, I'm reminded of just how exceptional Duke Parker was as a mentor. I probably need to thank God for the man all over again."

"You were blessed far more than you can imagine."

"And what about you? How were you broken?"

Jason lowered his half-eaten sandwich to the plate. He spoke slowly. "I'll just say that at one time I was a very blind and very mean pastor. I, myself, misled a lot of people. More than I or anyone will ever know. At the time, though, I would never have considered, not for a single moment, that I was possibly at fault—not until I drove both my wife and my daughter to their deaths. It sounds very similar to the losses you experienced. Anyway, my world fell apart. Along with my faith. And just as God used a chaplain to salvage your life, He used an old Burmese pastor in Oslo, Norway, to salvage mine." Jason paused. "It was during that time when I realized that church leaders who practice true biblical mentoring are as rare as gold dust." Jason picked up his sandwich again. "So, you dropped by this morning to find out about the motorcycle mission trip?"

Cole's thoughts stumbled at the mental jump. "I did, but if you don't mind, I'd like to hear the rest of your story."

Jason nodded. "Let me go ahead and tell you about the motorcycle adventure. And perhaps I can share my story at another time."

As they finished their sandwiches, Cole learned that the motorcycle mission trip would be in mid-August, just two months away. It would be twelve days long, would involve approximately a dozen men, would cover an estimated 1,500 miles to north Georgia and back, and would include projects such as doing minor home-repair projects for needy families, leading church services, and perhaps visiting a foster home. "Plus," Jason added, "the trip will give me the opportunity as the new pastor to get to know some of the men. We'll have a sit-down session for the group each night where I will encourage the men to open up and share their hearts."

"So you'll be going along."

Jason took the last sip of his iced tea. "Yes, I will."

"And you ride a motorcycle?" Cole asked, hearing the doubt in his own voice.

Jason's face brightened. "I was introduced to the sport of motorcycling back in 1975 on the Mediterranean island of Cyprus. I've ridden bikes on and off ever since."

"Really? I just assumed that motorcycling was somewhat off limits for pastors. You know, the hoodlum image and such. But I think that's great! What kind of bike do you ride?"

"A 1996 Suzuki Intruder 1400. She's a wonderful old machine."

Cole laughed on the inside when he heard Jason refer to the bike as a *she*, as if it were an animate object. But he understood; it was a biker thing. Cole felt that he had found a kindred spirit. Besides, since his release from prison, he had not met a single pastor or church leader who touched his heart and mind like the chaplain. Not until now. The old man looked and sounded as if he had walked countless days in the shadow of the Almighty's tutelage. A man of authentic faith, deep wisdom, and obvious love. Someone very special. Cole felt his heart being drawn to the old disciple. "I'd like to join you guys, if it's okay," he said.

* * *

Cole continued to rent a cabin at the Orlando campground, thinking he would stay in the area until the motorcycle mission trip. But the cloudless skies and unbearable summer heat conspired against him. When he was inside air-conditioned buildings, he could manage. But when he was riding and suited up in his helmet and black jacket, he was pushed to the limits of discomfort.

He was pinged by conflicting desires. He wanted to load the Scrambler and head northward to cooler States. Yet, he also wanted to hang around. Pastor Faircloth, with his engaging and transparent style of leadership, had won his admiration and interest. The man's recent Bible studies on "Disciple Making and How Pastors Seldom Get Around To It" and "The Uniqueness of Each Congregation and How Pastors Need To Work With That Uniqueness" had been masterpieces of Biblical insight and group interaction. According to the attendees, the elderly teacher had been able to clearly define what they had abstractly thought but had never been able to put into words. Cole had never seen so many people in one group delving into the Scriptures with such keen fascination. He was captivated by what was unfolding under Jason's pastoral model. Plus, he had been more than entranced by his one-on-one conversations with the man during a couple of long evening strolls.

Should he leave Orlando or stay? He could always journey northward for a few weeks and then rendezvous with Jason and the men somewhere in north Georgia.

On Friday afternoon, Cole was weighing the pros and cons when he heard a car pull up outside his cabin. It was Jason.

Jason didn't get out of the vehicle. "I'm just on my way to help a couple of the motorcycle guys resolve a long-standing conflict," he explained. "But ever since hearing the full version of your story the other night, I've felt the urge to ask if you would sing and play for us on Sunday. I think your style of music will nurture the people with a sense of...what shall I say....divine peacefulness. And that's something the church definitely needs right now. If you're willing, I'll just introduce you as CJ."

Cole stared at the pastor through the open window and considered the invitation. If he obliged, he would be bound to the city for another two days. But certainly he could make that sacrifice for the endearing old church leader, couldn't he? "Sure, I can do that," he said softly.

65

Mysterious Lady in hand, Cole stepped into the Sunday morning crowd that was once again bunched around the platform at the front of the auditorium. Many were sitting on the carpeted floor. It was Cole's first time to play for an audience jammed together so closely that people could literally reach out from several directions and touch him.

He closed his eyes and laid the Mysterious Lady on his shoulder, the bow suspended above the strings. He waited for a few seconds until the whole room was quiet. He then broached the first note with a reverential push of the bow. He held his eyes closed throughout the two instrumental pieces. The last note of the second song was followed by a silence so pronounced that it was striking, intensified by a few teary sniffs.

Cole felt awash in God's overpowering presence. He then sang. In the spirit of the moment, his words seemed to be lifted to a level of grandeur by the treasured violin. Near the end of the lyrics, his voice faded into a soft, broken sob. God's goodness in his life over the last twelve years suddenly overshadowed his mind and heart—irrepressible, unquenchable, and incontestable. He folded beneath the graciousness of the Father. He moved to his knees and wept. The people around him, unfamiliar with the details of his story, supported him with touches of kinship. They too wept—for their own reasons.

The intense outflow of hushed emotion lasted for five minutes or so. A lady's voice suddenly broke through the quiet. "Forgive us, oh God!" she cried out in prayer. "We are a miserable people. We are critical. We are selfish. And we are unworthy of your consideration. And I personally stand at the bottom of the heap. Please forgive me for my disgusting attitude over the last year. I've been appalling. And I can't stand it any more." The lady burst into sobs. Then she stood and made her way through the crowd till she was face to face with one of the few remaining deacons at the church. "Forgive me, Marvin," she wept. "I've been a member of this church for so long that I've been determined to fight for every decision that I've felt was best for me. Not you. Not the leadership team. Not the congregation. I've resisted you every step of the way when you were only trying to help. I've gossiped. I've promoted disharmony. And I'm ashamed. I'm sure that some of the people who left the church last year did so because of me." She gasped. "I just can't go on like this. I want God to correct me. I want Him to teach me. I want to obey Him. Will you forgive me? Please! Will you forgive me?"

Marvin's expression revealed both his shock and his

uncertainty. He stood a good foot taller than the weeping woman.

Nearly everyone in the building was holding their breath. Cole saw Jason bow his head.

Marvin's face was a shade of angry red. He lingered in uncertain silence. The heavy quiet seemed to stretch completely around the room, near the breaking point. "Honestly, I...I..." He stopped. He took a difficult breath. "All right," he said at last. "I'll forgive you." He embraced her with a strong and lengthy hug. New tears erupted throughout the crowd. Stillness wrapped the room, except for some sniffling.

In the flow of the moment, the two motorcyclists Jason had counseled two nights earlier stood to their feet. They humbly announced their reconciliation. They publicly shook hands as a sign of their personal settlement. Additional tears flowed from the audience, even from several tough-hearted old men.

For the next hour or so, a host of other men and women followed suit and apologized for their personal offenses— and asked forgiveness. Forgiveness was granted throughout the hall, though easier for some than others.

For Cole, it all felt like a New Testament story, rare and divinely miraculous.

"As the interim pastor," Jason proceeded worshipfully, "I think I can safely say that today will be a new beginning for this congregation. Realistically, what has happened here this morning should be a normal event in church life. Unfortunately though, because of the egocentric nature of the human heart, the church seldom, if ever, witnesses such a divine obedience to God's Spirit. Therefore, I want to commend every one of you who confessed your hurtful deeds and words. And I want to thank every one of you who extended forgiveness. You have done nothing less than bring God's favor upon our church. This will—" Jason interrupted his thoughts to acknowledge a hand that had been raised. "Yes, sir?"

A man—blonde and in his late thirties—stood. "Many of you know me. My name is Steve Rove. I've served as a missionary to the street kids of Recife, Brazil, for over six years. I was ordained here at this church. I was sent out by this church. This church has been one of my biggest monthly supporters. I'm currently back in the States for an extended four-month furlough. But, like many others here at the church during the last several months when things have been disintegrating, I have seriously considered moving on and looking for a new church family. But after seeing what has happened here this morning, and after sitting under Pastor Faircloth's ministry for the last two weeks, I realize that I need to be—and that I want to be—part of our church's healing, not part of its unraveling. I say all this to say to Pastor Faircloth: I'm planning to stay put, and I want to make myself available to help in any way I can."

Someone applauded. Others joined in the gesture of affirmation.

"Will you be around during the motorcycle mission trip?" Jason asked.

Steve nodded. "Yes, I'll actually be in town during that time."

"Then will you plan to join us? I believe that this getaway in particular will be an opportune time for the men of our church to touch hearts in a unique way, to reunite as a family, and to build a mutual vision for the future of our congregation. And, as one of our missionaries, your participation, I believe, would be a real asset."

Steve pondered. "Yeah, I guess I can mark the dates on my calendar. Would there be room for me in the support vehicle? I don't have a motorcycle here in the States."

"We'll make room," Jason promised.

Cole had never met, or even seen, a foreign missionary as far as he knew. Yet, he found himself drawn to this man, Steve. Maybe it was because the guy worked with street kids, something Cole would like to hear more about. Maybe it was because Chaplain Duke Parker himself had been the child of foreign missionaries. Or maybe it was because the man chose to speak honestly from his heart and be helpful.

Cole raised his hand.

"Yes, CJ," Jason said.

Cole didn't bother to stand. "Steve, do you ride motorcycles?"

"I have a small bike in Brazil. It's actually been my main mode of transportation for the last three years. Just a 125 cc."

"If I arrange to get a bigger bike for you to use on the mission trip, would you be comfortable with that?"

Steve's surprise showed. "Uh...yeah, if I could get in a few days of practice with it before the trip, I think that would be fine."

"Then consider it done."

Steve nodded enthusiastically. "Thanks! I don't know what else to say. Just...thank you, man."

Jason wrapped up the service with a few additional words about the profundity of forgiveness, then led the group in a time of mutual prayer.

At the end of the dismissal prayer, Cole felt as if he had been immersed in the heavenlies. He wanted to remain seated and bask in the moment. Yet he also wanted to talk with the missionary. He stood and approached the man.

Within ten minutes, Cole had learned that Steve was single, that he ministered alone to over a hundred kids between the ages of two and twelve who had been abandoned by their parents, that he enjoyed his small scooter and hoped one day, when he could afford it, to replace it with a more substantial bike. While in the states, he was house-sitting for a family in Melbourne, sixty-five miles away on the Atlantic coast. Cole felt an unspoken connection with the brother, both spiritually and socially. Besides, any man who would give the best years of his life to assist needy kids had to be an exceptional individual— the kind of person Cole wanted to get to know.

As they talked, Cole led the way outside till they were standing beside the Scrambler. "Here," Cole said, placing the ignition key in Steve's hand, "Take her for a ride around the block and see if you're suited for a bigger bike."

Steve asked three or four questions about the bike, then cautiously mounted the big machine. He started the parallel twin and slowly pulled out of the parking lot. When he returned a few minutes later, his face shone with undisguised pleasure. "This is one awesome bike!" he raved. "She feels a lot lighter than I expected. And she handles like a charm." He laughed. "Well, I guess that means that I am suited for a bigger bike!"

Cole laughed with him, and they exchanged a high-five.

"The bike that you're planning to borrow for me—is it anything like this one?" Steve asked.

"Borrow?"

"Loan, rent, whatever it is that you're planning to do."

"Do you have some free time on either Tuesday or Wednesday?" Cole asked.

Steve thought. "I have an appointment on Tuesday morning. But I could be free after lunch."

"Do you think you could meet me here at the church between one and one-thirty?"

"Yeah, I think I can manage that."

"Good. I'll plan to meet you here then. Oh—by the way, I'm just curious. What kind of bigger bike have you been eyeing down in Brazil?"

"Well, there are a lot of unpaved roads in Brazil, even around the cities. So the bike I have now is a dirt bike—it's more practical, and in Brazil we're allowed to ride dirt bikes on the street. So even though I would love to have a big street bike, I'll probably end up replacing my little dirt bike with a big dirt bike. But what kind? I'm not sure. I haven't had the time or money to do any serious shopping. It will probably be a Japanese bike, though. A European bike like this one, or an American bike, would be just too tempting for the thieves. And in Brazil, there wouldn't be a lot of mechanics to work on them."

"All right. Well, since you're more experienced on a dirt bike," Cole said, "what I would like to do is arrange for you to ride a street-legal dirt bike on the August trip, one that will be big enough and powerful enough to keep up with all the street bikes. So between now and Tuesday afternoon, do some research and make a list of the three or four Japanese bikes that interest you the most. And bring the list with you on Tuesday."

66

On Tuesday afternoon, Cole was as excited, or more so, than Steve. He could barely contain his giddiness.

When they were strapped in their seats and ready to roll, Cole asked, "Did you have a chance to make a list of the big dirt bikes that pique your interest?"

Steve pulled out a sheet of paper. "I did, actually. Here's what I came up with."

Cole took the paper, which listed four models.

Kawasaki KLR650
Honda XR650 L
Suzuki DR650 SE
Suzuki V-strom 650

Cole had already scouted out the Japanese dealerships and noted their addresses. "All right, let's head over to Highway 50," he said.

When Cole pulled up to the first bike shop, he and Steve jumped out of the car, and Steve—referring to his list—said, "Are you really going to try to rent one of those bikes?"

"No, sir," Cole said. "I'm not going to try to rent one of those bikes. I'm planning to buy one of those bikes."

Steve twisted in mid-stride and stopped on the sidewalk. "Buy one? Just for a two-week road trip?"

"No, sir," Cole answered again, pausing at his friend's side. "It's going to be for longer than that. I'm actually going to buy a bike for you to take back to Brazil with you. It's going to be a personal gift from me to you."

Cole was sure at that moment that he saw Steve wrenched by a surge of emotion.

Steve finally managed to wheeze out the words, "A personal gift? To take back to Brazil?"

"Listen, I could tell you my story. And then you would understand my heart. Maybe we'll do that later. For now, I just know that foreign missionaries must be very dedicated people. And when I heard that you work with homeless kids, I knew that I wanted to help you somehow."

Steve bent over at the waist and tried to anchor his emotions again. "Yeah, but a new motorcycle? That's a lot of money! I don't want you to do anything that would become a burden to you financially. I—"

Cole raised his hand. "Trust me. It will not be a burden. Not in any sense of the word."

Overcome, Steve covered his face with both hands. "Excuse me for breaking up like this. It's just that this has totally rocked me." He removed his hands. "The only reason I'm back in the States is to try to raise additional funds for my ministry. And yet, I continue to feel guilty by being here.

I don't have anyone to fill in for me on the field while I'm away. So the longer I'm here, the longer my kids have no one to father them or care for them. I've been begging God in the last few days to show me if I should just return to Brazil without all the funding I need and trust Him to provide for me in His own way, or if I should continue to stay here until I've raised all the additional support. And then—this happens! You, a virtual stranger, offer to buy me a new motorcycle that I can use in my ministry. Whew!" Steve raked his fingers through his hair. "It looks like God has just answered my prayer. I mean, this can't be just a coincidence. I think He's just demonstrated to me in a big way that He's more than capable of providing for me—anywhere, any-time, even in the most unexpected and extraordinary way." Steve chuckled. "Nothing like this has ever happened to me before. Thank you, man! I'm...I'm just completely floored. Absolutely, totally floored."

Cole placed a hand on Steve's shoulder. "However you interpret it is between you and God. I'm just honored to help. More than you know." Cole grinned. "Someday, I really would like for you to hear my story. I think it would offer you a lot of encouragement. But first, let's go get you a bike!"

* * *

After four hours of comparative shopping at two motorcycle shops, Steve finally made his choice—a new 2009 Suzuki V-Strom 650. In person, it was one of the ugliest motorcycles Steve had ever seen, but after being persuaded by a salesman to take it for a test ride, he was smitten. Within the first hundred yards down the street, he knew it was the bike he wanted. Ergonomically, it fit him to a T. It was strong. It was light on its wheels. It was easy to balance, even across a sandy lot. And it was smooth. He also seemed influenced by a story the salesman told about a pastor friend—a Mr. RT Wadland—who lived in Calgary, Canada, and owned a 2007 model, which he had ridden from Calgary to Atlanta, Georgia, and then back to Calgary—via Arizona, a trip of 7,500 miles. The bike had never skipped a beat. Steve was also impressed to hear that the motorcycle magazines rated the bike as one of the best all-around bikes on the market.

Steve and Cole agreed—the V-Strom was an excellent pick.

To Steve's ongoing surprise, Cole added a tank bag, two saddle bags, a full-face helmet, a motorcycle jacket, leather gloves, and motorcycle boots to the purchase. And paid for everything in cash.

Steve thus became the proud owner of a gray V-Strom 650 with a lot of accessories. He had never before in his entire life owned a new vehicle.

Before they left the store, Cole even purchased insurance for him. Steve was speechless.

* * *

Cole decided, at Steve's insistence, to stay in Florida until the August mission trip and share the four-bedroom Melbourne house. The sizable abode, just one block off the beach, afforded plenty of private space, around-the-clock AC, and a welcomed nightly breeze that blew in off the Atlantic.

During the weeks leading up to the motorcycle mission adventure, Cole basked in the opulent surroundings and simply relaxed. Steve was often away meeting with pastors, mission directors, and personal supporters. But when he was at the house, the two of them meandered in and out of fascinating conversations and frequently took rides together on their motorcycles—exploring, laughing, and talking.

Steve was splendid company and a more-than-worthy conversationalist. Cole enjoyed the regular companionship for a change. As a bonus, Cole learned a great deal from Steve about foreign missions—especially about the spiritual needs of Recife, the city where Steve ministered in Brazil. He learned that the city possessed the largest population of abandoned and homeless street kids in the country, maybe in the world. And that those kids, boys and girls alike, were the regular victims of murder, rape, abuse, and human trafficking—criminal acts perpetrated typically by adult men, including members of the nation's police force. Steve described how he provided a place of refuge for many of the children in his apartment, how he met daily with as many of the little ones as possible at city parks in a staunch effort to provide food, love, and encouragement, and how he even conducted Bible studies with a select few in his home on Sunday mornings. Steve lamented that he worked without help and that he always felt hampered by his limited resources.

Cole's heart was tugged by the awful plight of these kids that he had never seen. It bothered him that they were considered a public scourge. And it disturbed him equally that Steve had no partners or associates to help in his herculean efforts with the kids and that he was constantly short of funds. He bombarded Steve with questions: Why were so many children in Recife abandoned? Was it the same in other Brazilian cities? How young were the youngest ones? Why were they preyed upon by adults? Did the city fathers have any programs to provide shelter, food, and protection for the children? Why was this more of a problem in Brazil than other countries? Were policemen truly guilty of murdering and raping these kids? Were any western countries crying out against these inhumane crimes? Were there any other missionaries in the city doing similar work? Did the churches of Recife use any of their resources to help rescue their city's children?

Cole was haunted by many of the answers. He found himself several nights praying for the children.

One morning as he and Steve shared breakfast—with the Florida sunlight beaming through the kitchen windows—he followed the urge to pray for Steve out loud. "Father, I thank You for my brother and for his willingness to do what ninety-nine percent of the church would never do. I thank You for his faith, his obedience, and his fortitude. I beg You right now to hold him in Your lap and whisper Your words of encouragement to him. He has honored You. I pray, therefore, that You will honor him. Invigorate him today with special grace, energy, vision, hope, and love. Continue to build a fire in his heart for the children of Brazil, a fire that will continue to motivate him and embolden him. Back his efforts, his voice, and his spirit with Your authority. May he sense that authority. You have called him to an elite mission. So equip him in an elite way as he soon returns to Brazil and stands against the enemy that hates him, hates his purpose, and hates his mission. Surround him here, and there, with miracles that will lift him above the mundane. Fill his days, especially on the mission field, with unforgettable adventure, with exciting contacts, and with enduring fruit. I ask this in the mighty name of Your Son. Amen."

Steve looked up teary-eyed.

Cole slid a check for $80,000 across the table. "Maybe this will help you get back to the field earlier and fulfill some of your ministry dreams."

Steve glanced at the check and shook his head as if he doubted his eyesight. He looked two more times to make sure the number was in focus. He stood, his eyes as big as golf balls. "This isn't a joke, is it?"

Cole shook his head.

Steve closed his eyes and wordlessly tried to digest what was happening. He rubbed his forehead with his palm. With his eyes still shut, he wept, "Who are you? How can you manage something like this? Why would you even volunteer to give away such an unimaginable amount. I'm not sure I'm even worthy of this kind of gift!" He sat and massaged his face. "I'm dreaming, aren't I?"

Cole began to speak. He unfolded his whole story from beginning to end, revealing his identity along the way. "I've forgiven myself," Cole said softly, "for taking the lives of the two little ones. And, of course, I know that God has forgiven me. But I find that I'm always driven to make it up to them by helping as many other young kids as I can. And I believe that my son in heaven would be pleased to the max that I'm helping you out like this."

Steve sat dazed. "You know...I thought I was speechless before. But this is...almost beyond belief. I've just discovered that I'm living with a pop star, a pop star who has given up his celebrity and career to live on the road and give all his money away to children's causes. And he gives me...a nobody...eighty thousand dollars. Eighty thousand dollars! Life doesn't get any stranger than that. I...I'm still in shock. I think you need to pinch me."

Cole offered a sober grin. "Accept it with God's blessings. Just feed, clothe, shelter, and protect as many of the boys and girls as you can."

Steve clenched his teeth and nodded. He closed his eyes for a moment, then reopened them. "I know this sounds rather bold, but if I'm going to accept a gift of this magnitude, then I really believe you need to fly down to Recife before the end of the year and survey my ministry and help me decide how to spend the money. I really think it would be wise for you to have a say. I would definitely be more comfortable."

Cole started to insist that such a trip wouldn't be necessary, but then realized that a personal visit to Steve on the field might encourage him even further. Plus a trip to Brazil would give Cole a firsthand education, which he both needed and desired, regarding foreign missions. He agreed.

After that, on their frequent motorcycle outings together, Cole was bombarded by Steve's questions about his youthful dreams to be a famous fiddler, his musical training, his church experience that left him disillusioned and angry, his first record deal, his family, his eleven years in the correctional facility, and his audacious decision to walk away from stardom.

In return, Cole asked Steve about his parents, his salvation experience, his call to be a cross-cultural missionary, his theological training, and his reason for choosing Recife as his place of ministry.

Each of the men developed a newer and deeper respect for the other.

Three days before the motorcycle mission adventure— as they waded in the ocean—Cole said, "Since the weather here in the South will be cooler in September and October, I'll just hang out here in the Gulf Coast region after the motorcycle mission trip and wait until you fly back to Recife. Once you've been back for a week or two, I'll leave my bike with Jason and come down for a short visit."

* * *

In the dim light of his car, Jesse Rainwater stared at the $30,000 in cash crammed inside the unzipped duffel bag. Payment received for another blonde beauty, this time from the Czech Republic.

Jesse conjured up an image of the girl in his head. The

idiot. The skank. She should have been content with her own country, her own village, her own men. She should have learned long ago that you never trust strange men, especially in the perverse world of the Internet. She just couldn't say no, could she?

He noticed a car running parallel to him in the next lane. As it pulled slowly ahead, Jesse saw two little boys staring at him through the back window. One of the boys pecked at his own face and then made a show of disgust, responding to the horrendous display of acne on Jesse's face.

Jesse showed his teeth. The little dirtbags! If he wasn't hauling $30,000 in his car, he would be tempted to run them off the road.

He stewed all the way to his apartment.

He hid his cash in the heating and AC vent in his bedroom, then stared at his reflection in the bathroom mirror. He rubbed his fingers across the ugly pits that splotched his face.

Before his encounter with the little turds, he had intended to go out later in the evening and celebrate his windfall, maybe do a little flirting. "But why should I even try?" he whispered to the empty room. "I'd just be wasting my time." No girl was ever going to be attracted to him for any length of time, no matter what. His last three dates had already proven that fact. He would never forget how the last girl, when discovering his long-held secret, nervously laughed, slowly collected her things, and backed her way out of his apartment.

He sighed and looked at his bulkier physique.

He stripped off his clothes, turned the lights off in his room, and laid back across his bed naked.

He felt so empty. So hopeless. Maybe he should just hang himself. Not a soul would miss him.

To make himself feel better, he thought again about the girl he had just sold. The fool. The European piece of trash. Whatever was happening to her right now, she deserved it. And more.

67

Cole glanced wide-eyed at the bedside clock—1:30 Monday morning. He just could not sleep. The start of the motorcycle mission adventure was only nine hours away, and he was too stoked to relax. He would soon be living on the road again. After two months of staying put in central Florida, he was ready to lift the kickstand and head northward. He rolled onto his back and stared at the ceiling, reviewing the checklist in his head one more time: bike washed; gas tank filled; tire pressure regulated; chain adjusted and lubricated; oil and filter changed; all nuts and bolts tightened; brake pads checked; brake fluid level checked; sleeping bag strapped over the headlight; tank bag holding the rainsuit secured atop the gas tank; waterproof duffel containing clothes, toiletries, tent, and Bible bungeed to the passenger seat; and the Mysterious Lady snug in her backpack sitting at the front door. Everything was ready.

He was sure that Steve, at the other end of the house, was as pumped as he was. About four hours before, when they had completed all the preparations with their bikes, they had both just stood and gawked at the loaded machines, envisioning the adventures that lay ahead. Steve had thanked him exorbitantly for making the trip a possibility for him.

Cole rolled onto his stomach and prayed into the mattress. "Thank You, thank You, thank You again," he said, "for giving me the freedom to roam at will. I thank You for every adventure I've been able to enjoy along the way. I especially thank You that I've been able to meet Jason and Steve. I thank You for their inspiration. I thank You for this upcoming trip. I suspect that all of the men joining us are overdue for something like this. I pray that the whole experience will be unforgettable—for all of us, and for all the right reasons. I pray that the group will experience harmony and true brotherhood. May our ministries influence the lives of many. Use us to change one another for the good." Cole laughed into the pillow. "I know I must sound like a kid. And I guess I'm acting like one too. I just thank You that You understand. And that You meant for us to sometimes feel this way."

* * *

"All right, gentlemen," Jason began. He was outfitted in jeans and a T-shirt. For a man his age, his physique looked lithe and fit. "It looks like everyone is here."

The men, collected at the front of the church auditorium, settled down.

Cole rolled his hands inside each other, the image lingering in his mind of all the different motorcycles outside laden with saddlebags, rolled-up sleeping bags, waterproof satchels, tank bags, helmets, and jackets. It looked like a dude ranch on wheels. And judging by the facial expressions and the nervous excitement, everyone felt the same.

"First of all," Jason continued, "I want to thank each of you for setting aside the time to spend the next twelve days together. I'm aware that several of you have taken precious vacation time to do this."

He smiled. "Perhaps you already know this, but to occasionally step out of our routine is necessary and educational. Over the next two weeks, our hearts, minds, and bodies are going to be challenged. We will feel feelings we haven't felt in a long time. We will think thoughts we haven't thought in a long time. And we will ask questions that maybe we have never asked. We're going to laugh together. We're going to cry together. We're going to build memories that we'll take with us for the rest of our lives. Savor every single second. Live in the moment and squeeze from it everything you can."

Jason reached behind him and picked up a sheet of paper. "Okay, here's our schedule. Tonight, we'll stay in cabins at a campsite in St. Augustine. Several of you have expressed an interest in hearing about my life's journey. So, after dinner tonight, I'll tell you my story. On Tuesday, Wednesday, and Thursday nights, we'll stay at a state park in Savannah, Georgia. We'll pitch our tents under oak trees covered with Spanish moss. While in the area, we'll assist two elderly widows with some home-repair projects. We'll divide into two teams. One team will help build a wheelchair ramp and replace a rear deck for one of the ladies. The other team will work with the second lady and help repair a leaking roof and replace a living-room ceiling that is collapsing. On Friday, Saturday, and Sunday, we'll be in Suches, Georgia, in the foothills of the Blueridge Mountains. We'll camp there in tents at a motorcycle-only campground. During our stay, we will help a grandmother who is raising a mentally handicapped granddaughter. We'll try to cut a winter's worth of firewood for her. We'll also lead a Sunday School class and a worship service on Sunday morning in a nearby church. I would like for twelve of you to be ready to speak for about five minutes each—six in the combined Sunday School class, and the other six in the worship service. I want everyone who speaks to focus on the theme of *influence*. Simply tell about the individual, the group, or the church that influenced you to take your pivotal step toward Christ."

One of the men raised his hand.

"Yes, sir?" Jason said.

"Put my name on the list."

"Thanks." When Jason saw another two hands go up, he said, "First, let's finish going through the schedule. Those who want to volunteer to speak can just let me know over the next couple of days."

The hands lowered.

"Okay—on Monday, Tuesday, and Wednesday, we'll move up into Franklin, North Carolina. There we'll stay in a hotel."

One of the men gave an exaggerated sigh of gratitude when hearing the word *hotel*. Several of the men laughed.

Jason continued. "There, it's been arranged for us to meet with a couple of pastors along with their wives and children. Our hope is to encourage them by taking them out for a meal and praying out loud for their families, their ministries, and their personal lives. We'll then turn southward and head for Warm Springs, Georgia, where we'll spend our final two nights. We'll stay in a hotel there as well. At that stop, everyone will have free time to visit the Little White House and ride along the ridge of Pine Mountain.

"As I've said several times, each night along the route we'll have an organized sit-down time just for our group. Each of you will have an opportunity to share whatever is on your heart. And we'll pray for each other." Jason returned the sheet of notes to the stage floor. "Now, before I say more about the trip, let's have a round of introductions. I would like for each of you to simply give your name, your occupation, and the kind of bike you're riding. We'll start to my left and move clockwise. Tommy, you go first."

"All right," a husky man with a strong southern accent bellowed, "My name is Tommy Bauer. I'm a bounty hunter. And I'm riding a 2003 Gold Wing."

Jason nodded and pointed to the next man.

"My name is Robbie Bauer. I'm Tommy's son. I work with my dad. And I'm riding a Honda ST1300."

"Geoff Merritt. I own and operate a chicken processing plant. I ride a BMW R1200GS."

"I'm Randy Maner. I supervise a small group of men at a chemical plant. And I ride a Harley Davidson Super Glide."

"A Harley?" one of the men laughed. "We'll never complete our itinerary now. We'll be parked on the side of the road dealing with mechanical problems the whole time."

As fast as the hilarious remark came his way, Randy Maner returned it. "Whoa, my friend. You need to understand right now that Harleys are not the problem; they are the solution."

Groans seeped across the pews.

The next man lowered a map he had been examining. "I'm one of the new guys. My name is Ric Kennedy. I'm a chemistry professor. I live in New York City. I've been a longtime member at the Liberty International City Church where Jason pastored for many years. I'm here at his invitation. Like some of the other men, I'm riding an 1800 Gold Wing."

Eleven other men introduced themselves—a couple of policemen, a detective, a psychologist, a journalist, a videographer, a real estate developer, a recording engineer, a jet fuel specialist, a retired contractor, and a carpenter. Then it was Cole's turn.

"I'm also a new guy to the group," Cole said. "My name is CJ. I'm a drifter. And I ride a Triumph Scrambler."

"Whoa, whoa," someone said. "A drifter? You've got to be more specific than that."

Jason intervened. "We'll give CJ the opportunity in one of our evening meetings to tell us more about himself. Let's move on to the next man."

"Steve Rove. I'm a career missionary. I'm home in the States for just another month or so, and then I'll be moving back to Brazil. Thanks to a very generous individual, I'm riding a new V-Strom 650. So, I'm probably more surprised to be here than anybody. I'm looking forward to it."

"Tim Royston. I operate a roofing business. I'll be the driver of the support vehicle. And if we need it, I'll be pulling a trailer that will hold two bikes."

"We'll need it for the Harleys," someone yelled.

The comment set loose another round of quips.

Jason clapped to restore everyone's attention to the front. "Thank you, gentlemen," he grinned. "In just a moment, I'll ask Tommy—our designated road captain—to come to the front and tell us about the group assignments and to also share a few guidelines. Thanks again for being here. I really, really appreciate it. I'll be out there with you on two wheels some of the time. When I'm riding, I'll be on my Suzuki Intruder 1400. At other times, I'll be in the truck with Tim." Jason stepped backward and leaned against the edge of the stage. "Tommy, go ahead and share. And try to have us on the road in fifteen or twenty minutes."

Cole had counted twenty men, including himself. This was going to be awesome!

Tommy, the bounty hunter, moved like a bulldozer to the front—slow, strong, and intimidating. "All right, for those of you who have traveled in large groups before, you know it's dang near impossible to hold the group together. Everybody has a different riding style. Some like to ride fast, some like to ride slow. So the group tends to spread out. When that happens, bikes get separated at traffic lights, bikes miss a turn and get lost, cars weave in between the bikes. It becomes a real hassle to get everybody back together again. Riders start losing their patience. So to help prevent all that, Jason has asked me to divide our group into small teams of four or five. Here are the group assignments. Robbie, Terry Ray, RD Dodge, and Jeff Sweeny will ride with me. Jim McFee will be the next group leader. Jim, raise your hand. DW Sunn, Jason, CJ, and Steve Rove will ride with him." Tommy revealed the final two teams, then added, "Tim will follow in the truck. Before any of you ask, I've already given the group leaders detailed maps that outline our route. They've also been given the names and phone numbers of our campgrounds and hotels. So if the groups get separated, don't panic. The group leaders will be responsible for getting their teams to the designated stops. Understood?"

* * *

After Tommy had issued a few instructions for group riding, and answered questions from four or five of the men, Jason led the group out into the parking lot. The morning air had already reached 90 degrees and was climbing. Jason gathered the men in a circle. He prayed briefly for every man by name and asked God to overshadow them with His incomparable greatness.

Cole continued to be impressed by the old sage. He thought once again that this getaway, with Jason at the helm, would probably be extraordinary, if not outright life-shaping. He looked forward to hearing the man's story later in the evening.

"All right," Tommy Bauer shouted, "helmets on! Group

leaders, get your groups together. We're pulling out in five minutes."

Everyone quickly donned jackets and helmets.

Motorcycle engines fired up all around the parking lot.

Cole straddled the Scrambler and started the parallel twin. When the exhaust note came to life, it seemed to snort anxiously, like a racehorse at a starting gate. Cole adjusted his backpack so that it was snug. He secured the goggles around his eyes and slapped his thigh with excitement. Jim McFee, his group leader, pulled his Mean Streak out into an opening and motioned for his team to fall in behind him. Within minutes, Cole, Steve, Jason, and the other man called DW were bunched one behind the other ready for departure.

About four minutes later, Tommy Bauer, at the head of the lead group, hoisted his hand, held it still for a moment—and then chopped it through the air like an officer leading a cavalry charge.

The moment had finally arrived. The trip was on.

68

$\mathcal{F}$or Cole, the first two-hour surge up I-4 and A1A was as thrilling as an adolescent boy's first date, minus the angst. His sixteen months of scooting solo had provided incalculable joy almost every mile of the way. But blasting up the highway in a group of nineteen bikes and a truck produced a new and different kind of rush. An invisible pledge of brotherhood was already understood, though some of the men had not even had the chance to speak to one another. Nineteen motorcyclists. Four groups. Yet, one team. Threading together through the interstate traffic. On a mission.

Cole stood up on his pegs out of sheer celebration. Steve pulled up beside him, gave him a thumbs up, and hung there for a quarter of a mile or so.

When they stopped for a late lunch at a picturesque cafe along A1A, it took at least twenty minutes for the men to make their way into the restaurant. The men stood talking throughout the gravel parking lot, enthralled in pockets of exuberant animation.

*   *   *

It was late in the afternoon when the four groups of bikes and the truck pulled into the campground in St. Augustine.

As the men checked in and dispersed to their cabins, two of the guys took the truck and ran to a local grocery store, returning with all the foods and condiments for grilling. Later in the evening, Tommy Bauer served up the biggest burgers that any of the guys had ever seen. He christened them the "Bauer Burgers".

After the meal, the men sat around in a common area on benches and patted their full bellies. Eventually, Jason stood and said, "Since I've volunteered to be your spiritual shepherd for a couple of years, I want to honor your request that I share some of the details of my history."

Eager to hear the man's story, Cole lay back in the grass and made himself comfortable.

"I chose to follow the Lord Jesus Christ when I was seventeen," Jason commenced. "I was primarily influenced by a radio pastor. One evening after listening to this man deliver a fiery sermon about the wrath of God, I knelt in a cornfield near my home and cried out for God to have mercy on me. The focus of my life was immediately altered. I became so serious in my newfound faith that it didn't take long for the other believers in my high school to spot me. A couple of young men invited me to attend church with them. I did. And I was smitten by their pastor's dynamism. He was smart. He was loud. He was forceful. I had never met anyone with such an overture of righteous authority.

The man became my hero. I sat at his feet and devoured every sermon, every prayer, and every display of brash leadership. I eventually enrolled in the same Bible college that he had attended. And then the same seminary. And in my naiveté, I cheerfully allowed those institutions to take my heart and mind and shape me into an authoritarian much like the pastor I had so admired. Upon my graduation, I was quickly scooped up by a church in the same ultra-conservative denomination."

"Where was the church?" one of the guys asked.

"Atlanta, Georgia," Jason said, looking as if his mind suddenly registered too many heavy memories. "Anyway, I served as an assistant pastor at the church for two years. Then the senior pastor died from a heart attack. The church asked me to step up and fill his position, and I did. I wish I could tell you that I became a loving, altruistic leader. But I didn't. I became a spiritual dictator. For eleven long years I imposed on my people—including my wife and daughter—an ironclad list of do's and don'ts that stretched one's imagination. I whipped everyone into action, using the tools of fear and guilt. I built a church that rested on the cusp of blind and unquestioning allegiance to me and my believe-the-way-I-believe-or-be-damned vision. I actually disciplined people out of membership if they opposed me. I eventually became known not as the Pastor or the Reverend, but as the General." Jason paused. "My daughter, however, was not a *yes* person. She refused to be suffocated by my mindless rules. So, at the age of—"

"I'm just curious," one man interrupted. "What were the do's and don'ts and mindless rules you're referring to?"

"No dancing. No rhythmic music. No drums. No electric instruments. No movie theaters. No form of alcohol whatsoever. No card games. No dice. No piercings. No tattoos. No mixed swimming. Church attendance every Sunday morning, every Sunday evening, and every Wednesday evening. Mandatory tithing. Only the King James Version of the Bible. Hawkish patriotism. Military-style haircuts for men and boys. No beards. No mustaches. Knee-length dresses for women and girls—no slacks. Suits and ties for the men at church gatherings. Shall I go on?"

"That's enough," responded the questioner. "You've already raised my blood pressure and just about worn me out."

Laughter encompassed the group.

"Anyway, as I was about to say," Jason proceeded, "my daughter decided at the age of seventeen that she could not subject herself to my kind of tyranny. So she ran away. My wife and I didn't see her again until a year and a half later, when her body was delivered to our local mortuary. She had died in Miami, Florida, giving birth to a baby girl. She had warned the baby's father to never make contact with me, but I went to Miami and tried to find them. The search was fruitless. My wife became severely ill shortly thereafter and died. In my despair, I began for the first time to question my beliefs and my style of merciless leadership. I became so disgusted with myself that I eventually left the ministry."

Cole had heard only a snippet of Jason's story before, and he was glued to Jason's words. The lost child. The lost wife. The disillusionment. The resignation. The similarities between their stories were uncanny. Cole wondered if any of the other men in the group had shared a similar journey.

"Through sheer stubbornness, I finally managed to track down my son-in-law's address in south Florida," Jason continued, "but by that time he had moved. I learned from his neighbor that the young man wasn't functioning well as a single father, that my granddaughter was most likely being physically and emotionally abused because of her father's alcoholism."

Cole was now more attentive than ever.

Jason went on to tell about his search for his grandchild, a search that spanned eighteen years and four different countries. He mentioned a spectacular motorcycle adventure that he had experienced along the way, a prison sentence on the Turkish side of Cyprus after being set up to unknowingly smuggle drugs across the Green Line, and a daring escape off the island that involved a motorcycle.

Several hands shot up. The men, with their warrior fantasies, insisted on hearing more about the prison escape.

Jason laughed and answered their questions.

Cole listened, totally fascinated.

After satisfying the group's hunger for details about the nail-biting escape, Jason explained that he eventually found his granddaughter. But in the process, he was radically influenced and changed by a long-term encounter with an old pastor in Norway. "The man modeled for me what it means to be a truly wise pastor, mentor, and friend. God used that pastor to pull me back from the threshold of spiritual anarchy. Because of him, I dared reenter the ministry after so many years of being a Christian vagabond. I was actually serving as the interim pastor at my church in New York City when I found my granddaughter." Jason shared only a brief synopsis of the miraculous convergence of their two lives, yet several of the men—especially the grandfathers in the group—found themselves wiping dampness from their eyes. The report that the girl had been a rape victim, a drug addict, a prostitute, and almost a suicide victim—by the time he found her—only heightened their emotion. Everyone was thrilled to hear that the girl, Daytona, had found her way to Christ and had been baptized under her grandfather's care and that she was currently serving in full-time ministry at the Liberty International City Church in New York. "So, I've shared my story with you for three reasons. Number one, you have asked me to share it. Number two, I want to emphasize the life-changing influence of a single individual, such as the old pastor in Norway. And number three, I want to encourage you to never, never lose your heart for God."

Reacting to Jason's story, the men quickly leaned into pockets of animated conversation, but Tommy Bauer raised his hand and shouted to reclaim everyone's attention. He then spoke loudly so that everyone could hear. "As I was listening to Jason tell about his granddaughter's conversion and baptism, I was hit with the reminder that I've still never been baptized as a believer. I've always felt guilty about it. So I'm thinking it's about time." Tommy then zeroed in on Jason. "What about it? Would it be okay for you to baptize me?"

"Here? Tonight?" Jason asked for clarification.

"Is there a better moment?"

Jason smiled. He asked Tommy a couple more questions

and, when satisfied that the moment was indeed right, said, "Gentlemen, I'll need for ten to twelve of you to ride your bikes down to the riverbank and be ready to give us some light. CJ and Steve, I'd like for you to get ready to go down into the water with me."

Cole was caught off guard. Did the old pastor want him to provide a special song, perhaps? By the time Cole headed toward his cabin to fetch a towel and a change of clothes, everyone else was already on the move. The ethos of the group had been transformed from a reflective seriousness to a hallowed excitement.

The river scene slowly came together like a movie production set. A portion of the river's edge was sectioned off by the headlight beams of thirteen manly machines, waiting for the main actors to take their places.

Jason eventually gathered Cole and Steve in a huddle at the riverbank and explained that he wanted the three of them as invested ministers to share the honor of lowering Tommy into the water and raising him up again. Jason then stepped first into the lazily flowing river, followed by Cole and Steve.

Tommy, when beckoned, entered the flow. All the men waded a few feet out until they were waist deep.

Jason spoke a few words about the significance of baptism to give Tommy a chance to savor the moment. Then all three ministers held the back of Tommy's shoulders, elbows, and head and lowered him into the water. When they lifted him back to the surface, in the brilliance of the motorcycle beams, Tommy gasped, his face transformed by joy.

Cole swallowed with emotion. On the bank, sixteen men began singing *Amazing Grace* in absolute jubilation.

Tommy grabbed Jason and gave him a heartfelt hug. He then reached for Cole. "Thank you, thank you," he sniffled as he squeezed him in a passionate embrace. He turned to Steve and did the same.

Tommy's display of sudden gratitude was truly moving.

Cole was pleased to discover that Derek Atwood, the videographer in the group, had captured the entire event on film.

* * *

Around midnight, when everyone was bedded down in their cabins and fading into sleep, Cole looked up into the darkness from his bunk and reflected on the day. He savored every memory, especially the joyous baptism. But the story of Jason's granddaughter, Daytona, had been exceptionally mesmerizing for him. Blood connections, Cole had personally learned, were often the making of historic and epic tales. And then, as if he were a deer in the path of a rushing locomotive, he was slammed breathless by the memory of his other son, the one he and Jana had given up for adoption before they were married. It had been a while since the child had crossed his mind. What kind of young man had he become? He would be...what...almost twenty-five now? Was he living somewhere in the South? Or elsewhere? Was he a believer? He wondered if, like Jason, he should pursue contact. He fell asleep wondering if he should even be thinking such thoughts.

69

Jesse balled his fist once more.

"Go ahead, hit me again!" the girl screamed. "Does that make you feel big and strong?" Her left eye was black and swollen. Her upper lip was bleeding. She rubbed her tongue across her upper teeth, then sneered, "You're the most pitiful human being I've ever met! And believe me, I've met some pretty raunchy scum!"

Jesse felt tension in every muscle of his body.

The brunette stood toe to toe with him. She didn't even raise her hands to defend herself. She just locked eyes with him in defiance and waited.

"Just get out!" Jesse growled. His hate for human life was so complete that he didn't know why he let the whore live. "Don't ever let me see you again! Do you hear?"

She pivoted, scraped up the rails of cocaine and the cut straw from the table and stormed out of the hotel room. She slammed the door behind her.

Jesse clenched his jaws and stared at the door. He had paid to be with the fiery female twice before. This time, however, as he'd stepped out of the bathroom he had caught her attempting to steal extra cash from his pants draped across a chair.

He felt alone and empty. It was the same feeling of darkness and all-consuming weariness that in the past year had begun to progressively overshadow his day-to-day existence. He walked back into the bathroom and looked into the mirror.

As the rhythm of his breathing moderated itself, he watched the reflection of his index finger making slow slashing movements across his larynx. He had long since learned to psychologically outwit the physical pain of self mutilation. Now he wondered what it would be like to cut his throat all the way through. And watch while he did it.

* * *

Cole and Steve awoke in their cabin at dawn to the explosive rumble of a large-bore V-twin motor somewhere in the campground. An early bird in the group must be heading out for breakfast.

Within an hour and a half, all twenty men were gathered around their loaded bikes in the sandy parking lot, ready to pull out of St. Augustine. Jason prayed for their day's journey. Tommy Bauer informed everyone that a thunderstorm was bearing down on them, and they would need to leave pronto and ride hard to stay ahead of the rain. The next rendezvous would be in Brunswick, Georgia, a hundred and eight miles up the coast. "See you there!" Tommy hollered. He sped away with his designated group of four.

Cole and his group were ready to follow, but Jason—on his Intruder—got off and made a last-minute jaunt back into the campground office. Jim McFee waited patiently. The group was finally able to leave about five minutes behind everyone else. Once underway and out of the city limits, Jim pulled the bunch into an extremely tight formation and picked up speed. Cole had never ridden in such a close-knit pattern. At such high speeds, there was no margin for error. His concentration and adrenaline were energized to the fullest. He squeezed the handlebars and thanked God again for the adventure.

Cole's group had covered no more than twenty miles when huge raindrops started to pelt them. Jim led the group into a gas station, under giant eaves. Everybody dismounted and dug for raingear. A few mocking remarks were made when DW, the retired contractor, produced a bright yellow suit—a size too small—and fought to wiggle into it. When everyone, amidst the bantering, was finally suited and giving thumbs-up signals, Jim led the way out into the now pouring rain.

This time, the five men unreeled into a stretched-out formation and rode in a nebula of spray.

Cole had learned a long time ago that the pounding of heavy rain on his suit, helmet, and goggles while moving at highway speeds provided an unmatched cocktail of physical, aural, and olfactory sensations. He actually enjoyed it, especially like now, when the rain and the air were warm.

The storm, though, quickly brought unwelcome dark clouds, blistering crosswinds, and thunder. The men endured nearly seventy miles of it. By the time they pulled into the designated convenience store in Brunswick, Georgia, the storm had already moved out over the Atlantic. All the other groups were already at the store, enjoying the calm and the sunshine.

As Cole slowed the Triumph inside the parking lot, he saw one of the men rolling on the concrete. He felt a jolt of alarm until he saw that the man was laughing. It was the journalist, RD Dodge. He then saw one of the other guys, Lynn Newton if he remembered correctly, draped in a shredded green rain suit and standing conspicuously at the center of the commotion. Lynn looked as if he had survived a category-five hurricane. One sleeve on the suit was completely gone. The other was dangling by a tiny piece of plastic at the elbow. All the snaps were ripped apart. The hood was nearly torn off. And the pants looked worse. Lynn's clothing beneath the suit was drenched.

Cole snickered as he got off his bike. He learned that Lynn had bought his rain suit at a convenience store when his group had stopped to gear up for the storm. The cheap suit had lasted about ten miles before starting to come apart. The teasing and knee-slapping laughter continued for several minutes. When RD Dodge was finally able to stand and compose himself, the group settled down and moved next door to a restaurant for lunch.

The laughter returned later in the afternoon when the whole crew pitched their tents at the State park just outside Savannah. Tim Royston, who had never camped before, became absolutely perplexed when he laid out his tent pieces. As he read the step-by-step instructions and began connecting the parts, it became obvious to him that something was not right. When he asked for help, his good Samaritans realized immediately that Tim had not bought a tent, but rather a portable gazebo. The merciless ribbing persisted until Tim went off to buy a proper sleeping tent. One of the men laughingly accompanied him to make sure he bought the correct item.

The mood of the group became deadly serious, though, at the evening session. "A large number of men," Jason reminded the guys, "live clandestine lives, meaning they conceal a significant portion of their thoughts, fantasies, feelings, doubts, fears, and pains behind a mask that is nothing more than ornamentation. They live in isolation. Some men live this way for years, some for decades." He shared examples from his own life, then read two verses from the New Testament—Hebrews chapter ten, verse twenty-five, and First Thessalonians chapter five, verse eleven. "These inspired words instruct us to encourage one another. Now, how do we know who to encourage, unless those that are discouraged raise their hands and say, 'I'm discouraged'? We don't. So the implication here is there must be an element of honesty in the church, that we must slowly start to come out from behind our masks."

Jason paused, then added, "I want to emphasize that the Scriptures are not telling those who are discouraged to completely divulge all the details of their lives. That's not prudent. It never has been and never will be. But the Scriptures *are* saying that perpetual isolation isn't healthy for one's soul. God, after all, designed us to be social creatures, to be interactive, to live in community. And in order to function in that capacity, we should have the freedom when we are hurting to at least stand up and say so. And to know that our circle of brothers will rally around us, pray for us, and encourage us—even if they don't know all the details."

Jason then asked if any of the men indeed felt isolated behind a mask. There was a haze of silence. Jason, nevertheless, waited.

One man finally lifted his hand. Then a second man. And a third.

* * *

By 10:00 that evening, nine men—trying to use discretion at Jason's prompting—had opened up and revealed personal pains regarding family, marriage, depression, and faith that momentarily held their lives hostage. One of the men had even told about his lifelong struggle over the fact that his mother had never loved him, simply because he was a male. In the end, each of the men had received support, insight, and prayer.

Cole had seldom witnessed such a rich outpouring of truthfulness and brotherhood. He wondered if some of the men—before tonight—had ever witnessed it. Jason, however, looked blissfully pleased as if he had experienced it many times.

When Cole crawled into his tent around midnight and stretched out, he knew he would sleep well. *"But let all who take refuge in you, rejoice;"* he quoted from Psalm chapter five, *"let them sing joyful praises forever."*

70

 *T*he following morning, Cole sat alone with Jason at a breakfast buffet. "Last night," he said, "you emphasized that there should be an element of honesty in the church. At the same time, you said it was never wise for a Christian to publicly reveal all the details of his struggles. Yet several of the men were very forthcoming with details. And it appeared that their transparency made it easier for the other men to open up. So, I'm just curious—where does one draw the line on sharing details?"

Jason took a sip of juice. "On one level, it's true that honesty breeds honesty. And when it happens in the confines of a single meeting and everybody is comfortable, it can be very contagious and therapeutic, as we all witnessed last night. But sharing openly in public is always risky. Why? Because it seems that every Christian and every Christian group has subjectively set a bar of righteous expectation for other Christians. Some set the bar unreasonably high; others set it very low. And as long as their friends and acquaintances live above that bar, everyone will be accepted without question and will be shown grace. But..." Jason took another swig of juice. "But...the moment anyone in their circle of associates drops below that bar, even if the drop occurs through publicly confessing too many details about their lives, the guilty one will almost without exception be treated differently. At that point, he is no longer given grace. Rather, he is given ultimatums. If he doesn't rise quickly back to the bar of expectation, he will eventually be set adrift and blacklisted. When that happens, the church ceases to be a brotherhood of love and grace and becomes a brotherhood of rejection and abandonment. Tragically, Christendom is littered with hundreds of thousands of individuals who have been dropped, as it were, and broken. And they've simply been left unrepaired. It's one of the greatest tragedies of the Christian church. So where does one draw the line when it comes to sharing details?" Jason stared out the window as if conjuring up a memory. "If you want to find the edge of human grace, then—honestly— you never know if you've gone too far until you've gone too far. That's why discretion should always temper one's honesty."

Cole took a bite of egg. As he chewed in silence, he thanked God again for Chaplain Duke Parker, who had so graciously helped him repair his own broken life without ever issuing a single word of judgment or condemnation. He thanked God as well for the grace that the men had, so far, extended to one another in the motorcycle group. How beautiful it was!

*   *   *

When Jesse crawled out of bed a little before noon, he decided that he would accept the invitation from the guy named Cruz he met last night at the bar. He would go to Stone Mountain and hang out with the bro and his buddies and waste the day drinking, laughing, and trying to have a little fun.

It would at least get him out of the apartment.

Before he headed for the shower, though, he sat down groggy-eyed at his computer. He typed "Cole Michaels" into the search engine. Only one new paragraph was listed. It showed up on five different websites.

> Cole Michaels' CD *Oasis Blues* continues to hover in the top of the music charts, having now sold over two million units. Industry insiders express amazement at this milestone, considering there has been no tour, video, or public appearances by the artist. It is rare, they say, when music alone can generate these impressive numbers.

But nothing about where the man was now. One day, there would be an announcement of where Michaels had chosen to settle. And when that word came, Jesse would move as quickly as a shrew to capitalize on it.

* * *

At 5:30 PM, Randy Maner, the leader of Cole's home-repair team, spread the word for everyone to wrap up their work for the day. The leaking roof had been repaired, and the two pieces of water-damaged drywall in the living room ceiling had been ripped out and replaced. Every piece of furniture in the living room was draped with sheets of polyethylene, now smattered with drywall debris and old pieces of insulation.

"Tomorrow morning," Randy told the makeshift crew, "we'll prep and paint the new ceiling and replace the molding. We'll then clean everything up. We should be finished by noon."

The lady of the house, a skinny African-American widow in her 70s, threw her arms above her head and said, "Lordy, Lordy, it's looking so good."

During dinner at a mom-and-pop seafood restaurant, the two work teams gave reports. The other group had finished a wheelchair ramp and set the posts for a rear deck. They would try to finish by noon the next day as well. They were elated that the widow who lived in their house, a retired schoolteacher with severe arthritis in her knees and hips, had already used the ramp five or six times, with both her walker and her motorized scooter. "This is freedom!" she had whooped over and over.

The joy of helping those in need was celebrated several times in the evening's sit-down session.

So was the value of transparency and grace, as another

man opened up, sharing his ongoing guilt, and need for advice, regarding his colossal failures as a father.

* * *

The next afternoon, when the two work projects—interspersed with a few pranks and a lot of laughter—had been completed, Jason suggested to the men that they all stop at a nursing home on their way back to the campground and seek permission to mingle with the residents. "If we're allowed to visit, we can split into pairs and encourage the residents for a few minutes with some conversation and prayer."

The men liked the idea.

The director of the nursing home, as it happened, was a strong-looking woman in her fifties. Jason made his request on behalf of the group. The woman drilled him with questions, then asked to meet the men. "I wouldn't normally allow a group like this to just pop in with no advance notice," she finally said, "but considering that you're on a church-related mission, I'll give you permission to talk to the residents in the hallways only, not in the rooms."

As the men scattered throughout the corridors, Cole and Steve paired up. After fifteen minutes or so, as they finished praying with a wheelchair-bound grandmother, Jef Cass, the recording engineer, swept past them and said, "You need to make your way to the dining hall—all our guys need to see this."

Cole and Steve went to the big room, where Jeff

Sweeny, the real-estate broker, stood in the middle of a ring of people, talking loudly to one of the residents—who, they quickly learned, was a hundred-and-one-year-old man named George. Wisps of white hair crowned the old gentlemen's head as he sat wide-eyed in a cushioned chair.

"How long were you married before your wife passed away?" Jeff asked.

"Sixty-eight years," the man replied in a sweet but strained voice.

"How was it that you guys managed to keep the marriage together for so long?"

"We both learned to be good forgivers."

"Do you remember your first car?"

"A Ford Model T."

"Do you remember its top speed?"

"Thirty-five miles-per-hour."

"That wasn't very fast, was it?"

"It was if you had been used to walking all your life."

People chuckled.

"Who has been your favorite president through the years?"

"Franklin Delano Roosevelt."

"Any reason why?"

"He signed the Social Security Act. And those payouts have kept me alive for thirty years."

Again, amusement rippled through the crowd.

"To what do you attribute your long life?"

"Ginseng and golden root. I've taken them every day of my life since I was a teenager."

Jeff motioned for other men to chime in if they wanted.

Cole leaned forward. "Have you ever ridden a motorcycle, George?"

"No, never have."

Cole looked around at the guys and then back at George. "Would you like to?"

George squinted. A wave of expectation rose in everyone's eyes.

"Well...are there any Harleys out there?"

Randy Maner stepped forward and said, "Yes, sir. This motorcycle group wouldn't be a valid group without a few Harleys, now would it?"

The old man smiled.

Cole reclaimed the old fellow's attention. "George, if we can get permission to put you on the back of this man's Harley, and if he promises to ride real slow, would you like to take your first ride?"

George's brow wrinkled once, then twice. "Yes, sir, I think I would."

The man's six-word response ignited an instant whirlwind of excitement. A few men darted off to the front office to ask permission.

Within a few minutes, the director of the home, with two assistants at her side, appeared. "George, is this something you really want to do?" she asked.

George nodded. "Yeah, I might as well do it while I have the chance."

The director looked at the men. She posed several safety-related questions and then concluded, "All right, but only if you promise to stay in the parking lot."

Within seconds, Cole and some of the men were helping George make his way to the main entrance. Derek Atwood was running to get his video camera. Randy Manor was bringing the Harley to just outside the front door. Steve Rove fetched his helmet for the old man to wear. One of the office workers, notepad in hand, asked Tommy Bauer for information about the group to put into a county newspaper article. Other office workers grabbed cameras and made their way outside. Residents everywhere shuffled toward windows that offered views of the front parking lot, as if they had just been told that a Christmas reindeer had landed outside.

When George finally stood beside the Harley, with a man on either side to give him support, cameras started flashing. Jeff Sweeny placed the helmet on George's head, assured him that Randy was an experienced rider, and explained that four of the men would help lift him onto the bike's passenger seat.

George offered a sweet, nervous grin.

Randy Maner mounted the bike, raised it upright, then patted the pillion seat.

With George helping all he could, four of the men lifted him and positioned him on the bike. Cameras flashed, and Derek Atwood zoomed in with the video camera.

Before Randy could turn the ignition key, George spouted two words audible to all those standing nearby. "A Harley," he announced, as if this were something he had thought about all his life.

As Randy fired up the V-twin engine, Jeff Sweeny told George to hold onto Randy's shoulders.

When Randy activated the clutch and pulled away, all the men burst into spontaneous cheers.

When the grand ride was over, all the men were thanked enthusiastically by residents and staff alike.

As the team rode back to the campsite, Cole figured it must be a rare and impressive sight for an individual, or a group like the nursing home staff, to see twenty men moving around the country doing ministry together. One thing was for sure—he was glad to be part of it.

71

When the men gathered for their evening session, they made themselves comfortable as Jason stood and led in an opening prayer.

"Father, we thank You for all the great memories we've collected in the last four days. Each one has been a cherished gift. I know the men are filled with anticipation about what will happen in our meeting tonight. But whatever happens, please don't let us squander the next two hours. Help us to sense Your presence. Inspire us. Motivate us. Challenge us. In Jesus' name. Amen."

After a few opening comments, Jason sat, opening the meeting to whoever felt led to share.

Wasting no time, Ric Kennedy from New York said he had something to say.

Jason simply lifted a thumb of solidarity.

Ric began by thanking the men for welcoming him as an outsider and allowing him to be an accepted part of the group. "I really hope you make this an annual event. More men need to experience something like this."

"Hear! Hear!" someone shouted.

"Anyway," Ric said, "I'll jump right into my main

thought." He scratched at his eyebrow. "As Christian men, we have often heard claims in the church such as 'God told me', 'God led me', and 'God revealed to me'. We've heard phrases like 'God's relationship with me' and 'God's presence in my life'. It's much less common to hear Christians talk openly about their frustrations that God is silent, or distant, or that He just doesn't seem to care. Yet the Bible is very candid about this barren side of the God-follower's experience. King David, for example, tells us throughout the Psalms that he fought this private hell on multiple occasions. And he was a man after God's own heart."

Ric turned to Psalm thirteen in a small leather Bible and read all six verses, illustrating his claim about King David.

Cole removed a pen and piece of paper from his violin backpack and began taking notes.

"Now," Ric said, "let's keep in mind here that David was not an ordinary individual. Not only was David literate in a day and age when most people were not, but he was also a lyricist and a chronicler. In addition, he was handsome. He was fit and strong. He was famous. He was a hero on a national scale. He was financially secure, with gold and silver that weighed literally in the tons. He was powerful—with one sentence he could set new laws in motion or end a man's life. He was intelligent to the point that he could politically lead a nation. He was an orator who could speak to crowds of dignitaries or subjects. He was a musician and singer whose talents won the attention and vocal admiration of the masses. And he had plenty of wives that he could be physically intimate with whenever he wanted."

"Lucky man," one of the guys shouted.

Everyone laughed.

"In other words," Ric smiled, "David possessed everything that most people fantasize about and strive for. As an extremely fortunate individual, he had both hands on the rainbow. Both hands! Yet...the good looks, the charisma, the celebrity status, the abundance of wealth, the artistic skills, and the throne did not elevate him above feelings of loneliness, depression, and insecurity. His assets certainly did not lift him above the periodic feelings that God had turned a deaf ear and a calloused heart toward him. This knowledge alone should encourage each one of us. The reality is, life is a battle for everybody. Everybody! No exceptions! But—and here is the big question—how did David handle these seasons of darkness in his life? And can we learn from him?"

As Ric paused to order his thoughts, the group was silent and attentive.

Cole, impressed with what he was hearing, was still busy putting Ric's key points into writing.

"Here's *how* he survived the dry and torturous moments when he could have sworn God had left him. Quite simply, he would take a mental journey into the past. According to his own personal journal in Psalm chapter forty-two, verses five and six—written in conjunction with his chief songwriters—he would intentionally recall those times in his past when God spoke, intervened, provided, answered, and protected in undeniable ways. By journeying into his past, he revisited God's fingerprints that were all over his life. He reviewed the evidence that God had faithfully been present in his life. And, as you can understand, these remembrances assured him that even though God might seem distant or silent at any given moment, He really hadn't gone anywhere. He was still presently active in David's current circumstances. Always had been. And always would be. These remembrances gave him hope. And I've said all that to say this—each of us needs to nail down every God-known intervention, every protection, every revelation, every encouragement, and every answer in our past as a recognized memorial, a memorial that we can go back to over and over again as a reminder of His faithful involvement in our life. Such memorials will help us survive those dark, lonely, and scary days that we'll inevitably face. This motorcycle trip, for example, should be used as a memorial for each of us, as a red-letter week when each of us bathed in God's life-changing presence, as a steadfast reminder that we are indeed on His mind."

"Absolutely right on!" someone hailed as Ric sat down.

"I like it," declared another voice.

"Something we all need to learn," confirmed another.

Cole was still writing, lost in his own thoughts, when he felt Steve Rove nudge him. Steve motioned for him to look over at Jason.

Cole looked across the crowd and saw Jason gesture for him to take his turn. Cole slowly laid down his pen and paper and stood.

"Wait a minute," Jef Cass said. "Before anyone else shares, let me grab the bug spray to pass around. The gnats are starting to eat us alive over here. Hold on!" Jef ran to his tent. He was back in a minute or so, spraying his arms, legs, and face. He passed the can around to the group. Within a few minutes, the bug repellent made its circuit and the whole area smelled strongly of Deet.

"All right," Jef announced, looking at Cole, "It's all yours."

"Well," Cole said, "I want to thank Ric for that great teaching. I've already taken notes and intend to explore the idea further." He slowly squeezed his lower lip, lowered his head, then looked up. "Okay—Jason has asked me to tell you a little bit about my personal journey. I am, or was, a professional violin player. Some of you already know this. Others of you have probably seen me hauling around the fiddle in my backpack and wondered about it."

Revealing his true identity as Cole Michaels the music celebrity, Cole went on to tell the group about his early years as an unregenerate soul, his marriage to Jana, his first church experience, his debut record *Sweet Manipulations*, his son's death, his wife's death, his drunk-driving accident, his jail time, his spiritual renewal under the chaplain, his recent *Oasis Blues* CD, and his current status as a free-roaming ambassador for Christ.

As he concluded his story, he reached over to pull the violin from its pack.

"I thought I'd seen your picture somewhere before," Terry Ray, the psychologist, proclaimed during the lull. "It's on the back cover of the old *Sweet Manipulations* CD, isn't it?"

Cole nodded.

"Come on!" interrupted Ron Sasson, the carpenter. "And you're seriously telling us that you're also the singer of *Oasis Blues*?"

Cole again nodded, with a tinge of embarrassment.

"Well, I'll be danged—I can't believe it!" Ron said. "That's one of my favorite songs! It's in my iPod right now! I've listened to it a couple of times already on this trip!"

A few more questions were asked to confirm Cole's stardom. Someone then called out the CD's best-selling stats they'd recently heard on the radio. Three or four of the men asked if Cole would play and sing a couple of his hit songs, particularly *Oasis Blues*.

Before Cole sang, he told briefly how the song *Oasis Blues* was born. He also told briefly about the history of his beloved fiddle, the Mysterious Lady.

When Cole finally leaned into the fiddle and started playing, he noticed that the men seemed unusually hushed.

After three songs, the session ended. Almost on cue, the men scattered like quail and pulled out their mobile phones. Snapshots were taken with phone cameras. And a bevy of calls were made to share the surprise with wives and kids.

72

*T*he next morning before the group pulled up tent pegs to make their 331-mile trip to Suches, Georgia, Cole was stopped by Jason just outside the showers. "I've never been a musician," Jason told him in the quiet of the dawn, "but I've always been an avid listener of music. And in my opinion, the violin—when it's played poorly—is one of the worst-sounding instruments in the world. But when it's played well, it produces one of the most beautiful sounds in all creation. And you, my friend, play more than well— you play magically. You make the instrument come alive, almost with a soul of its own. God has blessed you with a magnificent gift. Thanks for sharing it with us last night. Every man in the group benefitted from hearing you play."

Cole meekly thanked the old mentor.

An hour and a half later, when bellies and gas tanks were full, and the group was within minutes of departing, Ron Sasson, the leader of Derek Atwood's team, let it be known that Derek had not yet returned—that he had rushed back to the nursing home to inform the staff that a Nashville celebrity had been in their group yesterday afternoon and that they might want to highlight that in their newspaper article about George and the out-of-town bikers. "Derek said he wanted to make sure the article lets people know that Cole Michaels is out here helping people when he doesn't have to, and that he's the real deal."

Cole, for the second time that morning, was humbled by the words of affirmation. He thanked the men. "But," he said, "just because I can play the fiddle and sing doesn't mean that my contribution to what we're doing here is any greater than what you're contributing. Most of you have accomplished far more in life than I ever will."

Later that morning, when the motorcycles had logged about a hundred miles, Tommy Bauer led the pack into a convenience-store parking lot to let the guys stretch their legs. While most of the men topped off their gas tanks, purchased sodas and snacks, and used the restroom, Cole took the occasion to do a bit of business that had recently been pecking away at his mind. He borrowed one of the men's cell phones and called the SpiritMark office.

"Hello, this is Cole Michaels. Can I speak with Roland Powers, please?...Sure, I'll hold."

"Cole!" Roland's voice soon zipped through the line. "What a surprise! What a surprise! Are you back in Nashville?"

Cole explained that he was on the road in central Georgia with nineteen other men on a twelve-day motorcycle mission trip. He had a spare moment, and he just wanted to find out about Lindsey. He had been thinking about her lately. Was she doing okay in the engagement? Was she still living in Nashville, or had she moved to Memphis? What was the latest news about her?

Roland teasingly reminded him of his great loss and told him that Lindsey had persuaded her fiancé to buy them a condo in New York City so that she could try to get a foothold in the modeling industry. The last Roland had heard, she had signed a contract with a small agency for some catalogue work. "You know Lindsey, though—she'll keep pushing until she makes something bigger happen."

Cole sighed, fighting feelings of jealousy. Had he made the right decision to give her up? Could he have possibly influenced her if he had married her and settled down?

"By the way," Roland said. "Congratulations on the sale of another million CDs."

Cole recoiled at the number.

Though distracted by the news about Lindsey, Cole engaged in business talk for four or five minutes. No, he still wasn't ready to go on tour. Neither was he ready to give interviews for television and radio. He would be forever thankful, though, for the recording opportunity SpiritMark had given him.

After his conversation with Roland, Cole made one more call, this time to his bank. He learned that the balance of his account was now $2,237,366.45. He breathlessly sat down in the grass. Nearly two and a half million dollars!

He deeply inhaled.

He sometimes thought in secret that his choice to walk away from a public life of fame, adulation, and riches and to give away his existing cash bit by bit was admirable. Yet, as he looked around at his motorcycle buddies pumping gas, catnapping in the sun, conversing on cell phones, and nibbling snacks, he sighed in humility. In truth, many of these men, along with a host of other Christian men around the country, would be equally as generous in their own way if they possessed his bank account.

Nevertheless, he pulled a blade of grass and thanked God again for his particular freedom to just drift and share his resources.

*   *   *

Over the course of the next week, the motorcycle group dynamics continued to add to the legend of road-trip moments.

One afternoon, Cole's group reached the bottom of a long descent on a narrow country road and was brought to a halt by a cow that had escaped its pasture and was standing astride the center line. The cow's calf was trapped in the roadside ditch—the mother was simply protecting her young one. While Cole's group patiently waited, the group led by Ron Sasson, the carpenter, arrived behind them. Ron, on his Harley, rumbled to the front, read the predicament, then accelerated slowly toward the cow to chase her off the highway. To everyone's surprise, though, the cow lowered her head at Ron, snorted like a bull, and dragged her hoof threateningly across the asphalt, daring Ron to move one inch closer. With everyone laughing in the background and getting poised to abandon their bikes, Ron stopped, did a double take, and instantly back-shuffled his 700-pound Harley.

At the next work site, when the men arrived to cut a winter's worth of firewood for the widowed grandmother raising a mentally retarded granddaughter, Randy Maner bypassed the uphill driveway. To everyone's amazement, he diverted his Harley Super Glide, slipping and sliding, through the ditch and up a steep grassy knoll like a stunt rider and dismounted in the yard with a brazen grin on his face. Cole heard someone say, "He used to be a dirt-bike racer."

Cole, during his solo travels, had accrued more than his share of precious and exhilarating memories, but the combination of multiple men, multiple bikes, multiple roads, and multiple days had, in his opinion, served up a gourmet platter of classical stories that would come around only once in a lifetime.

Just when he thought the moments they'd already experienced could never be topped, he heard Lynn Newton—one of the policemen—tell a portion of his story. "When I was seventeen, I did a lot of skydiving. I normally rode my Honda 250 to and from the airfield. And I normally wore my parachute on my back. One afternoon, when I was on my way home from the airport, it dawned on me that dragsters deploy a parachute to come to a stop. Curiosity got the best of me. On a two-mile straight stretch of road near my house, I twisted the throttle. When I reached the bike's top speed of eighty-miles-an-hour, I reached back and pulled the ripcord on my chute. Before I could get a grip on the handlebars to brace myself, I was launched straight up into the sky. I was at least thirty yards up in the air when I saw my bike wrap around a tree. Fortunately, I landed safely. But later, when I told my dad what had happened, he shook his head and said, *Son, tomorrow I want you to march straight down to the insurance office and deal with it.* That night, I didn't sleep very well. I racked my brain, trying to decide what I should tell the insurance agent. The next day, I went to the insurer and showed him a picture of the bike bent like a horseshoe around the trunk of the tree. He asked me how it happened. As I stuttered and stammered, he looked me up and down and said, *And pray tell me how you managed to walk away from this accident without any injuries.* When I reluctantly told him the truth, he leaned back in his chair and roared. He then slapped his desk and, still laughing, said, *Young man, I'm going to buy you a new bike, just simply for not lying to me. But don't ever pull a stunt like that again.*"

The men were already hooting and hollering before Lynn finished his last sentence. And they couldn't stop. "What a story!" "Can you believe that?" "Unbelievable!" "Sheee..." The men would never forget that story—they were all sure of it.

Then there was the Sunday morning church service. As planned, six of the men shared, one after the other, in Sunday school. And six men shared, one after the other, in the worship service. At Jason's request, all the men focused on the subject of "influence". They told about the individuals, experiences, or churches that had been the single greatest influencers in their lives. Near the end of the service, Jason asked the pastor and his wife to stand at the front of the auditorium. "I'm just curious," Jason said to the congregation. "If you're here today and your life has been influenced by this pastor and his wife, I would like to invite you to stand up and take a minute or two to let them know how they've influenced you."

For at least thirty minutes, men, women, and young people generously voiced their appreciation of how the shepherding couple had contributed personally to their faith, discipline, and growth or had earned their admiration and respect. Several spoke through tears. Nearly all extended their thanks.

Cole saw that many in the audience were deeply inspired by the session, including some of the motorcycle team. He suspected that the congregation had never before done this—a suspicion later confirmed when he overheard the pastor's adult son in the parking lot tell Jason, "Thanks for what you did in there today. My dad has actually been going through a dark season, wondering if he's wasting his time here and should possibly step down. I think this was the first time he actually heard the people give him any kind of public affirmation. And he needed it more than you can imagine. This might just revitalize him and keep him going for a few more years." The words of appreciation reminded Cole again of just how refreshingly different Jason's leadership style was compared to the average Christian leader.

Cole, to his intense satisfaction, witnessed a display of those differences again in the final days of the trip when the group, by appointment, met with three separate pastors and their families—one in a park, one in his parsonage, and one at a lakeside—and lifted them up in group prayer. The motorcyclists prayed for all aspects of the lives of each member of the family. Those families wept with gratitude for the unconventional encouragement. "It's not every day," one of the pastors said, "that a group of twenty men sweeps by like an angelic army and reenergizes you for battle."

As the trip came to an end, Cole tried desperately to stretch every mile and every hour. But on Friday night, the men gathered in a circle for their final time together. "All right, it's time to debrief," Jason said. "But first, I want to say how pleased I am with each of you. You have carried the name of Christ honorably throughout the last twelve days. You've helped...you've inspired...you've encouraged... and you've built memories. In all honesty, I've been swayed to be a better person because of your fellowship. Plus, it's been a long time since I've played so hard and had so much fun. I'm indebted to each of you for making this trip such a wonderful success."

All the men shared similar sentiments. They spotlighted the great roads, the superb riding, the life-changing camaraderie, and the remarkable ministries. And they each related a story or two that stood out to them.

The teams thanked their team leaders. They thanked Tim Royston for driving the support vehicle and hauling around tons of their camping gear. And everyone thanked Jason profusely for coordinating the adventure and for modeling real ministry for them.

DW Sunn, the retired contractor in the group, summed up the trip for everyone. "We've been given an awesome opportunity here. I, for one, just can't imagine never doing this again. I know the trip has been billed as the 'first annual' such trip, but let's make sure it really happens every year. And let's please, please make sure we introduce a lot of new men to what we've sampled." DW paused as he fought his emotions. "It's been absolutely unforgettable. And more men need to experience it."

The men gave each other hugs. And whispered words of promise.

Before Jason officially closed out the trip, he led the men in one final ride. It was over the ridge of Pine Mountain in the Franklin Delano Roosevelt State Park. Together the men watched a spectacular sunset and wondered why life couldn't grant more such grandiose and gracious adventures.

PART 4

73

On a rainy afternoon in early fall, Jesse was flipping through a sample inventory of designs at a dingy tattoo parlor, getting increasingly bored and impatient—and agitated at the incessant chatter of another client.

He found a pay phone in the back hallway and called the office of Cole's music label. "Yes, I've called a couple of times over the past year-and-a-half trying to book Cole Michaels for an event in Birmingham, Alabama. Both times I was told he wasn't available. Can you tell me if that's changed?"

When he heard the words, "I'm sorry, sir, but Mister Michaels is still not available for bookings right now," he slammed the phone back into the cradle. Was the man still wandering the country after all this time? Or was he back in Nashville, trying to protect his privacy?

Maybe the SpiritMark office was lying to him. He decided to leave the next morning to return to Nashville to do some more spying.

* * *

After two hours of walking with missionary Steve Rove along the back and side streets of Recife, Brazil, Cole was discouraged by the size of the slum districts, or *favelas* as Steve called them, and the number of dirty children, apparently homeless, wandering the cityscape.

In Cole's mind, the city of two million people was stretched along the Atlantic beach like a paradox of humanity. Tall, modern buildings that spoke of money and architectural ingenuity proudly marked the city's skyline. Yet, only blocks away were favelas, smelling of garbage and open sewage, where people lived in huts made of scrap boards, mud, and cinderblock.

Cole was reminded by Steve that most of the city's abandoned kids came from the favelas and that many of those children were often the victims of rape, abuse, and human trafficking. With his brain trying to grasp the inequity of what he was seeing, Cole accompanied Steve to a park where he was introduced to ten or twelve of the kids that Steve had loved, taught, and encouraged for nearly four years.

"Steve!" the kids screamed, throwing up filthy arms and running into his hug.

Cole watched as Steve enthusiastically greeted the children in Portuguese, rubbed their heads, and bent down to talk to them face to face. The only word Cole could decipher in the flurry of interaction was his own name. As he heard his name spoken, he saw Steve point to him. About twelve pairs of brown and hazel-colored eyes instantly looked his way.

Cole smiled and waved. Before he could ask Steve what

was happening, a runt of a boy, looking no older than six, ran over and grabbed his leg in a lingering embrace. Cole rested his palm on the little fellow's head.

"I just explained that you're the very generous man I've told them about. That it's because of you I was able to come back early. That it's because of you I will be able to help them with more food and more clothes."

Cole looked down at the little guy gripping his thigh.

"He's usually not so outgoing," Steve said.

"What's his name?"

"Lino. L...I...N...O."

"Lino," Cole repeated.

The young boy, dressed in a tattered and dirty T-shirt, looked up into Cole's eyes. And lifted his arms for Cole to hold him.

Cole fought back tears as he lifted the kid into his arms and allowed the youngster's body odor to fill his nostrils. He just couldn't imagine such a tiny boy living on the streets without parental care or protection. It was opposed to Cole's idea of justice, of what it meant to be human. As Cole scanned the group, looking briefly at each child, he felt his sense of manhood and fatherhood surge to the forefront. "Steve," he said, "is it okay if we go buy a few sacks of food and come back and feed these kids?"

Steve broke away from a conversation with one of the older boys. "Yeah, we can. I usually purchase food from the grocery store for them. It's more affordable. But, what do you have in mind?"

"I was thinking fast food. Burgers. Fries. Sodas."

Steve grinned, turned back to the kids, and spoke

loudly in Portuguese. In less than five seconds, Cole was rendered speechless by a cacophony of hoorays and yells, followed by a rush of hugs around his legs and waist.

Steve told the boys and girls to stay put. He explained that he and Cole would try to be back in about thirty minutes.

Cole tried to lower Lino to the ground, but the little fellow clung to him. "Can I take him with me?"

Steve exchanged words with the other kids, then turned to Cole and nodded. "Yeah…let's go."

As they left the park, Cole thought of how the little boy willingly let himself be carried off in the arms of a total stranger—and realized just how vulnerable these children were to would-be abductors.

His heart broke even further.

* * *

Jesse rose early the next morning and made the four-hour trip to Nashville. He checked into a cheap hotel that smelled of curry. He grabbed a sandwich at a drive-thru and proceeded to the SpiritMark office just off Music Row. He parked his car about thirty yards down the street from SpiritMark's front door.

For two hours, he waited inside his car and watched as several people entered and exited the SpiritMark building. Then he left the area for a while, for caution's sake, and came back during the final hour of the business day. A small group of people vacated the building at closing time, but again, Cole was not among them.

Determined, Jesse drove the short distance to the townhouse where he had seen Cole's motorcycle a year and a half before. Again, he parked catty-cornered across the street in the commercial parking lot. There was no motorcycle anywhere on the site.

Within the hour, the same two girls he had seen move into the house eighteen months before reappeared, unlocked the front door, and went inside. Room lights came on throughout the abode.

Jesse flopped his head backward against the headrest and pressed. "Where is he?"

That evening, Jesse found himself in a small country-music honky-tonk. Around midnight, an ugly woman about ten years older than Jesse said, "You wanna take me home with you?" She was half drunk. Jesse looked her up and down. *Yeah, I wanna take you home with me,* he thought. *I want to use you, and then I want to put a plastic bag over your head and watch you fight for your life while I suffocate you.*

Jesse set his glass down on the bar, stood, and said, "Not tonight, lady." He turned and walked out of the club, leaving her stammering.

Lying in his hotel bed an hour later, Jesse couldn't wipe the smirk off his face. He had actually done a good deed. A heck of a good deed. And somebody should give him credit for it!

* * *

Over the next three days, Cole was baptized deeper into the world of Recife's abandoned children. He saw, and even sat for awhile, inside the culvert where Lino slept at night with eight other kids. He learned that each child on the street was a member of a gang or "family", and that each kid, no matter how young, somehow contributed to the welfare of the gang. He learned that the leaders of the gangs carried guns, and used them on occasion to protect themselves and their turf. He watched groups of kids scrounge for food in the city's landfills. He saw children eat out of garbage cans. He heard about kids selling drugs and firearms for adults in the underworld of crime. He saw kids contending with fevers, allergies, and sicknesses, yet with no access to medical treatment—unless they shoplifted medicine from pharmacies. He even saw a few children here and there with fresh gunshot and knife wounds.

Who was accountable for this? The government? The churches? The culture? The more he saw, the more his heart cried out for the children. He was just thankful that a few people, like Steve, were on the streets dispensing food, love, and education, at least for a few hours a week.

But how could the $80,000 he had given Steve best be spent? How could the money be invested to achieve the greatest and most enduring impact? Cole spent hours with Steve, even late into the evenings, discussing possibilities.

74

After three days of fruitless stakeouts in Nashville, Jesse returned to Atlanta. On Saturday night, he searched the Internet again for new entries pertaining to Cole Michaels. He was cautiously upbeat when he found a new article from a newspaper in Savannah, Georgia.

> The Suncoast Nursing Home received a pleasant surprise last Thursday when a Christian motorcycle group of twenty men dropped by from Florida. The group was led by Pastor Jason Faircloth from Genesis Bible Church in Orlando. The men were on a twelve day mission trip, primarily doing home repair projects for the needy. The men blessed our residents with their company and conversations. Our oldest resident, George Mills, at a hundred and one, was even

given his first motorcycle ride.
To everyone's surprise, one of
the motorcyclists was the famous
Blonde Fiddler, Cole Michaels. Our
residents are still talking about the
event and how special it was for
everyone.

Two pictures accompanied the article. Jesse barely
glanced at the first photo that captured the male centenarian
on the back of a Harley. He focused more carefully on the
second photo, the one that framed the group of bikers
posing outside the nursing home.

There he was, at the back of the pack! Unmistakably!
Cole Michaels.

Jesse's heart raced. *Whoa, whoa*, he told himself. *Calm
down. This might lead to something, or it might not.* He
grabbed a pen and paper and wrote down the words:

Pastor Jason Faircloth
Genesis Bible Church
Orlando, Florida

Jesse noticed the date of the article—mid-August,
five or six weeks ago. He quickly typed "Genesis Bible
Church Orlando Florida" into his Internet search engine.
The church's name and phone number appeared on the
screen, but no website address. Had Cole decided to settle
in Orlando? Or had he just been passing through? Was this
Pastor Faircloth a longtime friend, or a new acquaintance?

Jesse buried his face in his slightly shaking palms. Should he rush to Orlando? Or would he just be wasting three days? Or a week?

He copied the church's phone number. He then looked at the computer clock: 8:21 PM Saturday, October 3, 2009. Would anyone be at a church office on Saturday night? What kind of story could he offer that would persuade religious crackpots to put him in touch with Michaels?

More importantly, how many more opportunities would he have to find him? How much longer could he afford to be so cautious? He squeezed his forehead hard. Maybe now was the time to throw caution to the wind.

He made the call from a pay phone down the street. When the phone rang on the other end, he tried to subdue his breathing. But no one answered. He called three more times after short waits. There was still no answer.

After a night of sleeplessness, weighty decisions, and self-mutilation with a carving knife, he returned to the pay phone the next morning and called again.

"Good morning, Genesis Bible Church," a female voice said.

Jesse took a deep, silent breath. "Yes, can I speak with Pastor Jason Faircloth, please?"

"Hold on, let me see if he's arrived yet."

Jesse wrestled with his decision. Should he? Should he not?

"All right," the lady's voice returned. "Give him just a second and he'll be right with you."

Was this it? Was he about to achieve the goal he'd worked so hard for?

"Pastor Faircloth speaking; how can I help you?"

"Pastor Faircloth, I'm calling from Atlanta, Georgia. I'm trying to contact a man named Cole Michaels. I understand that he rode with you on a motorcycle trip a few weeks ago. Can you tell me if he's still in Orlando? If he is, can you tell me how I can reach him?"

"And who am I speaking with, please?"

Jesse closed his eyes.

It was time.

"Yeah, my name is Jesse. I'm a son that Cole gave up for adoption twenty-five years ago. He's the biological father I've never seen. I've been trying for several years to track him down. Any help would be appreciated."

There was silence on the other end.

"Cole is not here this morning," the clergyman finally replied. "And I'm getting ready in a few minutes to lead a church service. Can I have your last name and phone number? And I'll personally make sure Cole gets the information."

"If you don't mind," Jesse said, intentionally smoothing out his voice, "I'd rather give out that information only to Cole. Can you simply contact him and ask if I can call him?"

"Sure...I'll be glad to."

"When should I plan to call you back, then?"

"Give me about...four hours. Call me back this afternoon at the same number, at around two o'clock."

*   *   *

On Sunday afternoon, after the in-house Bible study

with twenty children in Steve's apartment, Cole went for a long, private walk. He meandered through the favelas and city streets and allowed the uninterrupted sights and smells of unchecked poverty to charge his creative thinking. The situation, particularly for the homeless kids and their long nightmare, was incomprehensible.

Considering his commitment to help children in need, Cole didn't believe that his introduction to Steve Rove and the street kids of Recife was a coincidence. But even if it was, he now knew too much to blankly walk away.

He opened the ragged Bible that he'd brought with him for the walk. He turned to the Gospel of Mark, chapter nine, verses thirty-six and thirty-seven. He read them quietly as he ambled along: *"Taking the child in His arms, Jesus said to them, 'Anyone who welcomes a little child like this on my behalf welcomes me, and anyone who welcomes me welcomes my Father who sent me.'"*

"Oh, God," he prayed, "You love these street kids more than anyone in the whole world. How can I show them your love? How can I help cut through the betrayal, the abuse, and the exploitation that has dominated their lives, and introduce them to you in a way that will lift you high above every lie they've ever believed?"

He continued to walk as he prayed. And brainstormed.

Should part of the $80,000 be used to help Steve rent a larger apartment so that ten children could move in with him? Perhaps to hire a live-in nanny and cook, along with a teacher to offer reading, writing, and arithmetic classes every day. Perhaps two large apartments could be found side by side that would house twenty kids.

Cole kicked a piece of gravel. But would a triage to help just twenty of the kids even be fair? What about the remaining hundreds?

Or, as an American, was he being totally naive? Would the kids, after carving out a routine life on the streets with freedom and independence, even want to move into an apartment where they would be subjected to rules and regulations? And even if they wanted to, could they? Would they need psychotherapy to even begin to make the jump from one value system to the other? Plus, what kind of duress would Steve be placed under if he lovingly tried to assume the moment-by-moment responsibilities for twenty troubled kids? Could he manage?

Oh, God, we really need your help here! he pled.

As he rounded a corner, he was caught off guard by the sight of a young boy who looked about eight years old crawling out of a storm drain at the side of the street. Then he heard a gaggle of childish voices echoing from somewhere inside the drain. He stopped and watched as two more grimy-faced boys and a mop-headed little girl hauled themselves up out of the drain and onto the cobblestone road.

Cole shook his head. A surge of broken-heartedness nearly paralyzed him as he drooped his head and sighed. The quartet of young vagabonds ignored him as they walked barefooted toward a major intersection. He sighed again. No matter how badly he felt, he couldn't help but be impressed by the youngsters' adaptation to their circumstances.

Obviously, he realized, these castaways did not need U.S.-style accommodations. So what were their basic needs that the $80,000 could help accommodate? Food and clothing, of course. Medical treatment. But what else? As Cole headed back toward Steve's place, he framed an answer. Besides the basic needs, the street kids needed adult role models who would love them, provide an element of security and protection for them, and teach them. They needed to learn to read and write. They needed to learn relevant trades. And they needed to learn that God's truths would set them free from darkness, fears, and insecurities— truths that would guide them and give them hope.

Food, clothing, and loving teachers.

Should he help build a school for them?

He was walking down the street next to a tall plywood wall covered with graffiti when a truck horn trounced his attention. He looked ahead. A tow truck was turning across his path into a gated entryway of some kind. The truck was pulling a wrecked van. When the truck and its haul cleared the sidewalk, Cole walked on. As he passed the iron gate, he looked inside. He saw a junkyard full of wrecked cars, vans, buses, and trucks.

He took another twenty steps and stopped. He backtracked to the gate and looked into the junkyard one more time.

His mind lingered, then sparked. What if...? Nahhh.

But the more he explored the idea, the more excited he got. But did the idea have any real merit, or was he just being silly? The more he probed the idea, the more convinced he was that it was either ingenious—or ludicrous. Either way, he had to share it with Steve.

75

Cole was excited and ready to talk when he entered Steve's apartment. The moment he walked in, though, Lino ran full-speed into his arms, shouting, "Cole!" Cole's name was the only English word the little fellow had learned. Cole grabbed the boy and twirled him, then gave him a long embrace.

"Hey, guy," Steve shouted from across the room, where he was playing a board game with two boys and three girls, all preteens. "Pastor Faircloth called from Atlanta about half an hour ago. He wants you to call him at the church as soon as possible. He says it's urgent."

Cole was immediately concerned. "Did he say what it was about?"

"Nope. He just said it was urgent."

"All right; will you explain to Lino that I need to be alone in the bedroom for a few minutes to make the call? And then when I'm finished, I need to bend your ear for about twenty minutes. I have a bizarre idea that I think might help a few hundred kids."

"Really? All right—well, I'll be right here." He then spoke Portuguese to Lino. Lino hesitantly let go of Cole's neck, as Cole lowered him to the floor.

Cole went into Steve's bedroom and closed the door. He used the land line and called the church number in Orlando.

Jason answered after only one ring. "Jason speaking."

"Jason, this is Cole. I just walked in the door. Steve said I needed to call you right away."

"Ah, Cole. Are you alone?"

"I am," Cole answered slowly.

"Do you remember telling me in passing about the baby boy you gave up for adoption right before you got married?"

Cole felt a sudden ball of caution in the pit of his stomach. "I remember."

"Well, a young man named Jesse called the church office about three-and-a-half hours ago. He claims to be that child. He said he's been trying for a few years to make contact with you. He wanted to know if I could give him your phone number. I didn't think it was prudent to assume anything, so I told him I would call you first to get permission. He's supposed to call me back in about thirty minutes to find out if you're willing to give him the number. Listen—I'm not sure what it all means. But I just wanted to get the message to you pronto."

Every other thought, including his idea for helping the children of Recife, flew out of his head. "He...who...what? Are...are you serious?"

"I wouldn't joke about this."

"The child we gave up for adoption?"

"The child you gave up for adoption."

"He wants to call me?"

"Yes, he wants to call you."

"Like...today, now, this afternoon?"

"That's the impression I got."

Cole looked out the bedroom window. His mind instantly recalled the day nearly twenty-five years ago when Jana was taken to the hospital with a fully pregnant belly and then was brought home childless. "What's his name again?"

"Jesse. That's all he said. He didn't give me a last name."

"Jesse. Did he say where he was calling from...or how he even knew to contact you?"

"No. To be honest, he was reluctant to give me any information other than his first name. He just wants to know if he can have your phone number."

Cole knelt beside the bed. "All right...sure...of course. Give him this number. And just pray that if he does call that God will give me the right words to say. Wow...I'm ah...I guess I'm in shock." Cole felt an uncertain excitement start to build. "Can you pray with me?"

Cole listened intently as Jason prayed that God would grant him special grace, understanding, and wisdom in choosing what to say during the phone call.

"Thanks," Cole said. "That means more to me than you know."

Within seconds, Cole was alone in his retrospection. He sat on the edge of the bed and gawked out the window. Had he and Jana made the right decision to give the baby up for adoption? Had the boy grown up in a nurturing and stable home? Was the young man trying to make contact now out of curiosity about his biological parents, or a need to trace his genetic identity? Whatever the answers, Cole wondered tentatively, yet excitedly, if there might be an opportunity here to forge a new and long-term relationship.

After ten minutes or so, Steve poked his head into the room. "Is everything okay?"

"Yeah, I'm just waiting for another call. It might take a few minutes. But I'll tell you about it later.

In about twenty minutes, the phone rang.

* * *

Steve, sitting on the sofa watching cartoons with a little boy nestled in his lap and four other kids snuggled all around him, was tempted one more time to get up and go check on his friend. He was definitely growing concerned. Cole had been in the bedroom engaged in phone calls for forty-five minutes or more. Was something wrong? Had there been bad news of some kind?

Right when he started to excuse himself from the sofa, he saw the bedroom door open. Cole, looking perplexed, stepped out of the room and rambled clumsily to the kitchen.

When Cole didn't say anything, Steve said, "You look a little strange, bro. Do you need to talk about whatever just happened in there?"

Cole gulped water from a plastic cup. "It looks like I'll be taking a trip back to the States."

Before Steve could ask additional questions, Cole moved closer to the couch. "There's a part of my story that I never told you," he said, raising his voice to compete with the TV.

Steve promptly softened the TV volume with a remote.

"Before Jana and I were married, we had a baby out of wedlock, a little boy. We were high-school seniors. With our consent, the little guy was taken straight from the delivery room and given to an adoptive family. We never even got to look at him. Well," Cole said, then paused, "it seems that the little boy has grown up and has tracked me down. He's living in Atlanta. And he wants to meet."

Steve peeled away the kids and took a break from the sofa. He led Cole outside onto a tiny balcony just off the kitchen.

"And?" Steve prompted.

"And I've agreed to meet him. I'm supposed to rendezvous with him this coming Friday at a hotel in Gainesville, Florida. He's a freelance architect. He'll be flying out of Atlanta on Monday week for a month-long project on the West Coast. He wants us to meet, if possible, before he leaves. He has this next weekend free. So, he's going to drive down from Atlanta and I'll ride the bike up from Orlando. And we'll have a whole day, or more, together."

Steve was awkwardly speechless. All he could say was, "Wow."

"I'll leave here on Wednesday," Cole said. "Okay if I come back the following week sometime?"

Steve placed a supportive hand on Cole's shoulder. "By all means!"

76

*T*he next morning, Cole bought a ticket for a flight leaving Brazil in forty-eight hours.

His mental focus tilted from the street kids of Recife to his own flesh-and-blood offspring. What a surprise, after so many years of living with no family, to now hear the breathing voice of a son he had biologically fathered. Would the boy look like him? Or more like a grown-up version of Shay? And would there be an opportunity here to redeem himself as a father?

He really wanted time alone with his violin, just to play and think. But the Mysterious Lady was back in Orlando at Jason's place.

He did manage, though, in the midst of his mental turmoil, to share with Steve a dulled-down version of his idea for the kids and the junkyard. He was too distracted, though, to gauge Steve's response.

Even so, out of nervous energy, he tracked down the owner of the yard. When he finally found the man the evening before his departure, he asked three important questions: Can you legally sell the land *as is* to a private buyer? Would you be interested in selling the land *as is*? And, if so, what would be your price?

The owner of the yard, a middle-class hardworking ruffian, said in extremely shattered English that he, of course, would be interested in selling the plot of land *as is*. But only for a minimum of 1.3 million dollars. He did not know, however, if he could legally sell the property to a private buyer, especially a foreigner. He could make a few calls to find out. But he was sure it would take a few days to get an answer. In the meantime, he was certain the city government would not even consider giving their permission until they first knew the intentions of the buyer.

So Cole shared with the man his preliminary vision.

The man threw up his dirty hands and laughed. "I don't know what to say, man! You Americans sometimes...how do you say...a little strange."

Cole told the man he would contact him again in a few days, when he got back from the States.

The next morning, Cole said goodbye to Steve and took a taxi to the airport.

Once he was in the air, he rested for the first time in three days. As he listened through an airline headset to some chill music performed by an up-and-coming European group called the Sugarbaker Ladies, he managed to sleep a portion of the way to Orlando.

* * *

"The young man called again," Jason told Cole when he

arrived at the airport in Orlando on Wednesday evening. "He says he's reserved room four-forty at the Red Roof Inn. He'll meet you there on Friday evening at six."

Cole had initially intended to use Wednesday evening and all day Thursday to just lie around Jason's place in Orlando and relax. But he was too antsy. His ever-increasing anxiousness regarding the meeting with his son stimulated his brain like amphetamines.

By noon on Thursday, he couldn't just hang around any longer. He loaded up his bike, strapped on his violin backpack, and headed out of Orlando.

He had a day and a half before the meeting, so he pointed his beloved Scrambler westward toward the Gulf Coast. He would take the long way to Gainesville.

Once he exited the city limits, he turned onto back roads. What a joy to cruise along on two wheels at one's own pace. As he roared along the asphalt in the 80-degree weather, he let his mind savor the memory of his high-school days with Jana—the accidental pregnancy, the day of the delivery, and the whole adoption affair. He remembered that at the time he had been thankful that someone else would assume responsibility for the child. He wondered now if he would make the same choice if he could be transported back in time.

By late afternoon, he found himself in the coastal village of Bayport. He followed signs to Bayport Park where he walked out onto a fishing pier and dangled his feet out over the seawater. He pulled the violin from its backpack and played a Russian classical piece, then another and another. He lost himself in the melancholy tunes.

After four or five songs, he lay back on the pier, looked up into the sky, and wondered if the upcoming rendezvous with his first son would be such a remarkable reunion that it would somehow graft the young man back into his life. Would they ride motorcycles together one day? Take a cross-cultural mission trip together? Perhaps to Brazil? Hopefully, the young fellow was a Christian. Maybe Atlanta would become a regular stop for Cole. Maybe, at some point, he would even settle down there.

Massaged by his fantasies, he fell asleep on the sun-faded boards.

When he awakened a couple of hours later, he sat through a glorious sunset, then checked into a nearby hotel.

77

On Friday morning at an Atlanta gun show, Jesse purchased all the separate parts for a Browning .22-caliber whisper pistol and a silencer. Later, at a department store, he bought five rolls of standard duct tape.

Back at his apartment, he assembled the gun, then stashed the tape, handgun and silencer, Reunion Registry documents, and copy of his biological mother's death certificate into a leather satchel.

After showering, he packed a change of clothes and a bottle of steroids in a small suitcase. He threw the suitcase and satchel, along with some beef jerky and a bottle of water, into the car and headed south on I-75 toward Florida.

* * *

Late Friday morning Cole aimed the Triumph in a northerly direction. As he scooted through the natural-springs area of central Florida, he thought of two more things he wanted to ask Jesse. Was the young man married?

And did he have any children? Cole smiled at the thought that he—the Blonde Fiddler—might just be a grandfather. Wow! What a multilayered surprise that would be! He laughed. He couldn't think of a grander twist of fate!

When he reached Fanning Springs at around 1:30 he turned the bike inland toward Gainesville. A few miles later, when he reached the town of Trenton, he stopped on impulse at a quaint-looking cafe. He really wasn't hungry, but he was only an hour out of Gainesville and he needed to burn some time. To curb his anxiety, he ordered and then slowly nibbled away at chips and a chicken-salad sandwich. Afterward, he took a casual walk through a hardware store and a gift shop. He wondered if he should give his son a gift of some kind, but decided that such a gesture might be a little too premature for the circumstance.

At 3:00, he mounted the Scrambler for the last leg to Gainesville.

He arrived at the popular college town shortly before 4:00. He asked for directions and quickly found the Red Roof Inn. He was too early, of course, for the 6:00 rendezvous. And he didn't want to assume that Jesse would be comfortable if he checked into the same hotel. So, after a few minutes of thought, he checked into a hotel diagonally across the highway.

Once in his room, he began the minute-by-minute countdown to 6:00 PM. Time seemed to pass excruciatingly slow. To occupy himself, he wiped down his bike, took a long hot shower, and viewed a television news update. At 5:40, he dressed in a clean set of clothes and left his room.

Out in the parking lot, he walked to the edge of the

highway, the Red Roof Inn visible on the other side. "Oh, Father," he prayed as he scanned the Friday evening traffic, "I feel like I'm in a daze, or a dream. I'm not sure what to expect here. Or what to hope for. Just give me the insight to speak healthy words. And to make amends if that's necessary."

During a break in the flow of vehicles, he sprinted across the three lanes of asphalt. When he stepped onto the Red Roof Inn parking lot, he felt his pulse start to jackhammer. Around the corner from the lobby, he stopped and took multiple deep breaths. "All right," he said, "room four-forty. Let's do it."

When he entered the hotel lobby, he felt that his mind was suddenly and strangely filled with fog. For a few seconds, he totally forgot all the questions he was supposed to ask, and everything he wanted to say. He simply found the elevators and whirred up to the fourth floor. He floated down the hallway toward the room. At the end of the hallway, he found room 440. The door was standing open.

He was suddenly overcome with joy. His mind started to clear.

He took another deep breath, whispered an additional prayer, and knocked.

"Come on in," a voice shouted. "I'm in the bathroom. Just close the door behind you."

* * *

Like a predator waiting for the precise moment to strike, Jesse was poised and ready.

When the man crossed into the room and turned to shut the door, Jesse struck with the speed of a cobra. He bludgeoned the man behind the ear with the butt of his Browning .22 and watched with pleasure as the music star crumpled to the carpet like a load of bricks.

Jesse stepped back for a second and observed. Every nerve cell in his body, it seemed, was zinging with electricity.

78

Cole felt like he was looking into a dark well. He tried to move, but couldn't. He tried to talk, but couldn't. Where was he? What was happening? The pain in his head was horrendous! But why? What was the cause? He was seized by fear and panic. He was sure he was going to throw up. He tried to break free of the catatonic blur—and then everything went blank.

For a sudden moment, there was another dull haze. And more excruciating agony. How long? Then the darkness snuffed out everything again.

When Cole's eyes finally opened, it took him several horrifying minutes to focus. His brain struggled like an animal in quicksand to interpret what was happening. His eyes burned. He felt like he was trying to crawl out of a tunnel. But he still couldn't move. Then, like fog dissipating from a windshield, his vision slowly, slowly captured a sight that set off new panic alarms throughout his system.

Was he hallucinating? Imagining? He closed his eyes and reopened them. He squinted. Again. And again. The vision before him was incomprehensible. He was looking at...his own image reflected in a mirror. He stared at the reflection and willed it to be only a dream.

Then he looked down at his lap, and realized that the image was true. He was sitting in a chair. And he was duct taped. A strip of the silver adhesive was wrapped around his head, across his mouth. From his shoulders all the way down to his waist, including his arms, he was completely bound by the tape. Was he even wearing a shirt? He didn't know; no fabric could be seen. His knees and his ankles were wrapped as well.

His memory was beyond hazy, but the throbbing pain at the back of his head combined with the massive tape job told him he had been on the receiving end of either an elaborate hoax or an unimaginable act of treachery.

But who or what...

He had...he had been on his way to meet someone.

He tried to loosen the grip of the tape, but it constricted him as if he were cast in cement.

He twisted his neck and looked around.

A hotel room.

Yes, that was it! He had been coming to a hotel...to meet...to meet his son.

But that made him even more confused. He groaned as loud as he could to attract someone's attention.

He tried to wiggle free again. But it was useless.

Had he stumbled into the wrong hotel room? Had he been mistaken for someone else? Had he stepped accidentally into a foul plot that had gone awry?

Just as he decided to try to throw himself to the floor

and slither across the carpet to the door and pound it with his feet, the door opened.

"Well, well, I see you're still in the land of the living," said a young man. The guy closed and locked the door behind him.

Cole stared long and hard at the man, feeling a rush of enormous anger. Then with a jolt he realized that he was looking at a younger clone of himself. The height, the build, the hair, the shape of the face—it was all nearly an exact replication of his own. There was no other explanation—this had to be the son he had come to meet, the son he had fathered in high school. Plus, the voice was the one that had spoken with him over the phone.

"All right," the young man sneered. "We'll begin the fun now."

Cole watched in abject disbelief as the guy balled up his fist and brutally slugged him across the jaw. Cole heard himself moan explosively in pain as his head was thrust sideways. He was sure something had broken. But before he could string words together in his mind to form another thought, he was slapped from the other direction with the full swing of an open hand.

As Cole shook his head in an effort to clear his brain, he was sure he heard the attacker's voice say, "Question number one. So, dad, why in the sick and hellish name of *family* did you father me if you had no intention of keeping me?"

Cole tried frantically to process the question. He then tried to move his lips beneath the tape to demonstrate that he was willing to talk.

"Second question. Did you know that I was a freak of nature when I was born? Is that why you threw me aside like a piece of trash?" The man raised a clenched fist again. "You're going to die anyway, so you *will* tell me the truth."

Cole felt his eyes flinch. He was going to die anyway? What was...?

"Third question. Do you have any idea whatsoever how utterly and completely you destroyed my life?"

Cole watched as the young man walked over to the bed and pulled a pistol out from under one of the pillows. *Dear God,* he prayed. *I'm in the dark here...I'm not...*

The young man returned to the chair and pressed the barrel of the pistol against Cole's left temple.

79

God forgive me, Cole prayed. He closed his eyes. But before he could think another thought, he felt a tearing burst of pain unlike anything he had ever felt. The duct tape was violently ripped from his face, pulling facial hair and skin with it. He tried to scream. His mouth, though, was instantly capped by the abuser's strong hand.

"My name is Jesse," the young man said, squeezing Cole's mouth. "And I've waited over half my life to hear the answers to these three questions." Jesse then pushed the gun nozzle into Cole's thigh. "And I'm absolutely ready to torture you for as long as it takes to get straight answers. As you can see, the gun is equipped with a silencer. So I can shoot the crap out of you and no one will ever hear anything. Plus, we're on the top floor, in the end room, and you're facing an outside wall. Now I'm going to slowly let go of your mouth. And if you try to scream or call for help, I'll simply wrap the tape around your face again. And then I'll beat you so badly that you'll wish you were a pile of BS in a farmyard. Is that clear enough for you?"

Cole nodded that he understood.

The hand gradually unclasped Cole's mouth.

Cole slowly wrenched his jaw from side to side in an effort to alleviate some of the pain and decipher if anything was broken. The sharp throb, though, did not subside. And a portion of his jaw indeed felt as if it had been knocked out of alignment. One of his upper teeth had been loosened. And his mouth was full of blood.

"Can I ask a question?" Cole slurred. But no sooner had he spoken the last syllable than he was slapped silly again.

"I don't think you understand," Jesse said. "I'm the one asking the questions. You're the one answering them.

Cole rolled his tongue around on the inside of his mouth and tried to forget about the screaming pain. "All right, remind me of the first question again."

"Why did you father me if you had no plans to keep me?" As Jesse spat out the words, he rested the pistol on the bed and pulled out an official-looking document. He snapped it open in front of Cole's face. "The Adoption Reunion Registry in Atlanta has confirmed that I'm your son. This is a copy of my birth mother's death certificate. Your former wife! And it should be obvious just by looking at me that you're the father. So, I ask again; why did you allow me to be born if you knew you didn't want me? And I want an honest answer!" The demand was delivered with jarring profanity.

Cole quickly glimpsed portions of the purported death certificate. It looked authentic. Cole had never heard of the Adoption Reunion Registry, but clearly the organization had made a correct connection between the birth child and birth parents.

Cole looked fully into the young man's eyes for the first time. He unexpectedly winced. He had never before glared into a pair of eyes that looked so...empty, so hollow, so haunted. His fear intensified. "All right," Cole mouthed awkwardly due to the agony in his jaw, "we had you out of wedlock when we were still in high school. All the adults in our life at the time persuaded us to keep you through full term and then give you up for adoption. We were told this would be the best decision for everyone, especially you. We were young and naïve, and uncertain of our future together, so not knowing what else to do, we did as we were counseled."

Jesse huffed. "So I was a freaking accident?"

Cole hesitated. He had never thought about whether the twenty-five-year-old decision might have caused long-term damage to anyone. "An accident?" he finally answered, "Yes, in the sense that we were not trying to have a baby at the time. But no, not in the sense that God didn't plan from the beginning of time for your arrival. He knew—"

Jesse raised a hand for him to stop, then retrieved the pistol. "You know," he growled, "I think I'll shoot you in the freaking bow arm just for the fun of it."

"Bow arm," Cole repeated. Was the guy talking about the violin bow? *Oh no...not the arm...Oh, God, please help me...*

The pop of the muted gunfire was followed by a thud, then searing pain in his upper right arm. Cole contracted every muscle in his body. He squinted through half-closed eyes at this right arm. The bullet had pierced the tape at close range just below the shoulder. Blood oozed like evening shadows to the surface of the tape. Cole closed his eyes. How could this be happening? Thoughts flashed in his head of his carefree life, the open road, his friends, Brazil, his plans for the Recife street kids. Was this how it was all going to end?

"All right, question number two. And please do not use the word 'God' again. It pisses me off. Now, did you know that I was an absolute reject, a bona fide freak, when I came out of your lover's belly—and is that the reason you didn't want me?" Wearing a sadistic smile, Jesse pressed the loaded gun into Cole's forehead and waited for an answer.

Distracted by the gunshot wound, immense fear, loss of blood, and his own list of questions, Cole desperately tried to focus. "We never even saw you when you were born. I swear. It had been prearranged for you to be taken immediately from the birthing room and turned over to the adopting couple. We weren't allowed to see you, hold you, or talk to you. And we were told not to ask any questions. So, I honestly have no idea what you're talking about when you say you're a reject and a freak. That's all I can tell you. That's the absolute truth as I know it."

Jesse turned and kicked a plastic trash can against the wall. Through his teeth, his hissed, "So, you had no part in the decision?"

Cole was confused. "Yes," he stammered, "whether it was right or wrong; we were the ones that chose to give you up."

"NO, You Fool! I mean the surgery!"

Cole shook his head. "I…we…didn't know anything about any surgery."

"Then let's just play a game here," Jesse snapped. "Do you know the word *hermaphrodite*?

Cole needed medical attention pronto. He shook his head again. "No. I'm sorry—I don't."

Jesse swiped his hand across his mouth in a gesture of frustration. "It's a mix up of chromosomes, a freaking accident of biology. It's a cruel, malicious joke of nature when nature can't decide if a baby should be a boy or a girl. So, it equips the little monster with the reproduction organs of both."

Cole was without words. He felt himself sweating.

"Do you know how often such a mutant is born?" Jesse demanded.

Cole managed a weak "No."

"One out of every ten thousand births, or point-zero-one-percent," Jesse said. "And your little baby happened to have the distinct horror of being the one-in-ten-thousand. So had you decided to keep me, like any decent and loving parent should have done, how in the name of your pitiful, powerless God would you have handled it?"

Praying frantically behind his words, Cole said, "First of all, I don't know that I could give an answer without knowing more about the disorder. But I'm sure I—"

Jesse snorted. "I'm born; the doctor throws me in your arms; says, 'Uh oh, we've got a real problem here'; shows you the little mix up; and says, 'You can choose now if you want it to be a boy or a girl, *or* you can wait a few years, for God's sake, and see if it carries more testosterone or estrogen, to see if it becomes more of a boy or girl, then consult its opinion about what seems natural, and then decide if surgery is needed.'" Jesse stuck his face into Cole's face. "So, what would you have done, Mister Blonde Fiddler?"

All of Cole's senses, physically and mentally, were on overload. "I'm…I'm sure I…we…would have done the latter. But that—"

"And you would have loved me anyway, even though I was a freak?"

"I can't imagine that we would've hesitated for a second."

Jesse ground his teeth. "That's what I thought you'd say. So that brings me to my third question. Do you have any inkling of an idea how you stole from me everything and anything resembling a normal life?"

Cole stumbled. "I still don't understand."

"The man that adopted me, you freaking moron!" Jesse shouted. "He decided that day in the hospital that he wanted his wife to have a baby girl. So I was emasculated there on the spot. But what do you know—I grew up and became a man! Yet, because of their decision, I've never been able to *be* a man!" Jesse placed his index finger forcefully between Cole's eyes. "And I blame you!" he growled as he shoved with his full strength.

Cole's head snapped backward, raising the front legs of the chair off the floor. Cole felt his pulse racing. When his chair slammed back to the floor, he said, "I'm at a loss here. I'm not—"

"I am a man with a woman's genitals!" Jesse yelled. "I'm a circus freak! A misfit! A throwaway! An *it!* I'm something that nobody has ever wanted. Or ever will want. I am a monster! And it can all be traced back to you. So, the next question is, am I going to kill you quickly, or am I simply going to let you sit here and bleed to death and give you time to think about what you've done?"

Cole was left momentarily speechless. Somewhere deep inside him, he registered for the first time the stark and ugly truth behind the young man's unfolding words…the words of his own flesh and blood…his biological son. And those words of revelation kick-started a father's protective passion. He lowered and raised his head. He sighed. "What if *I* want you?" He felt the power of the words even as he spoke them.

Jesse instantly froze. He then tilted his head backward and howled in laughter. "Oh, that's good! Really good! I certainly didn't see that one coming!"

"I mean it," Cole said. He then hung his head in genuine shame. "I really do. At the same time, I agree with you—I deserve to die, just as you've said. In all honesty, I've felt that way for years. And believe me, I've only lived as long as I have because of grace…God's grace. So if today is my day, then I'm ready. And I guess I had rather it be… at your hands than in any other way." He started to weep out of fresh guilt. "And, no, I cannot begin to imagine the heartache, the trauma, the confusion you've been forced to live with because of my decision. All I can do at this point is to say that I'm sorry. I'm truly, truly sorry. I had no clue." Having surrendered to whatever was going to happen, all fear left him. "Please forgive me."

"What's *this* crap?" Jesse retorted, sounding now less sure of himself. "I'm facing a man down with a gun. And he's not afraid to die." He paced the length of the room and back. Then in an explosion of anger, he thrust the pistol up to Cole's arm and shot one more time.

Cole grimaced and screamed.

Jesse stood there breathing like a wild horse. "So—do you still want me now?" he yelled.

Contorting every muscle in his head and upper body, Cole gasped deeply and said, "I would like to die knowing that you've heard me apologize with all my heart for the wrong I've caused you and for you to know that…yes…the man who fathered you would still like to be your friend... and father...in spite of who you are or what you've done. Even if you want to kill me."

Jesse was clearly shaken. He lowered the pistol to his side and turned away. "So you would just like to go ahead and be my friend," he mocked. "You don't even know me! You can't mean that!"

Cole had never felt more at peace. "Yeah, actually, I do," he sniffed. "With the help of my God, I mean it more than you can imagine." He sniffed up some of his tears.

Jesse snarled, "And I'm hearing this now, after I've lived with unspeakable abuse, rejection, and loneliness my whole life! And you actually try to make it sound genuine?"

Cole stumbled for a response. He then heard Jesse mumble, "So, tell me, mister fiddler—what about your life?" Jesse turned and snapped, "All love and roses since you found God?"

Cole rolled his head. "He's definitely rescued me out of a lot of pain, heartache, and misery."

"And so what have you been doing since you got out of prison?"

How does he know I was in prison? "I...uh...I've just been roaming the country. Helping people. Trying to repay some debts."

"Helping people?" Jesse laughed a hideous laugh. "What if I told you that I've spent the last year of my life only hurting people."

"Like I said, God is a God of grace. He can forgive. That's what He's known for."

Cole felt the barrel of the pistol jammed into the back of his neck.

A strange pause followed.

The reflection in the mirror showed Jesse suddenly drop his head. "So you want to be my friend?" Jesse said. His voice, for the first time, was less harsh. Almost lifeless. "Well, it's too late. So let me hear you beg before I pull the trigger."

Cole hung his head. And whispered. "I only beg that God will forgive you...just like He's forgiven me." Cole stiffened as he felt the pistol drive deeper into his neck. "During my wretched life I've caused more harm to more people than you will ever know. And I thought I had paid most of my dues. But, I see now that I was wrong." Cole now wept freely, out of guilt. "I'm tired. And I'm broken. And I'm truly sorry. All I've ever wanted in the last ten years is to be a vessel that God could use to make a difference. But I guess I've run my course. So I'm ready whenever you are." He closed his eyes and waited for the final bullet. And realized that it would be welcomed.

Seconds ticked by in slow motion. With his eyes clamped shut, Cole sat in silence. He was ready. He wondered if bleeding to death would really be so bad. In his last moments, he tried as a father not to focus on his newly discovered failure, both gargantuan and irrefutable. It was too much to ponder in the throes of death.

"Then may your God of grace forgive me!" Jesse finally whispered.

Cole heard the shot and jumped like a sprung mousetrap. But he didn't feel the bullet.

He cracked open his eyes and looked.

He saw the mirrored image.

Lying on the bed bleeding profusely, Jesse...his firstborn son...had blown a hole in his own head.

In disbelief, Cole froze for a second. He then cried like he had never cried before. He felt his shoulders bounce up and down like misfiring pistons as he started yelling uncontrollably.

"No, God!" he finally screamed plainly for the heavens to hear. "Don't do this again! I can't handle it! I should be the one this time—don't you understand?" He thrashed violently in his chair for nearly a minute, then went limp. His head drooped to his chest. He tried to catch his breath. He looked at Jesse again. "Save him! You can't let him go like this!" And in a burst of energy, he threw himself to the floor. Pushing with his bound feet, he managed to scoot to the door. On his back, he pounded the door with his feet as if he could overpower the wood.

As he pounded, he bellowed, bellowed, and bellowed for help until he was nearly hoarse.

80

As soon as Cole was given permission to leave his hospital recovery room, he hurried to the Intensive Care Ward to take up vigil at Jesse's side.

As he maneuvered through the hallways, he was careful to guard his right arm that hung in a sling. It had been fractured in two places by Jesse's bullets. Titanium plates and screws had been surgically inserted to align the broken sections of bone and hold them in place until they could fuse.

"I'm not convinced," the orthopedic surgeon had said, "that you will ever regain full range of motion in the arm. But in due time, maybe in four or five months, you should certainly be able to play the violin and ride your motorcycle again. In the meantime, you'll have to wear the sling twenty-four/seven until your next visit."

His jaw had also been x-rayed. Fortunately, nothing had been broken or damaged long-term. But he still suffered from sharp pains whenever his mouth settled or twisted in certain motions. The doctor's prognosis was that within the week the jaw would feel normal again.

The duct tape had been taken off his shirtless body while he had been anesthetized for the arm surgery. The nurses had removed the complicated mess slowly, using a special lotion to minimize damage to the skin. There were hairless sections across his chest and a few raw areas around the torso that were still sensitive, otherwise, the tape was history.

As he entered the ICU, he quickly asked for an updated report of Jesse's medical condition.

"He's still in the coma," the head nurse informed him. "The blood transfusion initially helped stabilize him. But for the last four hours, his vitals have been dangerously weak." The nurse explained that no surgeries were planned—that none could even be implemented at this point. It was now just a waiting game.

Cole learned that the attempted-suicide bullet had entered the roof of Jesse's mouth, clipped the base of his brain, and exited his body just behind the top of his right ear.

Cole asked, "Will he come out of the coma? Will he live? Will there be any temporary or permanent brain damage if he does live?"

"Only time will tell," was the prevailing answer.

* * *

Cole reflectively pulled a chair up to the bedside and sat. The quiet of the room transformed the space into a sanctuary for him. He reached out and slowly touched the hand of his boy. For the first time, he saw the scars of self-mutilation all over the young man's arms. He slowly lowered the sheets and found additional scars on the chest and legs. He realized then that suicide had probably never been a distant thought for the young man. "Oh, my God, what have I done?" He squeezed Jesse's hand. "Why did I ever give you up?" He hung his head and poured out his guilt-ridden apologies. Over...and over again.

For three days he stayed at the bed around the clock and petitioned God with tears, like David of old, for the survival of his son. He even went so far as to demand a miracle.

But in the early morning hours of Tuesday, October 13, Jesse slipped away into eternity.

For an hour after the corpse had been removed from the room, Cole sat like a stubborn troll and stewed in grief and anger.

* * *

Jesse's death was quickly ruled a suicide by Florida's District Eight Medical Examiner. The Gainesville Police Department filed no charges against Cole.

DNA tests revealed that Jesse Rainwater had indeed been the biological son of Cole Michaels.

Feeling totally lost, Cole spent the next four months, until he could ride his bike again, in Orlando. He attended Jason's church but didn't say much. Jason, the congregation, and the guys in the motorcycle group cooked a few meals for him. Otherwise, they all gave him the space he needed to grieve.

Jason did tell him one gorgeous February afternoon, in response to some feelings Cole shared, that "the life-changing education of the heart and soul is not in the already knowing, but rather in the strain of learning." Cole tried to keep the words close to heart.

As soon as he was able to ride again, Cole packed the Scrambler with all his belongings and for five months laid down a trail of restlessness and loneliness all over the great Midwest.

In an effort to feel like a productive human again, he occasionally worked temporary jobs along the way—at a loading dock, a horse ranch, a recycling plant, a limousine rental company, and an amusement park.

Sometime in mid June, after sitting through many sunsets and mulling over the unpredictable intricacies of life, he started thinking back to the motorcycle mission trip and Ric Kennedy's message about memorials. And then, with a new vision rising in his head, he started focusing again on Steve Rove and the kids in South America.

On a hot morning, with the Recife kids in mind, he mounted the bike and—motivated by his new vision—pointed the wheel southward toward the Mexican border.

He ended up riding all the way to Panama, then flying from there to Brazil.

*   *   *

Cole rode back into Orlando in late November of 2010, with a reinvested spirit.

And also with a monumental request for Jason and his men.

"I've just made a huge purchase for Steve's ministry in Recife," he explained, "and I'm looking for at least five men to travel with me back to Brazil in January and do some serious manual labor for two weeks."

To Cole's surprise, Jason Faircloth, Derek Atwood, Tommy Bauer, DW Sunn, Terry Ray, Ron Sasson, and four new men from the Genesis Bible Church agreed to join him.

In January, a little over a year after Jesse's death, Cole flew the group of men down to Recife and checked them into a nice hotel.

For eight to ten hours a day, the group, including missionary Steve Rove, labored in the junk-car yard that Cole had acquired from the city for a price of $1,500,000.

In accord with Cole's step-by-step plan for the project, the men first cleared the four acres of walled-in yard of every piece of debris not attached to a wrecked vehicle.

Loose cans, bottles, wrappers, wheels, boards, mats, tires, window glass and all other scraps of metal, plastic, rubber, wood, and glass were collected and hauled off to a city landfill.

The ground was then swept clean.

A standing one-room block house that had been used by the previous owner as an office was gutted, refurbished, and repainted. A small kitchen was added.

Two fork-lift drivers were hired to reposition all the junked vehicles into neat rows. Adequate walking space was created between each of the rows and each of the vehicles.

One large corner of the property was cleared and left bare.

The inside of each truck, van, bus, and car was then cleared of all trash, dirt, glass, and bugs, and washed with soap, water, and disinfectant. All broken windows were demolished and every sliver of broken glass was removed. Waterproof tarps were purchased and erected over each vehicle with missing windows.

A huge circus tent was bought and set up by hired hands in the vacant corner. Four rolling chalkboards and a hundred and fifty chairs were placed strategically into four groupings under the big top.

The front gate of the property was replaced with a 14-gauge powder-coated steel frame and a three-quarter inch plywood barricade.

A small wooden house that could seat four people was built just inside the front gate.

On the eve of the group's departure, Cole treated Jason and the men to a celebratory steak dinner and thanked them a thousand times over for their invaluable labor. He promised to keep them updated with his and Steve's progress.

* * *

A week later, electricity was cabled to the big tent by contractors. Ceiling fans were installed, and thirty electrical outlets were wired and activated.

A cinderblock water house was built near the tent by another group of contractors. There was a boys' side and a girls' side. Each side housed ten sinks, ten showers and ten toilets.

New pillows, sleeping bags, and foam-rubber pads were placed inside each wrecked vehicle.

Finally, four Christian teachers were hired full time for $350 a month—a female reading teacher, a female Portuguese teacher, a male math teacher, and a male science teacher. Two Christian cooks were also hired.

When the overall facility was ready for use, Cole designed, crafted, and hung a huge sign on the front gate: *Jesse's Town.*

By early March, Cole was ready to open the front gate for ministry. He had drained his personal bank account from $2,200,000 to $600,000, only to learn that another $900,000 worth of royalties had been deposited into his account during the previous twelve months.

He figured he could keep the ministry going for at least ten years out of his own pocket.

* * *

On a gorgeous Brazilian fall day, a few weeks before Easter, the twenty homeless kids from Steve's ministry, including little Lino, were the first children invited to make *Jesse's Town* their new home. The kids, with smiles as big as fajitas, were allowed to choose the vehicle of their choice to be their personal sleeping quarters.

It was explained to them from the offset, though, that in order to stay long-term, they would have to attend the classes offered under the big tent Monday through Friday, and that each person would have to contribute to the *town's* maintenance and well-being by carrying out assigned jobs. All twenty kids accepted.

By Easter, 150 children—from ages 4 to 15—filled all available sleeping spots.

Cole made sure that the first priority for the on-site teachers was to teach each of the children to read. The tent was filled every day with eager students.

On Sundays, the big tent was used for church services. Steve faithfully shared the Gospel during the services so that every kid could grasp the meaning of God's redeeming love.

The ministry, like the bud of an exotic spring flower, quickly transformed into a gorgeous and exquisite bloom.

One afternoon, Lino—as naturally as honey dripping from a honeycomb—gave Cole a hug and for the first time called him *Papai*, the Portuguese word for *Daddy*. Within a day or two, all 150 kids had adopted the new name.

Epilogue

During the first week of May, 2011, Cole pulled out the Mysterious Lady—which he had brought back to Recife with him—and played for the first time at the *Jesse's Town* weekly church service. For days afterward, he was astounded at the number of kids who expressed an unquenchable interest in the instrument.

Prompted by a new and lingering question, Cole purchased ten beginner fiddles and, to his shock and surprise, quickly discovered that at least five of the kids—three girls and two boys—had a natural talent for the instrument. Within a month—after practicing nearly every day with the five eager learners—Cole was amazed that all five children could play a pretty clean rendition of *Twinkle Twinkle Little Star*.

Promptly deciding to add music classes to the *Jesse's Town* curriculum, Cole hired three music teachers and a choir director.

By September, Cole was wrestling with a new conviction. He had clearly seen how God had used his music talents to literally transform the lives of dozens of kids—those who were learning instruments, as well as those who were participating in the growing choir. The music had given the kids a new focus. Something productive. Something promising. Something joyous.

Believing that he was hearing God's whisper, Cole surrendered to the understanding that it was perhaps time for him to put his music skills back to work on a large, public scale.

He took a lot of deep breaths.

He wanted to call Roland Powers in Nashville and pitch a new idea, but would Roland even be open to such a wild dream?

Cole kept procrastinating.

And then, in November, two of the world's largest television news agencies produced a news report about *Jesse's Town* and its innovative way of helping solve a serious problem.

The news item highlighted Cole—the "Blonde Fiddler" and told about the reading, math, science, and music classes being offered, and the daily meals. It also told about the newly planned cooking, gardening, wrench-turning, wood crafting, and art classes that would soon be introduced. It showed film clips of a doctor and dentist who served at the compound twice a month. It especially focused on the kids and the jobs given to them to help instill a sense of ownership and responsibility—assisting the cooks, serving meals, collecting daily garbage, guarding the main gate, cultivating the garden, cleaning the toilets, policing bullies, and running errands for the teachers and cooks. There had even been a committee made up of older children, the report emphasized, to help serve as a decision-making body for the "town".

Within hours of the first television broadcast, monetary donations started to pour in from all over the world. So did offers to volunteer: teachers, doctors, dentists, cooks, musicians, and builders.

Not long thereafter, the *Jesse's Town* mailbox received letters from the city fathers of Guatemala City, Guatemala and Bangkok, Thailand, asking several questions. After hearing about the success of *Jesse's Town*, they too were interested in converting several of their cities' salvage yards into towns for the homeless.

One of the most interesting letters to show up, though, was delivered to the town mailbox on December 1, 2011.

> Dearest Cole,
>
> I recently saw the TV report about you and your new work in Brazil. I was really touched.
>
> I just want to let you know that I'm back in Nashville, and I'm working at SpiritMark again. My engagement to Rod didn't pan out. I finally admitted to myself that I was marrying him for all the wrong reasons. Anyway, it's a long story. But suffice it to say, the relationship is over.
>
> As I'm sitting here writing this letter, I need to let you know that

I've never stopped thinking about you. It might be a shock to you, but after all I've been through, I'm even starting to see life through different eyes. Who knows, maybe I'm finally growing up.

Anyway, I can honestly say that I appreciate you now more than ever. Actually, you're the only man I've ever felt that I could trust. And I am learning that this is far more valuable than any amount of money in a bank account. Men like you, I am realizing, are very few and far between.

Thank you for the ways you've contributed to my life. I'm extremely proud of you. Please know that you will always have a huge place in my heart.

Sincerely,

Lindsey

P.S.-The enclosed check is for your ministry. Use it as you wish.

Cole read the letter at least two dozen times and stared over and over at the $1,500 check.

He held the letter for two full days, then picked up the phone and called her. Within minutes, he sensed a difference in her heart—a remarkable difference. To his relief, the call turned out to be quite blissful.

After several highly enjoyable calls over a two week period, he—like any broken and lonely man longing for a gracious lover—asked if they could meet.

With new found excitement and hope, they agreed to meet in Nashville at the SpiritMark office on Monday, January 9, 2012. They decided they were both ready to once again talk about a possible future together. One, this time, that would include serving others.

Cole couldn't have been more thrilled.

Then, finally yielding to the flame that had recently started burning in his soul, Cole called Roland Powers.

"Hi, Roland. This is Cole Michaels calling from Brazil."

"Well, well, if it's not our long lost wandering spirit. How are you, man?"

"I'm okay. Do you have a moment to talk?"

"For you, my friend, I'll take the time."

"Are you sitting down? I think this might be the call you've been waiting on for a long time."

"Whoa...are you going to tell me you're ready to hit the stage again?"

Cole cleared his throat. "I am. But with some new twists."

"All right; I'm listening."

"I'll sign a contract to do ten to twenty live concerts, with unlimited media interviews, over any six-week period of your choice."

"And?" The excitement was rising in Roland's voice.

"And I'll have company."

"Go on."

"There will be twenty kids with me."

Hearing a curious and inviting silence on the other end, Cole gave details of his Recife ministry, about which Roland had only heard vague reports, and explained that he would feature the twenty young musicians and vocalists, on at least two different songs, at each concert. And that he would use the events to help raise money to build more "towns" for more homeless kids. If everybody at SpiritMark agreed to the concerts, and the concerts went well, then he would be willing to discuss the possibility of doing a similar tour each summer for the next four or five years. And, hopefully, he would bring a different group of kids each time.

Cole knew he shouldn't be, but he was surprised to hear Roland enthusiastically say, "I'll start working on it today."

"If you don't mind," Cold added, barely managing to contain his euphoria, "will you step down the hall and pass the news to Lindsey?"

"Will do. And, oh...one more thing."

"Yeah?"

"Welcome back."

Cole had finally found his place in the world.

*   *   *

"Even though the fig trees have no blossoms, and there are no grapes on the vine; even though the olive crop fails, and the fields lie empty and barren; even though the flocks die in the fields, and the cattle barns are empty, yet I will rejoice in the Lord! I will be joyful in the God of my salvation. The Sovereign Lord is my strength! He will make me as surefooted as a deer and bring me safely over the mountains."

Habakkuk
Old Testament Jewish prophet
Habakkuk 3:17-19

Acknowledgments

Chapters 17 and 18 of *Forgotten Road* were written in memory of James Michael Martin, a two-year-old killed in a similar bush-hog accident in 1986. This accident is the most tragic story I have ever heard. James was the son of my longtime friends, Jamie and Vicky. Our prayers are still with you, my friends.

The forms in Chapter 29 are taken word-for-word from actual documents from the Georgia Adoption Reunion Registry.

The words from "The Forgotten Road" pamphlet in Chapter 43 are an altered version of an original writing penned by Melanie Barber, a friend of my youngest daughter. Melanie permitted me to edit her words and use them in a fitting context in my story.

The "Bible Handkerchief" letter in Chapter 43 is a tweaked version of an actual letter that arrived in my mailbox when I was in the process of writing this novel. I gladly give the original author credit for the script.

Ray and Fay Christy are dear friends in Maine with extraordinary testimonies of God's grace and mercy. They gave me permission to use altered versions of their names and stories in Chapter 60. I continue to be inspired by their testimonies and talents.

The AOK guys, to whom this volume is dedicated, are my longtime riding buddies. These gentlemen gave birth to the characters who take part in the motorcycle mission adventure in Chapters 67 through 72. The guys even permitted me to embellish stories about our numerous motorcycle road trips together. The real riders are Tommy Brewer, Robbie Brewer, Geoff Marott, Randy Maney, Glenn Martin, Lynn Newell, Terry Day, Jeff Swaney, Derek Arwood, Jef Bass, Ric Kinne, Gary Waldron, DW Senn, Steve Bove, Ron Sisson, Jim McGee, and Tim Boynton. Other riders in the group who have contributed to my life are Wayne Cone, Cornel Unteanu, Richard Woodlands, Dan Langley, Anthony Davis, Todd Hughes, Benny Wayne Ford, Barney Sallee, Beetle Bailey, Roger Blankenship, George Clamser, Joe Watkins, Ray Seaton, Keith Hayes, Brandon McGee, David Daniell, Gene Ross, Kent Kelsoe, Brian Cunningham, Bob Brown, Jim Sansone, Tommy Nowell, Bill Cline, David Arwood, Ron Ray, and 'Pops'. Thank you, men.

Special Thanks

To my oldest daughter, Heidi, who designed the front and back covers of *Forgotten Road*. Of all the cover designs used on my books throughout the years, this is my all-time favorite. Heidi also designed and built the RandallArthur. com website. Thank you, girl. Your artistic skills are more than impressive.

To the eight test readers of the original draft. They scoured the pages with the eyes of their professions and made sure my statements and descriptions were plausible. Their feedback and corrections were more valuable than they know. Those test readers were:

Linda Foltz—Psychologist
Tommy Brewer—Bounty Hunter
Sherri Dodd—Missionary and Life Coach
Sonja LaVigne—Vocalist
Billy Lord—Musician and Worship Leader
Steve Usury—Pastor and Bible Teacher
Neil Brown—Pastor and Administrator
Misti Atwood—Attorney

And to the multiple test readers of the second and third drafts. Your feedback was spot on.

Thank you again. Forgive me if I allowed any false statements to slip through.

To the Nashville DA, James Sledge, for taking my numerous phone calls and providing important answers regarding Tennessee laws. He was more than gracious.

To my niece, Autumn, and my friend, Linda Foltz, for their pivotal suggestions.

To Merrilyn S. for her beautiful desktop-composition work.

And finally to Dave Lambert, my editor. A manuscript is always enhanced by the sharp eye of a proven editor. This is certainly the case with *Forgotten Road*. Dave's editorial skills are superb. And more than right on. Thank you, thank you, thank you.
